SIEGE OF
HEAVEN

Also by Tom Harper

The Mosaic of Shadows
Knights of the Cross

TOM HARPER
SIEGE OF HEAVEN

arrow books

Published in the United Kingdom by Arrow Books in 2007

9 10 8

First published in the United Kingdom in 2006 by Century

Arrow Books
The Random House Group Limited
20 Vauxhall Bridge Road, London SW1V 2SA

Address for companies within The Random House Group Limited can be found at:
www.randomhouse.co.uk/offices.htm

The Random House Group Limited
Reg. No. 954009

A CIP catalogue record for this book is available
from the British Library

ISBN 9780099454755

Typeset in Minion by Palimpsest Book Production Limited,
Grangemouth, Stirlingshire

The Random House Group Limited supports The Forest Stewardship
Council® (FSC®), the leading international forest-certification organisation.
Our books carrying the FSC label are printed on FSC®-certified paper.
FSC is the only forest-certification scheme supported by the leading
environmental organisations, including Greenpeace. Our
paper procurement policy can be found at
www.randomhouse.co.uk/environment

Printed and bound in Great Britain by Clays Ltd, St Ives plc

                    so over many a tract
Of Heav'n they marched, and many a Province wide
Tenfold the length of this terrene: at last
Far in th' Horizon to the North appeared
From skirt to skirt a fiery Region, stretched
In battailous aspect, and nearer view
Bristled with upright beams innumerable
Of rigid Spears, and Helmets throng'd, and Shields
Various, with boastful Argument portrayed,
The banded Powers of Satan hasting on
With furious expedition; for they weened
That self same day by fight, or by surprise
To win the Mount of God

                              – *Milton*, Paradise Lost

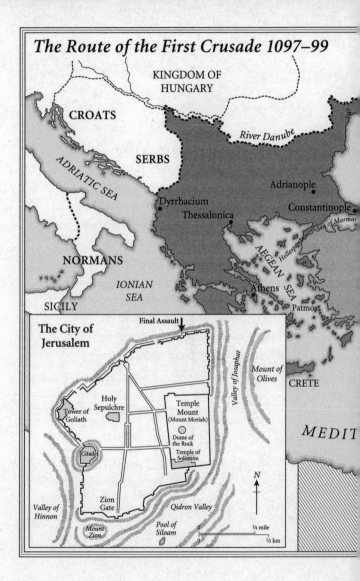

The Route of the First Crusade 1097–99

KINGDOM OF HUNGARY

CROATS

River Danube

SERBS

ADRIATIC SEA

Adrianople

Dyrrhacium

Thessalonica

Constantinople

Sea of Marmara

Hellespont

NORMANS

IONIAN SEA

AEGEAN SEA

SICILY

Athens

Patmos

CRETE

The City of Jerusalem

Valley of Josaphat

Final Assault

Mount of Olives

Holy Sepulchre

Tower of Goliath

Temple Mount (Mount Moriah)

Dome of the Rock

Temple of Solomon

Citadel

MEDIT

N

Zion Gate

Valley of Hinnon

Qidron Valley

Mount Zion

Pool of Siloam

0   ¼ mile

0   ½ km

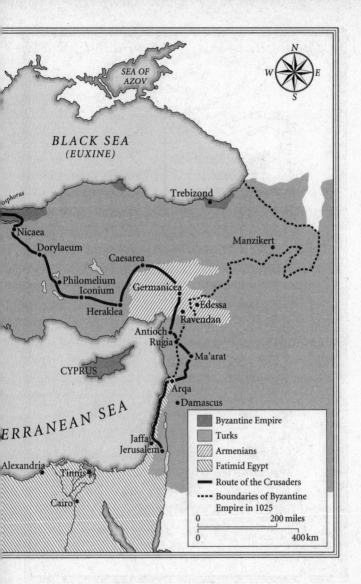

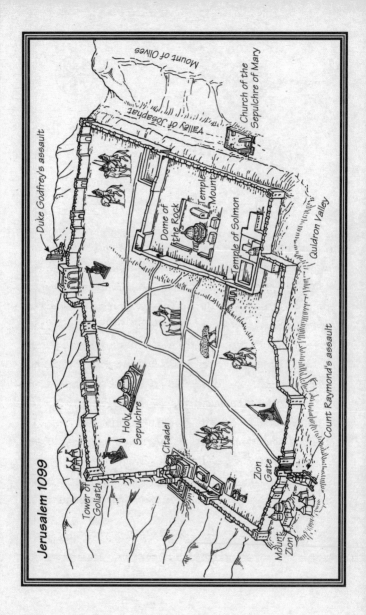

Jerusalem 1099

Duke Godfrey's assault

Mount of Olives

Valley of Josaphat

Church of the Sepulchre of Mary

Temple Mount

Dome of the Rock

Temple of Solmon

Quidron Valley

Count Raymond's assault

Tower of Goliath

Holy Sepulchre

Citadel

Zion Gate

Mount Zion

History

The fall of Rome was not the end of its empire: it lived on in the east, in the imperial city of Constantinople. A thousand years after the first Caesars, it remained the greatest power in Christendom. But new dangers threatened, and the old empire could no longer defend itself. In desperation, the emperor Alexios turned to the west – to the descendants of the same barbarian tribes which had overthrown the first Rome. He asked for mercenaries; but Pope Urban, seeing an opportunity for the papacy in its eternal struggle with secular authority, responded with something quite different. He preached a holy war, an armed pilgrimage that would fight its way to Jerusalem and free the city from the occupying Turks. All over Europe, men and women answered his call: knights and nobles, but also peasants in their ten-thousands.

The army reached Constantinople in late 1096 and, after negotiations which almost boiled over into war, swore an oath to yield up the lands they conquered to the emperor Alexios. In the summer of 1097 they stormed across Asia Minor, winning victory after victory, until at last they ground to a halt in front of the impregnable fortress city of Antioch. Eight months of gruelling siege followed until, on the cusp of destruction, the crusaders finally took the city. Not a moment too soon: within days, a vast Muslim relief army had arrived and trapped the crusaders in the city they had just laid waste. With no alternative, they broke out and despite overwhelming odds routed the Muslim army, breaking their power for a generation.

The battle for Antioch – the crisis of the First Crusade – had been won. But the Army of God was physically and psychologically exhausted, while its leaders quickly fell out over the division of the spoils they had won. The road lay open, but in August 1098, two years after the army had left home, Jerusalem still seemed as distant and impossible as ever.

I

Wilderness

August – December 1098

Requiem

∾∾∾∾∾

The crowds gathered early: they did not have long to live. They poured out of their hovels and their plundered homes, lining the street for a full mile to see the corpse. Infants who would soon be orphans sat on their father's shoulders, while children who would not outlive the harvest chased each other on hands and knees through the throng. Some of the more cautious tied scarves over their faces or bound their hands with cloths, but most people did not believe the threat – yet. They climbed onto the cracked roofs of the old colonnades, raised themselves on broken pillars and crowded the upper tiers of the nearby houses to see better. Many would die in the coming weeks and months, but none would enjoy as grand a funeral as this. Many would be lucky to get even a marker on their grave. So they massed in their thousands, craning for the best possible view, and perhaps understood that this one, magnificent occasion would suffice for them all.

We knew the procession had set out when the bells began to toll. Mothers hushed their children and the crowd turned its eyes to the south. The August sun had climbed over the shoulder of the mountain above the city, and there was no wind to raise the dust that clung to us. I hoped the pallbearers would not linger with the body in that heat.

Four priests swinging golden censers led the procession. Clouds of incense billowed from the wrought aureoles, hazing the fresh morning air and sweetening it. Next came eight more priests with long candles, their flames invisible in the brilliant glare of the sun. Following them, all alone, an oddity: a tall man dressed not as a priest but a pilgrim, the sleeves of his robe falling back where he raised his arms in front of him. He carried a golden casket inlaid with crystal and pearls, and his narrow eyes were closed almost to blindness by its dazzle. All in the crowd crossed themselves as he passed, for the casket contained the relic of the holy lance, the spear that pierced the side of Christ on the cross, and it was only by its divine power that we had conquered the city. So they believed.

Behind him, four knights carried the body on a bier. A white shroud wrapped it, studded with silver light where the shroud-pins fastened it. The sun breathed through the cloth and filled it with radiance, so that it became a gauzy nimbus around the corpse. I could see the outline of his body beneath it, the arms crossed over his chest. A bishop's mitre and a wooden cross were laid over him.

Unbidden, every man about me sank to his knees and joined the swelling antiphon chanted by the priests.

> *May angels lead you to Paradise,*
> *May the martyrs come forth to welcome you,*
> *And bring you into the Holy City,*
> *Jerusalem.*

Elsewhere, I could hear pilgrims invoking his name in whispered blessings and farewells. *Adhemar. God speed you to paradise. God bless you. Adhemar.*

A cool tear ran down my burning cheek. I had not known Bishop Adhemar well, but I had been with him when he died and had heard his last confession. I knew the efforts he had made to shepherd the Army of God, to hold together the bitter rivalries and ambitions that drove it. I knew the anguish he had suffered in that cause. That was what had killed him – and why so many men and women who had known him only by his sermons now wept. They mourned him honestly enough, but more than that they feared for what would come after him.

The prayers died suddenly. The catafalque had passed: behind it came a procession of men, each trying to outdo the others in the opulence of his funeral dress. First in rank and precedence came Raymond, Count of Saint-Gilles: a grizzled, one-eyed man with a grey beard that seemed greyer still as he hunched over his staff. He

7

probably meant it to appear as a pilgrim's staff, a pious crutch, but it owed more to the illness that had recently threatened to speed him to the same fate as Bishop Adhemar. Behind him, almost treading on his shuffling heels and not hiding his impatience, strode a younger man, Bohemond. He stood a full head taller than any of the others; his dark hair was cropped short and his pale face was ripe with unencumbered pride. There was something about him that drew men's eyes and held them, not just his size but some aura of power or danger. Certainly not love: faces hardened as he passed, and several voices took up another anthem in defiant counterpoint to the priests' chants. *The kings of the Earth are but dust.* Bohemond affected not to notice.

The third man in the party walked a little apart from the others, a fair-haired man with broad shoulders and a full beard – Godfrey, Duke of Lorraine. By most men's judgement he was the most powerful of the princes after Bohemond and Raymond, and more powerful still for being wise enough to keep out of their quarrels. He held himself stiffly, staring past the men in front of him and keeping his eyes fixed on the bier ahead.

The column passed on: counts and dukes, princelings and knights, bishops and priests. The crowds flooded in behind them as soon as they had passed. Ahead, the bier had reached the cathedral, and I could see the great, graven doors swing open to admit the body to the sanctuary. Above it, the church's silver dome reflected the light of heaven. The priests now had a new song:

You made me of the earth
And clothed me with flesh:
O Lord, my redeemer, raise me up
On the last day.

As the nobles took their places by the open grave under the dome, the mob behind struggled to squeeze through the doors. I was among them. A spiteful frenzy gripped them, more like rats fleeing fire than mourners entering a holy place, but I had earned my living long enough in the crowded streets of Constantinople and knew how to wield my elbows to good effect. Jabbing and poking, I crossed the threshold of the church and jostled my way across the sanctuary until the sheer choke of bodies blocked any further progress.

At the far end of the church, the burial had begun. The body had been lifted off its bier and now lay suspended over the grave on silken ropes, while the assembled princes knelt by the grave. Count Raymond had clasped his hands tight before him and rocked back and forth on his knees; Bohemond bowed his head, though it still twitched with surreptitious, guarded movements. Beyond them, I could see two dark figures waiting in the shadows with spades upturned like reaping hooks – the gravediggers. They would have had an easy time of it, for the grave had been excavated only seven weeks earlier. The relic of the holy lance, now cased in its golden reliquary, had been found at the bottom of the hole, though some said it looked more like a roofer's nail than the tip of a spear. Adhemar himself had struggled to believe it, had been almost embarrassed to endorse its power. I did not think he would have chosen to spend eternity buried in its place.

A silent chorus of marble saints looked down as the body descended into the pit. A groan rumbled around the silvered dome as the lid of the sarcophagus was drawn into place. At the head of the grave, the patriarch of Antioch made the sign of the cross, then threw a sprig of laurel into the hole, while the congregation sighed a wistful farewell, like the sound of a sword sliding out of a dying man's chest.

'May God forgive his sins with mercy,' the patriarch intoned. 'May Christ the Good Shepherd lead him safely home. And may he live in happiness for ever, with all the saints, in the presence of the eternal King.'

Amen.

A spade rasped on stone as the gravediggers began filling the hole with earth.

α

◠◠◠◠◠

They held the funeral feast at the palace, a sprawling accumulation of ramshackle courtyards and mismatched towers at the southern end of the city. A crowd of mourners had already gathered outside the gates, waiting for the scraps and crumbs to come after the feast, while a company of Norman knights leaned on their spears and glared at them. I was more favoured. I passed through the gatehouse into the outer courtyard, drawing mean glares from the Normans. I had my own place in the scheme of their enemies.

Priests and nobles of greater and lesser degrees thronged the courtyard, while smells of roasting meat and burning fat coated the hot air. I took a cup of wine from a servant and sipped it, keeping to the anonymous shade by the wall. I had worn my best tunic and boots, trimmed my beard, oiled my hair and tied a fresh bandage on my arm, but I did not belong among these people. I was too common – and, worse, a Greek. That I was there at all I owed to the cowardice of better men. I had come with the Army of God as an observer – a spy – but when my superior officer, the infinitely more glorious Tatikios, had departed Antioch in haste I had become, for lack of alternative, the emperor's ambassador. I even wore his signet ring, bequeathed to me by Tatikios before he fled Antioch in fear of his life. I would happily give up the role.

'Demetrios Askiates.' I turned at the sound of my name to see the patriarch of Antioch at my side. He had remained in the city throughout the Turkish occupation, even during the eight months that the Franks had besieged it, and he had paid terribly for his faith. At times the Turks had hung him from the battlements and invited our archers to attack; at other times they had caged him atop a tower, or burned him with hot irons. I could not imagine how he had endured it, but once we had driven the Turks from the city he had taken up his cope and staff and returned to his seat in the cathedral. Even the Franks, who despised and distrusted the Greek church, deferred to him.

He looked out across the courtyard. 'How many more times do you think we will see all the Franks gathered together in peace?'

I shrugged. 'As long as it takes to reach Jerusalem, I suppose.'

'I hope so. With Bishop Adhemar gone, they have lost

their guiding compass. There are too many among them with power, and none with authority. And they still have far to go.'

'Too far for me, Father.'

The patriarch lifted an eyebrow. 'You are not going to Jerusalem?'

'No.' I was defiant. 'By the time I get home I'll have been away for well over a year. I have two daughters I have neglected and – God willing – a grandson I have never seen. The road to Jerusalem only takes me further from home, and into worse dangers.'

'What will the emperor say?'

I did not answer. Any excuse would have sounded feeble – shameful, even – to a man who had endured what the patriarch had suffered. Mercifully, he did not judge me.

'God calls each of us on different paths,' he said. I could not tell if he meant it as a consolation or a warning. 'But before He calls you back to Constantinople, I have a task for you. There is someone . . .' He tailed off as his eyes darted across my shoulder; I half-turned to follow. A pair of Latin bishops were waiting there, evidently keen to speak with the patriarch. He gave them a pleasant smile and steered me aside with a gentle nudge of his elbow. 'I will find you later.'

I had no one else to speak to: the patriarch and I were the only Greeks there, and I was too insignificant to attract anyone else's attention. I could gladly have left that moment: left the decrepit palace, the city, the country itself, and run home to Constantinople. I longed to. But

I was the emperor's representative, however humble, and that brought certain obligations. Antioch had been a Byzantine city until thirteen years earlier, when the Turks captured it, and the emperor Alexios had not called this barbarian army into being just so that they should possess it in place of the Turks. He coveted it: partly for the riches of its trade, partly as the key fortress of his southern border, partly for pride. But Bohemond would sooner hand Antioch back to the Ishmaelites than surrender it to the emperor, despite having sworn an oath to do so. As long as I remained there I reminded him of his obligation, a human token for the emperor's claim. It was not a comfortable position.

I toyed with the signet ring on my finger, watching the sunlight reflect off its broad disc and play over the surrounding faces. I did not doubt the sincerity of their mourning but I could already see it fading, buried in the earth beneath the cathedral. One man looked to have been particularly quick to get beyond his grief – which perhaps explained why he stood alone. Tall, gangly and hook-nosed, he might have taken pride of place in the funeral procession, but here he was shunned.

His eyes met mine, narrowed with hostility, then relented enough to decide my company was preferable to his solitude. I might have decided otherwise, but before I could slide away he had ambled over and was peering down on me, hunched over like a crane.

'Peter Bartholomew.' I greeted him without enthusiasm. 'It seems we're both beggars at this feast.'

He bridled, as I knew he would.

'On this day of all days, they should remember me. Without the lance – the lance that *I* found – the bishop's legacy would be nothing but bones and dust.'

It was probably true. It was Peter Bartholomew who had received the remarkable – some said incredible – vision that told him where the lance was buried, and Peter Bartholomew who had leaped into the pit and prised out the fragment with his bare hands when everyone else had given up. The same pit that was now Bishop Adhemar's grave.

'The princes have short memories,' I said noncommittally.

'So short they even forget why God called us here. Look at Bohemond.' Peter gestured to his right, where Bohemond was deep in conversation with Duke Godfrey. Unusually, both men seemed to have dispensed with the hosts of knights and sycophants who usually surrounded them. 'He has Antioch, and that is enough for him.'

'Not if the emperor has his way,' I said. Peter ignored me.

'The army is greater than any of the princes. You saw the pilgrims at the procession this morning: they are already angry that we have not yet moved on to Jerusalem. With Adhemar gone, who will they trust to speak for them honestly when the princes meet?'

Unlike any army before it, the Army of God had not been summoned by kings or compelled into being by circumstance: it had been preached into existence for a

15

war of pilgrimage. Knights and soldiers had answered the call, but so had peasants, in vast numbers. They offered no service save drudgery, and required far more in supplies and protection than they earned. Yet in the strange world of the Army of God they were esteemed for their innocence; they had a righteousness of purpose that none of the knights or princes could claim, and were thus endowed with a special sanctity.

I stared at Peter. The naked hope was plain on his crooked face, and pitiable. For a few happy days he had been the army's salvation, the finder of the lance and the saviour of Antioch. Now the memory was fading and he was ebbing back towards obscurity. I could see how it wounded him, how desperate he was to snatch back his waning eminence.

'Other men have tried to put themselves at the head of the pilgrims,' I warned him, 'and it has never ended well.' The first man to do so, a self-styled hermit also named Peter, had led the pilgrims with assurances of divine immunity from swords and arrows. A single, terrible battle had proven the emptiness of that promise.

'God made you a vessel for His purpose and granted you a wonderful vision.' It was hard to believe that anyone would have chosen Peter Bartholomew for such a purpose – but perhaps it was ever so with visionaries. 'That is more than most men can dream of in a lifetime.'

He bridled again, snapping his head angrily, though this time I had not intended to provoke him. '*Most* men never dream at all. They crawl the earth like pigs, snouts

16

to the ground, never stopping to wonder why the farmer bothers to feed them. God's plan for me did not end when I found the lance – it has barely begun. And when it comes to His fullness, these fat princes will curse themselves for treating me like a peasant.'

His voice had risen, far louder than was wise in the company of the men he vilified. He realised it now, and stared around in wild defiance to see if he had provoked any reaction. To his immediate relief, and then anger, none of the surrounding lords paid him the least attention.

'They will notice me soon enough,' he mumbled. Forgetting me, he pushed away through the crowd.

I sighed. I knew too much of his history – the immoral diseases that ravaged his body, the flirtation with heresy that had almost cost him his life – to be taken in by his delusions, but I still pitied him. I could guess how he felt. Little more than a year earlier, I had walked freely in the halls of the palace at Byzantium – had even, for brief moments, been a confidant of the emperor. Now I lingered in the wilderness beyond the fringes of civilisation, not as punishment or in disfavour but simply because life had brought me there.

Talking with Peter Bartholomew had drawn me out of the shade, into the centre of the courtyard where the sun beat down. I looked for another cup of wine to cure my thirst, knowing I would regret it later, but there was none to be seen. I wandered along the fringes of the crowd, scanning for familiar faces and wondering what errand the patriarch intended for me.

17

'And will you go on to Jerusalem?'

The voice was so close, the question so much in my own mind, I thought it must have been spoken to me. It was only when I turned that I saw my error: the speaker was standing with his back to me, oblivious to my presence, while his companion stood beside him. Both were dressed in richly woven robes, and golden threads picked out the sign of the cross on their sleeves. With a start, I recognised Duke Godfrey and Bohemond.

'I took my oath to pray beside Christ's tomb,' Bohemond answered Godfrey. 'But I am not in a hurry. Too many questions demand my attention in Antioch for the moment.'

'Count Raymond may have his own answers to those questions.'

Bohemond made a swatting gesture with his hand. 'There will only be one lord in Antioch, and it will not be Count Raymond. Nor the king of the Greeks either.'

Godfrey made no sound of argument. Instead: 'The road to Jerusalem will be longer and harder without your army.'

Again, Bohemond waved his concerns away. 'Our victory over the Turks has broken them for a generation. With a strong Antioch defended at your back, you could be in Jerusalem in a fortnight. If you still mean to go.'

From behind, I saw Godfrey nod slowly. 'I will go.'

'To honour your oath?' There was a taunt in Bohemond's voice.

'To honour God – and to answer the destiny written for me.'

Bohemond laughed. 'Written in your book?'

'Written in my book,' Godfrey agreed. There was no laughter in his voice.

'And what book is that?'

The cheerful question rang out behind me. Godfrey and Bohemond turned with a start, and suddenly I was trapped between them and the patriarch, who had emerged from the crowd unnoticed and now stood there, smiling and expectant.

'A book of wisdom,' Godfrey answered brusquely.

The patriarch nodded. 'Good. We need God's wisdom to guide us, especially now that Adhemar has gone. He was a good and wise man. Your army will miss him.'

Bohemond pursed his lips and made a noise like a horse farting. 'A good man? You can't kill Turks and Saracens with goodness. Or even wisdom.'

'It takes wisdom to hold an army together – especially if it is to reach its destination.' The patriarch stared at Bohemond calmly. 'But perhaps that is no longer your concern.'

'As if it was ever a concern of the Greeks.' Without waiting for a reply, Bohemond drained his cup and barged away into the crowd. Godfrey waited a moment, fixing me with a harsh gaze of suspicion, before following. Though it seemed I had not been the only one eavesdropping: as Godfrey moved away, I saw Peter Bartholomew loitering artlessly nearby.

'Demetrios.' The patriarch was still there, watching me expectantly. 'Let me introduce you to . . .' He trailed off as he scanned the crowd. Whoever he was seeking, he did not find him; instead, on the other side of the courtyard, Count Raymond caught his eye and came limping towards us. The patriarch sighed.

'But here comes Count Raymond. He is upset to hear you will be leaving us.'

'I'm glad there will be someone who misses me.'

Count Raymond halted and swivelled his single eye towards me. Even after his illness it still retained a furious power. 'I have been your emperor's most constant ally, and it has won me few friends among the other princes. It has even tested the loyalty of many of my own men. If you leave now, you as good as surrender the city to Bohemond.'

'The emperor has not abandoned you,' I assured him. 'He has sent a new ambassador to Antioch. When he arrives, I will go home.'

'An ambassador? Not the emperor himself?' For a man who had fought more battles than Caesar, Count Raymond seemed suddenly vulnerable, like an expectant child looking for his father.

'The emperor has an empire to govern. He is needed in Constantinople, and cannot allow himself the journey to Jerusalem.'

'Hah. It will be a long time before we see Jerusalem. First we must decide what to do with Antioch. Bohemond will not surrender it easily.'

'Would you fight him for it?' I asked.

20

Raymond's eye narrowed. 'I have the noblest title, the largest army and the richest treasury. I have the support of both your emperor and the peasant mob. Most of all, I have the holy lance. It is a compelling claim. Hard to resist, if any man was so foolish.'

In my mind's eye, I saw Adhemar's shrouded body in the cold earth beneath the cathedral. These were exactly the wounds he had struggled to bind together: he would be turning in his grave to hear them torn open again so soon.

'If you are not careful, there will be nothing left to fight over,' observed the patriarch quietly. 'Adhemar will not be the last victim of the disease that claimed his life. In the fields outside the city there are already more gravediggers than farmers.'

I had noticed it too. Hardly had we seen off the physical threat of the Turkish army than a new, invisible enemy had insinuated itself into our ranks. At first in ones and twos, then in dozens and scores, men had started to sicken and die. Flush with victory, we had ignored it too long – and soon we would be dying in our thousands. Out of habit, I reached to my chest to touch the silver cross that had hung there but it was gone, gifted to a dead man, and could not help. *Grant me time enough to see my family again*, I prayed silently. *At least that.*

'Even Bohemond cannot fight the plague,' said Raymond. 'The rumour is that he will retreat up the coast until it has passed.'

'It would be unwise to try to take advantage of his absence,' warned the patriarch.

Raymond laughed, a wet and ragged old man's laugh. 'Never fear, Father. I have not survived sixty-three winters to throw my life away conquering a plague city. I will go south a little way, and watch Bohemond from there.' He swept his arm around the gathering. 'I will not be the only one. Now that the funeral is done, they will scatter. By nightfall there will not even be a squire left in Antioch.'

He excused himself to go and speak with some of his lieutenants. The patriarch watched him go.

'The sooner he reaches Jerusalem the better.'

'Why?' I asked. 'So that he and Bohemond are out of your way?'

The patriarch shook his head. 'Because otherwise he will tear himself in two. He has sworn to reach Jerusalem and free it from the Turks, and that is a sacred oath. But he cannot bring himself to let go of Antioch. He must choose between his conscience and his pride. I fear the choice may break him.'

'It had better not, he is the only ally we have here.'

'Then we must pray for him.'

For a few moments, we both watched the milling crowd in silence. Then, with a murmur of recognition, the patriarch tugged on my sleeve and led me briskly across to the colonnade at the edge of the courtyard. A tall man in a black habit lounged against one of the pillars, stripping a chicken bone with his teeth.

'This is the man I wanted you to meet – Brother Pakrad.'

The patriarch seemed delighted to have found him; I was more wary. He did not look much like the monks I had known during my own brief spell as a novice, fragile souls with faded eyes and stooped backs from their lifetimes of poring over manuscripts and prayers. The black stains beneath his fingernails and on his cracked teeth were not ink but grime, and there was a strength in his arms that had not come from carrying a breviary. The bald patch of skin on the crown of his skull seemed fresh and livid, with little welts of blood where the razor had cut.

'Brother Pakrad has come from the monastery of Ravendan. In the mountains, north-east of here.' The name meant nothing to me. 'It is in ruins. The Turks sacked it when they captured Antioch.'

I glanced at the monk. He was surely too young to have been even a novice at the time. Nor did the memory seem to stir him much.

The patriarch leaned closer, lowering his voice. 'The Turks razed the monastery and plundered it, but they did not find its greatest treasure. The relic of Saint Paul's hand.'

'His *right* hand,' added the monk. 'The same hand that held the pen that wrote the epistles.'

I sighed. I did not want to offend the old patriarch's faith, but nor could I hide my dismay. 'I have seen enough relics on this campaign.'

To my surprise, the patriarch nodded. 'Of course. The hand of a saint, even the greatest of saints, can only point a man towards God. It cannot make him holy. But sometimes we must be shown the way.' He gave a weary smile. 'I hold an ancient office, Demetrios, established by Saint

Peter himself. Compared to the men who have held this seat, I am like a child scrambling over his father's chair.'

'No one could fault you,' I objected. The words sounded clumsy.

He waved my intervention aside. 'Who can say how God will judge us? For now, I must try to rebuild the church in this ruined city. There is no lack of piety among the Franks, but they have little faith in Greeks.' He sighed. 'Saint Paul's hand will not make them love us, but at least it will add weight to our cause.'

The crowds around us had ebbed away, drawn towards the hall where the feast was almost ready. The three of us were alone in the sweltering courtyard.

'I need you to find this relic for me.' The patriarch fixed me with his tired eyes. 'Brother Pakrad knows where it is hidden.' He lifted a hand to halt my argument. 'Take a dozen men and travel quickly. You will need four days to reach the monastery, and four days to return. By then, God willing, your replacement will have arrived and you can go home.'

A bell tolled, summoning us to the feast.

β

∽∽∽∽

From the moment we arrived in Antioch, we had made our camp on a stretch of the western walls between two towers. At first it had protected us from the besieging Turks, though latterly it was threats from within the city we had to guard against. The walls made austere lodgings, but we had stayed there long enough now that their hard lines and heavy stones had taken on some of the comfort of familiarity. A faded eagle flew on a banner above the northern turret, and the sweet smell of figs was ripe in the afternoon air.

I climbed the stairs at the base of one of the towers, quickening my pace. I reached the guard chamber at the top and was about to step out onto the walls when a challenge rang out.

'Stop there.'

I stopped still. The voice was not the deep-throated bellow of a guardsman, but clear and delicate, a woman's voice. She stepped out from behind the door, watching me carefully. Her face was mostly hidden in shadow, but I did not need to see it to know it. The long black hair bound back with a ribbon, the quick eyes that forever seemed to see an inch further than mine, the lips that could smile or frown with equal force: they were all intimately familiar to me from long hours of contemplation. Anna.

She stood about three yards from me, as though an invisible orb surrounded me.

'You're late, Demetrios.'

'I'm sorry.' Even after eighteen months' intimacy, there were still times when she assumed the cool detachment of a physician with me. It always unsettled me. I was a widower and she had never wed: we should have married a year ago, but I had been ordered to follow the Army of God and there had been no time. I had gone with the army and she had accompanied me but even that did not soothe my anxiety. Every day we were away only stretched my fear that her patience would wear out.

She took two steps to her right, skirting an invisible boundary. 'Did you touch anyone?'

'I was in a crowd. It was impossible not to.'

'Take off your clothes.'

It would have been a ridiculous demand from anybody else but I did not argue. I pulled off my boots, then

26

unbuckled my belt and pulled my tunic and my undershirt over my head. Meanwhile, Anna had retreated behind the door and now reappeared carrying a wooden bucket and a sponge. Beyond her, loitering on the wall, I saw a group of fair-skinned men gathering to watch. No doubt they found it hilarious.

Anna stepped up to me and dipped the sponge in the bucket. I smelled the styptic fumes of vinegar, and my skin tightened as she began wiping it over my body. The soft brush of the sponge might have been erotic, but for the raw bite of the liquid and the stifled giggling in the background. When she knelt to dab at my groin, the spectators exploded with ribald mirth.

'If I get the plague, will you wash me like that?' one of the men called.

'Only once I've amputated the infected organ,' retorted Anna, who had spent a year living with soldiers and knew how to speak to them. She stood. 'Open your mouth.'

I obeyed, though I doubt she saw anything but a mouthful of dust. She peered closely at my face, then walked around behind me as if examining a horse at auction. At last she was satisfied.

'Did you eat at the funeral feast?'

'I said I was fasting.'

'Good.' She took a cloth she had draped over her shoulder and tossed it to me. 'A new tunic. I'll wash the other in vinegar.'

'As if I didn't stink enough already.'

Barefoot, I followed her onto the wall, into the next

tower and up to its summit. A troop of long-haired, pale-skinned barbarians lounged by the battlements. Some still wore their armour, though there had been no fighting in weeks, and most had long-hafted axes lying near them, the precious blades wrapped in fur coverings. They were the Varangians, the emperor's elite barbarian guardsmen, my companions.

One of the men was standing with a cup of wine in his hand. In a pack of wolves you would have known he was the leader by his size; in this pack of barbarians you could tell it by the easy arrogance of his face, the commanding set of his mighty shoulders and the thick gold band around his left forearm. He had taken it from a Turkish corpse at the battle of Antioch, though I was surprised he had found one that fitted the girth of his arms. He was called Sigurd – named, he had once told me, for a legendary dragon-slayer of his ancestors. Looking at him now, his beard the colour of fire, it was easy to imagine.

'Demetrios. Late, naked and stinking of old wine.'

'I'd rather be naked than dead.' I pulled on the new tunic and sat back against the wall. One of the barbarians passed me a flask of wine and I drank it eagerly.

'How was the funeral?' asked Anna, sitting beside me and squeezing herself into the crook of my arm. 'Did many go?'

'Thousands.' I wondered how many would die regretting it.

'And the princes?'

'They were all there. The one thing they feared more

28

than the plague was failing to parade their piety before the masses. I doubt a single one is left in the city now.'

'We should follow them quickly,' said Anna. 'The plague clouds are already gathering over this city. With no one to govern them, the mob will run riot.'

'The clergy will stay to minister to them.'

'Much good they will do. Those pilgrims and peasants have been too far from home too long. They are losing all restraint and reason. You can see it in their faces.'

I stretched out my tired legs. 'We've all been too far from home too long. Did any ships arrive today?'

'Three from Venice docked in Saint Simeon, I heard. They brought no one but pilgrims.'

I swore softly. Every day it was the same, waiting for the ship from Constantinople that would bring the emperor's new emissary and free me to go home with Anna. Every day that it did not come, my spirits grew more brittle.

'The patriarch spoke to me at the funeral feast. He has an errand for me.' Briefly, I repeated what he had told me. When I mentioned the relic, Sigurd snorted.

'The hand he used to wipe his shit. If the patriarch thinks that'll win the Franks' affection, he'll be disappointed.'

I had known Sigurd long enough that I should not have been shocked by his irreverence, but it still made me uneasy. 'It's a sacred object.'

'It's another week before we can go home.'

'But only a week.' Besides, in my heart, I knew that

Sigurd and I had not distinguished ourselves as guardians of the emperor's interests at Antioch. The Turks were gone, but to have Bohemond controlling the city in their place was hardly an improvement in the emperor's eyes. At least if we found the saint's hand for the patriarch we might salvage something from the campaign.

I looked to Anna, hoping for support. Her face offered nothing.

'If you die in some folly in the mountains, when you should both be sailing home to your families . . .' She stood. 'Anyway, while you go digging out old bones, I have living flesh and blood to attend to.'

I held her sleeve. 'In Antioch? What about the plague?'

She shook free of me. 'Even I know better than to imagine I can cure the plague. But there is a woman whose child is two weeks past due, and I promised I would see her.'

'Be careful.'

'You too. There are more than dead saints and ruined monasteries in the mountains.'

'We'll be back soon.'

'And gone sooner.' Sigurd rose. 'If we leave now, we'll have the cool of the evening to speed us on. *Aelfric!*' He beckoned to a sergeant playing dice on a board he had scratched into the stone rampart. 'Find a dozen men and have them ready to march in half an hour.'

He turned back to us. 'The sooner we go, the sooner we come back. And the sooner we leave this cursed city for ever.'

γ

༄༅

The Varangians could be entertaining travelling companions, but that evening they marched in single file and said little. Perhaps, after all the months spent waiting at Antioch, even they struggled to be on the march again. Perhaps it was the high rampart of the Anti-Taurus mountains looming ahead that dispirited them. Each hour that we marched, the mountains seemed to grow higher, but never closer. As for Brother Pakrad, he struck out ahead of us and stayed there, always fifty yards or so in front, his head bowed and his hands wrapped in his cowl. All I heard from him were occasional snatches of mumbled prayers when the breeze blew them back to us.

On the third day from Antioch, we reached the mountains. The air was cooler now, though the sun was no kinder, and jagged peaks towered over us. Crude terraces embanked some of the lower slopes, and a few hardy goats grazed the grass that pushed through the broken stones, but otherwise there were few signs of life.

'Are these your monastery's lands?' I asked Pakrad, when a particularly steep stretch of road momentarily closed the gap between us.

He nodded. 'Not rich, as you see. But we are simple men, and like the goats we find our living where we can.'

After a couple of miles, the valley opened out and forked into two still-higher valleys with a ridge of peaks between them. The road divided as well, and a ramshackle village had grown up at the junction. There was no inn, but we found the baker and persuaded him to sell us some bread and cheese for our lunch. We ate it in an empty field, just next to the place where the road forked. I noticed Sigurd looking at it unhappily.

'What's wrong?'

'We're not the first men to have come this way today.' He swallowed the last hunk of bread and pointed to the road. A thin stream dribbled across it, and in the surrounding dark earth I could see the churned impressions of many hooves.

I was too far away to see them clearly. 'Perhaps they were cattle.'

'Have you seen any cows since we came into the mountains?' Sigurd gestured a little further up the road, where low mounds rose like molehills in its course. 'I know you've lived in the city for twenty years, but even you must be able to recognise horse shit when you see it.'

I twisted around to look at Brother Pakrad, who was, as ever, sitting a little way apart. 'Which way to your monastery?'

He pointed right, to the north-eastern fork. 'At the head of that valley.'

'The horsemen went the other way.' I explained what Sigurd had noticed.

'Probably Franks. Perhaps they have heard of the relic and come for it themselves. We should hurry.' He looked up. It was only a little past noon, but a haze had clouded the blue sky and our shadows were fainter. 'It is not far now.'

Perhaps it was not, but it needed several more hours of painful drudgery to reach the monastery. The valley walls grew higher and steeper, funnelling us forward, while the hazy sky thickened into fat, dangerous clouds. We must have been very high, yet the air had not thinned. Instead, it felt heavy, pressing close around us. Pakrad was in a skittish mood, forever dancing ahead to spy out our path, while the rest of us trudged after him without enthusiasm.

After a time, Sigurd dropped back beside me and nodded at our sunken path. 'The road ended two miles back. We're walking on a river bed.'

'So?'

He nodded up to the clouds. 'So, if the storm breaks, where do you think all the water will go?'

I shouted ahead to Pakrad, 'How much further?'

In answer, he stopped where he stood and pointed forward. Just ahead, the two sides of the valley curved together to close it off, like a vast natural hippodrome. A sheer buttress protruded where they met, as though the seams of the mountains had been pinched together. Perched on its summit I could see the remains of jagged walls and towers.

'How do we get up there?'

'We climb.' Pakrad laughed, the first time I had ever heard a glimmer of humour from him. 'It is not as steep as it looks.'

That was true: it was not completely sheer, as it had seemed from the distance, but only immensely steep. A thin path threaded its way back and forth across the mountain face: in many places steps had been carved out of the rock.

'We'll never get the donkeys up there,' said Sigurd. 'Make them fast to those trees. Everybody else, get your armour on.' Pakrad made to protest but Sigurd silenced him with a glare. 'I don't want anyone losing his balance because he's got a load on his back. And who's to say what we'll find in the monastery.'

The men threw down their sacks and pulled out their armour. High above us, I could see eagles wheeling against the darkening sky. I wriggled into my mail shirt and drew it snug over my shoulders, then helped Sigurd lace his arm greaves. I buckled my sword belt around my waist and slung my shield over my back. Finally, I pulled on my helmet. Suddenly, the world was a confined and muted place – and even more stultifying than it had been before.

Sigurd scowled at the path. 'Up we go.'

As so often, the last part of the journey was the hardest. Despite the clammy heat inside the helmet, it at least trained my gaze straight ahead, always on the feet of the Varangian in front of me, preventing me from seeing the precipice by my side. The few times I did look out, I did not know whether to be terrified by the drop or dismayed by how far I still had to go. The shield on my back was forever unbalancing me, especially on the steps, which were worn smooth with age. Once the man behind me had to thrust out a palm to stop me toppling backwards.

At last, just when I feared my legs would give out completely and pitch me into oblivion, we halted. I had stopped even hoping for the path to end, and almost collided with the Varangian in front of me. At the head of the line, at the top of a last flight of stairs, Pakrad was standing in front of a door that seemed to lead into the cliff face itself. Only when I looked up did I see that, just above me, the rough rock of the cliff resolved itself into a sheer wall of square-chiselled stone. The masonry was so precise that I could hardly tell where nature's work ended and man's began.

'Is this the monastery's front gate?' asked Sigurd sceptically.

'Sometimes it is wiser to come in by the back door,' said Pakrad.

With the mordant creak of long-unused hinges, the

door in the cliff swung open. Just before I passed inside, I felt the first drops of rain begin to fall.

The Turks might have sacked the monastery but it would be many centuries – perhaps even to the great day of judgement – before the ruins were razed entirely. The foundations had not been erected by men: they had been carved out of the solid rock of the hilltop, so high that they towered over us as we walked through them. Together with the foundations they made a vast stone cauldron, crisscrossed with snatches of walls and strewn with megalithic rubble. They seemed even more mammoth in the wet gloom, while the walls stood stark against the leaden sky.

But someone must have been here since the Turks, for I gradually began to notice signs of repairs clumsily patched onto the mighty foundations. Cracks had been filled with bricks and mortar, while elsewhere wooden stockades had been erected in place of the old walls. A few of the chambers had even been re-roofed, with reed thatch instead of the shattered tiles that lay everywhere. I wandered through the ruins, frightening up a flock of nesting birds, but saw no one.

'Where is this relic hidden?' I called. The wind was stronger here on the summit, and colder, whistling through the glassless windows. My tentative words were snatched away almost before they passed my lips.

'Here.' Brother Pakrad's face appeared in a doorway, beneath a broken arch whose two stumps reached towards each other like claws. 'In here.'

I looked around. The rest of our company had scattered to search the ruins, not trusting our solitude, and I was alone. The rain was drumming harder now. Brother Pakrad beckoned me forward. 'Come. The relic is in here.'

I ducked under the broken arch, though I did not need to, into a rounded apse where the monastery church had once stood. A part of its domed roof still arced overhead, fractured like an eggshell, but otherwise it was open. Weeds had driven cracks through the tiled floor and the icons on the walls had crumbled, so that they represented not whole men but a dismembered host, the army of the saints as they might have appeared in the aftermath of a terrible battle.

'Over here.'

At least the remaining portion of the roof sheltered me from the rain. I followed where Pakrad led me, to a pedestal at the back of the church near where an altar must once have stood. It seemed far removed from God now.

'Pull that stone,' he ordered.

I knelt. It was easy to see the stone the monk meant. It had been cut to fit its niche, but not so perfectly as to hide the gaps where mortar should have held it in place. It rose slightly higher than the adjoining blocks as well, giving a purchase for my fingertips to press against. A small cross, weathered almost to invisibility, was carved in its centre.

It slid away easily when I pulled, revealing a small hollow behind. I reached in my hand and felt around in the darkness. The chamber was not large, no deeper than my elbow, and it took little time for me to establish its contents.

There was nothing there. The hole was empty.

Before I could wonder at it, a ticklish sensation under my chin caused me to raise my head. I suddenly went very still. Brother Pakrad had approached and was standing over me. He held a curved sword, pressing its blade so hard against my throat that I scarcely dared breathe.

My eyes locked on his. He carried the sword far more naturally than the cross: the blade barely trembled in his grip. In the distance, I heard sudden shouts of alarm, followed quickly by the ring of clashing steel, and the bellow of Sigurd shouting my name.

Pakrad moved the blade against my throat. It cut close as a razor – though thankfully no closer. 'Answer him.'

I had no time to obey – or defy him. Before I could speak, a barrage of heavy footsteps ran up the passage outside the church, paused, and rushed in. Kneeling with my back to the door I could not see anything, but I heard the commotion that accompanied them, then an abrupt halt and Sigurd's bewildered voice calling, 'Demetrios?'

'Put down your weapons,' Pakrad shouted. 'Put them down, or your friend will be the first to die.'

I could not hear if they obeyed, for suddenly the room became a pit of noise. Twisting back my head as far as I dared, I saw a small knot of Varangians surrounded on all sides by a press of armed men. More enemies were perched on top of the walls with bows in their hands, black as crows. Rain poured into the roofless church, plastering men's hair to their heads and making their weapons slick in their hands. Those bows would be almost useless, but that would not turn the odds in our favour. Above me, the rain drummed on the fractured roof so hard I thought it might crack and bury me.

Sigurd, standing at the head of the Varangians, caught my eye. He gave a resigned shrug, though I saw he had not put down his axe. A nudge on my throat from Pakrad's sword forced my head back around.

'Put down your weapons,' Pakrad repeated. The men who surrounded the Varangians were becoming agitated. *'Put them down now.'*

Over the pelting rain, I heard the defeated clatter of a heavy axe falling on stone. And then, very suddenly, a rushing of air and a sound like damp wood being chopped. The sword that had been against my neck fell to the ground as Pakrad reeled back. Blood cascaded down his cowl, pouring from the gash where a small throwing axe had almost severed his arm from his shoulder.

Instincts learned in the imperial armies and honed fine in the last year took over. I lunged for the fallen sword, snatched it up and swung it at Pakrad. But he had stumbled back, clutching his wound, and the blade swept wide. I had no time to chase him. Every man in that room had been poised a hair's breadth from violence; now, the battle erupted. I charged back to the centre of the church, ducking away from the blades that stabbed at me, and threw myself into the besieged knot of Varangians.

39

'We have to get out,' I shouted in Sigurd's ear. I shrugged the shield off my back and slung my arm through its straps. From the corner of my eye I saw a spear-point driving towards me and I rolled my wrists so that my blade knocked it wide. One of the Varangians behind me caught hold of the shaft and pulled it forward, unbalancing the man who held it: as he stumbled forward his head went down and exposed his neck. My sword flashed in the rain and he was gone.

A cold and bloody rage overtook me: rage that I had ignored my misgivings and walked into this trap; rage that I might never see Anna again; rage that Pakrad had betrayed us. I could see him across the room now, white-faced and bleeding but still shouting orders at his men. They must have outnumbered us at least threefold, but they did not have the discipline of the imperial armies. A wall of shields held them at bay, and the Varangians took savage delight in battering aside the spear-thrusts and chopping off the arms that held them.

'We have to get out of here,' Sigurd shouted from some-where beside me.

'How?'

'Back to the gate. We'll—'

Sigurd broke off as our enemies pressed home another attack. I could hear their spears smashing and splintering on the shield rim that cased us.

Suddenly, a bright chink appeared in the dark world of our defensive circle. One of the Varangians must have dropped his guard, for a spear had transfixed his throat and blood was pouring out of it like a spigot. He dropped to his knees but could not fall, for the spear held him upright like a man at prayer. The men beside him were desperately trying to close ranks but, even in death, he blocked them. It was all the opening our enemies needed: a wedge of men and spears drove in, prising us apart, and suddenly we were in a crazed mêlée of open combat. On my left, two of the Varangians dived towards the door but were stabbed back. I knocked aside a spear-thrust with my shield but did not have the strength to counter-attack; instead, inexorably, I gave ground, my eyes flitting over the battlefield in search of allies. Where was Sigurd?

The winnowing of combat had begun to separate our sides once more. Pakrad's men had managed to form a loose cordon that blocked off three sides of the room, forcing us back near the altar and cutting us off from the door. *Where was Sigurd?* The spear-thrusts were less fierce now, as if our enemies knew we were beaten and were content to prod us back into our pen. They were no less dangerous for that, and I was constantly on my guard, swatting and chopping at the stabbing points. Still they forced us back.

I saw Sigurd at last, and in my shock was almost spitted by an oncoming spear. He was not among the few Varangians beside me frantically fending off the closing noose: he was lying on the floor behind the line of our enemies, rolling and screaming in a lake of blood.

An unbidden silence suddenly gripped the bloody chamber. The line of Saracen guards stepped back, keeping their spears angled towards us, while the Varangians and I clustered together and lowered our weapons. There was blood on my hands and my armour – even, when I licked my lips, on my face – but little of it was mine. The coughing of exhausted warriors and the drumming of the rain dinned my ears after the clamour of battle.

Pakrad stepped forward. He had torn a strip from his cowl and tied it over his shoulder to stem the bleeding, though he had to lean on a spear to stay upright. 'Surrender now.'

I spat a bloody wad of phlegm onto the floor. 'What terms will you offer?'

That provoked a laugh. 'Terms? When you are wriggling on the points of my spears, then I will talk of terms. Otherwise, all I offer is that if you surrender, I will spare you – for now.'

I could see by their faces that the Varangians beside me did not like that. 'These men would rather die now than have their throats cut in your prison. You must offer them more than that.'

'Would you believe me if I did?'

Behind Pakrad, Sigurd struggled to raise himself on his elbow. He mumbled something that was too faint to hear, though every man among us knew what he meant. More than anyone, Sigurd wanted to die well: he would not surrender. All the time I had known him he had seemed invulnerable, an animal spirit from one of his boreal legends. Seeing him now left me wanting nothing more than to empty my stomach onto the ground and weep.

42

Pakrad had raised his sword. 'If you do not surrender now, I will kill the wounded first. Then I will finish you one by one. You, Demetrios, will be the last.'

'That is barbaric,' I muttered.

'It is war.'

Beside Pakrad, one of his men dangled his sword like a pendulum over Sigurd's throat. 'Well?'

I dropped my sword, pulled my left arm out of my shield straps and let it fall to the ground. Sigurd groaned; the other Varangians looked at me with despising, hate-filled eyes. One of them – a young man named Oswald – could not stand the wound to his pride: he ran towards the line of Pakrad's men, bellowing a war-cry and lifting his axe to strike. A long spear ran him through before he was within four feet of his enemies. He was lifted clear off the ground by the force of the blow before falling, gurgling, on his back. A second spear finished him with a thrust between his eyes.

None of the other Varangians had moved to follow him, and none did so now. Whether cowed by his fate or sickened by the waste, they threw down their axes.

With supreme derision in his moment of triumph, Pakrad turned his back on us.

'Lock them away.'

δ

∞∞∞∞

They stripped us of our armour and herded us out of the church, into a small adjoining room. Once it had probably been a chapel; now, with iron rings driven into the walls and lengths of rope and chain lying in the corners, it had become a prison. The only mercy was that it had a roof. The thatch was black with mould, and allowed a steady dribble of water to drip through, but it kept the worst of the rain off us.

Our captors tied our wrists, then made us fast to the wall on short ropes just long enough that we could sit. They treated the wounded no more gently – even Sigurd, whom they had carried there and who slumped unconscious against the wall. All told, nine of us seemed to have survived. With brusque tugs to make sure our bonds were secure, they left us alone.

I sat in the darkness, tipping my head back against the cool wall to lessen the strain on my shoulders. Despair squeezed me so tight that my body longed to empty itself: the food from my guts, the tears from my eyes, the blood from my veins. Only the presence of the Varangians kept me from collapse. The sour smell of blood overwhelmed the room, and the wounded groaned out their pain. I closed my eyes, though it made no difference.

After about an hour, Pakrad came to visit. The monk's habit had gone, replaced by a grimy grey tunic and a leather hauberk. Three knives hung from his belt, another jutted from the top of his boot. Of his monastic disguise, only the tonsure remained – an incongruous crown to his vicious appearance.

'We need a doctor,' I said. 'And water.'

Pakrad looked down on me with a sneer. 'You will get what I give you. After you have given me what I want. He pointed to my hands, tied in front of me like a supplicant at prayer. 'Give me your ring.'

I looked down at my left hand, to the finger where I wore the imperial signet ring. *Was that what this battle was about?*

'Give me the ring,' Pakrad repeated. He reached out his left hand, while with his right he pulled one of the knives from his belt. The blade was dull in the dim light as he slapped it impatiently against the flat of his hand.

'Give me it.'

Instinctively, I tried to make a fist, but Pakrad was faster and had pressed his blade into my palm so that I could not close my fingers without cutting myself. He lifted the knife, so that I had no choice but to raise my hand. With a grunt of satisfaction, he twisted the ring off my finger and jammed it on his own.

'Is that all you wanted?' I asked in astonishment. A little ring – a ring I would gladly have thrown into the dust at the roadside to be free of my obligation to the emperor. Why had it brought me here?

Pakrad sheathed his knife and stared at the ring on his hand, admiring his trophy. I saw that he winced whenever he moved his shoulder, and I took a small measure of satisfaction from that.

'We need a doctor,' I said again.

He looked up. 'Do you know what dogs do when one of their pack goes lame? They tear him apart and eat him. There is no doctor here.' He paused, savouring my misery. 'But I will do what I can for your friend. He will be worth less injured, and nothing at all if he dies.'

'Worth less to whom?'

But Pakrad only laughed, and left us in our prison.

None of us spoke. A wave of desolation broke over me; I no longer even had the hope to pray. I had abandoned Anna and forsaken Sigurd, the two people I loved best in the world after my children – and all so that a treacherous bandit could steal a worthless ring. I wished he had stolen the ring from my campfire, or even cut it from my finger at Antioch, rather than luring me to die in this remote monastery. *Not to die*, a voice whispered – if he'd wanted

46

me dead he could have had me impaled on the end of a spear hours ago. But I feared there was little kindness in his mercy.

If I kept thinking those thoughts I would have dashed out my brains on the wall behind me by morning. With a great effort of will, I forced myself to concentrate on my surroundings. It must be night outside: I could hear the tramp of guards on the walls, muttered watchwords and spears clattering against stone; water dripping on the floor and a horse whinnying near by. Around me, the Varangians muttered prayers, though whether for themselves, their captain or their fallen companions I could not tell. I wondered which god they prayed to.

My shoulders were beginning to go numb. I wriggled in my bonds to try and work some feeling into my limbs, and as I did so I noticed something in the corner of my eye. To my right, a small spot glowed silver in the dark wall. I twisted around, trying not to make a noise. There was a hole in the wall, no larger than a walnut, but big enough that if I put my eye to it I could see through into the room on the far side.

It was the basilica, the church where we had fought and lost our battle, now washed in moonlight. I could see the stone I had pulled away on the altar dais still lying where I had left it, and the pile of armour taken from the Varangians. Most of the blood had been cleaned away by the rain, though dark splashes still stained some of the walls. Otherwise, the room was empty.

I rolled away and settled myself in the least uncomfortable position I could manage. Then, God knows how, I slept.

When I opened my eyes, bright light poured through the holes in the thatch, and I could see my surroundings clearly at last. Immediately, I looked across the room to Sigurd. He lay still under his blanket, eyes closed, the only sign of life the shallow rising and falling of his chest beneath it. Thankfully, he did not seem to be bleeding.

Later in the morning, our guards brought breakfast: a cold corn-meal gruel that they slopped into our mouths. At least it seemed they meant to keep us alive – though to what purpose, I did not dare guess. After that, we were left alone again.

The storm the day before might have cleared the air, but the respite did not last long. The thatched roof stifled us like a blanket, heating the dank air until the stench and the steam became almost unbearable. For a time, the Varangians talked hopefully of escape and tugged on the iron rings that locked them in place, but even their strength could not dislodge them. They soon lapsed into silence. We lolled against the walls, occasionally shrugging our shoulders to try and keep some life in them, and sweltered.

With nothing else to do, I spent much of the time peering through the hole in the wall – though always on edge lest one of the guards catch me. There was plenty to see. Pakrad seemed to use the derelict church as his headquarters. He sat behind a broad table he had erected in the shade of the domed roof, while his men lounged in the sun and a succession of visitors came and went. They spoke Armenian, and though I did not understand a word they said it was easy enough to work out what was happening. Men and women, mostly peasants, would enter the room with eyes lowered and an offering held before them: baskets of eggs or olives, two chickens in a wicker cage, jars of wine and oil, even a full-grown sheep. Every one of them trembled as they came in – particularly the women. They would deposit their gifts in front of Pakrad, bow low, and mumble some plea or homage, which Pakrad would then consider, or debate with his men, or dismiss with a scornful wave of his hand. Some of the petitioners went away smiling with relief, others weeping or with their heads buried in their hands. Some were less lucky. In the middle of the afternoon I watched as a peasant girl harangued and pleaded with Pakrad, refusing to accept his obvious rejections, until eventually his men dragged her away. Her screams echoed through the monastery for a full hour afterwards.

I did not watch any more after that. I had seen enough to get the measure of Pakrad. He took homage and distributed justice like a lord, but in truth he was nothing more than a brigand, and the monastery his ramshackle castle. What had happened to the monks, I did not like to think. Nor could I tell why he should have troubled to lure us there, or what he intended with us.

*   *   *

Late in the day, when the light had softened to a peach-tinged glow streaming in over my head, I heard a shout from the courtyard, the creak of a heavy gate and the clop of hooves. A greeting or a challenge was shouted, though I did not hear the answer.

I twisted around and put my eye to the hole in the wall. A fire had been built in the nave of the church; beyond it, I could see Pakrad pacing behind his table. He was almost unrecognisable from the cocksure brigand I had watched that afternoon. He seemed off-balance, nervous, constantly smoothing down the folds of his tunic.

There was a noise from the unseen door and his head snapped around. I heard footsteps, then saw a dark figure stride past the fire. He wore a riding cloak with the hood pulled up, though he must surely have regretted it with the heat of the fire so close and the heat of the day not yet faded.

Like all the suppliants I had seen that day, he brought a gift: a heavy bag tied with rope, which he deposited on the table. I heard the muffled chink of coins settling as he put it down. It must have been a rich offering, but there was nothing subservient in the man who brought it. He stood tall and superior, surveying the bandit from under the shadow of his hood. Though I could not see his face, there was no doubting his authority over Pakrad.

Pakrad reached into one of the folds of his robe and pulled out something that he handed to his guest. Sparks of firelight reflected off it, and though it was too far and dim to see clearly, I knew what it was. The guest examined it, slid it onto his finger and held up his hand, twisting it this way and that so that light played on the filigrees of the imperial seal. Then he pulled it off and dropped it into a pouch around his neck.

'That was what you wanted?' Pakrad seemed hesitant, eager to please, though at the same time jealous of his visitor's status. With a shock, I realised he had spoken in Greek.

The hooded guest tapped the bag on the table. 'That is what I paid you for. Did they put up much of a struggle?'

He had spoken in Greek too – but more than that, there was something familiar in his voice. Could I have heard it before?

'They fought,' Pakrad admitted.

'I told you they would. But you overcame them?'

'You got your ring.'

The guest rounded on him. 'That was not all we agreed. You swore not one of them would survive.'

'None of them escaped.'

The evasion was as obvious as it was misjudged. In answer, the guest reached under his cloak and pulled out a long, straight-bladed sword. Pakrad recoiled, reaching for one of the knives in his belt, but before he could seize it the guest had stepped forward, put the tip of his blade against the bag on the table, and whipped it upwards to sever the rope that held it shut. The folds of cloth fell open like the petals of a flower, revealing a small mountain of gold within. Pakrad stared.

51

'I paid you and I paid you well. The ring – and no one to tell the tale.'

Pakrad picked up a coin and rubbed it between his fingers. The touch of gold seemed to give him new strength. 'These are dangerous times. The mountains are full of enemies – Franks, Arabs, Turks from the defeated army . . .'

'And thieves,' said his guest drily. Pakrad ignored him.

'Those prisoners will fetch a high price in Damascus or Baghdad. Death would be a waste.'

The guest still had his sword in his hand. Though he held it still, the reflected firelight made the blade look as though it danced and writhed in the air. For a moment, I thought he might cut down Pakrad where he stood. Then, to my surprise, he shrugged.

'Do as you want. They are not my concern.'

'I promise you they will never be heard of again,' Pakrad assured him.

The visitor looked around. 'Are they here?'

It was a casual question, but whether by chance or some devilish intuition, his gaze came to rest right on the stretch of wall that housed my peephole, so that he seemed to be staring straight down the stone tunnel into my eyes. Terror seized me; I almost jerked away, but then he would have seen the movement. I forced myself to stay still and prayed he had not noticed me.

Oblivious to my terror, Pakrad was answering the question. 'The prisoners have gone. I sold them this morning to an Arab.' The lie came fluently; I wondered what he

52

would have said if he had known how close his guest was to seeing the truth.

'Very well.' The guest nodded at the gold. 'I will not forget your service.'

'And you will see that the Franks do not come here looking for the Greeks?'

The visitor laughed softly. He had started to move to the door, was already almost beyond the confines of my view, but he turned back to answer Pakrad. The glowing fire threw up a monstrous shadow on the walls behind him.

'Nobody will come to look for the Greeks.'

I barely heard the words. The firelight that cast shadows behind him also banished the shadows that hooded his face, so for the first time I could see it clearly. Of course I knew his voice – the only reason I had not recognised it sooner was that I had not heard it speaking Greek before. Nor had I ever expected to hear it speaking the treachery I had just witnessed.

It was Duke Godfrey.

3

∽∾∽∾∽

It was hard to fall asleep that night. I squatted by the wall, my arms bound before me, trembling as my mind burned with thoughts of the treachery I had witnessed – the treachery that had snared me. Again and again I saw Duke Godfrey framed in the stone barrel of my peephole, his pale skin and golden beard turned orange by the firelight. Why had he done this? I knew he did not love the Greeks: at Constantinople, his army had even come to blows with the imperial forces. But that quarrel was long settled, and since then Godfrey had seemed a model of restraint, free of the tempestuous ambitions that shook the other princes. Why had he done this to me?

But of course, he had not done it to me – or not for my sake. I was merely a casualty, an inconvenience to be removed. He wanted the ring. For the rest of us, he did not even care enough to have us murdered. The thought only made me angrier: I raged against Godfrey, against Pakrad, against Tatikios who had abandoned me at Antioch and the emperor who had sent me there. But the heat of anger could not burn through my bonds or the walls that trapped me, nor lift the crushing weight of my insignificance. Few things make a man feel more alive than death, but now Duke Godfrey had robbed even that of meaning.

Eventually, fingers of sleep began to creep over me. The boundaries of the world dissolved: the things I saw and the things I dreamed and the things I feared mingled freely together in the dark room. Anna was there, though she would not talk to me, and Zoe and Helena my daughters. Helena held her newborn son and pointed to me, the grandfather he would never meet. Sigurd moaned, while Godfrey bent over him and laid gold coins on his eyes. I could see Antioch in the distance, and a terrible battle being waged before its gates. In an instant, I seemed to be in the midst of the battle, throwing up my shield while my enemies battered it with their blows.

I opened my eyes. Someone was jabbing me in the ribs, though without malice. Aelfric. With his hands bound in front of him, he could not reach me with his arms, but had swivelled himself around to poke me with his foot. Otherwise, everything in the room seemed normal: nine of us tied fast to the walls, moonlight filtering through the thatch, and the door still bolted shut.

'What is it?'

'Listen.'

Almost at once, I heard it. Shouts, the pound of running feet, and beyond it the drum of horses' hooves. A group of men – three or four by the sound of them – ran past our door. I could hear their spear-hafts dragging on the floor behind them.

'Is it a rescue?'

But even as I said it, I remembered the truth of Duke Godfrey's words. *Nobody will come to look for the Greeks.*

Whatever was happening, there was nothing we could do. We were like slaves in a galley, locked in place and powerless against the forces raging around us. We sat in the darkness, pale faces straining to understand the mysterious sounds that drifted down to us, and waited.

Outside, the uproar was rapidly building into the tumult of a full-blown battle. Bows cracked; arrows rattled against stone like leaves before a gale. The pitch of the shouts rose. Then men started screaming, and I knew the battle had been joined.

I wriggled around to see if I could see anything through my spyhole. The church was empty. The sack of gold was gone from the table, and the fire had all but burned out – though not long ago, for even through the dank stone wall I could smell the lingering tinge of smoke.

Another kick in the ribs from Aelfric drew me back to our room. His face was ashen in the moonlight.

'Do you smell that?'

After a day and a half being confined in that hot room,

unable to move more than a few inches, the stench was terrible. But beyond the rank smells of men, there was something new in the air. Smoke – not drifting through my spyhole, but pouring in through the holes in the thatch and seeping through the cracks in the eaves.

In an instant, the sullen resignation in the room turned to panic. The monumental stones of the monastery's foundations might be immune to fire, but the ramshackle wooden superstructures that Pakrad had built on it would burn like kindling. The Varangians turned to the walls and heaved with all their might on the ringbolts; they flexed their wrists and tried to pull the ropes apart with brute strength. Nothing would give. The smoke thickened; through the hole in the ceiling I could see sparks and embers dancing on air in the night sky. If a single one fell on the dry-baked straw roof . . .

'At least we won't be tied up much longer,' muttered Aelfric. He had lifted his hands to his mouth and was trying to gnaw through the bonds like a rat. He spat out a wad of fibres. 'If the roof drops on us, it'll burn these ropes clean through.'

'And us with them.' I had found a corner of stone that protruded from the wall and was rubbing my wrists against it, trying to saw through the rope. It did not even dent it.

With a squeak and a bang, the door flew open. A murky, light filled the corridor beyond like dawn, though we were still hours from sunrise: one of Pakrad's men stood silhouetted in its glow. His hair was dishevelled, his eyes wild with surprise; he had not even had time to put on armour or helmet, but the long, curved knife in his hand was steady enough. He took two steps into the room, towards the nearest prisoner – but whether he came to execute or to free us we never learned. Shouts from the corridor stopped him mid-stride. He turned back to the doorway, but his way was blocked, and this time the man who stood there had not forgotten his armour. He wore the coned helmet of the Franks, though with sackcloth hanging from its rim so that only his eyes were visible, and a loaded crossbow was wedged to his shoulder.

I did not know who fought this battle but it hardly mattered: we were merely spectators. The guard sprang towards the door, then seemed to halt, caught like a spark on a breeze. The crack of the bow still echoed around the chamber as he staggered back, clutching his breast where the bolt had struck, and collapsed. The knife dropped from his hand and skidded across the smooth-worn floor.

The Frank stared into the room. Eight pairs of captive eyes stared back in silence. Behind the sackcloth veil, I felt his eyes fixed upon me as he slowly put the curved end of the bow on the ground, held it down with his foot and leaned over to haul the string back into position. Even in that brief motion, he seemed to fade before me. Tears stung my eyes and I felt ashamed. Was this how I would face my death? At least Sigurd would not see me: through all the commotion he still lay unconscious under his blanket, eyes shut. Though he, too, seemed to be fading away from me. Is this how death comes, I wondered, the

58

world gradually thinning to a mist as we recede from it? Warmth suffused my body; my head felt light, while at the door the knight loaded his bolt.

A ball of fire fell like a star from the sky and I looked up in horror. Death was reaching out for me, but it would not be the quick passage I had hoped for. A gaping hole had opened in the roof, fringed with a jagged halo of burning straw spreading ever outwards as it devoured the thatch. Flames licked high above it.

Whether the Frank with the crossbow decided the fire would do his work for him, or whether he simply did not see us in the smoke and darkness, I never found out. He loaded his bow, then turned and disappeared down the corridor. In the madness of those moments I almost called him back so I could die quickly, but he would not have heard me. And I would die soon enough.

Ash and soot rained down on us, as if we sat in the grate of an enormous hearth. Across the room, I could see one of the Varangians stretching forward like a horse pulling its reins, still trying even now to escape. The swirl of smoke and flame made illusions of the world, so that for a second I could almost imagine that he had managed to free himself. Shadows rose above him so that he seemed to be standing; they moved across the room, shifting and turning as if ducking away from the falling embers.

A hot shard pressed against my wrist, searing flesh already chafed raw by my bonds. The roof-beams had started to burn, and a piece of debris must have fallen on me. I screamed and squirmed, trying to dislodge it, but it had a will of its own and would not go away. It writhed against my skin; it slithered back and forth, so I could almost imagine it was eating away at the ropes that bound me.

'Get up.'

The smoke and tears that clogged my eyes had all but blinded me. Now I forced my eyes open and looked up. One of the Varangians was standing over me. His bonds were gone, and in his hand he held the long-bladed knife Pakrad's guard had dropped.

'Am I dreaming?'

'You will be if we don't hurry. Come on.'

One by one, he knelt in front of the others and cut the ropes that bound them. I followed through the heat and flame, trying to coax life into limbs that smoke and despair had left numb. Last of all, we came to Sigurd. His face was peaceful, and he seemed to be sleeping beneath his blanket. We cut through his shackles as carefully as we could, then I gently slapped his cheek.

'Can you hear me?'

He groaned, but did not open his eyes.

In a torrent of confusion and haste, I beckoned two of the Varangians over. They slid their arms under his shoulders and lifted. As Sigurd rose, the blanket slid away leaving him entirely naked, but there was no time to dress him. Choking and coughing, we stumbled out into the corridor. Aelfric was the last through the door – and not a second too soon, for an instant later the makeshift beams gave way and the entire roof crashed down into our gaol. A cloud of sparks and burning straw blasted out through the door like dragon's breath, blackening the stones and singeing our heads.

Two of Pakrad's men lay dead in the passage, pierced with crossbow bolts, but there was no sign of any enemies living. Looking up into the sky, I could see that the ancient monastery had become a cauldron of fire. Even the stones seemed to burn.

'This way.' A dark blizzard of ash and soot assailed us as we staggered down the passage into the old monastery church. At least here there was little for the fire to take hold of, and the remaining portion of the stone roof might shelter us from the burning missiles raining down. We hurried into its shadow.

'Where now?' I bellowed in Aelfric's ear.

'Up there.'

In the curved bay at the end of the church, a high window looked out to the east. Its lower half had been blocked in with stones and mortar, but there was still enough space at the top for a man to squeeze through. If he could reach it.

'How do we get there?'

'On the shoulders of better men.' In a niche in the southern wall, a life-sized statue of the prophet Daniel watched over the monastery's desolation. Rain had smoothed his features to the primordial canvas of the first man, birds had fouled him, and white pock-marks on his chest showed where Pakrad's men had used him to prac-tise their archery, but he still stood. No wonder: it took

61

six of the Varangians just to pry him from his alcove and drag him to the space under the window. I watched the door, praying the invaders would not drive Pakrad's men back to this place. It was hard to believe any could have survived the inferno, though every so often the hot wind still carried the cries of men and horses to my ears.

A thought struck me. 'What's on the other side of that wall?'

But there was no time for doubts. One of the Varangians made a stirrup with his hands and lifted me up; another kept the statue from toppling over as I scrabbled for balance on its shoulders. From that height, I could just stretch my hands to the rough lip where the window opened. A day and a half in bondage had left my wrists raw and my arms numb; there was little power in them, but somehow I managed to keep my grip and haul myself up: first my chin, then my chest, and eventually my whole body. Urgent shouts from below spurred me on, though I did not have the strength to care what they were saying.

I reached the crumbling window ledge and crouched under its arch. Behind me, high tongues of flame licked into the night – ahead was only darkness.

'Go on!' shouted Aelfric's voice below. 'Out of the way.'

I jumped. It was the leap of a madman: from a high window, on a cliffbound mountain top, into darkness. If I had fallen a thousand feet and impaled myself on jagged rocks, it would have been no more than I deserved. But God was with me that night. The ground was hard, but not far. I struck it with a yelp of pain, jarring my knees, feeling my ankle turn beneath me, and rolled away in a cascade of dust and pebbles until a thorn tree brought me to a stop. After the inferno in the monastery, the night seemed cool and quiet. The smell of sagegrass filled my senses.

'*Demetrios!*' A voice from above was calling my name. 'Is it safe?'

I do not know what I answered – I was almost past thinking. I lay there, while one by one the Varangians crawled out through the window and dropped to the ground. Somehow they managed to manhandle Sigurd's naked body onto the ledge, and then lower it down. By that time, I had recovered enough that I could stand and hobble over to look at him. His face was deathly pale, scratched and bruised from being squeezed through the window.

'Sigurd?'

Whether he understood, or whether it was just reflex, his eyes flicked open. They looked vague and distant, but after a moment they seemed to focus on me.

'Demetrios,' he said, and I felt a thrill of hope. 'You shit.'

5

We had escaped – but not far. In the darkness, our heads still reeling from the smoke we had breathed, we did not dare try to find our way down. Even if there had been a path, we could never have managed to carry Sigurd. We found a small ledge in the mountainside, almost hidden by the gorse bushes that fringed it, and settled down to wait.

The monastery burned on, lighting up the western sky with its glow and filling the night with the crashing sounds of ruination. The noise wrought havoc on my nerves as I sat hunched on my rock: with each falling beam or collapsing wall, I was convinced I heard the footsteps of an unseen enemy about to discover us.

Eventually, when the fresh light in the east matched the

sullen glow in the west, I left our hiding place and crawled back up the slope. I could see the high wall of the monastery church and the window we had escaped through towering above me. I skirted around it to the north, then crept up to a hollow just below the summit where a tree-stump offered some cover. Even that was not entirely safe, for a spent arrow, a relic of the battle, lay planted in the earth by my feet. I pulled it out, snapped off the shaft and gripped the arrowhead like a dagger. Then I peered over the rotting tree-stump.

I had come around to the front of the monastery. As we had guessed, the steep path that Pakrad had brought us by was not the main entrance. Here, the mountain sloped away more gradually towards a high valley. A road ran up to a broad gate in the monastery wall; the gates had been thrown down, and through the arch I could see the ruins of the monastery still billowing smoke. Yet for all the desolation, it was not abandoned. Some fifty Frankish knights were arrayed in a wide cordon on the open ground before the gates, some mounted, others on foot; some watching outwards and some facing the centre of their circle, where a knot of men was gathered beside a smouldering heap of coals. Duke Godfrey stood among them. He had removed his helmet, so that his tousled hair blew freely in the morning breeze, and his face was streaked black where he had tried, unsuccessfully, to wipe away the soot stains. I thought of the ring he had taken from me, and wondered where it was now.

In front of Godfrey stood the defeated men from

Pakrad's garrison. A dozen Frankish spear-points held them back, though there was little defiance now in their wretched faces. Many were wounded: one had lost an entire arm, so that his captors could not shackle him but had been forced to tie him to the man next to him.

Two knights dragged one of the prisoners forward and flung him onto his knees in front of Godfrey. It was Pakrad, I realised, though he was hardly recognisable from the cocksure bandit who had betrayed us. He had lost his armour and his tunic, leaving only a dirty cloth around his hips to cover him. Terrible burns covered his naked chest and arms, and flaps of charred skin hung from his body like feathers. He was weeping.

'Did you think you could cheat our bargain?'

The breeze blew Godfrey's words over to my hiding place. Beside him, a man with his back to me stirred the coals with his sword. A flurry of sparks flew up, and the air shimmered above it. Pakrad trembled.

'Please, Lord,' he pleaded. 'I did everything you asked. I brought you the ring. I killed the Greeks. I—'

'You told me you sold the Greeks for slaves.'

'It is the same thing.' Pakrad glanced back over his shoulder at the ruin of his fortress; I wondered if Duke Godfrey had noticed. 'They are surely dead now.' He lifted his bound hands and pawed at the hem of Godfrey's tunic, but Godfrey stepped back with a snort of disgust and Pakrad almost fell on his face.

'You are a worm,' Godfrey told him. 'A robber and a villain. This monastery that you made your lair – how many monks did you murder to take it?' He walked around behind his captive and seized hold of a lock of his hair, jerking his head back. He rapped his knuckles on the bare skin where the tonsure had been, and Pakrad screamed.

'Does it hurt?' Godfrey enquired. 'It should. It is the mark of God on a wicked sinner. You profaned the holy soil of the monastery with your crimes, and you mocked God Himself by putting on the habit of His servants to work evil.'

'On your orders, Lord,' Pakrad protested. Godfrey ignored him.

'Do you know what the crime of Satan was?' Pakrad shook his head in terror. 'He knew he could not surpass God, so he sought to overthrow Heaven itself and make himself lord over its ruin. He tried to mimic God, as a chained ape mimics a man. And do you know what befell him?'

Pakrad, his head still pulled back by Godfrey's grip, made an unintelligible cry.

'He was cast into eternal darkness.'

Godfrey released Pakrad and turned his back. The bandit's head slumped, but in an instant one of the knights had sprung forward and clamped it between his gauntleted hands, twisting it up towards the sky. The man by the fire turned towards Pakrad, showing his face to me at last, and I gasped. It was Tancred, the half-Saracen nephew of Bohemond. He pulled the sword from the coals and advanced a few paces towards Pakrad. The tip of the sword glowed a dull red – which bloomed to a burning orange as Tancred held it up to his lips and blew on it. Pakrad started to squeal; his body jerked and writhed, but the iron-clad hands that gripped his skull held it helpless.

Tancred drew back the sword. The red tip hovered in front of Pakrad's eyes for a moment, darting this way and that. Twice Tancred flicked it forward but checked the blow, laughing to hear Pakrad's desperate screams. Then he lunged.

My own eyes clenched shut involuntarily a split second before the blow, but I heard the hiss of the iron as it cut through the eyeball, and the shattering cries from Pakrad's wounded body, which doubled in their agony as Tancred stabbed his sword into the second eye.

'Take him away,' said Godfrey. As I opened my eyes I saw that he still stood a little distance from Tancred, his back turned on the torture. Pakrad was being dragged back into the circle of prisoners. He was trying to press his hands to his face, but with the ropes that bound them he could not reach.

I had seen enough: I crawled away, back down the slope to the hidden ledge where the Varangians waited. Even there, the screams from the mountaintop echoed down to us for hours afterwards – and still seemed to linger in the air long after we heard Godfrey's men ride away. Only near sunset, when we were certain they had gone, did we rise from our hiding place and set out for Antioch.

ζ

〰〰〰〰〰

A wall of death surrounded Antioch, far stronger than any ramparts of earth or stone, and a foul film hung above the city where the smoke of countless pyres stained the air. We marched along the river bank, barely an arrow-shot from the walls, and saw no one. Only the dead were in evidence. The soft earth of the meadow outside the walls had been carved into innumerable graves, some marked with stones but most of them anonymous. One by one, each of the Varangians crossed himself, and then made a surreptitious sign against the evil eye for good measure. I laid a thin cloth over Sigurd's face so he would not breathe the malignant air. We had carried him back from the monastery on a litter, and though he had gained some consciousness and could occasionally speak a few

69

words, he was still achingly weak. Sweat glistened on his face where the fever boiled it out of him. It was shocking to see him diminished like this – like seeing an ancient oak tree felled for firewood. In the wandering course of my life I had not had to suffer the decline and death of my parents, for I had left them far behind in Illyria and never returned, but I imagined this was how a son must feel to see his father on his sick-bed: an indomitable constant brought down. It was strange, for he and I were the same age.

A few miles west of Antioch, in the hills between the plain and the coast, we found the hilltop where the remaining Varangians – and Anna – had moved their camp from the plague-ridden city. We climbed eagerly, our burdens suddenly much lightened. At the bottom of the valley, far below, I could see the sinuous course of the Orontes hastening towards the coast and the ship that would take me home. The setting sun turned the river gold, while an eagle wheeled silently in the sky above.

We came around a bend in the path and I knew at once something had changed. The guard who blocked our way was not a Varangian – indeed, he probably came from the opposite corner of the earth. His dark face was too wide and too short, like a reflection in a polished shield, with narrow eyes and a broad mouth that almost vanished under the mane of his beard. His helmet tapered to a sharp point like an onion, with a chain hood hanging down behind his neck, while the square plates of his scale armour rasped and chattered as they moved against each other.

The long spear in his hands was angled across our path, though it was the horn-ended bow slung across his shoulder that was the real danger. He was a Patzinak, another of the emperor's far-flung mercenary legions.

'Who are you?' he challenged us in guttural Greek.

'Demetrios Askiates, with Sigurd Ragnarson and what remain of his men.'

The Patzinak nodded, without curiosity. 'Come through. Nikephoros is impatient to meet you.'

Our fortunes had changed in the ten days we had been away. We had left the company with little more than the blankets they slept on; now, two enormous pavilions with gold-fringed awnings and crimson walls stood surrounded by neat rows of simpler tents. Guards, more Patzinaks, stood at every corner. Judging by the size of the encampment there must have been at least two hundred of them. An old orchard had become an enclosure for a dozen horses, all fine beasts branded with the mark of the imperial stables, while through an open door I saw a store tent piled high with casks of wine and sacks of grain. I had not seen anything so organised in months.

Among the throng of stocky, dark-skinned Patzinaks, I found one of the Varangians we had left to guard the camp.

'What has happened here?'

The Varangian glanced anxiously at Sigurd's litter. 'The new ambassador came a week ago. What happened to you? Where are the others?'

'The monk betrayed us. The others did not survive it – and Sigurd may yet follow. Where's Anna?'

The Varangian's mouth dropped open, as if the sun had fallen out of the sky. 'Sigurd? Sigurd cannot die.'

'I hope not. But where is Anna?'

'Anna?' Uncharacteristically, the Varangian seemed to be searching for delicate words. 'She—'

A sharp voice behind me interrupted us. 'Are you Demetrios Askiates?'

I turned. Another Patzinak, this one with a loaf-shaped cap and gilt edging on the plates of his armour, was watching me.

'Nikephoros wants you.'

'Find Anna and get Sigurd into her care,' I told the Varangian. 'Tell her I'll find them afterwards.'

The confines of a former life seemed to rise up and envelop me as I stepped into the gilded pavilion. Ever since my superior, the general Tatikios, had departed Antioch in May, I had lived beyond the reach of the empire – a desperate, untamed life where we had slept rough, killed easily, and obeyed nothing but the dictates of survival and our duty to each other. Now the whole edifice of Byzantine civilisation, vast as the pillars of Ayia Sophia, seemed to have descended on the hilltop. Rich carpets traced designs of lions and eagles on the floor, echoing the mosaics of the great palace, while the silk walls of the tent glowed red, as if we stood inside the orb of a setting sun. Gossamer-thin curtains partitioned the different rooms, so that the slaves and clerks who scurried behind them became pale spectres of themselves. Mahogany trees held

72

golden lamps in their branches, and icons of the saints looked out from their gilded windows. Rich incense filled the air. And, in the centre of the room, two men sat on carved chairs, their feet elevated on cushions, watching me carefully.

I had not changed my tunic or trimmed my beard in almost a fortnight of marching and fighting in the August sun. I had not washed, nor mended the tears and burns our ordeals had left in my clothing. In any company I would have felt filthy and disgusting: here, I felt like a dung-beetle rolling its ball on a banquet table. Too late, I remembered I should probably have bowed, though my back and my pride were both too stiff to allow it.

'If you have been the emperor's only representative these last four months, it is no wonder our situation is so desperate.'

The words were spoken with immaculate condescension, but their effect was like a kick in the groin. Fortunately, I was too weary to retaliate in anger. Instead, I looked blankly at the man who had addressed me. Both he and his companion were dressed in long white robes, trimmed with heavy embroidery and studded with coloured stones. There the similarity ended: the man on the left, who had spoken, was tall and strongly built; he kept his hair in studied disorder, and his face would have been handsome but for its arrogance. Only his beard seemed out of place, recently grown and not yet thickened to its fullness, like an adolescent who has not yet summoned the courage to shave, or a guilty man trying to hide his appearance. His companion, by contrast, was slight and clean-shaven, with thinning hair and a permanently worried expression tightening his soft features. I guessed he must be a eunuch. In their company you could believe that the courtyards and fountains of the palace were just beyond the door, not a thousand miles away across mountains and desert.

'Has the emperor sent you?' I asked.

The larger man drummed his fingers on the arm of his chair. 'I am Nikephoros.' He nodded to the eunuch beside him. 'This is Phokas. We arrived from Constantinople a week ago. Where have you been?'

Evidently I did not merit pleasantries. 'At the monastery of Ravendan, in the mountains north of here.'

Someone must surely have told him as much already, but he affected indignant surprise. 'What folly took you there?'

'A terrible folly.' I guessed he did not want to hear the whole ordeal, that its filthy details would bore his refined sensibilities. I told him anyway.

'It was a trap,' I concluded. 'Set by Duke Godfrey in concert with the Armenian brigands. Tancred was there too.'

My voice died away. The two envoys stared at me, their faces as flat and all-powerful as the saints in the icons around them.

'You are sure it was Duke Godfrey?' the eunuch, Phokas, asked at last. His voice was high, though not shrill, pitched in that indeterminate range between a man's and a woman's.

74

'I stood as far from him as I am from you now.'

That did not impress Nikephoros. 'It was a fool's errand anyway. What did you mean by going to Ravendan?'

'I was trying to defend the church's interests – and the emperor's. I did not know that his so-called allies would use the opportunity to try and kill us.'

'It hardly matters.' Acid disdain etched his voice. 'Though it is a pity you lost the emperor's seal that was entrusted to you. He will not be pleased.'

Had I been half my age, I would have broken his nose for his snide dismissal of our sacrifices. As it was, the cowardice of wisdom stilled my hand – but I could not keep all the heat from my voice. 'Six days ago I watched Duke Godfrey and Tancred mutilate the survivors of the battle and leave them to die on a mountaintop. They would have done worse to us, if Pakrad's greed had not spoiled their plan.'

'Perhaps you have spent too long with the barbarians – what else did you expect from them? This does not change anything.'

'Four of the emperor's men are dead. Does that change nothing?'

'You cannot cleanse your mistakes by washing them in your friends' blood,' Nikephoros retorted coolly. 'Do you really think the empire's interests have changed because – you say – a Frankish lord took against you? The emperor does not put down his hunting dogs just because they snap at his slaves.'

An agonising rage gripped me. I clenched my fists and

75

dug my long nails into the palms of my hands trying to force a pain excruciating enough to match the pain in my heart. But the harder I pressed, the less I felt.

The eunuch must have seen my anguish. 'Do not blame yourself too much. You were swimming in seas too strong for you. You did not have the wit to see what should be done.'

I stared at him, wondering if he had poked my wounds in malice or just in clumsy kindness. His polished face revealed nothing.

'Have you come to replace me?' I asked at last. The audience had barely begun, but I already longed for it to be over.

Nikephoros leaned forward in his chair. 'We have come to supersede you. The emperor has placed you under our command.'

His words struck me like arrows. 'I thought . . .' *I wanted*. 'I understood I was to go home, once you had arrived.'

The eunuch spoke. 'Go home? You cannot go home. You have not finished.'

'Finished what?'

'Your mission was to see that the Franks reached Jerusalem – not settled themselves in Antioch.'

Nikephoros picked up the thread. 'That is why your expedition to Ravendan was worthless, even before it proved to be a trap. The emperor does not want relics and trinkets to make the Franks love the Greeks.' Suddenly animated, he thumped his fist on the arm of his chair. 'He

76

wants Antioch itself. For its strength, its commerce, its harbours and its lands – yes. But most of all because it is his by right, and the Franks swore to return it to him. If we wanted it owned by a rabble of hateful, godless barbarians, we could have left it to the Turks. The Franks will have Jerusalem, that will be their reward. But Antioch must be ours. That is why it would not matter if Duke Godfrey, Count Raymond and all the Frankish captains hung you from a tree and let the birds devour you inch by inch. The emperor would still smile, and pay them flattery and gold, and pray they dislodged Bohemond from Antioch.'

His smooth neck was suddenly lumpen with taut sinews, and his head jerked with emphasis on every word. The diplomatic reserve seemed stripped away, though I could not tell if that was a calculated effect. Nor did I care. I was still numb from the sting of what the eunuch had said. *You cannot go home.*

'I must go home,' I mumbled, pathetic and uncaring. 'I cannot stay here.'

Nikephoros gave me a scornful look. 'Go home – and then what? You will not have the comfortable life you imagine in Constantinople if you return now. The emperor is furious that the Franks hold Antioch. He is famously quick to forgive his enemies, but he does not lightly forgive those who fail him.'

'How have I failed him? Was I supposed to hold Antioch against the Franks with a few dozen Varangians and the force of an oath the Franks never meant to uphold?'

Nikephoros rolled his eyes. 'Do you know Pythagoras?

With a stave and sufficient distance, a single man can move a boulder that would resist the strength of armies.'

'Then why does he want me to stay?' Like a prisoner broken on the rack, I suddenly felt a disgraceful willingness to say anything, to admit any charge and suffer any insult just to go free. I hated myself for it – but I hated the thought of staying more.

The eunuch leaned forward. 'Because he is merciful.'

Craven desperation kept me from laughing in his face, though my disbelief must have shone through.

'Your superior, the general Tatikios, made a full report to the emperor after he left Antioch,' the eunuch continued. 'He left little doubt where the blame for the Franks' success should lie.'

I had suffered so many blows to my hopes and pride that I should have been immune, but I still felt the bruise in my gut. 'He blamed me?'

'Suffice it to say the emperor felt it would be kinder to you to give you a chance to redeem yourself, rather than allowing your return.'

'But surely he must know—'

The eunuch raised a sanctimonious hand, as if pushing me back from an unseen precipice. 'The emperor can only know what his subordinates tell him. Tatikios is a great nobleman: he has many allies at court to support him.'

And I did not. I had seen the emperor many times and inhabited his palace, had saved his life and once or twice even spoken with him almost as an equal. I did not think him a bad man, for what such judgements were worth.

But he had not survived eighteen years on his tenuous throne by bowing to sentiment. If Tatikios commanded a faction – and legions to boot – then the emperor could not antagonise him on my account. Perhaps he truly did believe it was kindness to keep me away from Constantinople.

'If the Franks leave Antioch, there will be no problem and no blame to be attached,' the eunuch concluded. 'The only lever we have to prise them out is Jerusalem. We must see that they get there.'

I bowed my head, as if putting it through a noose. 'How?'

Nikephoros barked orders to his slaves, who scurried from behind the gauzy curtains and brought a map, a table and a low wooden stool for me to sit on. After so long marching, its hard seat was like a feather mattress to me. Lamps were set beside the unscrolled map, flickering over the ragged oblong of the Mediterranean Sea and the three continents that bordered it to the north, south and east. Nikephoros pulled a golden pin from his robes and leaned forward, tapping the pin against the map to illustrate his narration.

'Antioch is here.' Tap. 'Jerusalem here.' Tap. 'The lands in between – Syria, Lebanon, Palestine – are controlled by the Turks and Saracens.' The point of the pin scratched back and forth over the Mediterranean's eastern coast. 'They are weakened by the Franks' victory at Antioch, but they still have castles and fortified cities all along the coast.' A succession of pinpricks perforated the paper between

Antioch and Jerusalem. 'And, of course, they have Jerusalem.'

That much I knew. Far stranger was the sensation of seeing the canvas of my life laid out before me, my past and future journeys drawn in inky lines. Too often, my eyes drifted north and west to the ornately painted cross at the junction of Europe and Asia. Constantinople.

'But beyond Palestine, the Turks and Saracens face an older enemy. The Fatimids of Egypt.' The pin inscribed a circle in the south-eastern corner of the Mediterranean, centred on the cobweb of lines that marked the course of the Nile. 'You know the Fatimids?'

I had heard of them, but ignorance was easiest. I shook my head.

'The Saracens consider them heretics – if there can be a heresy against a heresy – and hate them above all others. Once, they drove the Fatimids out of their kingdoms all the way to Libya, but the Fatimids regrouped, invaded Egypt and conquered it. They will not be content until they have imposed their faith all the way to Baghdad and Mecca. The Saracens, likewise, will not rest until they have destroyed the Fatimids.'

I had been drawn into the invisible, eternal quarrel between the different Ishmaelite creeds once before, and the wounds had only recently healed. Even without Constantinople tempting me home, I did not like the sound of this.

'If we can make an alliance with the Fatimids, then the Saracens will be trapped between enemies to their north and south. We can squeeze them out of Palestine and the way will be open for the Franks to seize Jerusalem. When they hurry south to claim it, Antioch will be ours again. The stain of your incompetence will be wiped clean.'

Whatever bitterness I felt at the jibe, I swallowed it. 'And how will we achieve that?'

In answer, Nikephoros jammed the golden pin into the map, at the place where the different strands of the Nile delta braided themselves into a single thread heading south into Africa. The pin stuck in the wooden table and stayed upright, its trembling shadow crossing over Egypt and almost touching Jerusalem.

'That is the Fatimid capital, al-Qahira. That is where we must go.'

η

~~~~~~

I came out of the tent in a daze, like a defeated soldier
leaving a battle. My soul was falling through an endless
chasm, and though it was sickening it did not hurt yet.
That would come when I hit the bottom. For now, I
wandered across the hill until I found the Varangians'
tents. Aelfric was there.

'How is Sigurd?' I asked, forcing the words through my
constricted lungs.

'Unchanged. The fever seems a little less.'

'Has Anna seen him?'

Aelfric fixed me with his uncompromising blue eyes.
'She isn't here.'

My tumbling soul knocked against a looming cliff,
careered off it and continued its descent. 'Where is she?'

Aelfric turned his eyes away, looking over my shoulder and into the darkening east.

'In the cloisters behind the cathedral.'

I stared at him.

'In Antioch.'

I ran.

Whatever excesses I had expected from the plague city – baying mobs hunting through the streets, doomed men and women tupping like dogs in doorways, corpses burning on open fires or lying unburied at the roadside – the reality was different. Moonlight washed over empty streets, and most of the houses were dark – though the city was not empty. Unseen creatures scuffled in shadowy corners. Shutters creaked, doors slammed, clay vessels shattered and steel rang on steel. And, more than anything else, there was a constant tapestry of mourning that hung in the background: soft moans of despair, shrieks of anguish, plaintive sobbing and quiet prayer. A profound and angry melancholy gripped the city – it was like walking through the sinews of a broken heart.

At several points along my way, carts and boxes and rubble had been tipped across the street to form makeshift barricades. Some were abandoned, others guarded, but Antioch was not a city made for containment and I always found my way around them, until at last I reached the cathedral and a small door in the wall behind it. A frightened voice behind the door answered my knock.

'I want to see the doctor – Anna. Is she here?'

'She's asleep.'

'Wake her. Tell her Demetrios is here.'

He did not answer, but beyond the door I heard receding footsteps. I waited in the dark for what seemed an age, each second lengthened tenfold by uncertainty. Eventually I even started to probe the tip of Aelfric's knife into the door jamb, wondering if I could force it.

I heard the footsteps returning and pulled the knife away. A bolt slid back on the other side of the door, though it did not open.

'Wait here for a hundred-count, then come through. She will be in the cloisters.'

Once more, the footsteps retreated. I doubted the delay was necessary, but I honoured the doorkeeper's request and counted to a hundred as quickly as I could. Then I pushed the door open, padded down a short passage and emerged into the broad colonnades of the cloisters. Moonlight shone onto the columns' faces so that they appeared like steel bars around the square, while behind them all was darkness. On the far side, directly opposite me, stood Anna.

She was thinner than I remembered, though we had been apart less than two weeks. In the hot summer air her white shift clung to her body, divulging every rise and shadow beneath: her dark hair was tousled wild by her pillow. She appeared like an icon of everything I loved and craved; I pulled off the cloth that covered my face and ran towards her.

'Stop.'

A large figure stepped out of the darkness behind her, levelling a silver-tipped spear towards me. Desperation almost overpowered my instinct for survival, but at the last I reined myself in and halted just short of the spear's point.

'Stay there,' the figure ordered.

I stared at Anna, bewildered. Why did she not come forward? 'What is this?'

She closed her eyes. 'My guard.'

'Against what? Me?'

'No – he is protecting you.'

'Against what?'

'Against me.'

I stumbled back, though the guard's spear had not moved. There were hot tears on my face.

'What could you possibly do to me?' Even as I spoke the question, I began to guess its answer, and dread it.

Anna folded her hands penitently before her. She was crying too: the moon caught her tears and scarred her cheeks silver.

'I have become a plague doctor.'

The last spark of hope died in my soul. A voice that was hardly my own asked, 'Have you . . . ?'

'Have I caught the plague?' Anna shook her head. 'God willing, not yet.'

I gestured to the guard. 'Then why is he here?'

'They insisted on it.'

'Who?'

'The Franks. They would not let me tend the sick

85

without a guard to make sure I didn't touch the healthy.'

'You volunteered for this?'

She gave a joyless laugh. 'Do you really think I'm such a saint? I had no choice. The woman I went to see the day you left, the one whose baby was overdue – she was infected. She was almost dead when I found her – the baby, too. The Franks barred the doors and would not let anyone leave the house. They only allowed me out when I agreed to tend the other victims. Then I came here.'

Anna's guard had moved around to my left, standing between us and a little way apart with his spear outstretched, while she and I faced each other across the cloistered square. I needed an iron grip over every muscle in my body not to run to her and embrace her, heedless of consequence.

In a firmer voice, she asked, 'Did you find your relic?'

'There was no relic. Ravendan was a trap. The monk attacked us and took us prisoner.' With the guard watching, I did not mention Duke Godfrey's part. At that moment, it hardly seemed to matter. 'We only just escaped.'

'Is Sigurd all right?'

'Barely.' I saw Anna gasp. 'He suffered a blow to the head, and has not risen since. He has a fever. You must see him.'

'What can I do?' She opened her empty hands. 'I cannot leave this cloister, much less the city.'

'You have to,' I repeated stubbornly.

'I can't.'

'I could bring him here.'

She stamped her foot in anger. 'Is that a joke? If Sigurd is so weak, the plague would kill him the minute he looked at Antioch. He must manage without me.'

We stared at each other across the square. The moonlight filled the space between us like glass.

'If I could, of course I would be with Sigurd this instant,' she said softly. 'But I do not have that choice. I chose to come to Antioch and I came freely, because of you. Because I loved you.' She flicked her hand to shush my embarrassed protest. 'Now that choice is made, we are each as helpless as the other. We are slaves to powers we cannot defy.'

More tears were tumbling down her cheeks and her eyes were dark with sadness. I longed to run across the courtyard, to hug her to me and crush away the distance between us. But the guard's spear was steady, hovering like a wasp at the edge of my gaze.

'The emperor's new envoy has come,' I said at last.

Anna brushed away a tear, rubbing her cheek with a loose lock of hair. 'Then you're free to go.'

'He has ordered me to Egypt.'

With all the passion wrung from it, my soul had become dry and calloused. I related Nikephoros' orders without emotion. Anna listened quietly until I was finished.

'Will you go?'

I hesitated. I had come there that night with wild plans of escape burning in my heart: I would take Anna out of Antioch, she could heal Sigurd in a secret place until he was well, and then the three of us would make our way back to Constantinople. It was a pleasant dream – but impossible. It was as Anna had said: we had made our choices, or had them forced upon us, and now we would suffer the outcomes.

'I will go to Egypt,' I said. 'Nikephoros has given me little alternative.' *And you have made sure of it*, I did not say. To stay in Antioch, waiting to see whether Sigurd's wounds killed him before the plague killed Anna – it would be like being milled between boulders. Against that, Egypt was almost an enticing prospect.

Anna nodded, as if she had known my decision before I said it.

'Travel safely,' she said simply. Her tears had dried up, and her face was calm again.

I could not bring myself to turn away, but stared at Anna as though – by the force and duration of my gaze alone – I could communicate all I felt. She matched my gaze, unyielding. Pity, kindness and desperate sorrow mingled in her face; I thought she might collapse into tears again, and I would have followed suit if she had, but she did not.

Without a word of farewell, she half-raised a hand in mock salute and turned away. The guard followed her as she disappeared between the pillars into the dark cloisters.

θ

⚭⚭⚭⚭⚭

We sailed for Egypt the next day. I had never been on a ship before, except to cross the few hundred yards of the Bosphorus, but I had always assumed I would hate it. For some reason, I did not. Perhaps I felt so wretched that the turbulent deep beneath our keel lost its terror, or perhaps the suspension of all cares and duties, forced by the confines of the ship, calmed me. It was as if I had been plucked out of my life, cut free of the ties and obligations that held me there, and set adrift upon the blank canvas of the sea. For the first time in months, or even years, I had nothing to do. I sat in the shade of the turret that commanded the centre of the ship and watched the crew, as idle and superfluous as the cat who ate the galley scraps.

Apart from the crew, we were nineteen passengers:

Nikephoros and his attendants; a priest; an honour guard of ten Patzinaks who spent most of their time being seasick; one Varangian and myself. The Varangian was Aelfric, the man who had led us out of the burning monastery. The rest of his company had remained with Nikephoros' colleague, the eunuch, who had the unenviable task of trying to persuade the Frankish princes to resume their march once the plague subsided.

As for Nikephoros, he did not find the same solace I did in the ship. He had commandeered the captain's quarters at the ship's stern, and though it must have been a dark and humid room he rarely ventured out. When he did, he had his servants erect a white silk canopy on the foredeck; he would sit there in regal isolation and watch the waves, or sometimes compose long documents, many pages in length, on his ivory writing desk. Though I was nominally his secretary, he never asked me to write them out or confided their contents to me.

One afternoon, two days out of Saint Simeon, I gained some insight into his foul humour. I was sitting in the turret's shadow, playing with a rope-end and fretting about Anna, when Aelfric came and sat beside me. That in itself was unusual, for he was a quiet man who mostly kept to himself, but I welcomed him. He was small for a Varangian, though large by any other standard. His lean face bespoke a watchful intelligence, and you could see him weighing each word thrice over before he spoke it.

'I've found out why Nikephoros is so grumpy,' he announced.

I looked up from the frayed fibres I had teased apart. 'Why's that?'

'The emperor's not pleased with him.'

'How do you know?'

'I heard it from one of his slaves. He made the wrong friends at court. He was an ally of the dead chamberlain, Krysaphios.' Aelfric squinted at me. 'You knew him.'

'I did.' I had witnessed his death – indeed, I had contributed to it. 'I'm surprised the emperor would trust this mission to someone associated with that faction.'

'Are you? Why not? If he's honest, he'll have to try twice as hard to prove it, and if he's not honest he'll be well out of the emperor's way.'

Another more unpleasant aspect struck me. 'And if the embassy goes wrong, or if our ship is lost at sea, Nikephoros will be conveniently removed from the court.'

'No wonder he scowls so much.'

'The Franks sent ambassadors to the Fatimids once,' I remembered. 'Five months ago. I was at the council where the princes discussed it.'

'What became of them?'

I shrugged. 'They never returned.'

We put in at Cyprus to take on supplies. The harbour was choked with commerce: it felt as if half the imperial grain fleet must be there, together with transports and galleys so thick you could almost have walked across the bay on their decks. Every deck, wharf, jetty and gangway was piled high with the material of war: barrels of fish, bales of hay, live pigs to feed armies and iron pigs to feed the black-smiths' forges. In one corner of the port, makeshift fences had been erected to pen in the vast herd of horses and mules who waited to be embarked for Antioch. The greater part of the goods, though, were inbound, destined to sit in stores and warehouses until the Army of God moved south. It was a vast operation, the fruits of the empire all gathered together to feed the campaign, and I began to realise how far afield the tremors of our war had reached.

From Cyprus we sailed south and then south-east, running before the wind. Now it was the sailors who worked while the rowers rested, and a new urgency gripped the ship. Even with a good breeze behind us, the air seemed to be thickening day by day. Whenever they were off duty the men would gather near the bow and stare out over the waves, waiting for the land to appear. Some of them reported seeing great fish many times larger than a man swimming beside us, though I never saw them.

Like a shadow travelling in advance of its owner, I knew the coast must be close when the sea began to fill with an ever greater number of small vessels. I watched them nervously, but they were merely fishermen and shallow coastal traders who gave us a wide berth. Soon afterwards the land itself appeared: a low and inviting strip of shore that turned out, as we drew closer, to be only the arms of a great inland lagoon. We passed through to a flat sea studded with fragments of islands; on one of these, still some way from the land, was the port of Tinnis.

I had believed that a man who had lived in

Constantinople could never find any place exotic, that every race and colour of men, together with all their works and produce, were to be found in that city. Tinnis, though, was different: the dhows and feluccas that swarmed around the island like bees in a hive; long poles with drying flax hanging off them like hair; the slender turrets of the Ishmaelite churches and the mysterious chants of their priests, which echoed across the still water five times each day. But even more strange than that, I suspected, was the knowledge in my heart that this was Egypt, a land that had been ancient even in the time of the ancients. Byzantine emperors had once ruled this land, and Romans before them – but they were mere footnotes in a history of infinite depth and magnificence.

Our unexpected arrival caused considerable stir. Two war-galleys rowed out to challenge us, and our sailors waited anxiously by the naphtha throwers while Nikephoros conducted a brisk exchange with the Fatimid captain through the stammering efforts of our priest. Eventually, we convinced them of our neutrality – though even when one boat returned to the harbour to deliver the news, the other hovered vigilant near by.

For three full days we hung there on our anchor, like a mote of dust caught in a sunbeam. The captain struck the sails and fashioned makeshift awnings to shade the deck, for the planks were beginning to warp apart in the glare. After the second day, I thought the sinews of my mind might be warping too. I watched the sun inch across the sky until my eyes burned, and found myself longing for each repetition of the plaintive Ishmaelite prayer-chant to mark the passing of the days.

By the fourth afternoon I was almost past caring. So I did not hear the measured splash of oars approaching, or the creak of the thole-pins, and only realised that the confines of our solitude had been broken when the sleeping crew about me suddenly leaped up and began to array themselves in formal display. Almost before I realised it, something thudded gently against our hull and dark hands reached over the side. Nikephoros strode out from his cabin, his jewel-crusted lorum draped hastily over his shoulders, as the Fatimid envoy hauled himself onto our ship.

Every man on deck fell silent. Most stared in astonishment, though a few dropped their eyes in shame or embarrassment. The colour drained from Nikephoros' face so that he seemed even more pale beside the visitor.

The new arrival was an African. To many of our crew that alone would have been an incomparable novelty. I had seen a few of his race in Constantinople – expensive slaves in the noblest households, or porters on the docks – but never any like him. Everything about him marked him as a lord or prince: his proud bearing, his extraordinary height, the rich golden bands around his arms and the yellow robe that hung to his ankles. He was so different to any other man that it would be hard to call him handsome, but there was something in his face – beside his strangeness – that attracted the eye and held it. His scalp was shaved clean and glistened like wet tar in the heat, while his strong features wore authority easily. Strangely, he reminded me of Sigurd, though he could hardly have been more different from the hairy, sallow-skinned barbarian.

He smiled – a broad, white-toothed smile that you immediately wanted to share – then said: 'Praise be to God, the Lord of the universe – and peace.'

Nikephoros remained obviously unmoved by the man's smile – indeed, he seemed to be speaking through a mouthful of barely swallowed anger. 'Who are you?' he demanded.

'I am Bilal al-Sud, captain of the Qaysariyya guard. My master, the caliph of the Fatimids, the Commander of the Faithful, has sent me to greet you. If you come in peace and honest friendship, you are welcome in his realm.'

No doubt he expected some piece of well-honed diplomatic courtesy in reply. In this he was disappointed.

'You speak Greek.' Nikephoros' tone suggested it was more a curiosity, like a dog trained to answer questions, than an accomplishment.

Bilal flashed his brilliant smile again, though this time the white teeth seemed somehow sharper. 'I learned it from Greek slaves. The caliph has many in his palace.'

The warning had its desired effect. Nikephoros mastered his sneer and assumed a more polished, tactful demeanour. 'I have gifts and messages for the caliph from my master, the emperor Alexios of Byzantium.'

Bilal nodded. 'The caliph is eager to see them. He has ordered me to escort you up the river to al-Qahira.' He looked around. 'Your ship is magnificent, but she will not manage the bends and shallows of the Nile. You will come in my barge.'

We left the comforting bulk of our ship behind and rowed across the lagoon. The shores drew closer and began to pinch together, though if you looked ahead they never seemed to join. At some point I suppose we must have entered the mouth of the river, though there was nothing obvious to define it: the land off our beams was still as distant as ever, far wider than the Bosphorus at Constantinople. I looked out across the brown waters, curious to see something of this fabled land, but all I saw was water and reeds.

We spent two days and two nights on the Egyptian barge. It was an eerie voyage, more like a dance: we often turned where no turn seemed necessary, so many times around that sometimes the current seemed to be pushing us upstream. I pitied the men on the oars. As the river banks drew closer I began to make out the features of the landscape: a dirty brown soil bristling with the stalks of harvested crops, and divided by low ridges like causeways through the desert. Sometimes, where they intersected, I saw villages, though many were in ruins and I spied few inhabitants.

'What are they for?' I asked Bilal, pointing at the ridges. They seemed too regular and evenly spaced to be natural.

'When the river floods, they are the only way to travel

the land. Every year, the Nile bursts its banks and waters the fields enough to sustain a whole year's crops.'

'And when does that happen?'

Bilal scowled. 'August.'

I looked back at the fields. Even from that distance I could see that they were the pale brown colour of clay, not the rich black of wet soil. A skein of cracks had shattered the hard earth, and nothing grew save a few strands of wild grass. Above us, the sun burned down from the cloudless mid-September sky.

'Sometimes the floodwaters come late,' said Bilal, unconvincingly.

On the third day, the river widened again as several strands of its delta came together. Just beyond, on the eastern bank, a host of towers rose straight against the desert sky, so many that they clustered together and almost became a perfect whole. White triangles of sail flapped beside wharves that bustled with commerce, and columns of dust billowed up from the heavy-laden roads.

'Is that . . . ?'

'Al-Qahira,' said Bilal, and the sounds took on a deep and savage mystery in his voice. 'Or, as your Roman ancestors called it, Babylon.'

1

～～～～

Until then, I had always imagined ambassadors to be like angels. They were higher beings, of less substance and greater power than mere mortals, flitting about the world impervious to threats of harm. There in Egypt, I realised the truth: ambassadors were little better than prisoners. The moment we set foot on the wharf we were hurried to a caravan of litters borne by bare-chested Nubian slaves, who carried us in curtained blindness to a secluded court-yard, and then up a stair to the quarters appointed to us. There were three interconnecting rooms, spacious and airy and lavishly furnished. But the ornate screens that curved and twined across the windows were iron, and when the caliph's attendants left us alone I heard the door lock from the outside.

The next day, almost before dawn, a slave arrived to announce that the Fatimid king, the caliph himself, would give us an audience that very morning. I had been lying on my mattress, savouring the feeling of solid ground beneath me and watching the sun stream through the iron screens over the window; with reluctant speed, I rolled out of bed and rummaged through my belongings for my cleanest tunic. Only when I had pulled it on, splashed some water from a bronze basin over my face and ploughed a comb through my hair did I notice Nikephoros. He was sitting on a divan in a plain white under-tunic, while one slave held a mirror in front of him like a votive offering and another trimmed his hair and beard. He was perfectly still, his face a passive mask, yet even that somehow conveyed scorn for the bustle and haste around him.

Thinking perhaps he had not heard the slave's message, I repeated it. The corner of his mouth turned upward in a sneer.

'When you have spent more time in palaces, you will realise that courtiers treat hours as you would treat minutes. There is no hurry.'

He kept his head still as he spoke, careless of the sharp razor darting around near his ear. I guessed the slave knew what would befall him if he cut his master's precious skin.

Without seeming to look at me, Nikephoros added, 'But if you do intend to be ready, you might dress in something that befits the occasion. I do not want the caliph to think that the emperor Alexios has sent a delegation of slaves and mercenaries to dishonour him.'

His words were cruel and true – it was the truth that stung more. I bit back an instinctive retort and said humbly, 'I have nothing better.'

'My attendants will find you something.' Nikephoros looked in the mirror. 'I cannot have the caliph judging the emperor by your shortcomings.'

All that morning I experienced the strange urgent indolence that is the lot of ambassadors. Every fifteen minutes another Fatimid messenger would bustle into our rooms to announce, either in broken Greek or by elaborate hand gestures, that the great moment for our audience was nigh, but even after Nikephoros had been shaved, dressed, oiled and perfumed with deliberate care by his slaves, we remained waiting in our quarters. After the first two hours, we learned to ignore the announcements. I stood by the window to breathe what little air blew through it, trying to see something of the surrounding palace and city. The iron screen cut the view into a mosaic of a thousand disjointed fragments: I could see high domes and minarets, corners of courtyards shaded with plane trees, but without any sense of how the pieces joined together. The sun rose high, and the tenor of the messages became more apologetic: the caliph was exceedingly busy, he wanted nothing more than to greet his friends from Byzantium but there was urgent court business he had to attend to; he would certainly see us in the next half an hour, perhaps sooner.

At last, when even Nikephoros' patience must have

worn bare, Bilal appeared. We had not seen him all day, though we had sometimes heard his voice in the passages beyond our room. He strode through the double doors, pushing them back with such force that the dust in the air was swept into great swirling vortices. He wore a ceremonial coat of armour whose silver scales were edged in gold, with a chain mail coif draped over his shoulders like the folds of a cowl. Strange designs were embroidered on the hem of his cloak, jagged lines that cut across the fabric like wounds. I had never seen anything like them, and they only served to heighten his dazzling barbarity.

'Come,' he said simply.

Bilal led us through a succession of gates and tiled courtyards to a stifling anteroom where he left us for some minutes. Nikephoros paced the small room without bothering to hide his impatience, and when one of his Patzinak guards ventured a question he snarled his reply. At one point his gaze settled on me, and I quailed, but it was only to bark a reminder: 'Heed everything the caliph says, and remember it faithfully.'

I nodded. Whatever calm I had found in the broad waters of the sea had boiled away in our confinement, leaving only sharp crystals of misgiving. I longed for this audience to be over so that I could return to Antioch and see Sigurd and Anna – but that was too much to think about now. I squirmed under the unaccustomed weight of the robes Nikephoros had lent me: I could not understand why they should feel heavy, for they were lighter than the armour I had worn often enough. Unease

101

magnified the discomfort. They were too large for me and too grand, though shabby enough to Nikephoros' eyes, and I felt absurd.

Bilal returned. Without a word, he led us back out through the door, down a short corridor, and into the caliph's audience room.

I had seen ambassadors received with the full ceremony of the imperial court in Byzantium: I suppose I should not have been overawed by the ritual of a lesser, pagan king. But in Constantinople I had watched from a distance, secure in the knowledge that every piece of pageantry and theatrical trickery only emphasised the grandeur of the Byzantine emperor and – by reflection – his people. Here I stood on the opposite side, and it was not a comfortable place to be. Unlike the open expanse of the emperor's throne room, the caliph's hall was supported by a forest of pillars, which stretched away in every direction and cast a maze of long shadows. The spaces in between were crammed with a throng of courtiers who lined both sides of the long aisle that led to the back of the room. There, raised on a stone platform beneath a domed recess, seated cross-legged on a low, bench-like throne, sat the caliph.

Bilal led us forward. It took all my courage, and the sound of the guards advancing behind me, to follow him along the corridor of onlookers, under the weight of their strange and foreign gazes, to the open space below the caliph. Gilded lamps hung from the ceiling, casting a pool of light into which we stepped, but that was a dim hole compared to the radiance that shone from the dais above.

It seemed to be bathed in sunlight, though I could not see any windows, so bright that I could hardly look directly at the caliph but had to keep my eyes fixed on the ground at his feet. It was covered in rich carpets, which in turn were strewn with the pale-yellow petals of narcissus flowers. Their ripe scent filled the air.

Whether Nikephoros was cowed by the surroundings, or whether he had mastered his pride in the cause of diplomacy, he showed nothing but deference to the caliph. Without prompting, he dropped to his knees and kissed the ground three times. Clumsily, I and the rest of his retinue, the ten Patzinaks, did likewise. Above us, I could hear someone – Bilal? – speaking solemn words in Arabic. When he had finished, I risked a quick glance upwards. The caliph had stood. A disembodied voice drifted down from the podium, echoed imperfectly in Greek by Bilal.

'Praise be to God, the Lord of the universe. In the name of God, the lord and giver of mercy, and Mohammed His prophet, peace be upon him, the caliph al-Mustali welcomes the emissaries of the emperor of the Christians. Peace be on you.'

Still on his knees, Nikephoros responded with a recitation of titles and credentials. When he finished, I saw him darting sideways glances to Bilal, waiting for some signal that we could rise. None was given.

'The emperor Alexios honours us with this embassy,' said the caliph. His voice sounded surprisingly young for one so exalted, though the foreign language made it hard to be sure.

'The emperor Alexios has always esteemed your friendship. Now he seeks an alliance.'

The mood in the room tensed as Bilal rephrased this in Arabic. The pillars stretched away all around us, and I began to feel like a lamb caught by wolves in a forest. The caliph leaned forward on his throne, blocking out the light like a cloud covering the sun.

'Who does he wish to make this alliance against?'

Bilal's voice was louder than the caliph's, and the vaulted roof spun his words about so that they seemed to come from all around us.

'Against the Turks of Palestine.'

A great agitation spread through the crowd of courtiers, as though the surrounding forest had come alive in a breeze. The caliph let it build unchecked for a few moments, then hushed it with an unseen gesture.

'I have heard rumours of a mighty Christian army,' he announced. 'Not Greeks or *Rum*, but *Franj*. What do you know of them?'

'They have come from the west to liberate the holy city of Jerusalem.'

'They are the emperor's mercenaries?'

Nikephoros hesitated. 'His allies.'

The caliph sat down, and let the full radiance of the invisible sun bathe his face. If I squinted, I could just make out his face beneath a white turban. His features were soft, though held fast by a furious effort of concentration. As I had thought, he seemed very young – not much past twenty.

'If the emperor Alexios has so many allies, why does he seek our help?'

'Because we have a common enemy.' Nikephoros rocked forward on his knees, and I wondered if they were beginning to ache as much as mine. Perhaps that was why diplomats wore such thick robes. 'Because the Turks have stolen their land equally from both of us. Our army is poised at Antioch to strike south; if the Fatimids could come up from Egypt, we would crush them between us.'

This time there was no murmuring from the crowd. All waited to see what the caliph would say.

'It is easy to speak of crushing the Turks – and far harder to achieve it. They have the full power of the court of Baghdad behind them.'

'And we have broken it,' said Nikephoros urgently. 'You have heard of Kerbogha the Terrible? Two months ago the Franks routed him in battle at Antioch. Palestine is open for the taking.'

The caliph's face remained impassive – too impassive, I felt, for someone hearing this news for the first time.

'If Palestine is laid open, why not take it yourself? Does the emperor always seek allies in victory?'

'All Christians should abhor war and unnecessary killing – as indeed do faithful Muslims.'

'*Fight in God's cause against those who fight you, but do not overreach yourself, for that is hateful to God,*' the caliph murmured.

'The stronger our army, the less we will have to use it.'

'But how, then, will you reward your allies?'

There was an undisguised sharpness in the question. Nikephoros considered his answer carefully.

'The emperor has no claim on Palestine. The Frankish army want only Jerusalem, and enough land about it to sustain themselves. For the rest, as much as we conquer can be yours.'

The caliph clasped his hands together and pressed them against his chin. He looked down on us from his height, while the crowded nobles around us craned forward. I could not look at the caliph: my eyes ached from the nimbus of light that surrounded him, and the heavy robes pressed down on me like lead.

'The emperor's friendship is a prize for any man,' he declared. 'But an alliance for war cannot be entered into lightly or in haste. I will think on your proposal, and give you my answer as soon as it is decided. In the meantime, you will stay in the palace. As . . .' There was a pause in the translation as Bilal – unusually – struggled to find a word.

'As my guests.'

'How was the audience?' asked Aelfric.

I unpeeled my borrowed robe and threw it over a wooden stool. In the adjacent room, I could see Nikephoros' slaves pulling off his opulent lorum and dalmatica, leaving only a loose white smock beneath. I was desperate to release some of the tension of the audience, but it was not easy with a company of Bilal's African guards stationed outside our door. And my head still ached.

I shrugged. 'The caliph saw us in person – he didn't defer us with some string of lesser officials. I suppose that was good.'

'Are you so dazzled by royalty, Demetrios?'

I looked up wearily. Nikephoros had left his attendants folding his garments and had come through into our room. He was sipping a cup of sherbet, though it did nothing to sweeten the look on his face.

'The king is not always the most powerful man at court,' he said, and I remembered that in Constantinople he had been of that faction that sought to make emperors the tools of their officials. 'The caliph has barely come of age.'

'He seemed well enough in command of his court to me.'

'Because his court wanted you to think so. There is only one man who commands the court, and it is not the caliph.'

'Who, then?'

'His vizier, al-Afdal. Nothing happens except by his authority.' There was genuine respect in Nikephoros' words.

'Was he there at the audience?'

'No. But I do not doubt he will have been watching and listening. He flatters us by granting an audience with the caliph, but it is only the first move of a long game. Knowledge is the root of all diplomacy, no less than war. At the moment, our positions are almost equal – we know as much as he does, perhaps more on some matters. But now he will lock us away – with silk cords and golden keys, of course – and starve us of information, while he learns everything he can and watches how matters develop. He will wait until the situation has swung to his advantage before he seriously negotiates with us.'

'And how are we to know what is in the emperor's interest then?'

Nikephoros gave a savage grin, perhaps the first time I had seen him happy. 'That is the game.'

ια

It was not a game I wanted to play, but I no longer had any choice – if, indeed, I ever had. We lived almost entirely in the three rooms we had been allocated, and wanted for nothing except freedom. After three days we were all like caged beasts alternately sulking in corners and snarling at each other; after a fortnight we had learned to contain our passions enough to feign peace. Occasionally Nikephoros would have me write a dispatch to the emperor, emphasising the Fatimids' hospitality and his sincere hopes for an honest alliance with them; for the rest of the time, I sat by the window, trying not to think about Anna and Sigurd, and observed the comings and goings of the palace. At first it was merely something to watch, a small corner of movement in an otherwise still existence, but gradually I began to notice patterns: the different attires and the deference each man drew, who bowed and made way for whom, which hours were busy and which quiet. Most of all, I noticed the guards. There were a great many of them: Africans like Bilal, Turkish archers, Armenian cavalrymen, and brown-skinned desert-dwellers who carried short, stabbing spears. As with the Franks, or even the emperor's armies, there seemed to be a great rivalry between the different races – and it seemed to be the Africans who suffered worst. Each time a detachment of Turks or Armenians marched through the courtyard, the Africans were forced out of the way, and if they were not quick enough they often suffered kicks and blows. I mentioned it once to Nikephoros, and drew a predictably condescending response.

'Of course they beat the Africans – they are the least of races, savages worse than Franks. Why do you think they appointed them to guard us, if not to demean us? Is that all you've noticed?'

I hesitated, unwilling to risk drawing his scorn again.

'Which race do you see least?'

'The Armenians?'

'Exactly. The vizier, al-Afdal, is an Armenian, and he rests his authority on a private army of his countrymen. What does that tell you?'

'That perhaps al-Afdal is not here?'

Nikephoros nodded. 'And that is more disconcerting than any amount of tedium. Al-Afdal would not remove himself from his capital this long without good reason. But what that is . . . I do not know.'

After that, I watched the numbers of Armenian guards more closely, for it seemed that until the vizier al-Afdal returned we would be condemned to our unchanging, stifling confinement. I never saw any change, but one day we were treated to a rare release – not only from our rooms, but from the whole city itself.

'The caliph fears you may soon leave us without ever having seen the grandeur of Egypt,' Bilal announced, with what might have been an apologetic smile threatening to overcome his serious expression.

Evidently the caliph did not count his own capital among the grandeurs of Egypt, for we were taken to the docks on the same curtained litters that had carried us to the palace and loaded onto a gilded barge, which quickly pulled away from the wharf. The other river traffic, I noticed, steered a safe distance away from it. Looking back, I could see the southern edge of the city receding, and the arid fields beyond the walls. A little distance beyond, to the south, I saw a second city, utterly in ruins. Flocks of birds wheeled over the remains, and a few thin trails of smoke told tales of thieves or fugitives squatting inside, but otherwise it was silent, and the fleets of boats that scudded along the river ignored its broken wharves.

I saw Bilal standing alone near our prow. 'What happened here?' I asked quietly.

'This was Fustat. One of our great cities.'

111

'Who destroyed it?'

Bilal's face creased with anger. 'We did.' He must have seen my bafflement, for he continued: 'A civil war.'

'Recently?'

'Before you were born.'

I considered this. 'Then why . . . ?'

'Why is it still deserted?' Bilal gave a grim, sad laugh. 'Before the war we had enough men to fill two cities. Afterwards, we only had enough for one.'

We beached our barge a few miles upriver. A squadron of Turkish cavalry was waiting for us, with half a dozen camels and twice as many slaves. Though I had seen camels often enough from a distance, I had never ridden one, and I must have entertained the guards no end in my undignified attempts to haul myself onto its rolling back. Hardly was I in the saddle than the beast unfolded its spindly legs and lumbered to its feet, tipping me about like a ship in a storm. A small boy, black as Bilal but half his size, held the reins. Beside me, I could see Nikephoros suffering similar indignities; Bilal, evidently more practised, was sitting as calm as a monk in his saddle. Our Turkish escort, all mounted on Arabian horses, watched with grim amusement.

As my seat steadied, I was able to cast my gaze slightly further afield – and gasp in wonder. Now I saw why the caliph had sent us here. A few hundred yards to the west the flat ground of the flood plain ended suddenly in a steep, stony escarpment. Atop it, looming over the river valley, I could see the peaks of fantastic mountains unlike any I had ever seen. They had no foothills, no ridges or ravines, but rose in an unbroken line from the earth. Their long slopes were so vast and perfect that surely only a god could have carved them. They seemed unspeakably ancient.

Bilal saw my astonishment and nodded. 'There is nothing else like them on earth. Come.'

With the awning slung low over the barge I had not seen the mountains from the river; now I could look at nothing else. Their immensity was hypnotic, and only grew as we approached across the parched flats of the river basin. There were three peaks in total, the third a good deal shorter than the other two. For a brief moment I was reminded of the three peaks of Antioch – though they could hardly have been more different.

I gestured to Bilal, riding between me and Nikephoros, and he guided his camel closer.

'What are these? Churches?'

'Tombs.' Bilal raised his eyebrows. 'You have not heard of the pyramids?'

'Of course. They were once reckoned among the wonders of the world.' Nikephoros swatted his cane at the boy who led his camel, and was obediently led nearer to us. '"*It is through deeds such as these that men go up to the gods.*"'

'Did the caliphs build them?'

Nikephoros laughed. 'It was the ancient kings of Egypt. Long before the caliphs, the Caesars or even Alexander. Scholars say that they were built by the Jews before Moses led them out of their bondage.'

We carried on, climbed a narrow path up the escarpment and emerged on the plateau high above the river. Once again, I was dumbfounded. Though parched by the drought, the valley's inherent fertility was obvious; here, only a few hundred yards distant, we were in a desert, a sea of sand and dust that stretched as far as the horizon and lapped around the base of the pyramids. And rising out of it like a sea monster, straight ahead of us, towered an enormous carved head surrounded by a stone hood. I started, frightening my camel, and the boy with the bridle had to run back and calm it before I was pitched over the cliff.

'That is Abu al-Hol,' said Bilal. 'The Father of Terror.'

I crossed myself, and gave the creature a wide berth as we picked our way across the sands. The head seemed to be attached to a body which, if anything, was even larger – but an animal's body, not a man's, stretching out behind the head like a crouched cat or lion. I could just see the ridge of its back bursting out through the enveloping sand. It almost made me forget the grandeur of the pyramids, which seemed even more vast now that I could see how close we were. Until then, I had thought that no man could build anything larger than the cathedral of Ayia Sophia, but these must have been more than twice its height.

And yet, as we came around the side of the middle pyramid I saw that it was neither so perfect nor so permanent as it had been made to look. Scaffolding had been erected up one side of it, and the heirs of pharaohs' slaves still toiled in the heat with chisels and hammers. But instead of building this monument to eternity, they seemed to be dismantling it. Huge blocks of dressed limestone had been carved away from the pyramid's side, exposing ragged tiers of crumbling rocks and mortar beneath. As I watched, they slowly lowered one of the blocks down a long wooden slide, straining on the ropes.

'What are they doing?' I asked in astonishment.

Bilal shrugged. 'The caliph needs cut stone for his new city, and it is easier to quarry it from the past than from the ground.'

We made our way into the shade at the base of the largest pyramid and dismounted. Bilal had brought food – figs and dates and cheese – and also wine and sherbet. The slaves laid carpets on the hot sand, and we sat and ate in the shadow of antiquity. Our Turkish guards stayed on their horses and ate in the saddle, watching us from a little distance.

'Do they expect us to steal a camel and escape into the desert?' I wondered, pulling a fig from one of the baskets. A little way across the sand, the African boy sat in the shade of his hobbled camel and watched us impassively. Impulsively, I threw him the fig and watched his squinting eyes widen. He snatched it from the air, peeled back the green skin and sucked out the purple flesh and seeds. A trail of dark juice spilled onto the desert beside him.

Nikephoros looked away, bored or embarrassed, and pretended to examine the construction of the pyramid. Bilal glanced at me approvingly. It was a rare moment of empathy after so many weeks of guarded emotion, and I was suddenly desperate to make more of it.

I swept my arm across the desert, and back towards the river valley. 'Is this your country?'

He shrugged. 'I was born here.'

That wasn't what I had meant. 'Where are your people from?'

'From the south.' He spat a date seed onto the sand. 'But that is not my country.'

'Why not?'

'My mother was brought to Egypt when she was a girl. I was born here. I have campaigned in Palestine, in Syria and in Arabia, but I have never set eyes on Zanj, where she came from. How could that be my home?'

It seemed a strange and rootless way to live. 'I was born in Isauria, but I have not seen it in fifteen years. The Turks have governed it for most of that time – the emperor only reconquered it this past spring. But it is still my homeland.'

'And when your emperor conquered it – what happened to all the Turks who were born there?'

'I suppose they went back to their homelands in the East.' I saw the look Bilal was giving me. 'They did not belong there. It was Byzantine land.'

'And Jerusalem. Is that Byzantine land as well?'

'It's Christian land,' I said defensively.

'And when did Christians last own it?'

'Hundreds of years ago. But that is no reason why they should not have it again. Otherwise, you have nothing more than the rule of conquest.'

116

Bilal leaned sideways and sketched an abstract circle in the sand next to our carpet. 'Of course I believe in the rule of conquest. Show me a soldier who doesn't.'

'A defeated soldier,' said Nikephoros, who had shown every sign of ignoring us until then. Somehow, his attention now cast a chill on the conversation, and we lapsed into silence.

After lunch, I excused myself from the party and wandered across the desert to the northernmost of the pyramids. The Turkish guards watched me go but did not follow. There was nowhere I could have escaped to.

The pyramid was so vast that long before you entered its shadow you ceased to see it for what it was. Its geometric perfection, so obvious from afar, distorted until it became nothing more than a huge wall lifting out of the sand. Only as I reached its foot did it change again, resolving itself into a giant staircase, which seemed to rise to the heavens. Captivated, I began to climb without even thinking. The stripped courses were pitted and irregular, and I had to scramble to haul myself over each tier. Before I was even halfway up, my tunic was filthy with dust and sweat. Too late, I remembered I was supposed to be a representative of the emperor and probably above such things.

I paused in my ascent and looked down, shading my eyes with my hand. The green-brown smear of the Nile valley trailed away to the north, a thin vein of life between two apparently endless deserts. I could see the towers of al-Qahira, and the sprawling ruins of Fustat, the ghost city, beside it. Ahead and to my right, the blows of the masons' chisels rung in the still air.

It was too hot to sit there long, but I did not want to go back to Nikephoros and Bilal so soon. I rose, and edged my way around the pyramid along the uneven course. As I came around to the western face I looked down, and saw two horses tethered to a fallen rock at the pyramid's base. Even in this alien place, it seemed the Turkish guards would not allow me too long a leash, though I could not see the riders.

Sweating profusely, I reached the next corner and turned onto the northern side. I paused. A few tiers below me, and not quite in the centre of the face, a large gap broke the regular lines of stone. At first I thought it must just be where the caliph's workmen had cut away a deeper layer, but as I scrambled closer I saw that it was actually a hole, the mouth of a sloping tunnel leading down into the unseen depths of the pyramid. The stones about it were jagged and raw, as if the pyramid had been smashed open, while the walls of the tunnel within were impeccably smooth, inviting and sinister. I shivered, despite the heat. I had pried into pagan temples once before and found nothing but blood and wickedness. On the other hand, confronted with a dark cave, who does not long to know what lies within?

It was then that I heard the scream. It shrilled out of the tunnel as if squeezed from the ancient stones themselves, as if the ghosts of the pharaohs had stirred in their

118

coffins. I stepped back, almost over the edge of the ledge, and flailed my arms furiously to keep my balance. The effort seemed to right my senses. I believed there were demons in the world, of course, and I believed that evil lurked in the pagan inheritance of our ancestors. Sometimes I had felt it. But along with the scream, just after it, I had heard something else: a voice raised in anger. And as I peered at the sand that had drifted into the entrance, I could see two sets of fresh footprints – and two snaking lines as if something, or someone, had been dragged between them. Ghosts and spirits might dwell in the pyramid, but the sounds I had heard were the sounds of men. Crossing myself twice, I stepped into the darkness.

I had expected that the monumental scale of the building would be matched within: I had imagined cavernous chambers, high galleries and vast columns rising into darkness. Instead, almost immediately, the passage tapered into a shaft so small that I had to first crouch, then crawl – though it was so steep that I was grateful to be able to brace myself against the low ceiling for fear of losing my grip entirely and sliding forwards . . . how far down? My misgivings mounted as the light from outside vanished behind me, but almost immediately my eyes seemed to adjust to the gloom. No – something was illuminating the passage before me. A flickering orange glow, a torch or a fire, licked up the tunnel walls from below. Blood rushed into my head, paining and dizzying me. I suddenly saw what a lunatic mistake this had been; I wanted to turn back, but the tunnel was so thin I did not have the space. Would it ever release me, or would I have to crawl on my belly all the way into the depths of hell? All I could do was hasten my pace.

At last, the passage opened out. The air inside was cool and stale, smeared with the oily smoke of a lamp set in a niche in the wall. By its billowing light I could see I had entered a chamber tall enough that I could stand. At the far end, a black granite boulder blocked the passage beyond, though a heap of rubble suggested someone had once tried to burrow around it. For myself, I no longer had any desire to penetrate deeper into the depths of the pyramid: I would have turned around and counted myself lucky just to see the sky again. But I could not. The smoky lamplight cast three shadows over the polished granite: two were Turkish guards, their swords and belts unbuckled from their waists and their robes hanging open; the third was the black-skinned boy who had led my camel, now lying cowering on the floor. He was completely naked, and I saw a balled-up cloth in a corner where his thin tunic had been ripped from his body.

I spoke without thinking if I would be understood, or what my words would provoke. 'Stop!'

The two guards turned. The boy, who had seen me first, lifted himself on his hands like a dog scenting his master, though there was little hope on his face.

'Stop,' I said again. The sudden act of standing up had left me dizzy, and there was less conviction in my voice this time. The guard to my left scowled, then stepped towards me and spat out a stream of angry words. I shook my head dumbly, understanding nothing but terribly fearful for what I had begun. I glanced back at the boy: he had crawled over to his discarded tunic and reached out for it, but as he did so the second guard stamped a heavy boot on his hand. The gruesome crack of bone echoed around the chamber; the boy howled, and flung himself back into the far corner where he lay, whimpering, not even bothering to cover himself. How old could he be – ten? Twelve?

'I demand you stop.'

The guards could not understand my words, but the meaning must have been clear enough. An ugly look spread across the nearer man's face. He stepped forward again, reaching for the sword he had unbuckled. He pulled it from its scabbard and whipped the blade towards me; I retreated, but almost immediately felt the cold stone of the wall against my back. I had no chance of escape. The only way out was the narrow passage, and even if I had managed to squeeze into it my opponents could easily have hauled me back out. And that would have meant leaving the unfortunate boy to his fate. Even as I watched, I saw the second guard lift him off the floor and spin him hard against the wall. Would they make me watch?

The nearer guard was still holding the sword, its point angled towards my heart. A part of my mind refused to believe it: I was an ambassador, after all. Surely they could not afford to sacrifice me so carelessly. But I was alone, deep in a dangerous, crumbling monument. They could kill me, bury me under the rubble and pretend I had suffered an unfortunate accident. Or drag me into the desert and let the sands bury me for ever.

I brushed away those thoughts. This was not the first time I had seen a blade held to my heart, and by more desperate men than these. I tried to swallow the pulsing fear which my heart pumped through me.

'Let me go,' I said. 'I am the emperor's ambassador. You cannot—' I broke off as I saw the bored incomprehension on the Turk's face. He inched closer, and raised the sword a fraction higher. I could hardly look beyond the silver spark of the hovering point, but beyond it I saw the blurry shadow of the second guard approaching the boy with outstretched hands. The muscles in my back tensed, and I had to fight back the urge to hurl myself forward. I would only have impaled myself.

Neither of us moved. The only sound in the chamber was a grunting, fumbling noise by the far wall. I closed my eyes. Then, suddenly, I heard a scraping by my feet, a trickle of cascading pebbles and a half-checked cry of surprise. My eyes flashed open, and before I could even look at what had caused the noise I saw that my opponent's gaze had been distracted. It was all I needed. I braced myself against the wall and lashed out with my right boot, hammering it straight into his groin. He squealed with pain, though he was too well trained to let go his sword. He bent double, which only served to present his face to my upswinging fist. His nose cracked under the impact.

The guard reeled away, clutching his face with his left

122

hand, and I turned belatedly to see what it was that had distracted him. Even with the blood of battle scorching my veins, I recoiled. A black demon had crawled out of the tunnel, the ghost of some long-dead denizen of this tomb. He stood almost as high as the ceiling; his yellow cloak swirled around him like fire, and his round head was black and featureless as shadow. The sword in his hands smouldered in the lamplight as he advanced into the room.

He turned to glance at me, and I saw with grateful relief that he was no demon. There were white eyes and a mouth in the black face, and the yellow cloak was real enough to have been smeared and stained by his passage through the tunnel. It was Bilal. He strode towards the second guard, spun him around and hurled him against the wall with such force that I almost expected to see the granite crack. He shouted in the man's face, a furious tirade that needed no translation, and I sagged against the wall in relief.

A shadow fell across Bilal's back, though he could not see it. The first guard had risen out of the gloom at the edge of the chamber, and if my assault had left him unable to move freely, he still had a sword in his hands and vicious purpose in his arms. I shouted a warning and sprang forward. Bilal turned. The guard heard me too, but that did not matter: he was committed to his attack and too wounded to change course. I struck him and ploughed him to the ground, desperately trying to pin down his sword arm. I could not reach. He reversed his grip and thumped the pommel into my shoulder, loosening my

123

hold. Wet blood streamed over his face where I had broken his nose, but he seemed impervious to the pain as he tried to throw me off. He had almost dislodged me: in a second, I would be on the floor, and he would be over me. I could not expect any help from Bilal, for I could dimly hear him struggling with the other guard behind me.

My tumbling charge had taken us near the pile of rubble at the end of the room. In desperation, I let go with my right arm and flung it out, scrabbling on the ground for a loose stone. One was too heavy, another little more than a pebble. Meanwhile, my one-handed grasp was not enough to hold the Turk. He heaved up and rolled me over, just as my free hand closed around a fist-sized stone. I barely felt the weight; I lifted it, and swung it against the side of the guard's head with every ounce of strength I could muster. It struck him on the temple and I felt his skull shudder; I struck him again, and this time the stone came away stained with blood. Perhaps the sight should have sickened me, but instead it gave a deeper, savage power to my blows as I struck him again and again, until at last he went limp and fell away.

I stood, trembling, and let the stone drop to the floor – suddenly, it felt like the foulest object imaginable. I looked around. Bilal was standing, wiping his sword on a crumpled object by his feet, the unmoving body of the second guard. The boy, no longer in danger, had crawled away and was struggling into his tunic. Bilal stroked his head and murmured a few gentle words, then turned to me.

'I followed them when I saw them come after the boy,' he said. 'I did not know you were in here too.'

'I heard the boy's cry and came to look.'

Bilal crossed to my side and stared down at the guard, though I could hardly bear to look at the matted stew of hair, blood and bone I had pounded out of his skull.

'Is he dead?' I asked.

Bilal gave no answer. Instead, he turned his back on me and knelt beside the wounded guard. He lifted the man's bloody head and cradled it on his knee, staring down into the slack face. He shook his head, then reached across and stroked his hand gently across the man's neck. It was only as he suddenly leapt back, and as blood and air began bubbling out of a broad cut he had left, that I saw the gleam of a small knife in Bilal's hand.

'You – you killed him.'

'Only to finish what you had begun.' Bilal removed his cloak and his outer tunic, folded them, and placed them in one of the stone niches in the wall.

'But what he did is a crime – surely, even here? Better that he should have been punished in public.'

Bilal glanced at me with contempt. 'Do you think we are barbarians? Of course it is a crime. But it is more ... complicated.' He turned away and crouched by the fallen masonry. 'Help me.'

The air in that deep chamber had become a heady potion of smoke and oil, blood and dust. Together, Bilal and I pulled away some of the stones, laid the two corpses by the foot of the wall, and heaped the rubble back over

125

them. There was not nearly enough to hide them.

'If they are found, it will look as if they were killed in a rock fall,' said Bilal.

'It must have been sharp rocks, to stab one and slit the other's throat.'

Bilal grunted. 'The desert is full of scavengers. In two days, all trace of their wounds will have vanished with their flesh.'

'And their companions, the rest of the guards? What will you tell them?'

'That the two men deserted.'

Slowly, my wits began to return. 'But they were criminals. They would have raped the boy and murdered me – and you, when you found us. Why should we have to hide them?'

Bilal was hastily pulling on his tunic. 'Do you remember Fustat? The ruined city you saw from the boat?'

'You said it was destroyed in a civil war.'

Bilal wrapped his cloak around his shoulders and clasped it at the neck. 'That was a war between the black legions and the Turkish legions in the caliph's army. It raged for years and desolated the country. Eventually the vizier, al-Afdal's father, stopped it by bringing in his Armenian troops who hated Turks and Africans equally. But the wounds are not forgotten. That is why no one must know that a black man has killed two Turkish guards.'

He spun around and advanced on me. 'I know it is probably to your emperor's benefit if we tear ourselves apart, but you must swear not to tell what has happened here. If you had not followed them . . .'

'Then the boy would have been raped in secret, and no one would have known or cared. Is that what you would have preferred?'

Bilal had come very close to me, blocking the light of the fading lamp. Once again, he looked as he had first appeared in that chamber, a featureless void in the shape of a man. I shivered. Then he smiled, his white teeth breaking the darkness, and touched my arm.

'I am glad you did what you did.'

'And I am sorry for what came of it. I will keep it a secret, you have my word.'

'Then we should leave this evil place.'

Dusk was falling by the time we arrived at the palace. A damask haze hung over the low water, while the sky flushed pink over the western desert. Even so, the royal wharf thrived with activity. A fleet of long ships, easily large enough to navigate the sea, had arrived – so many of them that they had to moor three abreast. Their sailors were still coiling ropes and furling sails, while on shore a great throng of soldiers milled about. There was no sign of the litters that had carried us to and from the palace, and little chance that they could have forged a way through the crowd in any event.

'We will have to walk,' said Bilal. 'It is not far.'

We could not even dock, but had to tie up alongside one of the outermost ships and clamber from deck to deck until at last we reached the wharf. Instantly, we were plunged into the bustle and jostle of soldiers, bewildering after the emptiness of the desert. A babble of voices filled the air – and it seemed to me that the language they spoke was not Arabic but something else, something I had heard before among Pakrad's men in the monastery at Ravendan. Our guards made a tight circle around us, while Bilal approached one of the soldiers and questioned him. The man answered so volubly that Bilal had to wave him to be quiet, indicating Nikephoros and me with a cautionary glance. The soldier giggled and put a calloused finger to his lips, then wheeled away to join the throng of his fellow soldiers.

'What was that?'

I suspected I was not supposed to know, and that Bilal would either ignore me or pretend not to have heard. Instead, after a moment's pause to frown in thought, he looked me in the eye.

'It is the vizier, al-Afdal, He has returned.'

ιβ

∽∽∽∽∽

The following evening we had our first glimpse of the man who held sway over the caliph. We were invited to a banquet – to celebrate his latest triumph, said the courtier who brought the summons, though when I asked where the victory had been won he retreated from the room. Meanwhile, I had other concerns: I had not seen Bilal since we returned to the palace, and I feared lest he had suffered some punishment or revenge for what had happened in the pyramid. I tried to ask our guards, but they spoke no Greek and could not answer.

The sun was setting when we left our apartments, though we could not see it for the high walls that surrounded the courtyard. I had spent most of the day beside the window, watching the comings and goings and looking in vain for Bilal. Even if I had not known that the vizier had returned, I would have recognised that something had changed, for there was a new sense of urgency and activity in the palace. Now it had subsided, and the loudest sounds in the courtyard were the muted splashing of the fountains and the slap of our footsteps.

The quiet receded as we climbed a broad flight of stairs. I could hear a babble of voices, and the fragile melodies of flutes and a lyre in the background. The noise grew as we came out onto an open balcony: it was surrounded on three sides by wooden screens in the shape of foliage, while the fourth side offered an unbroken view across the river and the plain beyond, all the way to the high peaks of the pyramids several miles distant. I shivered to see them, and turned away to take the cup of sherbet a slave was presenting to me. I was half a pace behind Nikephoros, as befitted my station, and could ignore the functionary who was busy greeting him in a flurry of solicitudes and bows. The dying sun washed Nikephoros' face; with his head held proud and stiff, he looked like some haughty, golden statue. I could not see his eyes, but the tight curve at the edge of his mouth suggested he was in his element, basking in the mastic of protocol and courtesy.

It was a scheme where I had little part to play, save to stand behind Nikephoros and make him seem taller by lengthening his shadow. Ignoring the functionaries, I skimmed my gaze across the terrace, searching for the vizier. There must have been well over a hundred courtiers in attendance, some with faces as dark as Bilal's, others as fair as Sigurd, all dressed in long robes trimmed with gold and embroidered with the sharp-edged letters of their scripture. I could not see the vizier – but at the balcony's edge I saw four men clustered together, watching the gathering with wary concentration. They stood a little apart from the main assembly, sipping nervously from their silver cups, lumpen and awkward amid the fluid ease of the other guests. They were Franks.

I slipped away from behind Nikephoros and made my way towards them. I lost sight of them in the bustle; by the time I emerged, they had noticed my approach. They turned to face me, squaring their shoulders and watching me cautiously as if I posed some unknown danger.

'You're far from home.' I spoke in the bastardised Frankish that had become the Army of God's common tongue. At the sound of it, nervous glances flashed between the Franks.

'Further than you.' It was the nearest Frank who answered, a strongly built man with russet-brown hair and a face that, while smooth-skinned, appeared neither youthful nor handsome. Perhaps it was because of his eyes, which seemed somehow too large for his face; they drilled into me with such fierce and unhidden suspicion that I was almost embarrassed to look at them.

'Further than me,' I agreed. 'I am Demetrios Askiates, from Constantinople.'

'A Greek – but you have marched with the Army of God?'

'All the way to Antioch.'

131

The intensity in his eyes seemed to focus still sharper. 'You came from Antioch? What is the news there? We heard that God had given us a great victory over the Turks, but that was months ago. What has happened since?'

'Little except plague and delay.' I spoke shortly; Antioch reminded me of too many things I could not bear to think of. 'But why are you at the caliph's palace? How long have you been here?'

'Almost six months.' He laughed bitterly as he saw my shock. 'You will soon discover that the Fatimids do not hurry their guests. We were sent here by the princes to make an alliance against the Turks, but so far . . .' He held open his empty palms. 'Nothing. We have been feasted and entertained, we have marvelled at the caliph's new city and the pagan marvels of the ancients . . . Have you seen the pyramids?'

He pointed back over my shoulder, though I did not look. 'I have seen them. Have you met with the vizier, al-Afdal?'

'Many times. He speaks constantly, sees everything and says nothing. He is the arch-deceiver.'

It seemed a dangerous thing to say at the vizier's own gathering, and I glanced around nervously. To my alarm, I saw a Fatimid courtier striding towards us, with Nikephoros close behind him. Although the two men could hardly have been more different, the disapproving scowls on their faces were almost identical.

'Demetrios.' Nikephoros twitched his head to order me back to my allotted orbit behind him. 'The chamberlain

132

was about to present us – but it seems you could not wait.'

I swallowed my pride and stepped back into Nikephoros' shadow, shaking my head in wonder. Yesterday I had shattered a man's head with a rock; today I was rebuked for anticipating an introduction. As for Nikephoros, he might stand in front of a burning house and his only concern would be to ensure that the inhabitants escaped in order of rank.

The Fatimid chamberlain had begun to make the appropriate introductions – flattering Nikephoros by presenting him first. Then he turned to the Franks.

'Achard of Tournai.' He bowed to the man I had spoken with earlier. 'He has been our guest some months now.' He introduced the other three, though I promptly forgot their names. None of them even pretended enthusiasm at meeting us.

'Why does the Greek king need his own envoys here?' Achard's staring eyes were trained full on Nikephoros, who stiffened as I translated for him.

'The Greek *emperor* sends his envoys where he chooses. Perhaps together we can succeed where alone we may have failed.'

'When you have been here six months you can judge who has failed,' Achard muttered in Frankish. I did not translate it.

'All that matters is that we reach Jerusalem and that we take it from the Turks.'

'On that we can all agree,' said the Fatimid chamberlain piously. There was something knowing in his eyes, an amusement that I could not understand, though perhaps it was just the studied artifice of a courtier.

Before I could ponder it further, a train of slaves with long tapers appeared at the head of the stairs, and the crowd began to drift down to the banquet.

I did see the mysterious and all-powerful al-Afdal that evening, though only from the distant corner of the banqueting hall where I ate. I suppose, having heard his reputation, I had expected a lean-faced schemer with a predatory hunch and hawkish eyes; instead, he seemed a jovial figure who filled out his robes, lounged easily on his seat and laughed often. *He speaks constantly and says nothing*, I remembered with a cold chill. The hope I had felt the day before, that al-Afdal's arrival would hasten my return to Sigurd and Anna, had all but died when I heard Achard's story. Though I could not deny a small spark of optimism when I learned, next morning, that al-Afdal would receive our embassy.

'This time, you will do well to keep your eyes lowered, your mouth shut, and your feet planted one pace behind and to the left of my own,' said Nikephoros, as a slave combed and oiled his hair. 'The caliph's palace is not a fairground – you cannot wander about it entertaining yourself as you please.'

I said nothing, but sullenly rinsed my hands in a bowl of rosewater. Nikephoros sighed.

'I know you have followed paths where aggression is

prized. But now you are in a different world, where humility and obedience are the chief virtues.'

'I didn't know I had joined a monastery again,' I said sulkily.

Nikephoros gave a short laugh. 'You saw how long those clumsy Franks have waited here. Do you want to waste as many months fretting away your life?'

I shook my head.

'The Franks were fools to send their embassy when they did, when their army was mired in a fruitless siege and faced every prospect of destruction. Of course al-Afdal would not accept their alliance in those circumstances. Now that the Franks have proved their worth at Antioch, our proposal is more compelling.'

'Do we speak for the Army of God?'

'We speak for the emperor, and the Franks are his tool. Though it would be easier if their own emissaries were not here.'

'Strange that we have not seen them before.'

Nikephoros snorted. 'Do you think it was a coincidence that we met them last night? Al-Afdal permitted it because it suits his purposes. There was no chance in that meeting. Now that we are aware of each other's presence, al-Afdal will seek to divide us, and profit by our suspicions. That is why we must finish our business as quickly as possible – if al-Afdal allows it.'

Footsteps in the hall outside announced the arrival of our escort to the audience. Bilal's face appeared around the door; he gave me a sad, private frown, then bowed to

Nikephoros, who was straightening the hem of his sleeves and did not notice.

'The vizier al-Afdal begs you to attend him at his home.'

Whatever schemes he might entertain, al-Afdal had no need of the petty delays that the caliph had inflicted on us before our first audience. The litter-bearers carried us through bustling, unseen streets and set us down in a small courtyard hung with silk awnings to keep off the sun. Four fountains rose in the corners, and ran through green-tiled channels to a shallow pool in its centre. On the far side of the pool, reclining on cushions on a low marble dais, sat al-Afdal, and although he sat in the shade, the golden threads in his ivory robe still caught the sun like ripples on water. The sight was so unexpected and peaceful – a man enjoying the comforts of his garden on a hot day – that for a moment I completely forgot his power. Then I saw Nikephoros stoop to one knee in front of me, and hastily followed suit. Nikephoros did not offer the full *proskynesis*, I saw – that was reserved for true kings – but he held his bow several beats longer than was necessary.

Slaves brought honeyed wine and almond cakes, and al-Afdal's chamberlain motioned us to sit. Al-Afdal did not say a word, but smiled kindly at us as he waited for the attendants to finish. I took the opportunity to study him: as I had seen the night before, he had the rounded figure of a man who enjoyed his pleasures unabashedly – though he would still sit easily enough on a warhorse, I guessed. His black beard was streaked with grey; the creases at the corners of his eyes gave him a benign, avuncular air, but the eyes themselves were as dark and impenetrable as onyx. When he lifted the cup at his side, I saw a fresh scar livid on the back of his hand, and I wondered again about the victory he had celebrated the night before.

He murmured something in Arabic, and the chamberlain stood. 'In the name of the Most Illustrious Lord, the Counsellor of the Caliph, the Sword of Islam, the Commander of the Armies, Protector of the Muslims and Guide of the Missionaries, al-Afdal Shah-an-Shah – welcome.'

I thought I saw a sardonic smile play over al-Afdal's lips as he listened to his titles – and it grew subtly wider as Nikephoros responded with the full litany of the emperor's honorifics, taking great care, I thought, to draw them out longer than the vizier's. When he had finished, al-Afdal sat back. It seemed strange that for all his magnificent titles he should not know Greek, when even Bilal had managed to learn it, but he spoke in Arabic and left the chamberlain to translate.

'An embassy from the emperor of the Romans always brings honour to our court. And we have much to discuss. I have heard that the emperor wishes to forge an alliance.'

'We have both suffered many defeats against the Turks – often because we could not unite against the common threat. Now that they are on the brink of defeat, they should not escape on account of our differences. We both have too much to gain.'

Al-Afdal smiled. 'It is true that we have both allowed

the Turks too many victories. But let us be honest with each other. It is neither Byzantium nor Egypt that has now brought the Turks low. According to what I hear, that has been accomplished by this army of *Franj* – the so-called Army of God.'

Nikephoros shifted uneasily on his cushions. 'It is true that the Frankish armies have done much of the fighting. But it has all been on the emperor's behalf. He called them into being, and they have sworn allegiance to him as their ultimate lord.'

'So do you speak for them?' Al-Afdal popped a sticky sweet into his mouth, rubbed his fingers together in a bowl of water, and let one of the slaves dry them. The question hung unanswered in the lazy air – though al-Afdal obviously guessed the truth well enough. He had had six months to learn all about the Franks from Achard, after all.

'Only the Franks can speak for themselves,' Nikephoros said at last. 'But the emperor is a valued ally and he has . . . influence. When he speaks, they listen.'

Al-Afdal nodded. 'It must be hard for an army to provision itself so far from home. And if he asked for Antioch? Would they surrender it?'

'The Franks do not want Antioch for themselves.' I marvelled that Nikephoros could say that with such conviction. 'They only need it as a staging post to Jerusalem.'

'Ah, Jerusalem.' Al-Afdal leaned forward and dipped a finger in the tiled pool, swirling it around until he had whipped up a vortex. 'Have you ever seen Jerusalem?'

'Not yet, my lord.'

'I have. Until twenty years ago it was part of our holy empire.'

'Your kindness to its Christian inhabitants then is well remembered.'

Al-Afdal ignored the flattery. 'It is a terrible place, without water or comfort. But do you know what it's greatest problem is?'

Nobody answered.

'Too many gods. Even the pagan Egyptians would have struggled to squeeze so many deities into such a small space. The city cannot hold them. That is why only a fool would seek to conquer it.'

I could see Nikephoros struggling to measure his words appropriately. 'The Franks believe they are ordained by God to retake Jerusalem.'

'So Achard of Tournai has told me – many times.' Al-Afdal smiled again. 'And the Byzantine emperor? Does he believe that he too must possess Jerusalem?'

'He is of one mind with the Franks.'

'Of course.'

Nikephoros uncrossed his legs and leaned forward. 'Thirty years ago, before the Turks came, Egypt and Byzantium lived peacefully as neighbours. When our pilgrims travelled to the holy places, you protected them, and when famine threatened the Egyptian harvest we sold you grain. The emperor wishes to return to that happy state.'

'But only if he extends his lands to Jerusalem.'

'If the Turks are eventually driven out of Syria and Palestine, it will be the Franks who have struck the most telling blow,' Nikephoros insisted. 'They will deserve their reward.'

'And they will accept nothing other than Jerusalem?'

'Their ambassadors have surely told you so.'

Al-Afdal furrowed his brow, and stroked his beard in mock concentration. 'So to enjoy the emperor's friendship again, I must allow his allies to take and hold Jerusalem.'

'And then, with your left flank secured, you could drive east to Baghdad – to Mecca, even.'

'And if I do not?'

To the guards standing by the gates and watching us across the courtyard, it must have seemed that al-Afdal was entirely overwhelmed by Nikephoros. His shoulders were hunched and his head bowed, his hands clasped penitently before him as if hoping for a benediction. I could see Nikephoros was no more deceived by the charade than I, but even so he could not resist raising his voice a fraction to drive home his point.

'The Franks have proved that there are few who can resist them. They are destined for Jerusalem, and – for all our sakes – the emperor would prefer that they came as your allies, to make the victory complete. But, whatever you choose, they are coming.'

A hot silence hung in the courtyard. Even the fountains seemed to have stopped their flow. Al-Afdal sat very still, while Nikephoros sank back onto his cushions. His diplomat's face was as composed as ever, but his eyes were strained with anxiety.

Al-Afdal looked up with an apologetic smile. 'That is a pity.' With a start, I realised that I was no longer hearing his words through the chamberlain's translation, but direct from his mouth in fluent Greek. 'Because, you see, I already possess Jerusalem. I conquered it from the Turks a month ago. That was the victory we celebrated last night.'

I was lucky; in my insignificance, no reaction was demanded of me. Nikephoros had no such comfort. Al-Afdal's sudden leap into Greek had denied him even the translator's delay, and every second that he did not respond only doubled the oppressive expectation on him. To his credit, he absorbed the full weight of al-Afdal's blow with little more than a tightening in his cheeks, and a narrowing of his eyes.

'I did not know you spoke our language so well. I am surprised you need bother with an interpreter.'

Al-Afdal gave an ingenuous smile. 'I would speak it more often, but it is hard for me. I would not want you to misunderstand what I say.'

'Your Greek is flawless. Everything you say is perfectly clear.'

Al-Afdal took another sweet from the tray and kept his eyes fixed on Nikephoros.

'Although the caliph's obligations to his people kept him from leading the campaign personally, he is delighted by its result. Jerusalem is the holiest city in the world after Mecca and Medina: possessing it exalts the caliph and disgraces the Turks with their heretic Sunni faith.'

Nikephoros glanced at the cup of wine in his hands, but did not drink. 'The caliph would be reluctant to give it up, even to a loyal ally?'

Al-Afdal nodded a profession of regret. 'If Jerusalem was yours, would you surrender it?'

'The emperor might – if he gained by the transaction.'

I glanced at Nikephoros in astonishment, then remembered my place and hastily hid my face behind my wine glass. How could he contemplate giving up Jerusalem, even speculatively? A cunning edge had crept into his tone; I could not understand it, but al-Afdal seemed to have noticed, for he was sitting straighter and nodding slowly.

'But – forgive me – I do not see how the caliph could gain by surrendering his claim to Jerusalem. What does the emperor have to offer besides promises and protestations?' He lifted a stout hand in apology. 'You understand the caliph does not belittle the emperor's promises of friendship; he cherishes them. But the two halves of a bargain must balance each other. A promise for a promise, a city for a city. A war for a war.'

Al-Afdal rearranged himself into a more elegant repose on his cushions. 'I am grateful for your embassy, but I fear that events have overtaken us. It would be cruel to keep you here pretending otherwise. No doubt you yearn to see your homes and families again, and autumn will soon close the seas. If you have nothing else to discuss with the caliph, you could start for the sea tonight.'

The strain of concentrating on the shifting conversation, the heat of the sun beating through the awning and the sour bite of the wine in my mouth had contrived to raise a throbbing ache in my skull. For the past few minutes I had been staring at the cool water running through the fountains, wishing I could forsake protocol and plunge my head in. But the vizier's final words swept away all pain and care in an instant: for the first time in weeks I could think of Anna and Sigurd with hope. I looked expectantly at Nikephoros.

But Nikephoros was frowning and shaking his head. 'I am grateful for your kindness, but our duty to the emperor must overcome thoughts of home. Your great victory over the Turks has changed matters, but I do not think it means we cannot be allies. Perhaps, by your leave, we could talk further on this. Who knows what common interests we may discover?

'In the meantime, if the caliph permits it, we would be honoured to remain here as his guests.'

ιγ

∞∞∞∞∞

I did not know then how Nikephoros thought he could persuade al-Afdal to give up Jerusalem, but he certainly had no lack of time to consider it. After that first audience, the vizier showed little interest in continuing the conversation. Days lengthened into weeks, and gradually we forgot even to think of expecting another meeting. It did nothing to ease the burdens on my soul. I found that I slept later and later into the mornings; even when I did wake, I would pretend otherwise. I began to hate our quarters, though on the infrequent occasions that we were allowed out I suddenly found the prospect filling me with dread. All of us suffered from the long confinement, of course, and the perpetual pressure of being among enemies, but I seemed to feel it worst. Perhaps I only handled it worst.

Even when we did venture out into the palace grounds or the wider city, we never saw Achard and the other Frankish emissaries. Had they given up when they heard of al-Afdal's victory and returned to the Army of God? Or had they concluded their own bargain with al-Afdal, one that would turn him against us? I tried to ask Bilal one day, but all he would say was that he had not been assigned to guard them. There was much more I wanted to ask him – had the murdered Turks ever been found? were we suspected? – but before I could think of a way to broach it, he put a finger to his lips and shook his head. He too seemed under strain – as did many of the Fatimid courtiers. If Nikephoros ever managed to speak with them to ask when al-Afdal might receive us again, their eyes would flicker in alarm and their faces crease with tight, automatic smiles. Al-Afdal had many things to attend to, they said: the welfare of the caliph's subjects demanded his full energies. He would see us as soon as he could be sure of giving us the attention we deserved.

In the meantime, we were cast adrift on a sea of supposition and conjecture. We did not know why al-Afdal continually deferred us, we did not know how he would respond to whatever Nikephoros offered him, we did not know if he even still controlled Jerusalem, or whether the Army of God might have finished their journey and captured it for themselves by then. In which case, I thought, we would be left as mere flotsam, thrown up on a strange shore by the currents of distant storms.

*   *   *

One question, though, we did eventually answer. The Frankish envoys had not departed, nor been murdered in their beds, but remained at the palace in much the same condition as we did. We did not discover it by accident; instead, we found them waiting for us at the royal wharf on a river barge. I remembered Nikephoros' dark warnings from before, that the vizier would not have allowed us to meet the Franks except to further his own designs, and wondered whether this portended some new change in our mission. Nikephoros himself was not there to see it – he had declined the invitation, claiming he had letters to compose, though he had not asked me to stay behind and write them.

Aelfric and I climbed into the boat and seated ourselves on cushions in the bow with Achard and another of his companions. Achard's staring eyes followed Bilal as he went aft to relay some orders to the steersman, and he crossed himself fervently.

'How can you stand to be around that black devil?' he whispered in my ear. 'To live among the Ishmaelite heretics is perilous enough – but I never expected to see the demons of hell walking the earth. The devil is gathering his strength for the final contest. When demons walk the earth, the last days are near.'

'Not too near, I hope.'

'Closer than you think. No man will know the day or the hour – but there are signs, for those who can read them.'

I looked at him in astonishment, wondering if the long

months of confinement had unhinged his mind. He appeared to be in deadly earnest, but before I could question him further Bilal returned, and Achard lapsed into a sulky silence.

As the barge crawled upstream, the brick walls of the city faded behind us and we came into the wasteland beyond. Saplings had already grown tall in the disused fields, and toppled waterwheels lay broken beside silted-up channels. In the distance, to the south, I could see the ruined walls of the abandoned city.

'*A destroyer of nations has come forth to lay waste your lands, and your cities will be ruins without inhabitants,*' Achard muttered. I glanced at Bilal, but he showed no sign of understanding the Frankish – only the weary indifference of a man used to half-heard whisperings behind his back.

If I peered out from under the barge's awning I could see the three fangs of the pyramids rising on their summit above the river valley. Closer to us, though, the river forked around a thin island, which seemed to have escaped or repaired the ravages of the civil war: low mud-brick warehouses lined the shore, and dozens of wooden jetties marched out into the water on stilts. Between them, a score of boats in various states of progress sat lifted on wooden cradles in shipyards. Some of them were little more than bare-ribbed hulls, but most seemed almost ready to sail to Constantinople if required. They were certainly large enough for the task.

I did not hear any order, but the boat suddenly slowed

147

and stopped in midstream. There was no splash of an anchor; instead, the rowers kept their oars in the water and manoeuvred them gently to keep us steady. Even with the river so low and sluggish, it was an impressive feat.

'Is this where we are going?' Achard did not look at Bilal as he addressed him.

'The caliph was keen that you should see his dockyards,' said Bilal heavily.

I waved towards the shore. 'All these ships are his?'

'Of course. They will be ready for the next campaign season, when spring opens the seas again.'

I looked again. Of the ships that were nearing completion, all had heavy rams attached to their bows and fortified towers amidships. There was no mistaking their purpose. 'I am not surprised he wanted us to see them.'

One of Achard's companions tapped him on the arm and whispered in his ear. I could not hear the words, but I guessed them. When the Franks advanced on Jerusalem – if they had not already – they would have to take the coastal road, for the emperor could only supply them from the sea. I remembered the vast supply fleet I had seen gathering in Cyprus, and tried to imagine these skeletal vessels of the caliph encountering them at sea. One, even larger than the others and wanting only her oars, had a prow carved like a ravening eagle, and a copper-tipped ram which gleamed with menace.

We sat awkwardly in midstream and said little, listening to the creak of the thole-pins, and the hammering and sawing and songs drifting across from the shipyard. We were well into October now, and though the temperatures had cooled a little since our arrival it was still almost too hot to move. At home, autumn would be descending on Constantinople with falling leaves and shorter days, but here the sun shone and the palm fronds stayed green as ever in the still air. Only a few wispy clouds, far off on the sky's horizon, hinted at a changing season.

I dropped my arm over the boat's side and dipped my hand in the brown water. The current was stronger than I had expected; I felt a spark of pity for the rowers and their imperceptible efforts to keep us still.

'No!'

I had been staring into the knots and whorls on the river's surface and could not see behind me. Suddenly, a strong arm reached around my chest and hauled me backwards, yanking my trailing arm out of the water. I fell on my back, paddling my limbs in the air like an upturned crab while Achard and Aelfric and the others stared down on me in surprise. I rolled away and looked back to see Bilal lifting himself off the deck and smoothing down his cloak.

'What was that for?' I asked, breathing hard.

'It is not wise to touch the river.'

'Why not?'

Keeping his arm well clear of the water, Bilal gestured over the side. 'Do you see that?'

I looked, but could see nothing in the swirling silt. Perhaps there was a dark smudge beneath the surface, like a fish or sunken log, but I could not be sure. It might have been the shadow of a cloud.

'The river is infested with crocodiles – and too many careless unfortunates have given them a taste for human flesh.'

'What are they?' I had heard the name of crocodiles, but only in the company of mythic beasts: leviathans, basilisks, griffins and the like. 'Is it a fish?'

'A lizard. Longer than a man, and with jaws that could tear a horse in half.'

Even in this strange and ancient land, where men built mountains and the seasons never changed, it was hard to believe. 'Do they really exist? Have you ever seen one?'

'I can see three at this very moment.'

The Franks, who had been pretending not to listen, glanced over their shoulders and shifted in their seats, away from the side of the boat. But Bilal's gaze was fixed on the far bank. With a tremor of terror I looked up, half expecting to see a trio of winged dragons snorting fire as they ripped a horse limb from limb. Instead, there was nothing – only the sloping shore and a few tree-trunks that had floated away from the shipyard lying on the mud.

'Are you trying to make fools of us?' Achard demanded.

'They are sleeping at the moment.'

'And do they become invisible when they sleep?'

'They lie still as logs.'

I pointed to the long shapes I had taken for fallen trees. 'Those?' I squinted harder, shading my eyes against the sun, but even under close scrutiny they looked nothing like the monsters Bilal had described. Their bodies tapered into what might have been snouts, and there were small bulges by their sides which could have been stunted feet, but otherwise they looked no more alive – or dangerous – than rotten wood.

Achard evidently thought so too. 'I have seen mice more dangerous than your monsters.' He leaned back against the side of the boat and draped an arm provocatively over its edge – though when I peered down, I saw that he took care to keep his hand just above the water. I wondered if he was trying to goad Bilal into an outburst he would regret.

Bilal simply looked at him seriously. 'I hope you never have to learn otherwise.' He glanced across to the island. 'But I think we have admired the caliph's shipyard long enough. There is something on shore you should see.'

He spoke a command, and the crew hauled the boat forward against the current. The island slowly slid past, ending at a wooded point with a slim minaret rising through the trees and a dock by the water. The barge steered towards it, and soon bumped up beside a flight of stone steps. Bilal stepped out and beckoned us to follow.

At the top of the stairs, a broad and well-paved path led between orange and citron trees towards an arched gateway. Here it was easier to believe that autumn was coming: the desiccated leaves had curled back on their stems, tinged with brown; others had fallen and lay in heaps at the side of the path. They barely rustled as we passed in the still air.

We halted at the gateway, though there were no gates to stop us. Stone walls led away in both directions, framing a wide courtyard. A small mosque stood in one corner, and a square tower rose on the far side opposite us.

'Wait here,' said Bilal. He disappeared through the arch.

The six of us – the four Franks, Aelfric and I – stood in silence. The heat in the air and the flies buzzing around us made a strange contrast with the dead leaves by our feet, as if we had entered a new world where seasons collided without reason. It was an uncomfortable feeling – not helped by the weight of Achard's unblinking eyes on me.

I had to speak eventually to dislodge that stare. 'Do you ever wish you'd taken the vizier's offer and returned home?'

Contrary to what I had intended, my words only seemed to double the force of Achard's gaze. 'What offer?'

I paused, wishing I had kept silent. I tried a noncommittal shrug, but Achard's interest was as fixed as his stare. 'Did the vizier say you could return to the Army of God?'

'There seemed little purpose staying here when . . .' In the back of my mind I could almost hear Nikephoros' jeering laugh as I plunged towards another indiscretion. I wished Bilal would return, but there was no sign of him. I took a deep breath.

'You know that al-Afdal has conquered Jerusalem?'

'Of course.' Achard's studied indifference could not have been entirely contrived, but I noticed that for the first time he had dropped his gaze.

I shrugged. 'There seemed little left to negotiate.'

'But you chose to stay.'

I didn't choose to stay, I wanted to scream. *I would give half my life to be back in Constantinople now.* 'While there is any prospect of peace, we must work to achieve it,' I said piously. 'Blessed are the peacemakers.'

Achard looked surprised. 'You cannot make peace with Babylon – only destroy her, as was prophesied.'

Now it was my turn to stare at him. Did he mean the abstract, biblical Babylon or the kingdom where we stood at that moment? Either way, it was a foolish thing to say, and I looked around anxiously. I did not know whether to be relieved or alarmed when I saw that Bilal had reappeared.

'Come.'

He led us across the courtyard to the tower opposite. As we approached, I saw that its walls were not the evenly cut masonry they looked from a distance, but were built from a host of different stones, which seemed to have been plundered from across the ages and hammered, chiselled or cemented into one. Some of the lower stones were carved with shocking pagan images: men with heads like birds and jackals; men bowing prostrate with sheaves of corn; crows and beetles. Others were decorated with scrolls and rosettes, and curved as if they had once framed windows or doors. One of the stones even bore an inscription in Greek, though so old I could not read it. It unsettled me to see it there amid all those relics.

An old man in a white robe awaited us by a doorway.

He bowed courteously, though there was anxiety in his eyes as he spoke to Bilal in Arabic. Whatever his concerns, I saw Bilal dismiss them with a shake of his head, and the man reluctantly stepped aside. Just before we entered, Bilal turned to us.

'This is one of the most important sites in Egypt. Few outside the court are allowed to see it.'

His words seemed at odds with the sight that greeted us as we ducked through the doorway. Inside was a dim, square-sided chamber that seemed to rise the full height of the tower and, more curiously, to drop away almost an equal distance below. Broad windows had been cut into the tower's walls, and though they seemed to admit less sun than they should it was enough for me to see that the entire tower was one tall shaft, with a staircase winding around its edges until it disappeared into a pool of black-brown water at the bottom. From its centre, an eight-sided column rose to a stone beam above our heads.

'Is this a well?' I asked. Now that we were all inside and the noise of our entry had subsided, I could hear the water lapping against the stones – and a steady gurgling, as if somewhere it was pouring through a spout.

'This is where we measure the rising and falling of the Nile.' Bilal pointed to the central column. Now that my eyes had adjusted to the light, I could see it was scored with hundreds of parallel lines, each a finger's breadth apart from the next. 'By this, we know how strong the harvest will be even before it is sown. Look.'

I peered down. The measuring marks reached right to

the top of the column, though if the river ever reached that high then there would be no hope of reading it, for the entire island would be inundated. That had evidently never happened, for the upper reaches of the column were clean and smooth, gleaming with a sheen of moisture from the damp air. Further down, the high-water marks of the past stained the marble a dirty grey, progressively darker as it descended. Finally, a still-living scum coated the pillar a few feet above the water where the river had only recently subsided. Even at its height, it seemed a great deal lower than the floods of previous years.

Achard coughed, perhaps overcome by the dank and spore-filled air. 'Is this what you brought us to see?' He glanced uneasily at the plaques mounted on the wall, filled with inscriptions in the Arabic script, as if they might be written with spells to damn his soul. 'I have seen villages with more impressive wells.'

'Perhaps you would like to wait outside. The air is cleaner there.' Bilal turned to me. 'But there are some carvings you have not seen. You will like them.'

'I do not need to see the works of demons and heretics,' declared Achard. With another fit of coughing, he led his Franks back out through the door. Aelfric looked after them, then back at me; I nodded to him, and he followed them out, leaving me alone with Bilal.

I sighed. 'I had forgotten how rude the Franks can be.'

Bilal laughed. 'And these are their diplomats. Come.'

He led me down, skirting the sides of the central well until the stairs vanished into the dark water. He sat down by the water's edge, a few steps up, and beckoned me to do likewise.

'I cannot see any carvings,' I observed.

'I needed to speak with you.' Bilal glanced up to make sure that we were not overheard; I could see the priest's shadow hovering by the doorway, but that did not seem to trouble him.

'You are not safe. None of you.'

'What?' I craned my head around and looked into his face. I saw no trace of deceit.

'The vizier's capture of Jerusalem has changed many things. There are voices at the palace who say that we are strong enough now to challenge all our enemies. They are stirring up old grievances to breed hatred – it is not difficult.'

'Does al-Afdal support this?'

Bilal shook his head. 'He knows our strength too well. It is those furthest from the armies who are keenest to use them.'

'But I thought . . .' I paused, unsure how frankly I could speak.

'You thought al-Afdal controlled the palace? He does. But there are many factions, and al-Afdal cannot always master them all.' Bilal looked across the water and gave the column an appraising look, as if counting off the exposed notches. 'And there are other pressures on our kingdom, too.'

A wave of bitter helplessness swept over me. 'Why have you told me this? Is there anything I can do?'

156

Bilal glanced up again at the shadow by the door. 'You can be careful. And take this.'

He reached inside his cloak and pulled out a short knife in a leather sheath. He handed it to me. It was a plain weapon, with no carving or ornament on its bone handle, but the blade looked sharp enough when I slid it out.

'Is this yours?'

'I bought it in the bazaar. No one will know where it came from, unless you tell them.'

'I will not tell them.'

'It will not be much use if the caliph's guards come for you, but . . . it may be helpful. I hope you do not need it.'

I tucked the knife into my boot, wondering if the bulge was too obvious. 'Thank you. You did not have to.'

A movement above our heads caught my eye, and I looked up. Nothing stirred, but it seemed that the shadow by the door had moved. Bilal noticed it too.

'We should go.'

As we climbed the stairs, I looked around the great stone well once more. Even in the time we had been there, the river level seemed to have dropped further down the column.

'How old is this measure?'

Bilal shrugged. 'Who knows? But it was here before the Fatimids came. Perhaps the same men who built the pyramids erected it.'

We came out into the courtyard. In the short time we had been inside, the sun had sunk lower and dusk was hastening on. I could see our companions loitering impatiently by the gate.

'Thank you for showing it to me,' I said.

'The vizier thought you would find it interesting. It is a shame your master Nikephoros did not see it. You should tell him about it.'

'I will give him a full account.'

We rejoined the others and walked down towards the boat, while a too-hot October sun stained the clouds with a mess of bloody colour.

ιδ

∾∾∾∾∾

I told Nikephoros everything as soon we returned. His impatience soon turned to interest, particularly the account of the Nile measure, though he rolled his eyes when I repeated Bilal's warnings of danger.

'That is just part of their tactics. Like the men in Constantinople who convince you your house is on fire so they can rob it when you flee.'

'He seemed serious enough.'

'Of course he did – there would be little point in the lie if he did not.' Nikephoros took a piece from the tray of sweetmeats before him. 'I am surprised the ape had the wit for it.'

He flashed a sly glance as he said it, quick as a razor,

but I did not rise to the provocation. Not that I let him see, anyway.

'But why show us that their harvest is failing?' I said. 'Surely that weakens their position?'

Nikephoros gave me a withering look. 'Is that all you saw? If you had looked out of the boat two months ago you would have seen as much.'

Even after so much experience of it, his vitriol could still sting me. I waited, wondering if he would explain himself or grow bored.

'Al-Afdal will negotiate.'

'How do you know?'

Nikephoros took the last two sweetmeats off the tray and crammed them in his mouth. 'Because he has finally shown us what he wants. And because he sent word while you were away. He will see me tomorrow.'

Whatever Nikephoros had to say to al-Afdal, he did not need me to hear it. He went alone, and when he returned a couple of hours later he said nothing except to call for wine and retreat to his own room. The meeting must have pleased him, though, for when he came out for supper he was in a better humour than I had seen him for weeks. The setting sun filled the room with a bright copper glow, moulded into intricate shadows on the wall by the carved window screens. The caliph's slaves kept us well supplied with wine, and the feeling in the room was of an army on the last night of its campaign. Even I found myself caught up in the false and easy camaraderie. I looked around at the laughing faces and thought that if this was to be our last night in Egypt, it was at least a happy ending.

Afterwards, like the others, I regretted drinking so much wine, but it was the wine that made me bold enough to question Nikephoros directly.

'What came of your meeting with the vizier?'

If the wine had made me incautious, it had evidently mellowed Nikephoros' humour. Or perhaps he did not want to cut into the good feeling. He waved an arm expansively and said, 'Good things.'

'Will he take our grain in exchange for Jerusalem?'

Even with the mist of alcohol in his mind, Nikephoros was alert enough to give me a keen look. I could see he was minded not to answer my guess, but eventually he acknowledged it with a shrug. 'He will take the emperor's grain to relieve the famine here.'

'And surrender Jerusalem in return?' I pressed.

'Al-Afdal has been called to Alexandria for a few days. When he returns here he will give me his answer.'

Aelfric, sitting in the corner, raised his cup. 'And then we can go home.'

I drank to that.

I woke craving water. Lifting myself from my mattress, I fumbled my way across the room and felt around until I found the alcove where the palace slaves had left a jug and a pair of cups. I splashed some water into the cup, spilling it in the dark, and drank gratefully. Between the privations we had suffered at Antioch, and the recent hospitality of

161

the Fatimids who seemed to drink alcohol rarely if at all, it had been an age since I drank so much wine. I shook my head to clear it, and immediately wished I had not.

I was about to return to my bed when a noise outside the door drove all thoughts of sleep from my head. I heard a rush of footsteps, and the ominous clattering of spear-shafts on stone. The guard in the passage issued a challenge, and was instantly answered by a sharp torrent of unintelligible words.

I did not know what was happening – I barely knew if I was dreaming or not – but I knew that I wanted to be armed. I let the cup drop from my hand and ran to my bedside, rummaging under the mattress where I had hidden Bilal's dagger. Around me, the others were stirring uncertainly, their dreams interrupted by the shattering cup and the noises in the passageway, but it was not until the double doors flew open in a blaze of shouts and torch-light that they realised what was happening. By then, I had managed to pull on one boot and slip the knife inside it.

A couple of our Patzinak guards managed to leap to their feet, but they were quickly pinned back against the walls by the incoming horde. They wore long hauberks of quilted leather and carried short stabbing spears with leaf-shaped heads. The caliph's personal bodyguard – not al-Afdal's men, but Berbers from the deserts of Africa.

Two of the guards tore open the curtain to Nikephoros' private quarters. I thought they would find him in bed, but either he had heard the intrusion and acted quickly, or he had expected it. He stood there dressed in a plain tunic, his arms by his side and anger burning across his face. He might be a bully, I realised then, but he was not a coward.

'What in Christ's name are you doing?'

The words were lost on the Berber guards. Their hard faces never flinched as they stepped forward and seized him between them. Nikephoros shrank instinctively from their grasp; then he mastered himself, and let them lead him with silent dignity. Two more guards took hold of me, while others rounded up Aefric and the Patzinaks and herded them after us with spears. It was too soon to feel shock: the whole business had taken barely a minute, and I saw men still rubbing the sleep from their eyes as they left the room. In the corridor, the guard who had been assigned to watch us – one of Bilal's men – stood back and watched in disbelief, his wide eyes like moons in the dark. He had not expected this any more than we had.

'Fetch Bilal,' I called to him as we passed.

The eyes blinked, but otherwise there was no acknowledgement.

The Berbers brought us quickly to the hall where the caliph had first received us. Circles of torchlight overlapped to form a bright arena in the open space before the dais, while the myriad columns stretched away like a forest at midnight around us. From above, the caliph looked down from his low throne, flanked by a chamberlain. His face was drowned in darkness.

163

'This is an unexpected honour, Your Highness.' Nikephoros could not disguise the fear in his words. 'With a little more warning, we might have prepared ourselves more as your dignity demands. As it is—' He broke off, as he saw the chamberlain had not bothered to translate his words. An ominous silence overtook the dark room. The caliph let it grow until even Nikephoros began to fidget. Then he spoke.

'The vizier, my loyal servant' – he sneered as he said it – 'has told me your proposal.'

Nikephoros licked his lips and glanced nervously around. 'The illustrious vizier had me understand you looked kindly on our offer, Your Highness.'

'Al-Afdal does not speak for me,' barked the caliph, and even before I heard his words transmitted into Greek, I heard the aggrieved petulance in his voice, and remembered how young he had seemed at our first audience.

Nikephoros offered a too-humble bow. 'Forgive me, Your Highness, I—'

'You are a snake, Greek – a snake and a liar. You glide into my court and offer sweet promises of friendship and aid, but you are lying, waiting to strike when I am vulnerable. Jerusalem belongs to *me*; I who am descended from the Prophet himself by the line of the seven true Imams.'

The caliph had leaned so far forward on his throne that his face was almost in the light. 'You have listened to the rumours spread by my enemies. The harvest is not failing. Not one of my subjects will go hungry this winter. *Not one!*'

164

'We – '

'And even if we did suffer famine, I would sooner scrabble for seeds in the ground with my own fingers than beg your emperor for relief. Do you think I have forgotten what happened in my father's time? All Egypt starved – even for a thousand dinars you could not find a loaf of bread. The Greek emperor offered to send us two million bushels of grain and we gratefully accepted – but the ships never came. He betrayed us to appease the heretic Turks. I would rather slaughter every horse in my stable to feed the poor, pawn my treasury and send my wives to work in the bathhouses than beg your emperor's help again. Who will he not betray if it is to his advantage? He is like Satan: he says to a man, 'Do not believe!', but when the man obeys and forsakes God, he says, "I disown you."'

The caliph stood, rising into the darkness. His voice had become a fevered shriek, a disorienting counterpoint to the calm monotone of the chamberlain's translation. 'You are faithless hypocrites. You say that if we are attacked, you will help us; but when we are attacked you soon turn tail and flee. Truly, it is written: "You who believe, do not take the disbelievers as allies and protectors."'

Nikephoros stepped forward and looked defiantly up at the caliph. Even stripped of his magnificent robes, with no jewelled lorum wound about him like armour, his pride was enough to clothe him in self-righteous dignity.

'We came in peace and friendship, as ambassadors of the emperor Alexios. It is unwise to renounce that friendship

– but if you do, I ask you to at least honour our safe-conduct as ambassadors. We will leave in the morning, as soon as you permit it.'

They were the words I had longed to hear for two months; now I barely noticed them. The caliph was still standing, though his twitching movements had calmed, and when he spoke there was more reason in his voice.

'You cannot leave. Winter has closed the seas, and all the harbours are shut.'

The words struck me like a blow to my stomach. Even Nikephoros looked uncertain now. The caliph continued: 'But you cannot stay in my city. I have issued an edict that all unbelievers must leave. Your presence here disturbs my kingdom.'

Nikephoros stared at him. 'Then where shall we go?'

'I have a hunting lodge on the western bank of the river. My guards will take you there immediately – your possessions will be sent after you in the morning. You will wait there until the seas open in the spring.'

Too much wine, too little sleep – and then the grim shock of being dragged before the raging caliph: a dark mist seemed to hang before my eyes as the guards bustled us out of the caliph's throne room. As we reached a turn in the passage, I managed to draw ahead of my guards long enough to catch up with Nikephoros. He glanced back over his shoulder and tried to force a reassuring smile. That worried me more than anything.

'Al-Afdal will be back within the week,' he said. 'He will bring the caliph to his senses.'

But there are many factions, and al-Afdal cannot always master them all. I remembered Bilal's words with a shiver as the guardsmen pulled me back.

Once again, a fleet of litters awaited us by the palace gate. I climbed into mine without resistance and settled onto the cushions – like a corpse being laid on his funeral bier, my mind whispered. I thought of Bishop Adhemar draped in his shroud, but that took me to Antioch and that was too much to bear. *Until the seas open in the spring,* the caliph had said. After my hopes had been raised so high, my soul flinched even to think of it. I looked out from under my canopy at the other litters – squat boxes scattered around the courtyard like tombs in a necropolis. *Why were all my thoughts of death?* Then a guardsman drew the curtains, and the view was shut away from me.

They carried us from the city at great speed, the litters swaying and shuddering: the streets must have been entirely empty that deep into the night, and we travelled them unseen and unseeing. When we emerged at the dock, though, all was bustle and activity. Torches had been lit, and a great throng of slaves and guardsmen milled about on the wharf. In a knot in their midst, I saw the four Frankish envoys and their attendants. They must have been hauled from their sleep as peremptorily as we had, for they wore the same disarray of under-shirts and mismatched boots, and the same harried confusion on

167

their faces. Achard stood among them, his head darting about like a cornered cat's.

Our guards hustled us towards the Franks and gestured us to wait. Out on the water I could hear the approach of splashing oars, and nearer to me, a low and ragged chant.

'*Help me, O Lord my God. Save me according to your steadfast love.*'

All of the Franks were murmuring the same prayer, intensity fixed on their faces. The sound mingled with the harsher, wilder voices of the Berber guards, different currents in the dizzying babble that washed over me, as inconstant and elusive as the flickering firelight. I was so dazed I did not even think to pray.

A dark and familiar figure strode onto the dock, his yellow cloak billowing around his shoulders and his gold armband shining in the torchlight. He passed by us without a glance, but my heart leaped all the same at the sight of him. An angry shout was enough to bring the Berber captain hurrying out; they met in the middle of the wharf, so close they could have whispered their conversation if they had wanted. Instead, they began a furious discussion, which every man on the dock could hear. I understood almost nothing, but I did hear al-Afdal's name mentioned often by Bilal, and the caliph's name invoked each time in reply by the Berber captain. A circle of the guardsmen formed around them, thickest behind their captain, and I saw Bilal begin to edge backwards. Even his commanding presence could not deter so many.

With a final, sharp comment, he turned his back on the guards and marched towards us. His face was grey in the smoke.

'I cannot counter the caliph's order,' he said loudly. 'Even if he has fallen under the influence of evil counsellors. I have sworn to obey him in all things.' Then, more quietly: 'They are taking you to your deaths. If you reach the far bank of the river, it will only be to step into your graves.'

He spoke so softly, almost conversationally, that I had nodded before I even realised what he had said. By then he had turned away and vanished out of the light, while a host of guards gathered about us and began shepherding us towards the river with their short spears.

'What are they doing?'

The voice, small and frightened, cut through the fog of terror that gripped me. Achard was beside me, shuffling forward and looking up with fearful expectation. His staring eyes had lost their intensity; now they only made him look horribly innocent. He had not heard Bilal's warning: perhaps that was a mercy.

Before I could answer, we were pulled apart again. We had reached the steps, and had to descend in single file. Three boats awaited us at the bottom, small craft, already half-filled by the slaves who sat by their oars. Their hunched backs gleamed in the dark. Without regard for rank or race, the Berbers herded six of us into the first boat: Nikephoros and Aelfric, Achard, two of the Patzinaks and me. An equal number of guardsmen accompanied us.

Even in our utter helplessness, they clearly had orders to risk nothing.

A hand closed around my arm, tight as a noose. 'What are they doing?' Achard repeated. 'What did the black savage say?'

'That we will be murdered.' I spoke furtively and in Frankish, praying none of the Berbers understood. As long as they thought we remained ignorant of our fate, I hoped they might postpone it.

Achard closed his eyes. 'Into your hands, O Lord, we commit ourselves.'

I wished I could share his faith. My hands were trembling, and I almost had to lean over the side of the boat to vomit up the bile that had gathered in my stomach. I started to recite a prayer in my head, but the familiar words were no comfort to me and I could say no more than the first line before thoughts of death crowded out thoughts of God.

The boat cast off – I could see the other Franks, and some of our Patzinaks, climbing into the next one – and we pulled into the river. I felt the force of the current immediately, far stronger than in the fat barges that had carried us before, and the rowers had to lean hard on their oars to keep a straight course.

I glanced at Nikephoros. He was sitting very erect in the stern of the boat, his eyes fixed on the darkness ahead as if he could already see the saints lifting back the veil to the next life. I was not ready to die with such composure. I looked to Aelfric, seated on the bench opposite me, and our eyes met in agreement.

Out in the night, the oars dipped and swept through the water; further off our bow, I could hear fish rising to the surface. We were in the middle of the river now: far enough from the men on shore, I hoped. Feigning only a touch more despair than I actually felt, I bowed my head and rocked forward so that my face rested on my knees and my arms dangled beside my ankles. My fingers dug into my boot and closed around the handle of Bilal's knife. My heart was beating so fast that I felt sure it must almost tip the boat over, and I heard a suspicious growl from the guard in the stern. This was madness – pure, desperate suicide. But there was no choice.

For a blissful moment, I prayed as clean and perfect a prayer as I have ever prayed. Then I straightened, lifted my blade and stabbed it into the neck of the guard beside me. His mouth sprang open, pouring out blood like a fountain, and in that instant Aelfric had lunged across the boat and snatched the short spear from his hands.

Everything after that was blind instinct and reaction. I saw the guard beside Nikephoros twist around to strike him, but the commotion in the boat unbalanced his arm and the spear thudded harmlessly into the transom. The guard was still trying to pull it free when one of the Patzinaks seized his legs and pitched him into the river. Something surged in the water; I thought it was the guard trying to clamber aboard, and stepped forward to knock him away. Then I glimpsed a vast, scaly body, ancient and terrible, rising from the midst of a cloud of foam in the water. Two jaws opened like shears, so close that I swore afterwards I could smell the rotting flesh between the teeth, and snapped shut in a spray of blood and screams.

Even with all that came after, it was the hardest battle I ever fought. Even in the worst battle, there are some certainties: the ground you stand on, the men beside you, the sword in your hand. Here, all those were gone. The boat bucked and squirmed like a fish on a line, and more than once I thought we would all be tipped into the river to die together. In those heaving confines, the battle lines stretched no further than the end of your arm, and if you waited to see if the man next to you was friend or foe he would most likely have killed you. A horde of monsters circled us in the water, snapping and tearing at any man who fell overboard. Most strangely of all, only half the men there actually fought. All the rowers stayed rooted to their seats, bowing over their oars and covering their heads while the battle raged over them. The briefest whimpers as boots stamped on stray fingers or spear-butts knocked against shoulders was all the contribution they made to the battle.

One of the caliph's guards drove towards me with his spear, holding it two handed. Without sword or shield I had only one resort: I dropped to my knees and tried to roll away – straight into the side of the boat. That was my saving. The guard's feet tripped over me and he sprawled onto the deck. Praying there was not another behind him, I rolled back, crouched astride him and reached round to slit his throat. I was too slow: with a great heave of his shoulders he shrugged me off, pinning my knife hand as he did. I lay beside him, clinging to his back like a lover, while he wrestled to free his weapon from beneath the tangle of limbs. Then a shadow fell over us, a spear stabbed down, and I found I could pull free from the suddenly limp body. I looked up to thank my saviour; instead of Aelfric or one of the Patzinaks, I saw a Berber guardsman holding the dripping spear. His young face was dazed with guilt as he realised his mistake – but there is no place for guilt in battle, or wars would never be fought. I did not trust my knife; I lowered my shoulder and slammed it into his stomach. He staggered backwards. The backs of his legs caught on the side of the boat and he tottered for a moment, before a last kick from my boot plunged him into the water.

'Demetrios!'

How many more enemies could there be? I swung around, stepping left and trying to keep my balance on the rocking deck. It felt like trying to stand upright on a charging horse, and barely wider. Thankfully, there was no enemy behind me – the shout had been for help. Achard was standing at the stern of the boat; he had managed to get hold of a short sword, and was frantically parrying a furious onslaught of jabs and spear-thrusts from the man opposite. After six months locked up in the caliph's palace, I was surprised he even remembered how to hold the sword; he did not look as though he would last much longer.

His opponent stepped back a moment, and he risked the briefest sideways glance. 'Help me!'

I began to move towards him. On any normal battle-field I would have been at his side in an instant, but here I had to contend with the rolling deck, the slippery planking slick with blood, and the tangle of oars, corpses and cowering slaves. Achard was only a few paces away, yet it could have been miles.

'*Demetrios.*'

The sound seemed to have come from out on the water. A bedraggled figure in a white robe lay half-submerged in the river, his hands clinging to an oar and his feet kicking frantically in the water. *Nikephoros.*

'For God's sake, get me out,' he bellowed. He reached to try and haul himself up the oar, but it was slippery with river water and he could not get a purchase.

I glanced around. At the stern of the boat, Achard was still fending off his assailant, though with a weary lack of strength in his arms. At the opposite end, in the bow, Aelfric and another man I could not see were wrestling with a guardsman. In between, apart from the slaves, I was the only man standing.

'What are you – ' Nikephoros' plea choked off as he swallowed a mouthful of water. For a moment I thought he had been seized by one of the river monsters, and that alone was enough to break my indecision. I knelt by the side, pressing my knees against the planking, and stretched out for Nikephoros like a pilgrim reaching for a relic. I was horribly vulnerable; I prayed that the others would keep their opponents away from me, and that there were none lurking in the darkness at the bottom of the boat. I

174

could hear shouts and screams above my head but I did not dare look. Nikephoros lunged for my outstretched hand, but desperation made him wild: he missed, knocking my hand away and bruising it against the pole of the oar. I groaned, and reached again.

This time Nikephoros mastered his panic. His hand closed around my wrist and hauled, with such strength that I was almost pulled into the river after him. With a final effort, I braced my feet against the planking and threw myself backwards. Nikephoros sprang forward as if he had somehow found purchase on the water itself, while I sprawled on the deck. The blow had knocked the air from my body, and I lay there a second with my eyes shut, before the realisation that I could no longer feel Nikephoros' grip on my wrists forced me to look. I almost wept with relief. Nikephoros' chin was resting on the lip of the boat, and his arms dangled over the side. He hauled himself inboard and collapsed in a heap beside me, spewing curses and river water.

I looked around, aware of a sudden silence ringing in my ears. Aelfric and one of the Patzinaks crouched in the bow, wiping blood from their blades with quiet satisfaction. Nikephoros and I were all who remained amidships, apart from the petrified rowers. And at the back of the boat –

'Where is Achard?'

There was no sign of him, nor of the guard I had seen him fighting. Aelfric shrugged, pointing to the river with grim resignation. Out in the night, I could hear roaring and splashes as the river monsters feasted.

Later, I might feel a prick of remorse that I could have saved Achard. But there was no time. We must have drifted well downstream, far from the following boats, but once they reached the opposite bank and realised we had not arrived they would come after us. No one asked if we should go back to rescue the others. Aelfric and the Patzinak began tipping the corpses overboard, while I searched out the lightest skinned slave and seized him by the shoulder. Glancing down, I saw why they had avoided the battle raging between them: they were all shackled to their benches.

'Do you speak Greek?'

He looked up at me, quivering with terror, and shook his head. Mutely, he pointed to a man two rows in front of him.

'You?'

The slave flinched. 'A – a little. Not in . . . much years.'

'Tell the rowers to pick up their oars and head down-stream.'

'Tell them to pull as if their lives depend on it, or we will throw them to the river monsters and row this boat ourselves,' growled Nikephoros. He spoke quickly, and his voice was hoarse from screaming through mouthfuls of water, but the slave must have understood the brutal sense of his words. As one, the rowers leaned over their oars and began pulling us down the river.

When the bodies were cleared, we gathered in the stern of the boat for a council. As well as Achard, we had lost one of the Patzinaks; that left the other Patzinak, whose name was Jorol; Aelfric; Nikephoros and myself. We huddled together, smeared with the stains of combat, while a thin mist began to rise off the river around us. The night was not cold, but I suddenly found myself shivering.

'How long until dawn?' Aelfric asked.

No one answered. There was no way of knowing how much of the night had passed: you cannot measure a nightmare.

'Not enough time to reach the sea, at any rate,' I said.

Perhaps, because I had just saved his life, Nikephoros held some of his scorn in check. If so, I did not notice. 'Reach the sea? Even if the night hid us for ever, we would never find our way through the tangled mouths of this river. And if, by God's grace, we did reach Tinnis, what would we find there? A chain across the harbour, and every ship hauled out of the water for winter. Did you hear what the caliph said? The seas are closed.'

Aelfric stirred. 'What about the ship we came on?'

'The emperor's fleet is no use to him penned up in an enemy port. The ship's master had orders to sail home if we had not returned when winter came.'

'It was the caliph who turned on us,' I said tentatively. 'Al-Afdal was willing to bargain. If we hide until he returns he may protect us.'

Nikephoros shook his head. 'Al-Afdal would have bargained with us, but now the caliph has declared war on us and we have killed Fatimid soldiers. He cannot protect us now.'

'Much good his protection did us anyway,' Aelfric muttered.

'If al-Afdal finds us, he will have to kill us.'

A glum silence descended between us. Oars squeaked, the rowers sighed the unheard sighs of slaves, and mist drifted across our bow. The moon had set, and though I could not see the stars I guessed that morning could not be far off.

'So what shall we do?'

Nikephoros, who had been idly stroking his fingers through the tendrils of fog, looked up. 'We cannot go north, we cannot stay where we are, and we certainly cannot go south. West only takes us further from home. We will go east.'

'I have heard that there is only desert to the east,' said the Patzinak warily.

'So there is. But it has been crossed before. And you know what lies beyond?' Sodden, battered and doomed though he was, Nikephoros gave a wolfish grin.

'The promised land.'

31

∾∾∾∾∾

We rowed on as long as we dared, then nosed the boat into a patch of reeds at the water's edge. Before we disembarked, I forced the point of Bilal's knife into the lock that fastened the slaves' chain and pried until it opened. A dozen blank-faced slaves stared up at me, apparently unable to comprehend their freedom; we almost had to haul them off their benches and drive them ashore. When the boat was emptied, Aelfric and I waded into the water, keeping a cautious watch for the crocodiles, and rocked it back and forth until we capsized it. Then, with a final heave, we pushed it out into the stream and watched it drift into the darkness.

'If we're lucky, they may think we were all drowned.'

'Or eaten,' Aelfric said.

Nikephoros snorted, gesturing to the muddy ramp we had trampled out of the river bank. 'And will they think that this was made by cattle? We should hurry.'

We left the slaves still huddled together in their herd and struck out across the adjacent field. Dark cracks split the ground at our feet, but despite the river's failure to flood, the earth was still damp, and we left a perfect trail of footprints moulded into the soil. It would have been easier to walk on the embanked causeway that rose to our right – but then we would have been exposed to pursuing eyes.

As we had seen by the pyramids, the fertile ground extended no further than the edge of the river valley. We scrambled up the escarpment where the fields ended, and paused. Directly opposite, on the far side of the world, the sun climbed over the rim of the earth and faced us. An amethyst sky soared above us, fragile and new, while pink and golden light flooded across the horizon. *The promised land*, Nikephoros had said, and at that moment I could believe it.

But before that was the desert. It sprawled as far as we could see, all the way to the glittering horizon, a desolate wilderness of sharp stones and dust. Soon the heat of the day would boil the dregs of moisture from it, softening the scene with a haze, but for now we could see every peak, crag and broken hillside with savage clarity. Beside me, I heard the Patzinak groan.

'Are we going to cross that?'

'The Israelites did,' said Nikephoros.

'The Israelites struck water from the rock,' I said. 'Will we do the same?'

'There is no need for blasphemy.' Nikephoros pointed to our left, to the next ridge, where the splayed legs of a wooden tripod stood silhouetted against the new horizon. 'We can drink at the well.'

But the well was not unguarded. As we came to the top of the rise, into the glare of the rising sun, we heard a splash, and moments later saw a woman standing by the edge of the well. She was dressed entirely in black, her hair covered with a shawl, so that only a single bone-white hair escaped. She must have seen us struggling towards her long before that, but she did not flee. She waited a moment for her bucket to fill, then began hauling on the rope. The sleeves of her dress rode up her thin arms as she struggled with the weight. Without a word, Aelfric stepped forward and took the rope. The woman edged away with a reproachful look but said nothing. Now that she faced us, I could see wizened cheeks and a furrowed brow in between the black wrappings.

Aelfric hoisted the bucket onto the stone rampart. Water spilled over its edge, but he steadied it with his hand and gestured the woman to take it. With a wary glance, she tipped the contents into a clay jar by her feet. Beside it, I saw two deflated goatskins lying on the sand.

The gushing sound of pouring water stirred my thirst. I took the empty bucket, threw it down into the well and drew myself a fresh draught. In my haste, the bucket came up half full, but I hardly cared. I tipped it to my lips and drank greedily, so fast that water splashed over my face and chin, dribbling down over my filthy tunic. I emptied it far too soon, and would have refilled it for myself had I not felt the envious eyes of my companions. Reluctantly, I let them take it in turn, while the woman crouched by her jar and watched cautiously.

I prodded one of the goatskins with my toe. 'Will you sell us this?'

Blank eyes stared out at me from beneath her shawl. Beside me, Nikephoros shook the water from his beard and sniffed. 'Do you think she will understand you? Why should she? What can she do against us if we take her goatskins?'

Ignoring him, I threw down one of the spears we had stripped from the caliph's guards. She stared at it in terror, and I realised too late I had forgotten to wipe the blood from its tip. Trying to smile, I reached down for the two goatskins and pulled them towards me. I pointed to them, then to myself, then to the spear and then to the woman.

She stretched a bare foot from under her dress and pushed the spear back towards me. The goatskins she left untouched.

'What use is a spear to her?' Nikephoros jeered. 'Do you think she will march to the palace and ask to join the caliph's guard?'

'He has some spaces in his ranks to fill after last night,' said Jorol, the Patzinak.

'The steel in the blade is worth something.'

'Only trouble.' Aelfric took the spear off the ground and earned a grateful glance from the woman. 'If the caliph's guards come chasing us and find that spear in her house, what do you think they'll do to her?'

'No worse than they'll do to us if we wait any longer,' said Jorol, looking pointedly over his shoulder. Long shadows stretched out behind us, but they were shortening every minute.

With an apologetic bow to the woman, Aelfric tossed the leather bucket into the well and drew three quick measures. When the goatskins were filled, he and Jorol heaved them onto their shoulders while I gazed uncertainly at the woman.

'What if she tells someone she saw us?' Nikephoros' voice was harsh.

Aelfric shrugged. 'They'll see us for themselves if we don't go soon.'

Just before we left, I reached into my boot and pulled out the knife Bilal had given me, which I had retrieved from the bilge of the boat after the fight. I was loathe to part with it now: it had brought me luck in battle, and might be needed again in the desert. But the woman had given us water, and bad bargains bring bad luck. Bilal had bought the knife from a market stall, he had said, and there was nothing to mark it as ours – or his. I threw it to her; she caught it in her bony hand, examined it, then tucked it into the folds of her dress. Nikephoros stared at me with bare contempt.

'If you have finished giving alms . . .'

We walked into the desert.

*　　*　　*

183

Fifteen months earlier, I had marched with the Army of God across the barren plains of Anatolia in August, when we chewed thorns for moisture and slaughtered dogs for food because the horses were already dead. Turkish cavalry had harried our column every day, ants trying to strip the army's body one crumb of flesh at a time, and we had left a trail of corpses on the road behind us, mile after mile, because we had neither the time nor the strength to bury our dead. After surviving that, I had thought nothing could ever be so terrible again.

But that misunderstood the desert. Heat, thirst and hunger can kill a man, but it is the everlasting emptiness that flays his soul. The desert draws up life like a sponge, sucking until the heart dries up and turns inside out. Then it confronts you with the skeleton that remains. Some men find their revelation there and become prophets; some are driven mad. Most do not survive the ordeal.

How did the Army of God survive the march across Anatolia? Not through strength or courage or faith, but merely because it was too big to kill. However much we suffered individually, the sheer mass of humanity around us, in all its lumbering, screaming, stinking pain, proved we were still alive. We drove a column of life through the desert, and the desert could not overcome it. Four men, battered and hungry, with barely a day's water between them, were a different matter. Almost immediately, the desert began to reduce us. My limbs shrivelled and burned like sticks in a fire as the sweat was wrung out of them; my tongue felt as though it was baking in my mouth. I tore a strip from the bottom of my tunic and wound it around my head to shield the sun, though it did little good. Jorol went further still: he pulled off his tunic completely and ripped it in two, draping one half over his head and shoulders like a woman's shawl and tying the other around his waist for modesty. It made him look blasphemously like Christ.

By midday, we could go no further. We staggered into the shade of a rock in a shallow depression and lay there, too tired to stay awake and too hot to sleep. Flies crawled out of the sand to bite us, and rivulets of sweat slithered over my skin like snakes. And always I was listening out for the drumming hooves or jangling armour that would spell the end of our mad flight.

We pretended to sleep until dusk. Then we rose, brushed the dust from our clothes, and continued on.

At first we navigated by our shadows, following where they pointed as the sun sank behind us. They became so long it seemed they must reach all the way home; then, abruptly, they vanished. Stars came out, impossibly familiar in that lonely place, and we struggled on, keeping the pole star forward and to our left as much as the fractured terrain allowed. We walked in a single column for the most part, but every so often a steep slope or high obstacle would knot us together again. At one of those places, I asked Nikephoros about our course.

'We have to reach the coast,' he said. None of us had spoken a word all day, and his voice cracked with exhaustion.

'What will we find there?'

'Water.' He tried to smile, but his dry lips would not oblige. 'And perhaps a boat.'

'Then what? None of us is a sailor. Even if we were, you said the sea is closed.'

'We can make our way up the coast. The Fatimids control it, but their ships will be in harbour.'

With good reason, I suspected. I did not ask any more questions.

The desert had been a hostile place by day; in the dark, it became a nightmare. A land that had seemed unable to nourish a single stalk of grass now brought forth a host of living beasts: strange, unseen creatures, which scuttled, squealed and grunted all around us. Soon I became convinced that if only we had had a lamp to kindle we would have seen ourselves surrounded by a writhing mass of all the carrion birds, flesh eaters, beetles, snakes and worms of Hell. As it was, we saw none of them, though once I felt my boot step on something furry, which screamed and squirmed under my foot before scurrying away. Somewhere, perhaps half a mile away, something like a wolf howled to the stars.

The air itself seemed to mock us. We had waited for dusk to avoid the heat of the day; what we had not expected was that the night could be so cold. The empty dark seemed to suck all warmth from the air, so that the clothes that had felt like plates of burning iron now seemed flimsy and inadequate. Jorol untied the torn half-tunic from his head and draped it over his shoulders; it did not reach as far as the loincloth at his waist, and in the dark the gap between the two pieces of white cloth made it look as though his torso had been sawn in half.

We marched through the night. When the blood-red fingers of dawn began to reach over the horizon, we found another shelter and curled up for the day.

Many men enter the wilderness seeking answers. Some, I suppose, find them. For myself, I found that the emptiness of the desert left only questions. Words and images tumbled unbidden into my mind, as if every thought and memory I had ever had was being flushed through me. I saw Anna and Sigurd, sometimes alive and sometimes as ghosts; I saw my daughters, as they were and as they had been, cradled in their mother's arms. I even saw my parents, though I thought I had forgotten what they looked like. In one memory, or dream, I had thrust my hand into a bees' nest; I ran down the hill between spring wildflowers, crying with pain even as I licked the honey from my stinging fingers. A woman hugged me, so close that I could not see her, and I dried my tears on the folds of her skirt.

I opened my eyes and was back in the desert.

The second night's march was worse than the first. A chasm of hunger had been opening inside me since the previous morning; now it engulfed me. Cramps of pain shot through my stomach and I was forced to bend almost double, leaning on my spear for support like an old man.

Halfway through the night we ran out of water. We had hoarded it as long as we could, taking sips so small they barely wet our lips, but even so we could not eke it out for ever. Unfortunately for Aelfric, he was holding the goatskin when it happened – and he did not help matters by upending the empty sack and shaking the last few drops out into his mouth. Jorol stared at him with covetous anger.

'Who said you should have more than your share?'

Aelfric met his stare with haggard eyes, but did not answer. That in itself was a goad to Jorol. The Patzinak stepped towards Aelfric, snatched the empty skin from his hands and dashed it to the ground.

'What will we drink now? Dust?'

'You can drink my piss if you like.'

Even through the haze of despair and exhaustion, Aelfric must have known what he said; indeed, his fists were already rising as he spoke. But Jorol was too demented by thirst to be satisfied with that. He swung his spear around and lunged towards Aelfric.

The sneer died on Aelfric's face and he flung himself away. He tripped on a stone, lost his balance and sprawled backwards. Jorol sprang after him, and the wild look on his face left no doubt what he intended.

A heavy staff swept through the moonlight, humming with its speed. It struck Jorol in mid-air, square on the chest, and he dropped like a bird felled by a sling. As he bent over in pain, Nikephoros slapped the spear-haft across his shoulder blades; then he turned to Aelfric, still lying on the ground, and kicked him hard in the ribs.

'If you lose your discipline again, it will be the sharp end of this spear you feel. Get up.'

The two men staggered to their feet, breathing hard. For a moment, I feared they might both attack Nikephoros, but the desert had not yet stripped all habits of obedience from them.

'If we quarrel among ourselves, we will never escape this desert,' said Nikephoros.

'We will never escape anyway. Not without water to drink.' Beneath the despair, I sensed a sly mischief in Jorol's words, like a child who cannot help provoking his father to beat him.

Nikephoros' shoulders stiffened, and the spear twitched in his hand.

'Say that again, and I will see your body rot in the desert.' Before Jorol could decide whether to test the threat, Nikephoros spun around to face me. 'We will take the waterskins with us in case we find another well. You will carry them.'

I started. 'Why me?'

'Because the others carried them when they were full.'

Behind him, I saw Aelfric and Jorol smirking with satisfaction. I did not think we would find another well, but I shouldered the two empty waterskins without a word.

The next day, we did not stop at dawn. Without water, every hour brought death closer. Nikephoros led the way, his hand perpetually raised to shield his eyes as he scanned the horizon. Aelfric followed, then Jorol, then me. Even empty, the waterskins I carried weighed as much as a coat of armour.

The desert had already broken my defences; now it began to devour me. My sight closed in, so that despite the glaring sun the world seemed indistinct around me. I could barely see beyond Jorol in front of me; he had lost the half of his tunic that covered his head and looked more like Christ than ever with only a single white cloth wrapped about his waist.

I began to hate Him. How could He have brought me to die in this wilderness? Surely even a grave in Babylon would have been better than this torment? After all my prayers, my faithful service, was this all I had earned at the close of my life? Did He delight in inflicting this pain on me – and on my family, my daughters, and the grandchild I would never see? Would He watch over Anna's shoulder as she stood at the harbour at Saint Simeon, day after day, searching in vain for the ship that would never bring me home? Would He laugh at her? How did I deserve this?

But you are a sinner, an unbidden voice hissed in my mind. *You have killed and lain with whores. What else do you deserve? Christ has turned his back on you and left you desolate. See?*

I lifted my eyes. The world was dark around me, as though a black cloth had been tied over my eyes, but through the haze I could see a hunched figure dressed only in a loincloth, walking away alone across the sands.

He looked back at me for a moment, and behind his ragged beard I thought I saw him smile. Then he turned away.

I would not let him abandon me. Anger seized my limbs and drove me forward; the soft sand swallowed the noise of my footsteps, and he did not hear me until I was almost upon him. He twisted around, just as my shoulder thumped into his side, and we went down together. He screamed in surprise, and screamed some more as I began beating him with my fists. Famished by the desert, I had little strength to punish him, but he had little more strength to resist. He wrapped his arms around his face and drew his knees in like a child, while I rained down feeble blows.

Strong arms pulled me back and wrestled me to the ground. I could not resist them.

'What are you doing?' Nikephoros was bellowing with anger, his face almost touching mine, but his words were faint and vague. I had lifted myself on one arm and was staring over his shoulder, to where a column of dust rose across the horizon behind us. I pointed.

'A pillar of cloud,' I murmured, dazed. 'A pillar of cloud to guide us.'

Nikephoros glanced back, then gave a savage laugh and kicked my hand out from beneath me, so that I collapsed back to the ground. 'Fool. That is not your salvation. That is the dust rising from beneath the wheels of Pharaoh's chariots. Our pursuers have come.'

Nikephoros was right: it was not a pillar of cloud, but

billowing dust kicked up by a squadron of horsemen. As yet they were little more than specks against the storm, but that would not last long. I turned around and looked east, as if some vestigial piece of faith still expected God to provide a refuge, a sea to cross or a flight of angels to carry us up. Instead, all I saw was a solitary rock, rising like a boil out of the desert a mile or so distant. I had not seen it before, though it was the only feature on an otherwise flat plain, and I realised that the impending danger – or perhaps the prospect of release from my suffering – had at last swept back the darkness that shrouded my eyes.

'That's as good a place as any to die,' said Aelfric.

At last I knew how I had survived Antioch. Not because I was stronger, or because my faith was more steadfast, but because I had no choice. How else to explain the new strength that seized me? After the shadows that had engulfed it, the world seemed bright again – brighter even than it had before. I dropped the waterskins in the dust, for we would have no need of them now or ever again, and felt that I grew instantly a foot taller. Even my stride seemed longer.

But wherever you look in the desert, the sights deceive you. The land between us and the outcropping rock was furrowed with row upon row of dunes and ridges: from a distance they looked like little more than ripples blown by the wind, but once among them we found ourselves toiling up and down long, grinding inclines. Even at their summits there was no respite, for there we saw how far we still had to go. And all the while, the pursuing dust-cloud menaced us ever closer.

Even fear can only drive a man so far. I found I could no longer breathe except in the shallowest gasps, as if my lungs had filled so full of sand that there was no room for air. My legs buckled and swayed; I fell, dragged myself to my feet, fell once more and might never have risen again if a firm hand had not pinched around my neck and hauled me up. Still holding me, Nikephoros spun my face so that it was barely an inch from his own. His eyes blazed with demented purpose; he did not speak, but pursed his lips and spat a thin gob of saliva straight at me. It landed on my lips, and before I knew what I was doing I had licked it off, sucking the moisture greedily in.

'*Come on.*'

We staggered forward to the top of the next rise and halted, leaning on each other for support. Even the desert could not disguise our situation now. From the ridge where we stood, a gentle slope descended away, until it ended abruptly in the sheer wall of rock, barely three hundred yards away.

I cannot tell where we found the strength to run, but run we did. Arms flapping, legs splaying, shoulders hunched and faces contorted in gruesome snarls, we ran like men possessed by demons. All I could hear was the thump of my footsteps and the roaring blood in my ears. Halfway to the rock I looked back and saw the dust cloud billowing up; when I looked again, the horsemen had crested the ridge. Lances glittered in the sun, while the

193

archers among them loosed a volley of arrows. They dropped harmlessly into the sand behind me – but near enough that I could see where the next flight would fall.

A square black banner waved them forward. The horsemen charged down the slope, and I ran.

More arrows flew; I could hear them striking the ground, stalking up behind me, drawing level and over-taking me. I thought to try and weave between them, to make a harder target for the archers, but that would have cost me precious speed. I had to hope my lurching progress was enough to confuse them. Now the sound changed: ahead of me, I heard the crack of an arrow striking stone. I looked up. A wall of rock rose before me – and splitting open its face, a ravine. I hurled myself in as a hail of arrows clattered on the walls beside me.

The world went dark again. The two halves of the frac-tured rock rose so steep and close that even the sun could not prise its way between them, except to touch the very tops of the walls high above me. As my eyes balanced the gloom, I saw where I had entered: a sandy lagoon cupped between the rocky walls. Grasses and flowers grew out of the rock above me – stunted and pale, but the first green things I had seen since the Nile. There must be water somewhere, though that was my last concern at that moment.

I had been the last of our company to enter the ravine. Ahead of me, where the gap widened, I saw Nikephoros and the others scrambling up the steep slope, trying to find a path to the top. I followed them, though it seemed a hopeless task. Even if we had the strength to climb this mountain, the Egyptian archers would shoot us off its side long before we reached the summit.

But not yet. Whether they feared to bring their horses into the narrow defile, or whether they had sent some men around the rock to be sure we did not escape through the other side, they did not follow us in straight away. Meanwhile, Nikephoros seemed to have found some sort of goat path up the cliff, and we climbed it desperately, crawling on our hands and knees as it steepened. How could goats ever have come here? I wondered.

About a third of the way up, the path ended. I would have surrendered there, but Nikephoros was already moving on, scuttling up the sheer cliff like a spider. I was astonished, until I saw what he had seen: a ladder of recesses and handholds cut into the cliff, rising straight to the sky. Some were so freshly made I could still see the chisel scrapes on them, though I did not think to question who had carved them.

Fifty feet below, the horsemen swept into the ravine and dismounted. With cruel deliberation, I saw the archers pull fistfuls of arrows from the quivers on their backs and plant them in the sand beside them. They would not need so many, I thought. The others were already halfway up the cliff, caught like flies, while I still stood on the ledge where the path ended. I was safer there from the archers below – but that was no solace, for soon the spearmen scrambling up the path would reach me. The sharp snap of bowstrings echoed around the ravine, immediately drowned by the quick-fire rattle of iron on stone. Not only stone – several hit flesh, and a mortal screaming joined the cacophony that filled the air. A shadow fell from the sky as the arrows plucked one of my companions from the wall above. I did not see who it was; he fell into the sand at the foot of the cliff, and in its soft embrace I did not even hear his neck break.

Pebbles rained down on me as my companions climbed on. To my right, the spearmen were only a few yards down the path, though something seemed to have delayed them. They crouched behind their shields, looking up and across the ravine. Following their gaze I saw the dark shapes of more archers silhouetted against the sky on the opposite summit. Now they could rain arrows on us from above and below. There would be no escape.

Yet even where there is no hope of escape, men will try beyond reason. I could not get past the spearmen; the only other path was up. I scooped a handful of pebbles and threw them down on the archers in the ravine, a vain gesture of defiance, then turned and began hauling myself up the cliff.

It was easier than I had thought it would be. Whoever had cut the footholds had placed them well, so that my feet found grooves and fissures exactly where they expected. I pulled myself up, hand over hand, deaf now to the sounds of battle, to the arrows around me, to the voice in my heart that pleaded this was madness. The discipline of climbing brought a rare order to my body, and I embraced it eagerly. Perhaps I might even reach the summit, I thought, though I did not know what I would do when I reached it.

An arrow tore into my shoulder, and as I screamed my hand let go of the rock. I tried to cling on with my other hand, but I did not have the strength. I fell, felt a rush of air and then a life-emptying thud.

I lay back, and let the desert take me at last.

25

~~~~~

Angels hovered over me in a golden sky, their faces still and solemn as they circled the bearded man in their midst. In his left hand he clutched a thick book, bound with many seals, while his right was raised as if in blessing or judgement. There was a seriousness about him, which I had expected, but also a sadness, which I had not: his mouth seemed to droop away from his gaunt cheeks, and dark bags ringed his sunken eyes. In the distance, and seemingly all around me, I could hear the quiet chanting of prayers.

'Christ?' I asked uncertainly. I had thought I would recognise him immediately, but now I was not sure.

'You are in the presence of Christ.'

His lips did not move, nor did the voice even seem to

emanate from him. Instead, I heard it whispering in my ear.

A bolt of terror sparked through me. I tried to bow, or kneel, but at once an invisible force pushed me back. I did not resist.

'Will you judge me, Lord?'

He chuckled, though his drooping mouth did not move. 'It is not for me to judge you. And your time has not yet come.'

'Not yet . . . ?'

'Wake up,' said the voice. 'Wake up, Demetrios Askiates.'

Christ seemed to recede away into the sky as a larger, gentler face leaned close over me. There was no ethereal stillness in this man's features: his head swayed from side to side, and his blue eyes darted about as if searching for something within me.

'Are you Saint Peter?' I guessed.

He chuckled – the same laugh as I had heard before, but this time his cheeks creased and his mouth opened wide with mirth. His breath smelled of onions.

'I am Brother Luke. The infirmarian.'

I tried to rub my eyes, though only one hand obeyed. The other seemed to be tied down to something. I turned my head to look.

The golden sky disappeared. Instead, I saw a row of stern-faced prophets lining a long wall, and afternoon sunlight streaming through the windows above their heads. In front of them, at my bedside, an elderly monk in a black habit was pouring something from a jug into a plain cup.

'Where am I?'

The monk set the cup down on a wooden table and turned back to me. 'At the monastery of Mount Abraham.'

'I thought I saw—' I broke off, uncertain if it was blasphemy. The monk, however, showed no offence.

'Perhaps you did. You were half dead when they brought you here.'

'Who brought me?'

'The *Nizariyya*.'

I did not understand, but before I could ask anything else he had crooked an arm around the back of my head, lifted it forward and was tipping the contents of the cup into my mouth. I tasted honey and rosemary, and something bitter I did not know. It was only as the cool liquid touched my throat that I realised I was no longer thirsty – or hungry.

'How long have I been here?'

'Three days.'

Unbidden, I suddenly pictured a dark chasm filled with screams and the hiss of stinging arrows. 'And my companions?'

The monk dabbed at my mouth with a napkin. 'They both survived – better than you. You will see them tomorrow. Now, rest.'

There was much more I needed to find out, so much that all the questions seemed to choke in my mouth and I could not say one of them. A heavy hand drew a veil over my eyes, and sleep claimed me.

*   *   *

The angels were flying above me again but now the sky was dark, illuminated only by a dim orange haze like sunset after a storm. I twisted in my bed, testing my invisible bonds. If I went to my right I could turn quite easily; if I tried my left, I could barely move without igniting a horrible pain in my shoulder. I looked to my right. Iron lamps hung from a high ceiling, and by their light I could see the columns and vaults of a spacious room, and the shadowy throng of prophets and disciples painted on the surrounding walls. I rolled up my eyes – there were the angels again, inlaid on a half-dome above my head, and the Christ in their midst. His hand was still poised in unmoving judgement, and his face still told unspeakable sadness.

'When will he be healed?'

The voice came from my left, where I could not see. I twisted my neck cautiously, trying not to disturb my shoulder, but all I could make out were two dark figures in shapeless robes, silhouetted in front of a brazier. One was short and round; the other, taller and leaner, towered over his companion and leaned forward with authority.

'It will take weeks for him to heal – if the wound does not fester,' said the shorter man. I recognised the kindly fastidiousness in his tone – Brother Luke, the infirmarian.

'He must be ready to leave tomorrow.'

This distressed the infirmarian a great deal. His head bobbed back and forth, and he twisted his hands together. 'He cannot leave. If his wound opens before the flesh has rebound itself, he will die.'

'They cannot stay. Even as much as we have done already threatens our community if the caliph hears of it.'

'But where will he go? Will you cast them out into the desert?'

'A caravan passes by here tomorrow afternoon. Bind him tight, and make sure he is ready.'

'And if he dies on his journey?' The infirmarian's voice tightened with anger.

'Then he will not lie on my conscience. He should have chosen a safer path.'

Brilliant sunshine beamed through the high windows; outside, I could hear a bell tolling the office of the day. I sat up in bed, supported by two novices, while Brother Luke unwound the bandages from my shoulder. I peered down, digging my chin into my collarbone. As the cloths came away I saw what they had bound: a round hole, so wide you could poke a thumb into it, about halfway between my nipple and the crook of my arm. I flinched even to look at it – a few inches closer in, and it would have passed clean through my heart. The cherry-red surface was waxy and cracked, but I saw none of the black rot that would have doomed me. Brother Luke examined the bandage, looking pleased enough, then took green ointment from a jar and smeared it over the wound. His fingers were merciless, pushing hard and pressing the medicine into every corner, and I had to bite my lip not to yelp. I wished it were Anna tending to me. When he had finished with my chest, he reached around, and I felt his fingers repeating the procedure on my back.

'Did the arrow go clean through me?' I asked, gasping out the words before the pain became too much.

Brother Luke pursed his lips. 'If you mean to ask whether it went *straight* through you, then almost: we had to push it through to get the tip out where we could remove it. As to whether it went *cleanly* through,' he shrugged, 'only God knows, and time will reveal. But I pray, and I am hopeful.'

I did not ask whether his hopes rested on his prayers or his skill.

When the ointment was applied to his satisfaction, he brought fresh bandages and wound them about me: first around my shoulder, then across my back, then around my upper arm to bind it to my side. By the time he had finished I was swaddled like a baby – and almost as feeble.

'Now . . .' Under his supervision, the two novices helped pull me around so that I could swing my legs out of bed. They tugged on my boots, then lifted me as I tottered to my feet. My vision darkened again and I swayed, as if my legs had forgotten how to stand during their three days in bed – I tried to thrust out my arms for balance, but only one was free to obey.

Trying to hide his smirk, one of the novices reached out and steadied me while the other fetched some clothes. I watched them – they must have been about thirteen, the same age as I had been when I had worn those robes. Now, more than twenty years on, it was as if time's edifice had collapsed, so that my past and present selves found themselves face to face inside those monastery walls.

And in the same clothes – for when the second novice returned he brought another grey habit like his own, which the two of them wrestled over my head. I managed to poke my right arm through the sleeve, though my left remained bound up inside the robe.

Brother Luke looked at me enquiringly. 'Does it fit?'

'A little tight.' I had been smaller twenty years ago.

He nodded. 'That will help support your shoulder.' He squinted at me, tilting his head right and left as though judging my balance. Then he picked up a wooden staff that leaned against the wall and placed it in my hand.

'There. Now you look a proper pilgrim.'

'But where am I going?'

Brother Luke pointed to a door under the windows. 'You can begin by getting some fresh air.'

I shuffled uncertainly to the door, onto a shaded balcony which ran along the front of a wide building. Behind me, regular doors studded the whitewashed wall, no doubt leading to the monks' cells and offices; over the balustrade, the rest of the monastery sloped away down a gentle incline, a jumble of squat buildings, domes and faded tile roofs. It was a true fortress of God, bounded by a massive mud brick rampart whose single gate might have been ripped from the walls of Constantinople herself. Beyond it, a few miles distant, I could see the solitary hump of the rock where we had fought our desperate battle. Otherwise, the monastery stood alone in the desert.

I heard the quick slap of sandals and turned, expecting

the infirmarian had come to examine me. Instead, I saw a monk I did not recognise, a tall man in a black habit, with a heavy gold cross swinging around his neck and a ruby ring on his finger. He walked with a brisk, confident stride, though his close-trimmed beard masked a face no older than my own. He came level with me and extended a rigid arm, holding his hand just low enough that I had to stoop to kiss the ring. It was an awkward movement with one arm tied to my side, and I almost overbalanced attempting it. He snatched his hand away with an affronted tut.

'Are you the abbot?' I asked.

He nodded, and tried to force a smile. It did not keep the disapproval from his eyes. 'How is your wound recovering?'

I touched my good hand to my shoulder. 'With God's grace the infirmarian thinks it will heal. Though he tells me it will take weeks.'

The abbot avoided my gaze. 'In a just world, you would of course remain with us until your wounds were whole.'

I thought I had recognised something about him, the way he stooped forward, too eager to cow you with his authority. I had seen him arguing with the infirmarian in the night. 'You want me to leave.'

'In a just world . . .' He twisted his hands together. 'Your presence here is dangerous. You must know that.'

'I don't even know how I came to be here.'

'The *Nizariyya* brought you.'

It was the second time I had heard that name. 'Who?'

205

'They are rebels . . . brigands. Your friends will explain. But when the caliph's men do not return, he will send others to search for them. If they come here and find you . . .' The abbot turned and stared out into the desert, as if he was expecting to see the full might of the caliph's army thundering across the horizon. But there was only a hawk, circling in the cloudless sky.

'It is not easy living as Christians in a heathen land.'

'I'm surprised the caliph allows it,' I said.

The abbot gave me a sharp look, alive to any insult. 'We pay our tributes, as he requires, and he leaves us to practise our vocation.'

I looked around at the encompassing wilderness, silent and vast. 'You found a good place for it.'

'Yes.' The abbot nodded eagerly. 'Yes. Here we can be apart from the world and live as Christ taught.'

'And did Christ teach you to cast out the wretched and wounded who crawled to your doorstep?' barked a voice from over my shoulder.

I turned to see Nikephoros and Aelfric walking towards me, and immediately had to stifle a laugh. Both of them were dressed as I was, in novices' grey habits, but where mine was a little snug across my shoulders, theirs rode high above their knees and elbows, more like labourers' smocks. Nikephoros, in particular, seemed utterly ridiculous – though his face was as proud as ever.

'My Lord.' The abbot bowed low – evidently Nikephoros had already impressed his rank on the man. 'My Lord, you know we have extended you every kindness. But we live here to escape the snares of the world. We cannot allow them to intrude in our community, or they will destroy it.'

'You will have to run further than this if you want to escape the cares of the world. How much do you pay the caliph to leave you alone?'

The abbot swallowed. He was young, and too used to ruling unchallenged over his little kingdom in the desert, I guessed.

'We render Caesar his due, as Christ commanded.'

'And if Caesar demands the three men who escaped his captivity?'

Three men? I glanced at Aelfric and mouthed Jorol's name. Aelfric gave a small shake of his head.

The abbot was backing away along the balcony. 'No. No! I would never betray fellow Christians to the Egyptians. It is for your own safety that you must go, as much as ours.'

Nikephoros stared at him and said nothing.

'A caravan will come past the monastery this afternoon. They will take you to the coast. There are men there – Christians – with ships.'

'And what use are ships in winter?'

'Winter does not trouble these men. They are accustomed to it. They will take you . . .' He shrugged, perhaps uncertain where three vagabonds who had crawled out of the desert might want to go. 'Home.'

Despite myself, my hopes leaped to hear it. Nikephoros, meanwhile, took two quick strides and stared close into the abbot's face. They were almost the same height, and for a moment their eyes met on a level plane.

'If you betray us, master abbot, or deal unfairly with us, I will personally march back across this desert with a legion of the emperor's troops at my back, and tear apart every brick of your monastery.'

The abbot dropped his gaze. 'I will not betray you. I only want peace, and for my community to be left to their Christian lives.'

Before we left, I sought out Brother Luke the infirmarian to thank him for his care.

'You saved me from death.' I wished I had something to give him but I had nothing.

The infirmarian smiled a gentle rebuke. 'God saved you; I merely dressed the wound. I pray it is enough. I have little call here to practise on the wounds you brought me.'

'You could come with us. Your skills would save many lives, especially among the Army of God.'

'My vocation . . .'

'It would not be betraying your vocation,' I insisted. 'It would be serving God – more than sitting comfortably in the desert and tending to men who have blistered their knees with too much prayer. It would be a mercy to many.'

Brother Luke looked down in embarrassment, and I realised I had spoken with too much passion. 'I'm sorry. I only meant – '

'I know what you meant. And what you say has its truth. But God has called me here to withdraw from the world. That is my vocation; whatever small skill I have to heal proceeds from that.'

A bell tolled through the high windows. Brother Luke gave a smile. 'Now, however, I am called to prayer.'

'Let me join you,' I said impulsively. For all the prayers I had hurled at God in recent days, it was an age since I had entered the warm womb of a church, wrapped in candlelight and incense. Suddenly, I longed for it.

But Brother Luke shook his head. Outside, down the hill, I heard the creak of a gate and the tramp of many hooves.

'I think you are called back to the world.'

Above us, the stern Christ stayed fixed in his firmament. One hand clutched the sealed book, in which were written all things; the other was raised, as if in farewell.

After the strange familiarity of the monastery, it was something of a shock to meet our new escorts: a dozen Saracens dressed all in black, with crooked faces and fearsome swords. They rode on camels, with another two score of the beasts roped together in a train laden with sacks and bundles. Just walking past them brought a feast of exotic scents to my nose: sweet, musky and forbidden. It was like walking up the eastern end of the main avenue in Constantinople, outside the palace gates where the perfume-sellers kept their shops.

'Who are these men?' Nikephoros demanded, bristling with suspicion.

The abbot sniffed. 'Spice traders from Arabia. They are on their way to the coast.'

There was a brief delay while the abbot negotiated with the Saracen leader. We could not understand a word, but the exchange of a purse full of coins seemed to decide the matter. The Saracen leader gestured to a riderless camel, and with much unloading and rebalancing of their burdens, two more were found for the rest of us. I noticed that a couple of the sacks were not reloaded, but remained beside the abbot. Servants filled the caravan's waterskins from the monastery well; then we mounted our camels and rode out. With only one arm free to cling to the reins, my balance was precarious, but I managed to turn myself enough to see the monastery receding behind us. Looking back, seeing it alone in the empty desert, its mammoth walls and towering gate seemed more folly than ever – defences against an invisible siege. Yet they had not been built against the armies of men, but against the world itself, and for that even those bulwarks were no more than sand before a tide. Perhaps mindful of that fact, the monastery's builders had sited it artfully in the lee of a low ridge, almost the same colour as the faded mud-bricks of the ramparts. It seemed extraordinary that anything so vast as those walls could disappear, yet already it was hard to tell where the walls ended and the ridge began. The next time I looked back, it had vanished completely.

Nikephoros must have seen my glance, for he brought his camel alongside.

'Fools.' He jerked his head back towards the monastery. 'If God was obliged to come into the world and toil as a human, I doubt he intended that abbot and his flock to be spared.'

'Perhaps.' I was unsure whether I envied the monks their vocation, or pitied them for it. I tried to change the subject, nodding towards our Saracen guards. 'Who are these men?'

'Smugglers.' Nikephoros' camel began to drift back, and he swatted it with a short stick to bring it level with me again. 'No doubt when we reach the coast they'll find some pirate who will spirit their cargo across the sea.'

'But they are Ishmaelites. Why should they have to skulk about in their own country?'

'Because Ishmaelites hate taxes just as much as Christians and Jews. And also because the Saracens of Arabia follow a different sect of Islam, the same as the Turks. They are the Fatimid caliph's bitterest enemies.'

'Are they the same as the men who rescued us from over there?' I pointed to the west, where the outcropping rock was now a small blot on the horizon.

'No. Those were *Nizariyya*.'

It was the third time I had heard that name. 'Who?'

'Four years ago, when the old caliph died, his chosen heir was his eldest son, a prince named Nizar. But the vizier al-Afdal, whom we met, preferred the youngest son who had only recently come of age.'

'He thought the younger son would be more easily governed?'

'And the boy was married to al-Afdal's sister. Al-Afdal installed the boy on the throne – the same throne where we saw him; Nizar fled to Alexandria, raised a revolt and proclaimed himself the true caliph.

211

'Al-Afdal crushed the revolt easily enough, but it was only half a victory. To the Fatimids, the caliph is not just their king but also their high priest, the *imam*. There can only be one lawful imam at a time, and each must proceed from the last. They claim that the line stretches unbroken all the way from the heresiarch Mohammed. Supporting a caliph is not only a question of politics, but also of faith. And that is much harder to defeat.'

I considered this a moment. 'What happened to Prince Nizar?'

'He was captured and disappeared.' Nikephoros grimaced. 'No doubt in the same manner, perhaps the same place, as we would have done if we had not escaped. Al-Afdal hoped he would be forgotten; instead, his partisans believed that Prince Nizar had been concealed by their God until he could return in glory and vengeance. Naturally, that only redoubled their determination in their war against the caliph, though they were scattered and weak.'

'And these partisans: they are the *Nizariyya* who rescued us?'

'They have a hidden camp on the heights of that rock. When they saw that we had been pursued by the caliph's troops, and fought against them, they spared us.' He laughed. 'They are also the caliph's bitterest enemies.'

'There seem to be many.'

'And more now that he has offended Byzantium. When the *Nizariyya* realised we were Greek, they brought us to the monastery. The abbot did not say as much, but I guess there is an understanding between the monks and their neighbours.'

'And Jorol?'

'He fell from the cliff. They could not say whether it was the fall or the arrows that killed him. The monks buried him in their cemetery.'

We rode for two days, resting in the hottest hours of each day and the darkest hours of each night. Then, just before dusk on the second day, we came to a rise and saw a sight I had almost forgotten existed. Trees. Olive groves scattered the valley before us, and on the opposite ridge I could see a row of date plams swaying softly in the breeze. The same breeze blew across my face – not a parching desert wind, but a cool, wet wind flavoured with salt and fish.

Even with one arm tied to my side, I would have flogged my camel bare to gallop across that final stretch more quickly. Instead, we had to endure the painstaking pace of the pack animals as they picked their way among the crumbling stone terraces and irrigation channels in the valley. Up the far slope the ground became sandier – not the floury dust that coated the desert, but paler and coarser sand, which ground and crumbled underfoot.

We reached the line of date palms I had seen and looked out, onto a few low sand dunes, a flat beach and the sea beyond. If I had been standing I would have dropped to my knees to thank God; as it was, I stared at the water, unblinking, until my eyes wept from the salt breeze. To our left, I could see a small village of ramshackle huts thatched with palm leaves. Children played in the sand dunes, while women knotted broken nets and men caulked the boats they had hauled up to the top of the beach.

But those were not the only vessels. Drawn up at the water's edge where waves rippled between their hulls lay five ships – much bigger than the fishing boats, with stout masts and high, curving prows. Their sails were furled and their oars stowed, but one flew a green banner showing a man with outstretched arms at her masthead. Seeing it, Aelfric gave a small cry; he leaped down from his camel, almost tumbling into the sand in his haste, and ran across the beach.

The men by the boats saw his approach and advanced to meet him. Some snatched up their swords, and several carried long axes. It did not deter Aelfric: he ran straight into the throng, shouting something I could not understand. The nearest man stared in astonishment – but it was the astonishment of recognition, not fear. He dropped his axe, spread his arms and wrapped Aelfric in an engulfing hug.

'What . . . ?' Nikephoros slipped out of his saddle and strode after the Varangian. For myself, I could not dismount unaided but kicked my camel forward, overtaking Nikephoros and reining in just behind Aelfric, who was now deep in conversation. I paused and listened. It was not a language I could speak or understand, but it was familiar to me nonetheless. I had heard it spoken among the Varangians many times.

Nikephoros pushed forward. 'Who are these men?'

Aelfric broke off and turned to us, his eyes shining with excitement. A circle had begun to form around us as the men from the ships gathered. Looking at the assembled faces, I saw that many bore more than a passing resemblance to Aelfric: fair hair, light skin tanned red by wind and sun, and broad shoulders, which held their weapons easily.

Aelfric pointed to the man who stood at the centre of the throng. 'This is Saewulf. These are his ships.'

The man called Saewulf stepped forward. His chestnut-coloured hair hung lank over his shoulders, tied back by a leather thong, while his beard was so thick it almost covered his mouth. He wore a green tunic and red leggings, and a dagger with a handle carved like a fish tucked into his braided belt. He stood with his legs far apart, his shoulders back and his chest out-thrust. I suppose it was a posture learned from many months balancing on a heaving deck, but the effect on land was vaguely obscene.

'Is he English?' I blurted out.

Aelfric nodded.

No doubt it would take many questions to establish why an English sailor and his fleet had made their camp on the shores of Fatimid Egypt. But at that moment, there was only one question that mattered, and Nikephoros asked it with his customary brusqueness.

'Will he take us home?'

١ζ
∽∽∽∽∽

That evening, Saewulf's men built fires on the beach and roasted goats. It was the first meat I had tasted since we fled the caliph's palace and I forced myself to eat it cautiously, though I could have devoured it in a mouthful. I licked the fat from my fingers while Nikephoros and Aelfric talked with Saewulf. He had avoided Nikephoros' question, insisting we could not speak before eating; and once we were seated around the fire he had asked to hear our entire story. Nikephoros told it, with some explanation from Aelfric in English but mostly in Greek, for Saewulf's voyaging profession had taught him many languages. For all his barbaric appearance he made a charming host: he filled our cups with beer, cut us the choicest pieces of meat, and gave us fresh cloaks and tunics to replace the ill-fitting novices' clothes we wore.

When Nikephoros had finished his account, he fixed his gaze on Saewulf. 'That is our story. But why has an English seafarer beached his ships on these shores, at this time of year? You are a long way from safe harbours.'

'So are you.' Saewulf grinned; the goat-grease on his teeth gleamed in the firelight. 'I came to fish.'

Nikephoros gestured towards the ships, though all we could see of them were high prows sweeping up into the darkness. 'Are those fishing boats?'

'For me – yes.' Saewulf leaned forward. 'I was in England when I heard that the Pope had preached his holy pilgrimage – '

'I thought all of your people had been driven out of England when the Normans invaded,' I interrupted.

'Even William the Bastard could not kill every Englishman. He needed us to plough his fields and quarry stone for his castles. And sail his ships.' He shrugged. 'I carry many cargoes, but I have never profited from carrying a grudge.'

Aelfric stirred. 'Sigurd Ragnarson would disagree with you.'

'Which is why I left the Varangians.' He saw my look of surprise. 'Yes, Demetrios Askiates, I have seen your city and stood beside your emperor, in the palace and on the battlefield. As close as I am to you now. But do you know

217

what I realised? That if I was to live under a foreign king, it might as well be in my own country.'

'Even though he raped that country?' Aelfric murmured.

Saewulf gave a harsh laugh. 'Better that than living in perpetual exile, brooding on injustices that will never be undone and pretending that I can atone for my country's shame by giving my life for a king who cared nothing for it. That was why I left the Varangian guard – it was like living in an open grave.'

'I wonder, was it as hard for you to live under the king who murdered your family?'

'Much harder. But wasting my life with anger would have been too easy.'

There was no amusement on Saewulf's face now. He glared at Aelfric, and the Varangian returned the gaze, both men trembling like drawn swords.

'Even so, you are a long way from England.' Nikephoros spoke with forced calm.

Saewulf spread out his hands, peering at them as if looking for signs of weakness. 'I am no longer a soldier. I am a merchant.'

Mercenary, I thought I heard Aelfric mutter, but the crackling fire drowned it out.

'But I am still in the business of war. Armies need food and weapons. New conquests open new opportunities.' He nodded to the Saracen camel-drivers, who sat by their own fire a little way down the beach. 'And in wartime, luxuries become dearer.'

'And tax-collectors less vigilant,' said Nikephoros.

The knowing smile returned to Saewulf's face. 'New opportunities.'

'And if the opportunity came to earn gold and the emperor's favour?'

Saewulf scowled. 'I told you: I do not serve your emperor any more.'

'But you sail in his waters, where his fleets patrol. One day, it may matter that he looks kindly on you.'

'And the gold?'

Nikephoros spread open his cloak. 'You see I have nothing – not now. But when I reach home – '

'No.' Saewulf cut through Nikephoros' calm persuasion. 'I cannot take you to Constantinople. It would take weeks, and with the winter winds against us we might not even be able to enter the Hellespont. You offer me an opportunity, Greek, but I think there are greater profits to be made elsewhere.'

Under the chill of his words, the fire seemed to dim and the night breeze grow sharper. Aelfric turned away in disgust, as if he had expected no less, while I held myself still. Only Nikephoros remained unaffected.

'I do not want you to take me to Constantinople.'

Saewulf looked surprised. 'Where, then?'

'We are going to Antioch.'

Saewulf rested his chin in his hands and stared into the fire. 'And what will you do there? The last time I passed by Antioch, Franks and Normans controlled it.'

'We will prise them out,' said Nikephoros confidently, 'and put them on the road to Jerusalem. With the caliph turned against us, there is no alternative.'

The next day we loaded the Saracens' cargo onto the ships, and set sail for Antioch.

II

The Golgotha Road

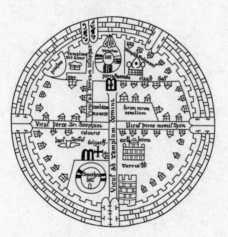

January – June 1099

η

∞∞∞∞

We returned to Antioch early in January. We were tired
from the journey: the endless days beating against sharp
winds, the damp and shivering, the constant watch for
pirates and storms. It was the very dead of winter, and a
freezing rain fell on us as we disembarked at the port of
Saint Simeon. On the higher ground there would be snow.
We stood by the empty harbour, three bedraggled figures
in borrowed clothes, with borrowed horses bullied from
the local innkeeper. Somewhere in the gloom, a church
bell tolled.

'What now?'

Nikephoros looked at the dreary town. 'We must find
out how far the Frankish army has advanced and follow.
With God's grace, they may even be at the gates of

Jerusalem.' He gave a cold laugh, like the drumming of raindrops. 'But we will ask at Antioch.'

For over a year Antioch had been the pole around which my life turned: by turns unattainable, irresistible and inescapable. Now I reached it for the last time, at a noon that was darker than dusk. The slopes of Mount Silpius rose up into the cloud, its triple-crowned peak invisible, while the city below lay still and sullen in the twilight. Whatever violence had been worked there in the past, it seemed peaceful enough now. That did not lessen my misgivings.

Though the rain had stopped, there was no break in the cloud, and it was not until we had approached within a bowshot of the gate that we noticed anything amiss. A red banner, as tall as a mounted rider, hung above the gate like a portcullis. Rain had wrung the fresh dye from the cloth, filling the ruts and craters below with crimson pools, but the design still stood clear. A white serpent, writhing down the middle of the banner like a tear or a scar.

I shook my head in confusion. 'This was Count Raymond's gate. Why is Bohemond's standard over it?'

Nikephoros trotted forward and thumped his fist on the gate. The age-blackened wood loomed above him, eternal and unmoving, and the sound of his knock quickly died. At the feet of the towers, beside the gate, white gouges pocked the stonework.

'Who are you?'

A suspicious voice rang in the still air. It must have

come from the gatehouse, but even when I craned my neck back I could see no one.

Nikephoros glanced at me and nodded. I licked my lips, then shouted: 'Ambassadors from the emperor Alexios.'

With a crack and a hiss, something ripped through the air and buried itself in the mud. My horse reared up; I flung my arms around its neck and hugged it tight, clenching my knees against its flanks. Beside me, I saw a small feathered arrow sticking up from the ground.

'Antioch is closed to you,' said the disembodied voice.

Nikephoros circled his horse back a little, trying to see between the battlements. 'Antioch belongs to the emperor. Who has closed it?'

There was no answer except the ominous creak of a bowstring being drawn back and snapped into position. A chill gust of wind blew over us, and the serpent banner flapped against the stone as the breeze lifted it.

None of us spoke as we rode south. It took all my concentration simply to stay in my saddle: my soul was trembling like a broken sword, while my body shivered in the deepening cold. I could barely keep hold of the reins. We forded the Orontes and rejoined the main road from Antioch, now rising towards the mountains. The rain had eased, but a thick, freezing fog replaced it as we climbed higher, and we had no warning of the men ahead until we saw dark shapes staggering through the fog.

It could so easily have been an ambush, and we would have been powerless to stop it. On the miry road and with flagging mounts, we could not even have run. But there was something shambolic and frantic in the shadows before us that did not speak of menace. We spurred our horses forward, and a dozen men turned in the mist to look at us.

They were not brigands. Nor were they Turks. All were dressed in mail hauberks, and most carried weapons, but they posed little danger. Dirty cloths and bandages hung off their bodies like flags; one man's head was bandaged thick as a turban where he had apparently lost an eye. Their faces were wretched: had they not been armed, you would have taken them for a slave coffle. Only the ragged crosses sewn on their sleeves told their true allegiance.

I gestured to their wounds. 'Where have you come from? Was there a battle?'

The foremost of the Franks leaned heavily on his spear, burying it in the mud. 'They attacked two nights ago. There was nothing we could do.'

'Where?' Had the Army of God been routed? Was this its last remnant, a handful of survivors spared to tell of its terrible fate?

'Antioch,' he mumbled. 'They have taken Antioch from us.'

'Who?' I could guess the answer, but I asked it anyway.

'The Norman traitor. Bohemond.'

Nikephoros twitched his reins. 'What did he say?'

I ignored him. 'And the Greeks in Antioch – what happened to them? What did Bohemond do to them? What – ' I broke off as I heard my voice become shrill

226

with panic. It did no good; the soldier dismissed my question with a careless shrug that was worse than any answer.

'And you – you are Provençals? Count Raymond's men?'

He nodded. Behind him, I could see his men shivering, and trying to keep their sodden bandages in place. There had never been any love between the Normans and Provençals, least of all between their leaders, but could Bohemond really have launched a war on his fellow Christians?

'Where is Count Raymond? Was he at Antioch?'

The Provençal shook his head. 'The count is at Ma'arat.'

'Where is that?'

'Further along this road.' Even in his despair, he seemed surprised that I had not heard of it. 'Two days' march from here.'

A cold gust of wind blew rain in my eyes, and my mount pawed at the ground in her eagerness to be moving again. *Two days' march*, I thought, listening to my own words as I translated for Nikephoros. We had been away more than four months, seen palaces, kings and wonders; crossed deserts and seas just to return. While in all that time, the invincible Army of God had moved just two days forward.

Snow fell in the mountains that night. Next morning, a brittle crust covered the ground, and our horses picked their way anxiously over the frozen ruts in the road. The skies above were grey, unyielding, but the air was clear. When we came to an outcrop on the mountain road, we could see a high plateau opening out below us. The whole earth sparkled white, made new by the snow.

'What's that?'

While I had been staring into the distance, Aelfric's practical gaze had been examining the road ahead. Immediately before us it plunged into a pine forest, but it emerged again below, heading south-east across the plain. At the bottom of the slope a river flowed around the mountains' feet, and where river and road met there stood a small town.

'Do you see there?' Aelfric was pointing to the meadows just beyond the town. I looked, but saw nothing. Squinting against the sullen winter light, I stared closer until suddenly, like a ship emerging from fog, foreground and background split apart and I saw what Aelfric meant. Tents – scores of them, white as the snow. Deceived by the distance, I had taken them for the furrows of some farmer's field, and the specks moving among them to be crows. In fact, they were not nearly so far off.

We had found the Army of God.

Whatever ordeals we had endured in the past months, the Franks must have suffered worse. As we rode through their camp towards the town we were surrounded by haggard faces and ragged bodies. Even in the midwinter cold, many did not have enough clothes to cover themselves: ribs like curved fingers pressed out against skin, while the bellies of the worst-affected swelled up in cruel mockery of satiety. Black toes and fingers poked from dirty bandages that had long since become useless, while twice I saw bodies so still they must have been corpses, lying unheeded and unburied in the mud.

Aelfric stared at the miserable faces, which turned towards us as we passed. 'Has nothing changed?'

I knew what he meant. There was a horrible familiarity in these scenes: we had suffered exactly the same way a year ago outside Antioch. It seemed almost inconceivable that for all the victories we had won in that time, the miracles that had sustained us, the Army of God now found itself suffering the same torments only a few dozen miles distant. Nothing had changed – except that there were many fewer tents now than there had been a year ago. The river of humanity, which had forced its way across deserts, broken down the walls of Antioch and swept away all opposition, had flowed into the earth. A few lingering pools were all that remained – and soon they, too, would drain away.

I glanced at Nikephoros, wondering how his life in the immaculate confines of the palace would have prepared him for this. He held his head rigid, his eyes fixed ahead, but it was not shock or compassion that his mask was worn to hide. The corner of his lip twitched, and his pitiless eyes stared on the wretches around us with something like disgust. And, I could have sworn, satisfaction.

Beyond the camp, at the entrance to the town proper, a guard challenged us. With relief, I saw he was a Provençal, one of Count Raymond's men.

'Is this Ma'arat?' I asked eagerly.

He looked puzzled. 'Ma'arat? Ma'arat is another day's march from here. This town is called Rugia.'

Two days' progress in four months, and now they had lost one of them. 'Has there been a battle? A defeat? Why has the army retreated here?'

The guard laughed at my panic. 'We have not retreated. The bulk of the army is still camped at Ma'arat.' He gestured at the rows of tents in front of him. 'Did you think this was all that survived of the Army of God? These are just the princes' bodyguards.'

'The princes?' My hopes rose. 'Is Count Raymond here?'

'They all are.' He gave me a crooked look, taking in our travel-stained clothes and weary faces. 'They've come here for a council – though to call it a parley would be nearer the mark. All of them: Count Raymond, the Count of Flanders, the Duke of Normandy, Tancred, Bohemond . . .' He paused, counting them off on his fingers. 'And Duke Godfrey.'

ιθ

∽∽∽∽∽

A Provençal knight led us to a high-walled villa in the centre of the town, where the blue banner of Provence and the white standard of the Army of God hung by the gate. Aelfric waited outside, while a small priest with a harelip brought us through many guarded doors to a wide chamber deep in the house. Rich carpets laid three or four deep covered the floor and lined the walls, steaming slightly where the lamps had been placed too close to them. A smouldering brazier filled the room with hot smoke; at the back, on a table of its own amid a constellation of candles, sat the golden reliquary with the fragment of the holy lance.

The harelipped priest motioned us to stay by the door and advanced to the middle of the room, where a slumped figure sat in a chair beside the brazier. A thick blanket was drawn over him, though he still seemed to shiver underneath it. The priest whispered in his ear, then beckoned us closer.

Whatever had happened in the months we had been away, it had not been kind to Count Raymond. He had always been the oldest of the princes – twice my age, I thought – but now the years showed. There was little trace of the vigour that had held together his army outside Antioch, and no authority in his bearing. His iron-grey hair had turned white, and his single eye was kept half closed.

'You have returned from Egypt,' he mumbled. 'I thought you had died there.'

Nikephoros did not even bother to bow. 'We nearly did. What has happened in our absence?'

'Bohemond has taken Antioch.' The cry rose from within him as if dragged out by torturers' hooks. Nikephoros remained impassive.

'I know. We were there two days ago.'

The count leaned forward, spilling the blanket off his chest. 'Then you know what must be done. In Constantinople, I bowed to the emperor as my liege-lord and offered him homage. Now is the time for him to honour his obligation and come to my aid.'

'The emperor knows you are his closest ally and most faithful servant.' Nikephoros contrived to look suitably sympathetic. 'But you forget, my lord count, that we have just returned from four months' absence. There are too many things we do not understand. Why you and Bohemond and all the Army of God are not at the gates of Jerusalem, for example.'

Count Raymond stiffened, but ordered his servants to bring us seats and hot wine. Nikephoros took only the merest sip.

'It is all Bohemond's doing,' Raymond began. 'Everything – or rather nothing – that we have accomplished since summer is his fault. It was madness to trust him – a man who came without an acre of land to his name; a man his own father disinherited. He never meant to go to Jerusalem. He has used us to sustain his ambition, and now that he has his prize he has turned on us.' Raymond gestured to the gilded casket behind him. 'He has even questioned the authenticity of the relic of the holy lance.'

Nikephoros drummed two fingers against his cup. 'This is not news. Bohemond had more than half of Antioch before we had even left. You were supposed to draw him out by leading the army on to Jerusalem.'

'That is what Bohemond wants!' Raymond thumped a fist on the wooden arm of his chair. 'Nothing would satisfy him more than if I set out for Jerusalem now. You have seen the state of my army here – and the rest, at Ma'arat, are no better. The Saracens would massacre them before we even reached the coast. Bohemond would sit safe in Antioch, unchallenged, and your emperor would have lost his last ally.'

Nikephoros pursed his lips. 'What happened to Phokas?

My colleague, the eunuch? He was supposed to stay here and advise you.'

'Much use he was. He should have advised himself to stay away. The plague took him almost before you'd left for Egypt.'

And what of Anna and Sigurd? I ached to know. But Nikephoros had already continued. 'And Duke Godfrey? The other princes? Where do they stand?'

'Hah! Without Bishop Adhemar, each looks to his own interests. Every day they come out and announce they want nothing more than to reach Jerusalem. Then they retire to their tents to sniff their own farts, trying to divine if it will be Bohemond or me they should support. I am sixty-six years old, and I am the only man with the balls to withstand him. Until the emperor comes.'

'No.' Nikephoros rose. 'Even if I could get word to the emperor straight away, he would not be able to come until the summer. You cannot afford to wait that long. You are locked in this struggle with Bohemond, but his feet are planted on the rock of Antioch and yours are in the mire of Ma'arat. You will not win this test of strength.'

'What would you have me do then?' Raymond's defiance was gone, and I heard only an old man's despair.

'If someone is pushing against you with all his might, it is easier to unbalance him by stepping backwards than forwards.'

'Not when you're standing on the edge of a cliff.' His words choked off in a fit of haggard coughing. He wiped his mouth on his blanket and continued. 'There are many voices that say the same as you. The soldiers offered to acclaim me as leader of the whole army if I would lead them to Jerusalem. Did you know that?'

'What did you say?'

'I accepted, of course. I *will* lead the Army of God to Jerusalem, and if God wills it we will take it for Christ. As soon as Bohemond surrenders Antioch.'

'You do not need Antioch,' Nikephoros persisted. 'It is a distraction.'

'Of course I do not need Antioch,' Raymond hissed. 'But that is not a reason why Bohemond should have it either.'

A thought struck me. 'What do the pilgrims say?'

The great swarm of peasants who followed the army like flies had never been happy with delay: rightly, for they only ever suffered or starved by it. At Antioch their frustrations had led many to question the authority of the princes – and some to ask still more dangerous questions.

'The pilgrims can afford a simpler view of affairs,' said Raymond shortly. 'They hunger for Jerusalem, but my priests trim their appetites with a diet of humility and obedience. And Peter Bartholomew holds great sway over their thoughts.'

'The visionary? The same Peter Bartholomew who found the holy lance?' I glanced at the reliquary again in its shining forest of candles.

Raymond's single eye swivelled towards me with suspicion. We both knew that Peter Bartholomew's journey to sanctity had been a circuitous one. 'The same.'

'Do you trust him to keep the pilgrims quiet?'

'I hold the lance: he is bound to me. Besides, what do peasants know? They are unhappy, of course; they always are. They say we should have taken Jerusalem months ago, and that all our quarrels are just the vanity. But these are the same simpletons who believed that God would give them an invulnerable shield against Turkish arrows. When I see spears and arrows bouncing off them like rocks, then I will let them dictate my strategy.'

'And if they do not let you wait that long?'

Nikephoros was giving me a strange look, irritated by my interruption but intrigued by my purpose. I kept my eyes on Raymond, who had half-risen from his chair in anger.

'I will wait as long as I choose, until the last peasant has rotted into the mud if necessary. I am the lord of thirteen counties, honoured by popes and the rightful captain of the Army of God. When Bohemond takes down his banners from Antioch and surrenders the keys to the citadel, and marches out his army, then we will join him on the road to Jerusalem. Until then, I will stay here and throttle him.'

'His fixation with Bohemond will be his ruin,' said Nikephoros darkly as we walked away. In a side-street, two women were fighting over what looked like a dog's leg. One held the paw while the other pulled on the haunch, their thin faces scarlet with the effort. The woman with the paw let go and her adversary tumbled back into the mud, screeching with triumph that turned to anguish as the first woman stepped over her and stole the trophy away.

'Does that matter?' All I cared about now was finding Anna and Sigurd – and then going home. Other men could quarrel over Jerusalem if they chose – though I doubted they would ever see it.

Nikephoros stopped in the road and turned to look at me. 'Of course it matters. Nothing has changed, except that we must try even harder to work Bohemond out of Antioch. And Count Raymond, Christ help us, is our last hope for doing that.'

I let my eyes sweep across the street, to the woman still lying in the mud lamenting her lost meal, and a ramshackle troop of Provençal soldiers picking their way up the slope. One had no boots and two others had no weapons. I gestured to them.

'Do you think we will take Antioch with those?'

'Of course not.' Nikephoros turned away impatiently and continued on. 'Did you listen to what I told the count? We must draw Bohemond out of Antioch.'

'How?'

'By going to Jerusalem.'

I ran after Nikephoros and stepped in front of him, blocking his path. 'Jerusalem is a myth, a lie concocted by priests and sold to peasants.' I realised that I was shouting, that passers-by were looking with crooked eyes at the mad Greek raving in a foreign tongue. I did not care. 'This army will die here. Not one man will ever see Jerusalem and even if they do, it will not solve one single thing.'

Nikephoros' cold eyes looked down on mine; clouds of air formed and dispersed between us as he breathed out.

'The man who conquers Jerusalem will be a legend through the ages – a hero to rank with Caesar and Alexander. His power and authority will be boundless.'

'Powerful enough to take on Bohemond?'

Nikephoros gave the cruel laugh I had heard so often. 'Powerful enough that Bohemond will not allow it to be anyone but himself. If he sees Raymond is about to conquer Jerusalem, he will flay his horse alive to be there first.'

'But if Bohemond takes Jerusalem it will be his power that is magnified.'

Nikephoros shrugged. 'What does it matter? He will be out of Antioch. That is all the emperor cares for.' He leaned closer, almost whispering in my ear. 'Yes, Jerusalem is a myth for peasants. But it is also a myth peddled to kings and princes, a myth that inspires men to greatness and folly. This army will reach Jerusalem. You and I will see that it does – even if we have to carry Count Raymond every mile ourselves.'

A gust of wind howled down off the mountains, whipping the snowflakes around us into turmoil. In the field beside us, a tent broke free from its guy ropes and billowed up, snapping like ravenous jaws, while men ran about in the firelight trying to hold it down. Nikephoros clapped his hands to force warmth into them.

'But hopefully it will not come to that. Not if we can persuade others to do our work for us.'

The snow was falling more thickly now, the flakes spiralling down like dust in the silver moonlight. The world closed off: the only sound was the faint protest as the snow underfoot yielded to our boots. I did not know where we were going, and I did not ask. How long had I been walking? I had marched across the plains and steppes of Anatolia in the legions; I had tramped the streets of the queen of cities, from sewers and slums to the imperial palaces, seeking wickedness and finding it all too often. I had walked – barely – over mountains, through the gates of Antioch and into the deserts of Egypt. Snow touched my face, melted, and ran down my cheeks like tears. Ahead of me, always two paces away, Nikephoros walked on. Snow had filled the folds of his cloak, so that spidery white lines crossed his shoulders like scars. He did not say a word to me, did not even turn to see that I was with him. I was a ghost, lingering unseen and unnoticed, haunting the footsteps of great men.

We passed shivering sentries and came to another field where scattered fires burned holes in the blanket of snow. In the centre, beside the largest fire, stood a tent so white it stood out even against the surrounding snow. A banner emblazoned with five red crosses – the five wounds of Christ – hung from a spear before it.

I stopped, as if the incessant press of snow had finally overwhelmed me and turned my soul to ice. Suddenly the smoke from the fire was no longer woodsmoke on a winter's evening, but the smog of smouldering ruins and burned flesh. As the wind moaned in the trees, it seemed to carry Pakrad's screams all the way from the mountaintop at Ravendan.

'That – that is Duke Godfrey's banner.'

Nikephoros paused and looked back. Beyond him, I saw the guard at the tent door ready to challenge us, caught off balance by the sudden halt. 'Of course it is Duke Godfrey's banner. Who else can help us now?' He frowned, remembering. 'Keep quiet – and if you ever hope to see Constantinople again, do not repeat your accusations.'

No doubt, in the village, counts and dukes would be feasting on roast boar, hot wine and honey cakes. Here, we might have been in a monk's cell. No rugs or carpets covered the floor – only a thin cloth, which bore the imprint of every rock and hummock beneath it. The sole concession to comfort was a small brazier in the corner, though it did not even give enough heat to melt the snow that weighed down the canvas ceiling. Otherwise, a handful of stools, a table that might have been dragged by its legs all the way from Lorraine, and a dusty book lying open on a reading stand were the only furnishings.

Nikephoros eyed our surroundings dismissively. 'Is the duke of Lorraine such a pauper?'

It was fortunate he had spoken in Greek, for at that moment one of the curtains swung back and Duke Godfrey strode into the room. I stared at him, unable to hide my hatred despite Nikephoros' warning. He had not changed much: the weatherbeaten face that seemed set in a permanent look of disapproval, the stocky shoulders more like a ploughman's than a duke's, the pale blue eyes. I tried to imagine him standing over the captives at Ravendan, watching his henchmen burn out their sight, but though the memory was sharp the details were clouded.

He looked at Nikephoros. 'Welcome,' he said courteously. He closed the book on the stand and covered it with a cloth. 'I had not expected I would host an ambassador of your rank on this frozen evening, or I would have made preparations. As it is, all I can offer you are the spartan comforts that I require myself.'

Evidently the attendant who announced our arrival had not troubled to mention my presence – why would he? – and Godfrey's noble gaze was well-practised at ignoring servants in the background. Only as I started speaking, translating his greeting, did his eyes flick across to notice me. I was ready for him: though my voice never wavered, I held his gaze and watched with savage delight as recognition bit. Even he, schooled in the wiles of courtly intrigue as he was, could not hide his shock. Just for a second, the mask slipped: colour drained from his face and his eyes widened in panic. By the time I finished relaying his welcome he had collected himself.

Nikephoros, standing in front of me, could not see my expression. 'Tell him I am grateful he has received me so late and unannounced.'

I repeated it in the Frankish dialect. 'No doubt you did not expect to see us.'

'You had been gone so long I feared you might be dead.'

'As you see, I survived.'

Two servants moved the brazier to the centre of the room, bringing chairs for Nikephoros and Godfrey and a wooden stool for me. Though outwardly calm, I could see the uncertainty in Godfrey's eyes as they darted between me and Nikephoros, gauging who was the greater threat. He had never seen me at the monastery, I realised; he did not know how much I knew or guessed of his role, and it troubled him. There at least I had the advantage.

He offered Nikephoros a taut, insincere smile. 'What brings the ambassador of Byzantium to my tent on this bleak night?'

'The same thing that has brought all the princes to this forsaken town.'

'The council?' He laughed. 'If you have come to persuade me to side with Count Raymond, you could have saved yourself a cold journey. I am not interested in who rules Antioch.'

'You swore an oath to return the emperor his lands.'

Godfrey's face soured at the memory. He had spent months trying to escape having to make that oath, and had only relented at the point of a sword. I wondered if his theft of the emperor's ring was somehow meant to revenge that defeat. 'Bohemond swore the same. If he has not honoured his word, it is a matter for his soul and conscience. Not mine.'

'Of course,' said Nikephoros calmly. 'The question of Antioch is a side issue – a distraction. As you say, it does not concern you.'

'No.'

'It concerns Count Raymond and Bohemond. But while they wrestle together, each trying to choke the other, we are all sinking into the mire.'

'Did you come all this way on a winter's night to tell me that?'

'Antioch is not worth losing this war for. Already, while you wasted the summer and autumn, the Fatimid vizier marched on Jerusalem and took it. He has already had six months to repair its defences and stuff it full of his men. If we wait another six months he will have made it impregnable.'

Godfrey leaned forward and stirred the coals with a poker, tapping it against the brazier's edge to clear the ash. I tensed, memories of Tancred and the blinding iron rushing back to me, then wondered if Godfrey had deliberately done it to provoke me. I glanced at him, but his expression betrayed nothing.

'Six months or six years or six thousand years: it does not matter. The caliph cannot make Jerusalem impregnable. Jerusalem is the city of the living God. He will deliver it to us in His own time.'

'Only if we reach it.'

'We will reach it,' said Godfrey stubbornly. He paused. 'Do you know the emperor Charlemagne?' He must have seen me perplexed by the barbarian name, for he added:

243

'The emperor Charles the Great. I know the Greeks did not recognise that title, but he was emperor of the west long after you had surrendered your right to it. He was my ancestor.'

With a solemn face, he stretched out his hand palm down. On his fourth finger, a black stone bulged from the heavy ring he wore, its gold scratched to an ancient dullness. Once again, I wondered if he was testing me by provoking memories of another ring. 'This was Charlemagne's ring.'

Nikephoros bowed his head in respect. 'I knew your own reputation, Duke Godfrey – long before I met you – but I admit I did not know your ancestry.'

Godfrey gave a smug smile. 'That was centuries ago. After his death there was not a man alive who possessed even half as much authority or ability. The empire he had ruled alone he divided between his three sons, who divided it among themselves and among their heirs until all that remained was my own duchy of Lorraine. But that is history. While he lived, the emperor Charlemagne made a pilgrimage of his own to Jerusalem. That is where he took the banner of the five wounds, which you saw outside. And that,' he concluded, 'is why you do not need to question my passion to see Jerusalem. I will never rule over the empire of my ancestors. I would not wish it and I doubt I could manage it. The world was smaller then, or the men bigger. But in this small thing at least I can follow his example, and honour his memory.'

Godfrey leaned forward on his stool, his eyes half closed, perhaps imagining the great exploits of his ancestor. Nikephoros pressed his fingers together.

'My master the emperor never doubted your zeal – or your faith. Indeed, he relied on you to carry this campaign forward when he knew other men would falter. Which is why – '

Godfrey held up a hand. Lamplight gleamed where it caught the band of his ring. 'When I go to Jerusalem, it will be of my own will and desire, not under duress from any man – Norman, Provençal or Greek.'

'What of the unity of the Army of God?'

'What of the unity of the Army of God? If there was such a thing, you would not be here now. When there is, I will happily follow the army where it chooses to go. But I will not drop to my knees and beg. When God ordains the time they will do what He requires.'

His tone was measured and his words precise, but there was no mistaking the unbending pride behind them. He rose; Nikephoros and I followed.

'Thank you for coming to speak with me,' Godfrey said, with the same efficient courtesy he had shown when we arrived. 'If we all spoke more often together, things would go better with us.'

'Then I will hope tomorrow brings accord.'

Nikephoros bowed again, and was about to go when Godfrey said, 'You said you were in Egypt, at the caliph's court. Did you hear any word of my liege-man, Achard of

Tournai? He travelled there nine months ago as part of our embassy, but I have heard nothing from him since the summer.'

Nikephoros halted in surprise, then crossed himself. 'While we were in Egypt, the caliph turned against all Christians at his court and tried to kill us. A few of us escaped; Achard did not. He drowned in the Nile while we fought the caliph's guards.'

Godfrey lowered his eyes. '*By the waters of Babylon I lay down and wept.* It was a risk he took, but I will mourn his loss. He was a good man and a zealous servant.'

'He fought bravely to the end.' Nikephoros, so practised in the nice phrases and smooth lies of diplomacy, sounded unexpectedly false when discussing a man's death.

'I am glad to hear it.'

Godfrey inclined his head to dismiss us and we retreated from the tent. We had not gone six paces when a servant scuttled out and called, 'You have forgotten your cloak, Demetrios Askiates.'

I touched a hand to my shoulders, feeling the thick wool of my cloak clasped where it should be. Nikephoros raised an eyebrow, but said nothing.

'I had better fetch it.'

Every muscle in my body tensed as I stepped back into Godfrey's chamber. He would not harm me with Nikephoros waiting outside and half the Frankish army camped nearby, I told myself. I still could not keep from shivering as I saw him standing over the brazier, stirring the coals. How many hours had I spent during our captivity in Egypt brooding over his treachery and pondering my revenge? Yet now that I stood face to face with him, alone, I could not touch him.

'Did I forget my cloak?' I asked.

'You were supposed to be dead.'

'By God's mercy, we escaped the Egyptians.'

'I was not talking of the Egyptians.' He raked me with a long, searching look. 'I do not know how you survived, or what you learned, but if you say one word against me I will make you wish you had died in the fires at Ravendan.'

I kept silent, fixing him with a stare of plain hatred.

'You do not want to make an enemy of me,' he warned.

'I never did.'

He banged the poker against the rim of the brazier. It rang with a mournful, hollow clang. 'You had something that I needed. Now that I have it, there is no reason for us to be enemies.' He jabbed the poker towards me and I flinched. 'Go home, Demetrios Askiates. Go home to your family. Leave behind these things that do not concern you. No good will come of it if you stay here.'

He nodded his head to dismiss me and I went. My last sight was of him pacing around the room, pinching out the candles with his fingers.

K

꩜꩜꩜

The princes met next morning. It was the last time they would all sit together under the same roof, though none of us knew it. Afterwards, we might look back and see the signs of what was to come, but on that dazzling morning there seemed genuine grounds for hope. The storm had passed: the morning sun shone gold on the dappled snow drifts, and pearls of ice hung from the trees like berries.

One by one, the Franks made their way to the centre of the village, striding through the knee-deep snow. They had been forbidden from carrying arms to the council, but they compensated by bringing hordes of their knights, who stood in small knots around the village square and glared at their rivals.

'They should have allowed the princes their swords and

forbidden them their followers,' said Aelfric. 'Then we would have been safer.'

'At least if it comes to a fight they'll have nothing more dangerous than snowballs.'

The bright morning did not last long. Clouds came up, chilling our spirits, and soldiers' boots soon ground the snow to a grey-brown gruel. Still we waited, all eyes watching the western road. Bohemond had not come. The princes clustered around the edges of the square, huddled with their men as they wondered what it signified. Only Raymond, standing outside the church doors flanked by his guards, did not seem troubled by the absence of his rival.

After half an hour, Raymond walked to the centre of the square and called the princes forward. I accompanied Nikephoros to translate for him; the others came alone. All were wrapped in vast thicknesses of bristling furs, swelling them to twice their actual size, and they sniffed at each other like a pack of wolves in the snow.

'Where is Bohemond?' said the Duke of Normandy. He was a stout man who had been prominent by his absence during most of the hard campaigning. Now his face was creased with worry.

'What does it matter?' Raymond's single eye swept around the gathering. 'I am too old to be kept waiting in the cold by a Norman whelp.'

'Without Bohemond there is nothing to discuss.'

Raymond's face flushed an angry red under his iron-grey beard. 'Are we beholden to one man? Are we children without Bohemond's hand to guide us? Bishop Adhemar, rest his soul, used to preach that the only commander of the Army of God is God Himself. I do not think that includes Bohemond – unless he has added divinity to his self-appointed honours.'

Several of the princes looked uneasy at the impiety of this suggestion. Tancred merely laughed, and murmured audibly, 'I would not put it past my uncle.'

His comment drew a disapproving stare from Duke Godfrey, and surprised looks from the others. Unabashed, Tancred continued, 'I agree with Count Raymond. If my uncle wishes to come then he will be here. He would not want us to delay on his account: he knows our cause is greater than any single man.' A smile curled at the edge of his lips. 'Even him.'

'Then it is decided.' Raymond turned and strode towards the church without looking back. The others hesitated, glancing at each other in indecision. No one made to follow Raymond until he was more than halfway across the square, a proud and lonely figure in the dirty snow. Then, like a gaggle of unruly children, they made their way into the church.

Once, during the great trials at Antioch, the princes' councils had been commonplace affairs, consumed with questions of detail and the care of the army. In those desperate times a short prayer from Bishop Adhemar had sufficed to consecrate the occasion, and the only men in attendance had been the princes and their closest aides. Now, a bishop led a full mass in Latin while all the princes' followers crowded into the church. When the service was over, a space was cleared in the middle of the church and the crowd penned back by four benches set in a square. In its centre, on a marble pedestal, sat the golden reliquary which held the fragment of the holy lance. I noticed many of the princes refused to look at it as they seated themselves, fidgeting under the eyes of the crowd and staring at the empty space where Bohemond should have been. I took my place behind Nikephoros, and thereafter whispered all that was said in his ear.

The bishop, whom I did not recognise but who sounded like a Provençal, began with a long and disjointed speech invoking the glorious deeds the Franks had worked. Had they not fought four great battles against the impious Saracens and – with God's aid – prevailed every time? Had they not taken the fortress city of Antioch, which all men thought impregnable, and then defended it against the mightiest army of Ishmaelites the world had ever seen? Had God not bestowed miracles – true miracles – to demonstrate His favour?

It was not an inspiring speech. After five minutes of it, Nikephoros signalled I did not need to translate any more. The bishop's oratory mixed extravagant hyperbole with flat-footed phrases, and dwelt too long on events that were known to every man there, so that it seemed even the most extraordinary feats must have been tedious and banal affairs. Each time the bishop mentioned Antioch, Raymond's head twitched with annoyance, and when he

251

invoked the holy lance as the climax of his argument, several of the princes smirked openly. In the packed space around us, I heard yawns and muttering.

A crack like thunder on the outer door shattered the tedium in the church and silenced the hapless bishop. The double doors swung in as if giant hands had thrown them open, and a dazzling light flooded in to the gloomy chamber. Silhouetted against the glare, the huge figure of Bohemond sat in the centre of the doorway on a pale horse. Even in a congregation of battle-hardened knights, several men cried out with fear.

Bohemond urged his horse forward into the church. Its hooves rang on the flagstones and echoed off the dome above. All the princes were on their feet, staring at the newcorner. He rode a little way into the sanctuary, then swung down from his saddle, thrust its bridle into the hands of a gaping bystander and strode through the throng. It opened before him like a well-oiled door. The mottled red skin on his face was livid, engorged by excitement and the attention of the crowd, while a wicked grin pinched the edges of his mouth. A blood-red cloak flowed from his shoulders, and where it parted over his chest a sliver of silvered armour gleamed through.

Count Raymond stood and faced Bohemond across the square, two bears in a ring. The old man's chest rose and fell under his fur cloak, his face riven with anger.

'Bohemond.' Stark syllables spat out the name. 'Are you so grand now that God Himself must wait for you?'

Bohemond shrugged. Rings of armour rippled beneath

his cloak like serpent's scales. 'If I have offended the council, I am sorry. Truly. In my haste to be here I lamed my horse and had to find another.'

Count Raymond stared pointedly at the horse, which still stood obediently in the doorway. It was a battle charger, a white stallion that had carried Bohemond into every battle we had fought. In the snow and ice that covered the ground, he would not have ridden it more than a hundred yards.

Duke Godfrey rose, stretching out his arms so that he bridged the space between the two antagonists. 'We are grateful you came. We will need our full strength if we are to confront the challenges God asks of us.'

Raymond looked as if he would happily have lifted Duke Godfrey and thrown him at Bohemond in fury. Instead, he swallowed his anger and sat back down on his bench. Godfrey and Bohemond did likewise, Bohemond taking his seat on the opposite side of the square to Raymond. When he had arranged the folds of his cloak behind him and smoothed them down, he turned to the bishop with a mocking gleam in his eye.

'My apologies, Your Grace. I think perhaps my late arrival interrupted you.'

The bishop's mouth flapped open; his head popped forward like a man trying to force a cough, but he made no sound.

'The bishop was reminding us of our sacred obligation to march on Jerusalem,' said Godfrey.

Bohemond looked puzzled. 'Had any of us forgotten

it?' His gaze touched on Count Raymond, who sat up with indignation.

'I have not forgotten my duty. *I* have not spent the last six months sitting in Antioch.'

'Only because my men threw you out.'

The crowd around us bridled at Bohemond's jibe, muttering their displeasure like spectators in the hippodrome. Though scattered among the jeers I heard laughter, and several men squawking like chickens. They could not have been Bohemond's knights, for he had brought none.

'Antioch does not belong to you,' snapped Raymond, upset by the noise.

'Come and claim it, if you want it. I will be ready for you.' Bohemond tapped a fist against his waist, where his sword should have been. 'But I did not come here to talk about Antioch. I thought our object was Jerusalem. Perhaps Count Raymond has forgotten that.'

'Antioch and Jerusalem are inseparable.' The Count of Flanders, one of the lesser princes, pronounced what everyone knew. 'If we cannot agree how to leave Antioch, then there is little point discussing how we reach Jerusalem.'

The hapless bishop, all but forgotten, rose to his feet. Raymond was quicker.

'Why dance around the truth? The Count of Flanders is right. Bohemond holds Antioch in defiance of our oaths to the emperor, and of all our claims. If he does not surrender it to us, we will stay here until he compels us.'

'Do not speak too freely for other men,' Godfrey

cautioned him. 'I besieged Antioch for eight months and led my men in the battle against Kerbogha. By rights of conquest, I have as much claim as any man to Antioch. But I renounce it. I would rather have ten minutes' prayer in the Holy Sepulchre than a lifetime owning all the lands and riches of Antioch. Who else can say the same?'

For a moment, his challenge echoed in the silent church. Godfrey's face shone with righteousness as he stared around at his colleagues, then looked down to his right where Tancred sat.

Tancred shrugged. 'I have no claim to Antioch.'

One by one, the princes repeated the declaration – some with careless ease, others, mostly those who had fought hardest in the siege, with obvious reluctance. Eventually only Raymond and Bohemond had not spoken. Godfrey looked to Raymond.

'We have all made our vow. For the cause of Christ and the unity of the Army of God, will you join us?'

Raymond stuck out his chin. 'If Bohemond renounces his claim.'

All eyes turned to Bohemond. He sighed.

'Nobody doubts Duke Godfrey's piety. But it is easy for him to renounce what he does not have. I possess Antioch, by right of conquest and of fact. I will not give it up.'

'Then I will stay here until you do.'

Three eyes – two hot with anger, one hard as iron – stared at each other. The lance's reliquary glittered on its pedestal between them, while murmurs of disappointment swelled all around. Most of it seemed to me to be directed at Count Raymond. Bohemond evidently thought the same, for the sound brought a cruel smile to his lips as he sat down again. Raymond remained on his feet, trembling like an oak tree under the first touch of the forester's axe.

'There will be a reckoning for this,' he warned. 'You are a thief, Bohemond – even your cursed father knew it when he disowned you. But you will not enjoy the spoils of your crime.'

Bohemond's face flushed crimson as his cloak, and though the smile remained fixed on his face I saw his curled fingers clenching involuntarily into fists. Even after rising from obscurity to become lord of Antioch and first among the princes, he could not forgive the father who had disowned him in preference to a younger half-brother from a second marriage. But he said nothing.

Godfrey rose. In the grey light of the church the princes' faces were dark and distraught – all except Bohemond, who seemed to glow with a savage energy. 'We came here to make peace: not to start a war. Have we grown so complacent since we defeated Kerbogha? We are beset by enemies on all sides. If you pursue this quarrel with Bohemond, Count Raymond, we will all die.'

'Not all of you,' said Bohemond. 'Only those who fight against me.'

'Jerusalem,' squeaked the bishop. 'Keep your hearts on Jerusalem. That is where we must go.'

'When we have finished our business here.'

The bishop stamped his foot, though you could not

hear it above the rising noise. He looked close to tears, as if he could not comprehend his impotence. 'In the name of Christ, I implore you, mend your quarrel and—'

'I will go to Jerusalem.' Bohemond's voice rose over the din and smothered it. 'I took an oath to capture the holy city or die, and I will fulfil it.'

The bishop stared at him hopefully. Raymond's face was dark with suspicion.

'But no army marches in January. Look out there.' He pointed through the church doors, which no one had thought to close since his entry. 'Can an army march through that? Let us wait until March, until the spring of the new year. When the earth has thawed and we can feed off the land, then we will go up to Jerusalem. I will lead the army there myself.'

'Hah!' Raymond strode to the centre of the square of benches and spun around, looking at each man in turn. He lifted the reliquary from its pillar and hugged it to his chest. 'It was a Provençal pope who preached this great pilgrimage, a Provençal bishop who guided us through our greatest perils, and a Provençal pilgrim who found this holy relic. It will be a Provençal who leads the army to Jerusalem, and it will be a Provençal who first stands atop its walls and looks down on the holy soil that Christ trod.'

He put the reliquary back down, hard, and leaned on its pedestal. His gaze bored into Bohemond, who did not quail but gave a short, dismissive laugh.

'I will not follow any man to Jerusalem. But I will go there with the Army of God.'

257

The Duke of Normandy stood. The worried expression that had creased his face from the start now threatened to fold it in two. 'I do not care who leads us to Jerusalem.' Approving cheers sounded around the church, though he did not seem to draw comfort from them. 'But I do not want to delay. In August we said we would wait until September. In September we delayed to November, in November we deferred to January and now Bohemond wishes us to wait again until March.' He spread his palms, showing empty hands. 'I mortgaged my dukedom to my dearest enemy, my brother the king of England, to pay for this pilgrimage. All I have earned by it are debt and suffering. If it brings me at last to Jerusalem, I will not begrudge one penny of it. But if our quest ends here, in pride and hatred, then my sacrifices and all our sacrifices will have been for nothing. Does any of us want that? I say we should march immediately, before I can no longer afford to keep my army.'

A wave of sympathetic murmurings echoed around the church. Embarrassed but grateful, the Duke of Normandy sat down and looked expectantly at Raymond.

Raymond hesitated. Without anger animating it, his face seemed old and haggard. 'I swear before Christ that I would march through storms and fields of ice to reach Jerusalem, fasting all the way. But I cannot leave injustice and usurpation behind. However . . .' He raised his arm. At the back of the church, I heard a commotion, and the grating of heavy boxes being dragged forward. 'If any man will follow me, then I will give him his reward.'

On cue, four knights appeared at the edge of the square of princes. Manoeuvring their way through a gap between benches, they manhandled two heavy strongboxes into the middle of the square. With fat keys they undid the locks that bound them, and pulled open the lids.

Every man in the church was standing, craning to see, as Count Raymond dug into one of the chests. A cascade of gold and silver coins fell from his hand as he lifted it.

'Who will join me in the battles to come?'

Bohemond moved forward, stepping around the reliquary so that he stood almost touching the count. Both men were tall but Bohemond had the advantage: he stared down on Raymond, cold scorn written across his face.

'It will take more than gold to buy you friends.'

'I did not offer it to you.'

'I would not have taken it.' Bohemond glanced around at the princes, perhaps sensing that he was looking on some of them for the last time. 'Take his money, if you like. Take it and make yourselves his servants. Feed his vanity and his envy. But when his gold runs out, or you tire of being an old man's pawn, come to Antioch and join me. I will be waiting there.'

He spun on his heel and walked to the door. Every footstep echoed like a hammer blow. He led his horse outside, hoisted himself into the saddle, and cantered away. The last I saw of him was his cloak swirling behind him, a blood-red stain against the white snow.

A cold breeze swept through the doors, as if the entire congregation had drawn breath. I glanced back at

Raymond, who stood still as a statue over his chests of treasure, his face vivid with triumph.

'We are well rid of him,' he declared, trying to force a jovial tone that did not suit the mood around him. 'But surely you will not spurn my generous offer. There is no shame in it,' he assured them.

The other princes glanced at each other uncertainly, refusing to meet his cajoling stare.

'I cannot take your gold.' All attention turned to Duke Godfrey. 'I refused the emperor of the Greeks when he offered his treasure, and now I refuse yours. I am the Duke of Lorraine from the line of Charlemagne himself; I cannot be any man's vassal.'

'You need not be my vassal,' Raymond pleaded. 'I do not need any return for my charity. All I want is the unity of the Army of God, and the speedy conquest of Jerusalem.'

'Then we want the same thing. But your gold will not make me want it more, and I can afford to pay my army myself. When you are ready to march to Jerusalem, and only then, I will join you – as a free man beholden to no one but God.'

Godfrey was not a natural orator: in public as in private, his manner felt brusque and detached. He had none of Bohemond's showmanship, nor the ability to whip up crowds to his cause. But his restraint, which too often seemed the product of arrogance, did confer a certain dignity. He bowed to Count Raymond, nodded to his fellow princes, and walked stiffly to the church door. His knights followed him out, threading their way through the thinning crowd.

'Duke Godfrey is right.' Now it was the Count of Flanders who spoke. 'I do not say that Bohemond is above reproach – but nor are you, Count Raymond. If you offer money to go to Jerusalem, then I am going there anyway; if you offer the money to fight Bohemond, then I reject it utterly.' He pushed his way out of the square, followed by his knights.

The triumph drained from Raymond's face though the smile remained fixed there, the skeleton of emotion. His hand trembled as he leaned on the reliquary's column for support.

'Is there any sensible man among you?' Desperation flecked his voice. 'Is there anyone whom Bohemond has not poisoned with his lies and malice?' As if to remind them of his riches, or perhaps out of nervous instinct, he dug his hand into the chest of gold again and let the coins trickle through his fingers.

'I will take your gold.' Tancred sauntered forward, immune to the stares of surprise and suspicion he drew. 'I am not too proud to accept aid if it will bring me closer to Jerusalem.'

He knelt before Raymond, putting his hands in the older man's. 'I swear—'

For the second time that day, the council was interrupted by the sound of hooves. Tancred broke off, while men looked back in fear lest Bohemond had returned with his knights to finish his feud. But there were no Norman hosts, only a single rider on a spent horse. Reining it in, he flung himself down and pushed his way into the church.

He wore no hat or helmet: his hair was tangled and filthy, and matted with crusts of ice. He must have ridden through the night.

He dropped to his knees before Count Raymond. 'Mercy, Lord,' he gasped, crossing himself. 'There is a mutiny among the pilgrims at Ma'arat. They have risen against your garrison and are tearing down the defences. They say they will not wait to proceed to Jerusalem, but must go immediately. God has willed it.'

ΚΑ

∽∽∽∽∽

The council ended in uproar. Count Raymond's men rushed to their camp and began pulling it down, churning the snow to slush, while grooms saddled horses and squires stuffed their belongings into saddlebags. With nothing to pack, I stood by my horse with Nikephoros and Aelfric and watched as, one by one, the princes hurried out of the town. Whatever hopes had existed for the union of the Army of God died in the snows of Rugia. Some marched north towards Antioch, others west to the coast. A few followed Raymond south to Ma'arat.

For all our haste, it was well after noon before we set out, and the sky was already darkening. Even then, we could not travel quickly. The fresh snow cast a treacherous veil over the ruts and holes in the road, and we had not gone far when we found it blocked completely by a fallen fir tree. I clutched my reins tighter, fearing an ambush, but it was only the weight of snow that had toppled the old tree. A company of Norman knights had already dismounted and were hacking at it with axes, while their captain walked his horse around them and shouted angry orders. He wheeled around as he heard our approach, and trotted up the road to meet us. Unruly curls stuck out from beneath his fur hat, and his dark eyes were alive with malice – which only deepened as he recognised me.

'Can it be Demetrios Askiates?' A soft, dangerous laugh. 'I saw you at the council. I had heard you were dead – or perhaps that you had gone to whore yourself to Ishmaelites.'

I fought back a wave of hatred and bile. I had not forgotten the vision of Tancred toying with Pakrad as he seared out his eyes at Ravendan. Nor was that the worst atrocity I had seen him inflict on captives during this campaign. I gestured to the tree. 'Has Count Raymond made you his forester, now that you have taken his gold and made yourself his servant?'

Tancred's horse shivered. Behind him, his men had managed to chop the tree free of its splintered stump. With a heave, they lifted the trunk off the road and rolled it into a ditch.

'You should be more careful when you address your betters,' Tancred warned me. 'Perhaps you do not know how much you have to lose.' Again the dangerous laugh. 'Have you had news of your family recently? They are not as safe as you suppose. If I were you, I would hurry to Ma'arat as quickly as I could.'

He had spurred his horse and was already moving, his last words almost drowned by wind and the beat of hooves. I kicked my own mount to follow, but she was a feeble creature compared with his. Before I had gone a hundred yards, he was lost from sight.

A chill dread held me in its grip for the rest of our ride. Night fell; further down the valley the snow had fallen as rain, turning the road to a bog, but Count Raymond insisted we press on through the darkness. Long before we reached Ma'arat, a writhing skein of flames in the sky ahead served as our beacon.

By midnight we had come close enough to see the individual fires burning ahead, and to make out the shadows of torn buildings around them. Soon, half a dozen fires seemed to break away from the main blaze like sparks, but they did not fly up and fade to cinders. Instead they drew nearer, growing larger and brighter until they resolved themselves into a troop of horsemen with torches in their hands. They halted before us and saluted.

'What has happened to my city?' Raymond demanded. 'Is this Bohemond's doing?'

The knight looked surprised. 'Bohemond has not been here. I thought he was at the council. This is Peter Bartholomew's work.'

Raymond pounded a fist on his saddle pommel, so hard that the horse below almost unseated him in its fright.

'Peter Bartholomew was under my patronage and my protection,' he raged. 'I sponsored his vanity so that he would keep the pilgrims obedient. Has he lost his command of them entirely?'

'Not at all. He preached this.'

All the men around Raymond edged back, anticipating another eruption of fury. Instead, he sat very still.

'It was yesterday evening, at sundown,' the knight continued. 'He summoned all the pilgrims and recounted a vision, how Saint Peter had appeared to him and revealed God's anger that His people suffered and delayed because of the avarice of princes.' The knight shot Raymond a fearful look. 'Forgive me, my lord, but that is what he said.'

'Go on.'

'He preached that a house built on error cannot stand. All at once a devilish madness seized the pilgrims and they spread through the town, grabbing mattocks and axes and firebrands – anything they could find that would destroy. They ran to the walls and began tearing them down, even with their bare hands.'

'And you did nothing to stop it?'

The knight swallowed hard. 'We tried, my lord. But the pilgrims were devious. Wherever we went they fled, only to reappear at another corner of the walls. We hanged any that we found but . . .' He shrugged. 'It has been going on a day and a night now. They are too many and we are too few. And there was nobody with your authority here to command them.'

Raymond heard all this in silence. The light from the

flickering torches did not reach his empty eye-socket, which loomed like a hole bored through his face.

'Come,' he said at last. 'Let us see what disaster Peter Bartholomew has worked.'

We rode on into the ruins of Ma'arat. Perhaps, before the Franks arrived, it had been a middlingly prosperous place on this lonely plateau; now it was a ruin. A ghoulish amber light filled the air like dawn, and by its glow we could see the devastation the pilgrims had wrought. At first sight, the destruction seemed wild, indiscriminate: some sections of wall were all but intact; in other places gaping holes rent the stone like cloth. Wisps of smoke rose from beneath the rubble, as though the very earth burned, and long stretches of the moat had been filled in with the debris.

Aelfric, riding beside me, gestured to the ruined defences. 'Frenzied peasants didn't do this.'

'No?' I was paying little attention, for I had other concerns. Tancred's taunt still echoed in my mind. What if Anna was somewhere in this smouldering chaos?

'Not unless the devil possessed them with the spirits of siege engineers. It takes more than zeal and a hammer to collapse ten-foot-thick walls, and I never heard of a wild crowd taking it into their heads to dig sapping tunnels. Look.' Aelfric pointed ahead of us, to where a felled gate now made a makeshift bridge over the moat. The towers that had flanked it were dissolved completely, and even the rubble had been carted away or used to fill in ditches.

'They couldn't have done that alone. Whatever the

count's steward protests, they had help from men who knew what they were doing.'

'Bohemond's agents, do you think?'

Aelfric shrugged. 'Perhaps.'

A sense of dread began to build in me as we approached the centre of the town. The streets were eerily empty, but the sounds of ruination were all around us: long screams abruptly choked off, shouts of alarm, the crackle of fire and the crash of tumbling stone. Somewhere near by we could hear singing, a sad sound like a lament for the ruined town. We followed the noise, listening to it swell as we rode down deserted streets. *Where was Anna?* I scanned every alley, every window and every door, desperate for a glimpse of her, but the shadows were too deep.

We came around a corner into the main square of the town. Suddenly, all the life that had been hidden in the empty town was thrust before us. A host of pilgrims packed the square, singing the mournful song that now engulfed us, staring at the church on the eastern side where two bonfires burned brightly. The flames played over the stone like sunlight on water, while a tall figure dressed all in white stood on the roof and stared down at the congregation. His hands were folded into his sleeves and his head was turned to heaven, as if it were he whom the pilgrims hymned.

Not one of the pilgrims turned around as Raymond rode in, yet they parted before him like waves before a ship's prow. Their song grew louder, almost deafening. I could not make out the words – perhaps it was a psalm, thought it might have been the tongue of angels for the fervour with which they sang it. On the dais at the front, Peter Bartholomew stood in a white robe.

Raymond had ridden to within about twenty yards of the church when suddenly he found the crowd would yield no further. He looked back, but that path had vanished. The pilgrim ranks had closed in, and he was marooned in their midst.

The man on the church stretched out his hands. For a moment it seemed that he did not have the mastery of the congregation I had expected, for they persisted with their song, rendering it louder still until the noise was almost deafening. And then, with a discipline so abrupt it left me breathless, they stopped, and there was nothing but an overwhelming silence.

A thousand pairs of eyes turned to Count Raymond. For a moment I feared he would buckle under the weight of their stares, but he recovered himself enough to call out in a ringing voice, 'Peter Bartholomew, what have you done?'

The man on the church stared down at him as dispassionately as an icon – though not nearly as beautiful. He had let his hair and beard grow long; his nose was misshapen where it had once or twice been broken, and the erratic firelight could not soften the hard pox marks on his face. Even so, he had climbed a long way since he crawled out of the pit at Antioch clutching the fragment of the holy lance.

'What I have done is God's will,' he declared. His voice was deeper than I remembered it, echoing off the surrounding walls. '*For lo, I will send a man to make straight the way of the Lord . . .*'

Raymond sat up straight. 'That is blasphemy.'

A quiet sigh carried through the crowd, and they seemed to press closer around the count. He looked down uncertainly.

'It is prophecy,' Peter answered calmly. He seemed to be clutching something in his right hand: a tablet, or maybe a book. 'Look around you. The Lord has sent these men out as sheep among wolves, and now their shepherd has abandoned them. You have tried to make your kingdom here, and forsaken the celestial kingdom that awaits us in Jerusalem.'

'I have not forsaken Jerusalem,' Raymond protested. His voice was brittle. 'I have the unity of the Army of God to consider.'

'Listen to your people. They are crying out to go to Jerusalem. You built your house here and they tore it down, stone from stone, because it was not built on the rock of faith. If you will not lead us to Zion then we will leave you here, abandoned and defenceless, for your enemies to pick over.'

'The time is not right,' Raymond murmured, almost to himself. 'It is madness to campaign in winter. None of the other princes will support this folly.'

'Then your glory will be all the greater.' Peter's voice was warm, the coaxing voice of a sympathetic friend. 'But if you do not go, your name will be ignominy, and your reputation dust.'

His hold on the crowd was astonishing. When he spoke kindly they stood there as docile and comforting as sheep, but as soon as he uttered a threat you could almost feel the anger ignite. I began to wonder what would happen to me if Count Raymond provoked Peter Bartholomew to violence.

Raymond looked away from Peter, scanning the crowd in the desperate hope of allies. Among the peasants' hoods and straw-brimmed hats I saw a good number of armoured helmets, but none of them showed the least impulse to help their lord.

'You have disobeyed my laws and offended against my authority,' he said, addressing the crowd directly. 'But disperse now, remake what you have broken and yield up the wicked men who led you astray and I will show mercy.'

It was a brave gesture from an old warrior, but he had been lured into a battle he could not win. Peter Bartholomew did not even need to reply: the sea of impassive, upturned faces around Raymond was all the answer he needed. From somewhere near the back a voice whispered 'Jerusalem', and very quickly the word spread until it resounded through the host like the crash of waves.

Raymond pressed his hands together as if in prayer, and bowed his head. At a sign from Peter Bartholomew, the pilgrims fell silent.

'Ready your arms and gather up what food you can find.' His voice trembled, perhaps from piety, though it sounded more like the edge of tears. 'In three days, we will march to Jerusalem.'

The chains of tension that had bound the crowd fell away, and all at once they erupted in a frenzied outburst of cheers, hymns and wild prayers. Banners waved in front of the fires, fanning the flames; Count Raymond was carried from his horse and lifted up to the church roof, where he stood beside Peter Bartholomew to receive the jubilant acclaim of the crowd. All memory of his reluctance was forgiven in an instant. Even those around me, at the very fringe of the gathering, had tears of joy glistening in their eyes as they prostrated themselves before Raymond and Peter.

I felt a tug on my stirrup and looked down to see Aelfric. I had not noticed him leave, but he must have gone somewhere and returned in haste, for he was breathing hard. His breath made clouds in the cold night air.

'Come with me,' he gasped. 'I have found them.'

κβ

∾∾∾∾∾

Aelfric led me to a door in a sandstone wall. I could not see the house above, but it seemed untouched by the mob – perhaps because of the two black crosses daubed in ashes on either side of the entrance. Aelfric thumped twice on the door. After a moment it cracked open, then swung in so fast I almost lost my balance. The room inside was dark; I could not make out the figure within, though I could see the gleam of armour and the familiar half-moon silhouette of a Varangian axe in his hands.

'Sigurd?' He looked slighter than I remembered, and I wondered how long it had taken him to recover from his wounds.

He stepped forward into the street. The glow from the fires that illuminated the night sky made his beard seem to copper, the same colour as Sigurd's – but it was an illusion. Instead of Sigurd's mane, his hair – which in daylight would be the colour of straw – hung in girlish curls to his shoulders. Instead of battle-scars, his smooth face was marked by nothing more than pimples and unpractised shaving.

It was a year and a half since I had seen him. Then he had been a boy, just starting to resemble the man he would become. Now he was almost unrecognisable.

'Thomas?' I stammered.

'*Petheros?* Father-in-law?'

Wary disbelief shrouded his face. We were close enough that his armoured chest almost brushed mine, but we did not touch.

'How . . . ?'

'The emperor sent my company from Byzantium. We arrived two days after you left for Egypt.'

'I wish you had not come.' Belatedly, and somewhat awkwardly, I clasped his arm. 'But it's good to see you. Have you had news of Helena and Zoe? How were they when you left? What of the baby? Was it delivered safely?' The questions poured out of me, a year's worth of hopes and fears written in each one. But Thomas was shying away. His eyes flickered down to the ground, then looked up defiantly as I fell silent.

'The baby is healthy, praise God. It was hard for Helena – especially the journey so soon afterwards – but she's well now. She will be happy to see you safely returned from Egypt. When we heard where you had gone, she was almost inconsolable.'

274

In the flood of emotion, it was hard to keep hold of everything he said. But even so, I could tell there was something wrong in what he said. 'How did she know where I had gone?'

I suddenly remembered Tancred's taunt on the road from Rugia. *Have you had news of your family recently? They are not as safe as you suppose.* I had thought he meant Anna, who was not family but should have been. Instead . . .

'Where are my daughters?'

Thomas stepped back. While we spoke, someone had lit lamps inside the room, and the household had gathered to see who had called so late. They stood in the middle of the room, staring at me. Sigurd, as vast and imposing as I remembered him, dressed in his armour even at that hour of the night. Anna, her dark hair tumbling loose over her face, not hiding the tears. And beside them, two smaller figures with blankets around their shoulders. One clutched a perilously small baby to her breast, and both were staring at me like Mary and Martha at Lazarus. My daughters: Zoe and Helena.

It was eighteen months since I had seen my children. When I left Constantinople Helena had been a bride, barely out of the church. Though only three years separated them, Zoe had seemed so young she might equally have been Helena's daughter as her sister. Now Helena was a mother: new cares had chiselled away the curves of her face, leaving it lean and serious, while a taut strength imbued the arms that cradled the baby. Zoe's face too was creased with concern, but in her it had the perverse effect of making her look younger, more innocent.

'What did you call the baby?' I asked at last.

'Everard. It was Thomas's father's name,' said Helena.

'Everard,' I repeated, manipulating the foreign sounds around my mouth. Thomas's father, the baby's grandfather, had been a pilgrim in the vanguard of the Army of God, part of a rabble who fell under the spell of a charismatic holy-man and believed they were invincible because he told them so. The Turks had shattered that illusion as soon as they crossed into Asia Minor, and paved a road with their bones. Thomas had been one of the few to survive: he had escaped to Constantinople, where I had found him and he had found Helena.

'Ever since I left home I've longed to see you,' I said at last. 'But not here. I was . . . on my way back to you. You should not have come for me.'

I saw immediately that I had said something wrong. Zoe took a bunch of hair in her mouth and began chewing it, while Helena looked up defiantly.

'We didn't come for you.'

'Then why . . . ?'

'We came because of Thomas,' Zoe blurted out. 'He made us.'

I rounded on Thomas. 'You? What have you done? My daughters—'

Thomas's face darkened. '*My* wife – and *my* son. Their place is with me.'

'Their place is in safety. At home.'

In my anger, I had spoken too loudly and disturbed the baby. He pulled away from Helena's breast and began to squeal, while Helena dabbed at his mouth and rocked him in her arms.

'I didn't marry Helena to lift her on a pedestal and then carry her with me in my memories,' said Thomas. 'I have left enough family behind. I married her to live with her. And this is where we are.'

'Only because you brought them here.'

'I am a Varangian now. I go where the emperor commands. Like you. You should thank me,' he added aggressively. 'If I had not brought Helena and Zoe here, you might never have seen them again. Or your grandson.'

I put out my arm and leaned on the door frame to steady myself. Outside, I could hear excited shouts echoing off the square, and the crash and tumble of more walls being torn down. It sounded like the end of the world.

'You should not have come,' I said again. 'In three days' time, Raymond's army will set out for Jerusalem. I will have to go with them – Nikephoros will not give me a choice. As for you ...' I tried to think my way out of the dark labyrinth I had fallen into, but every way I turned, the way was blocked. The Normans controlled the ports and Antioch, while Duke Godfrey's army sat camped on the road north. I could not send my family that way. Nor could I abandon them in the ruins of Ma'arat.

Sigurd laid his axe on the table and began unlacing his boots. 'It looks as though we'll all see Jerusalem.'

'Or die in the attempt.'

ΚΥ

∽∾∽∾∽

The smoke still rose over Ma'arat when we left it three days later. Defeated by Bohemond and humbled by Peter Bartholomew, Raymond had indulged his pique by completing the work the pilgrims had begun. He razed the town, so that none should have it if he could not. A chill fog came down, mingling with hot smoke from the burning until you could not tell one from the other, but walked everywhere wrapped in cloud.

Trumpets sounded, and after a few minutes a dim figure appeared as a shadow in the mist. He was on foot – barefoot, I saw as he drew closer – and the only sound he made was the slow staccato beat of his staff tapping the ground. He did not wear armour, nor any of his magnificent finery, but merely a grey pilgrim's robe. His bare head was slumped low, either in contemplation or because he could not bear to see his army watching him thus. With smoke in the air and a warm breeze breathing out of Ma'arat, he might have been Lot fleeing fire and brimstone in the punished city of Sodom. He did not look back.

Next, seated on an emaciated donkey, came Peter Bartholomew, carrying the reliquary of the holy lance on a purple cushion. There was no humility in his bearing, forced or otherwise: he stared at the soldiers lining the road with aloof dignity, almost defying them to adore him. None of the Varangians indulged him, but many of the Provençals offered shouts of praise or threw stalks of grass – there were no flowers – at his feet. Some even sank to their knees as he passed and offered ostentatious prayers for his safety.

Nikephoros, mounted beside me, leaned across and murmured in my ear, 'Count Raymond looks more like Peter's groom than his lord.'

I nodded, nervous of speaking ill of Peter Bartholomew among that crowd. 'At least he has done what we could not, and forced Count Raymond on to Jerusalem.'

'Hah.' Nikephoros broke off and inclined his head respectfully as the count came level with us. When he had passed, Nikephoros continued, 'Raymond should be more careful. If he allows himself to be seen looking like Peter Bartholomew's servant, soon people will start to believe it.'

'I think Peter Bartholomew already does.'

'All the more danger. And what do you suppose he intends next?'

I looked at Nikephoros in surprise. 'Intends?'

'He has a hold on the pilgrims' affection. Count Raymond has leaned on that as a crutch to his popularity for some time. Now that Peter Bartholomew has seen that he can bend the count to his will, do you think he will stop there?'

I shrugged. 'Something has changed. He used to be content with his fame, to soak up the adulation he earned by finding the lance.'

'Then perhaps he got a fright when it began to seep away from him.' Nikephoros gave a grim, self-mocking laugh. 'It can be a painful ordeal, losing the power you once enjoyed.'

For the next week the Army of God trudged south. There was little pretence at haste – some days we made so little progress that at dusk the rearguard pitched their tents where the vanguard had camped the night before – but day by day we inched our way further from Ma'arat, closer to Jerusalem. Peasants, priests and soldiers mingled freely, so that it felt not like a military expedition but as if a whole town had been uprooted and set in motion. Smiths loitered at the roadside offering to re-shoe horses or sharpen blades; peddlers and barterers conducted a lively exchange of clothes, boots, tools and gold; women brought baskets of bread or eggs or even chickens to sell, for now that we were out of the well-scoured lands of Ma'arat food was plentiful.

But for all we might be a wandering town, it was a town

under constant siege. Every day, bands of Saracens would descend from their hilltop castles to harry our column, peppering us with arrows, breaking our carts and stealing livestock or unfortunate stragglers. Once or twice Tancred's cavalry sallied out to try and punish the attackers and free the captives, but after two of his knights were killed he called off the sorties. It was even worse in the dark. However closely we huddled our camp together and however many fires we lit, each dawn revealed fresh losses: sentries with their throats cut, stores ransacked and women missing. Though I should have been happy to see my family again, it preyed on my nerves to have them there. I slept little, standing watch outside the tent into the dead hours until Sigurd or Thomas relieved me, then lying awake with my ears pricked open, trying to warm myself against Anna's body. At least Sigurd seemed restored to his natural humour. Moody and abrasive he might be, but against the uneasy cloud that hovered over my family he was a simple, reassuring bulwark.

Five days out of Ma'arat, we reached a place called Shaizar. High bluffs rose on either side of a broad river valley, and on a spur a formidable castle commanded the crossing. Sigurd looked at it from a distance and groaned.

'If we have to capture castles each time we ford a river or climb a mountain, Christ himself will have returned to Jerusalem before we get there.'

But for once his pessimism was misplaced. The local emir had heard of the Franks' exploits at Antioch and

281

Ma'arat, and drawn the conclusion that cooperation was his wisest course. He offered us safe passage through his lands and plied the princes with gifts.

We made our camp by the river that evening, in the shadow of the castle. While Thomas and Helena went to find firewood, and Zoe prepared food, Anna and I walked down to the river bank. In all the time since I had returned we had had few moments alone together, and even those had been fleeting and awkward. However much we might resist the idea, months of separation had driven a distance between us.

We clambered out on a rocky point and sat by the water's edge. A little way downstream a group of women were washing clothes, singing as they worked, but we were alone. I pulled off my boots and let the stream cool my weary blisters.

'I wonder what this river is called.' I leaned forward, scooping the water up in my hands and drinking. 'Is it one of the four rivers of Eden, do you think?'

Anna laughed, and wiped away the droplets that beaded my beard. 'Didn't you know? This is the Orontes.'

'I thought we had left it behind at Antioch.' I imagined kicking out into the river and letting it carry me back, beneath the walls we had besieged so long and all the way out to the sea.

Anna pulled up her knees and hugged them to her chest. 'Sometimes it seems we'll be wandering in circles for ever, until even the last of us is dead.'

It was unlike Anna to be so morose. I slipped my hand

into hers and held it. *Marry me*, I wanted to say. *Marry me now. Find a priest, even a Frankish one, and have him marry us before God.* I did not dare.

'At least we're on the road to Jerusalem again.'

'We've been on the road for the best part of two years.' Anna pulled her hand free. I edged away, pretending to peer in the water for fish.

'Two years of our lives,' she repeated. 'Two years when we should have been playing with our grandchildren and laughing with our families. And now that we have them with us at last, it only makes things worse.'

'You should have sent them home.'

Anna shook her head. 'They arrived just after you left for Egypt. I was in Antioch, caring for the plague victims. By the time I knew they had arrived there were no ships to take them away – and they would not have gone in any case.' She touched my arm gingerly. 'It is not what I would have chosen for them. But you must understand Thomas. He has already lost his family once; he could not bear to be parted from them again.'

'Even if all that meant was being with them at their death?'

'Even so.'

'He is not the only man who loves Helena.' I pressed my bare foot into the river bed, feeling cold mud ooze around it. 'And his son may have a Frankish name, but he has my blood in his veins as well.'

'Do you think I haven't told Thomas all this? And Helena, too. But she would follow him wherever he asked

283

– even if he didn't ask – and he loves her too much to let her go.'

'He'll be left holding onto her corpse if he clings so tight.'

Anna gave a sad smile. 'That is the risk we all take. But you should be kinder to him. When you were his age and the emperor's armies stormed Constantinople, did you send your daughters away to safety? Your wife?'

I had never been happy discussing Maria with Anna. It always felt that I was trying to squeeze them both into the same place in my soul, a place where only one could fit. I could see immediately from Anna's face that she regretted it, but that did not temper the anger in my words.

'I protected my wife and child in our home – as men are supposed to do. I didn't drag them a thousand miles *away* from home to die in a famished, plague-stricken wilderness of barbarians and Ishmaelites.'

Tears gleamed in the corners of Anna's eyes as she rose. 'It's too late to tell him that. Too late for any of us.'

I sat there for a time after she had left, until even the river no longer numbed my cares. Then I pulled on my boots and walked back towards our tent. It lay on the far side of the pilgrim camp: I tried to avoid going that way if I could, but night was hastening on and there was no good reason to fear anything – only a vague sense of unease. For so long the pilgrims had been an encumbrance, a mute and obedient shadow behind the main army. Now, in Peter

Bartholomew, they had begun to find their voice, and it was an unsettling sound.

I was almost at the far edge of the pilgrim camp when suddenly I came around a row of tents and found my way barred by a knot of peasants. They had gathered around a preacher: I did not think he was a priest, for he wore only a simple white tunic, but he held his audience rapt.

'Think of the mustard seed. When you sow it in the earth it is the least of seeds, yet it grows to greatness. In the same way, the kingdom of God will grow from the least of his people. The last shall be first, and the first last.'

I was about to slip away and find another route, when suddenly I noticed two familiar figures standing at the edge of the gathering. Thomas and Helena, watching intently. Helena held Everard in her arms.

'The time will come when the Lord will send two great prophets, Enoch and Elijah, back into the world. They will prepare God's elect for the coming storm with three and a half years of teaching and preaching. Three and a half years,' he repeated ominously. 'When did we set out from our homes?'

'Three years ago,' someone called from the crowd.

'Three years ago.' He leaned forward, lowering his voice. 'The prophets are already abroad. First Enoch – and now Elijah. There is not much time.'

I had almost reached Helena, when a voice in the crowd beside me asked: 'But where will we find the prophet?'

The preacher answered with a gap-toothed smile, as if

he had expected the question. 'Come with me, and I will show you. He has much to teach you, and little time.'

He beckoned them on. Several stepped forward immediately, hope bright on their faces; others hung back. The preacher gave them a pitying smile.

'Have you forgotten the prophecy of Isaiah? *You will listen but never understand; you will look but never perceive.* Come now and see.'

He turned around, and began shepherding his converts deeper into the camp. Some of the waverers hurried after him, while others – shamefaced and sullen – drifted away. Thomas and Helena looked as though they were about to follow, when my hands gripped their shoulders and spun them around.

'What are you doing here?' I demanded. 'You were supposed to be fetching firewood.' I pointed to their empty hands. 'Did you have nothing better to do than listen to charlatans preaching nonsense?'

Thomas's face hardened but he said nothing. Helena was less restrained. 'What are you doing spying on us? I am not your girlish daughter any more. I will go where I choose, hear what I choose and believe what I choose.'

I looked at Thomas. 'You, most of all, should know the dangers of following self-ordained prophets on the path to heaven. Your parents certainly found it out.'

Thomas looked at me as if he could have cut my throat. His hateful stare transfixed me, until at last Helena took his hand and pulled him away into the twilight.

*　　*　　*

286

Later that night, I crawled across to Helena's corner of the tent and lay next to her.

'I'm sorry. I should not have said what I did.' I spoke softly, trying not to wake the baby. For a long moment I thought I had been too quiet, for the only reply was slow breathing, but I did not dare repeat myself.

At last, still lying with her back to me, she whispered, 'You cannot teach Thomas the lessons of his own past.'

But why doesn't he learn them? I did not say it. Instead: 'I don't want you to die like his mother and father.'

'Neither do I. But he is my husband, and I am the mother of his son. You cannot expect me to live locked away from the world like a nun.'

I thought of the monks in the Egyptian desert, invisible to the outside world. 'There are places on this earth between the convent and the front line of battle.'

She rolled over. 'Not where Thomas is. And not where you are.'

We lay there in silence, facing each other a few inches apart. Once there had been no distance there, when she and her mother and a newborn Zoe and I all shared the same bed.

'I cannot make Thomas learn the mistakes of his parents, any more than I can make you learn from mine.'

Helena gave a small laugh, which reminded me of younger, happier times, then broke off as she remembered the baby. 'A lifetime would not be long enough to learn from your mistakes,' she teased.

'Probably not.' I fumbled in the dark for her hand and

squeezed it. 'I know Thomas has suffered pains and horrors I can barely imagine. He has my pity.'

In the darkness of the tent, I sensed Helena stiffen. 'He does not need pity. He needs love.'

'Love, too. But he must not let his hurt drive him to oblivion. He has too much to lose.'

On Helena's far side, the baby started to cough. She turned over, and I heard a tapping as she patted its back, like soft footsteps approaching.

Four days after leaving Shaizar, we reached a crossroads. To the south, a broad road followed the river valley; to the west, another road led towards the snow-capped mountains we could see in the distance and thence, our guides assured us, to the sea. Raymond summoned Tancred, Robert of Normandy and Nikephoros to debate our choice. As ever, I accompanied Nikephoros to translate. Though a month in the Franks' company must have taught him something of the common dialect, I think he would rather have cut his tongue out than allowed the barbarian sounds to touch it.

'The southerly road looks easier.' Duke Robert craned his head and stared, as if he might see all the way to Jerusalem if he looked hard enough.

'But that road goes by Damascus,' said Nikephoros. 'There you would find yourselves trapped before another Antioch. You could besiege it for a year and never take it.'

'Perhaps the lord of Damascus would give us safe passage, like the lord of Shaizar,' Robert suggested.

Raymond twitched his head to dismiss the idea. 'He might – if Bohemond had not slaughtered half his army at Antioch a year ago.'

'Then what lies the other way, past the mountains?'

'The coast,' answered Nikephoros. 'Go that way, and the emperor's grain ships can supply you from the sea.'

'If we can capture a harbour. The coastal road is guarded by a chain of fortified ports. Arqa, Tripoli, Sidon and Tyre, Acre, Caesarea, Jaffa.' Raymond's face darkened as he recited them. 'If we besiege every one of them, we'll have exhausted the emperor's granaries long before we reach Jerusalem.'

'We will not need to capture each of them,' said Tancred confidently. 'The reputation of Antioch and Ma'arat will carry before us and open their gates. Otherwise, we'll sack the first city we see, raze it to the ground and teach the rest what awaits them if they resist us.'

Raymond nodded absent-mindedly, distracted by a movement behind us. A rider had ridden out from the army to join us, with half a dozen acolytes scampering on foot behind him. It was Peter Bartholomew, who seemed to have exchanged his donkey for a full-grown horse, a snow-white mare. He perched awkwardly in the saddle, unaccustomed to the motion or the height, and struggled to rein in his mount as he reached us.

'Why have we stopped?' he demanded.

'We heard that the crown of thorns was hidden in a thicket near by, and thought you might be able to find it,' said Tancred.

Peter Bartholomew flushed, and made a fumbling sign across his chest to ward off evil. Saying nothing to Tancred, he turned and looked at the fork in the road. 'Which way leads to Jerusalem?'

'Both of them.'

Peter considered this for a while, staring at the different paths. It was the same gaze that he could fix on a man – frank, penetrating and overwhelming – as if you could not imagine the thoughts and judgements that passed behind his eyes. No one interrupted him, not even Nikephoros.

At last he blinked, and pointed towards Damascus. 'We should go that way.'

'Who asked you?' growled Tancred. He turned to Count Raymond. 'When I offered you my service I thought I would be led by the Count of Toulouse, not an ignorant peasant. Who is in command of this army?'

'The Lord God,' said Peter primly.

'*I am in command.*' Raymond's eye raked over the watching faces; no one, not even Peter Bartholomew, contradicted him.

'Then which way do *you* say we go?' A blade of insolence hovered under Tancred's question.

Raymond jerked his head around, first to the wending road to Damascus, then the steep path that descended past the mountains towards the sea.

'We will camp here tonight. I will announce my decision in the morning.'

κδ

∽∽∽∽∽

But there was no decision the next day, nor even the day after. Word went out that this was to allow us to replenish our supplies, for the inhabitants of this country had fled before our advance and abandoned their granaries for us to plunder. That was fortunate for Count Raymond, for even the most ardent pilgrim would not complain of the pause if given the chance to fill his belly.

'But he cannot delay much longer,' Nikephoros told me on the second day. 'Once the pilgrims have eaten, they will be doubly eager to march on to Jerusalem.'

'What do you think Raymond will decide?'

Nikephoros leaned forward. Even on campaign he wore a dalmatic sewn with a crust of gems, which stretched and sank above his shoulders as they moved. 'The road to

Damascus is a dead end: the only way we will ever reach Jerusalem is by the coast. Raymond knows that. He only delays because he is too frightened to contradict Peter Bartholomew.'

When did peasants learn to direct the affairs of armies? I wondered. Perhaps the preacher had been right: perhaps the meek had inherited the earth and the mighty fallen from their seats. Perhaps.

'Have you tried to convince him?'

'Every day.' Nikephoros snapped a stick of sealing wax in two. 'If force of argument could move a man, I would have propelled him all the way to the gates of Jerusalem by now. He will not listen to me.'

There was a pause. Nikephoros squeezed the broken wax in his hand, crumbling it over the desk.

'I could try,' I said at last.

He looked up. 'You? What could you say to Count Raymond that I have not?'

'Not Count Raymond: Peter Bartholomew.'

Nikephoros said nothing but gestured me to go on. The wax had stained his hand red.

'Peter Bartholomew has not always been the pillar of righteousness he is now. His past has been . . . erratic.' I shrugged. 'Perhaps if I remind him of it he will prove more amenable.'

I did not trust my powers of persuasion so much that I would go alone. I tried to find Sigurd, but he had gone foraging; instead, I took Thomas. We walked without speaking. The silence weighed on me desperately, but I could not think of anything to say that was not trite or patronising.

Soon we crossed the open ground that divided the two camps and entered the pilgrims' domain. A hostile atmosphere seemed to menace us all about. Even when we could see no one I felt the prickling sense of being watched; elsewhere, wide-eyed peasants sat under their makeshift shelters – sheets tied to branches, or awnings hung in the spaces between larger tents – and stared openly. But no one touched us or tried to stop us.

We found Peter Bartholomew in the very heart of the camp – but he was not alone. In a circle of open ground among the tents, a large crowd had gathered around a makeshift stage. A tall cross towered over it, high enough to crucify a man, and there, in its shadow, stood Peter Bartholomew. He was speaking, his voice reaching every corner of the crowd.

'This morning, before the sun was up, the holy Saint Peter appeared again before me.'

A murmur of expectation ran through the crowd.

'I had prayed, in all our names, that the Lord God would show His servant the way to Jerusalem.'

With Thomas behind me, I pushed my way into the crowd. It swayed and heaved as if possessed by a vital spirit all its own.

'And suddenly Saint Peter was there in a haze of golden light. Two keys swung from his belt, and he held the staff of judgement in his hands. I dropped to my knees.'

Enraptured by the memory, Peter sank to his knees. Every man and woman in the crowd did likewise.

"'Command me, Lord,' I said, and in an instant I was lifted up high into the air.' Peter stood and stretched out his arms; the crowd remained kneeling. 'The wizened earth lay beneath me, her mountains like pebbles and her oceans like pools of rainwater. In the south, a thin river snaked away towards a great city, from where I heard cries and lamentations.

"'What city is that?' I asked, and the saint answered, "Jerusalem."

"'And why does she cry out?'

"'Because the king of Babylon has come to her. He has set his throne in Solomon's temple, and has slain every true Christian who resisted him,' said the saint. "You must hasten and relieve her distress."

'We fell from the sky like thunder and were back in the tent. "This sacred journey is only for the pure of heart," the saint warned me. "If you wander and are lost, it is because there are sinners among you. You must root them out like weeds among the corn."

"'My followers are pure and devout,' I protested, but he silenced me with a flash of his eyes. "There are some among your flock who even now blaspheme and sin against the Lord," he told me. "This very night, the knight Amanieu of Vienne has lain in adultery with the wife of Reynauld the blacksmith.'"

Anger hissed through the crowd and they stood, as two people shuffled onto the platform. Both their heads were shaved bare: it was only when they turned to face the audience that I saw to my shock that one was a woman. She stood there in a flimsy grey shift, her eyes swollen and her skull scraped red. A young man, little older than Thomas, stood beside her in a similar state – only the rise of the woman's breasts under the shift marked them apart. Peter Bartholomew stood between them, holding out his arms so that it looked as if he embraced them.

'The penalty for adultery, laid down in the law of Moses, is death.'

The crowd stirred, nodding their agreement.

'But Christ taught us to love the sinner. That through true repentance, we could overcome the sinful clay of our flesh and perfect the spark of divine spirit within.'

He looked slowly at each of his prisoners in turn. Both stood there in silence.

'All sins must be laid bare.'

Rough hands reached forward, tearing away the grey shifts the adulterers wore. A gasp of sanctimonious delight shot through the crowd. The two lovers stood naked before them, trembling in the chill air but otherwise unmoving. The man wore a cloth tied around his hips, but the woman was entirely naked. Her breasts pricked up in the cold, while the white lines of childbearing spidered her belly like scars. I wondered if her children were in the audience now to see their mother's shame.

All around me I felt a charge in the air, the smouldering iron taste on my tongue I had sometimes felt before a storm or a battle. I turned to Thomas.

'Go and find Count Raymond,' I whispered. 'Tell him to come with his knights. Go.'

Thomas's eyes darted over my shoulder to the stage, mesmerised by the spectacle. I cuffed him on his cheek. '*Go.*'

He tore his gaze away and pushed out of the crowd. Back on the stage, the adulterers were now on their knees. Two men stood over them with switches in their hands, the green wood quivering.

Peter Bartholomew stepped back and lifted a hand as if in blessing.

'Thy will be done, O Lord.'

The hand dropped. An involuntary moan of excitement rose from the crowd and they pushed forward. The switches came down, rose, and dropped again, rising and falling in ever faster rhythm. The crowd had fallen silent, holding themselves still, as though they did not trust themselves even to breathe. Their lips and cheeks were flushed with blood, their bodies taut and erect. Even the women watched without modesty; many seemed more passionate than the men, flinching as each blow struck home. The only sounds were the hiss of wood in the air, and the abrupt snap as it cut into the naked flesh beneath. Soon every blow produced a spray of blood, though not a single droplet stained the whiteness of Peter Bartholomew's robe. His hands were crossed penitently before him, his lips parted in rapture, but he never closed his eyes or lifted his gaze from the punishment before him. Where was Raymond?

I suppose I had seen many men beaten in my time, but this sickened me. I could not watch the naked wretches, for even that felt like complicity. I looked over my shoulder, praying that Raymond would come. When I turned back, my gaze involuntarily fell on the stage. The noise of the blows had stopped, and the beaters had lifted up the victims to display their punishment. It was a gruesome sight. Blood had run down their sides and embraced them all around: it trickled down the woman's breasts, smeared her belly and matted in the fair hair between her thighs. With her bare head, she reminded me terribly of a newborn baby fresh from the womb. The man was in little better state.

Peter stepped forward. He held himself very still, the quivering restraint of a man who knew the slightest touch might cause him to disgorge himself. A bead of spittle dribbled from his mouth.

'Truly it is said, there is more joy in heaven over one sinner that repents than ninety-nine who never strayed.' He stretched out his arms again. 'Do you repent?'

The battered man cleared his throat, spitting gobs of blood on the stage. 'I repent,' he croaked.

'And you?' Peter turned to the woman, struggling to keep the leer from his face. 'Do you repent of your sins?'

She mumbled something I could not hear. It evidently satisfied Peter. He crouched down, and appeared to draw or write something in the blood on the stage with his finger. 'Your flesh has been made clean, purged with suffering and redeemed in blood.'

He crooked a beckoning finger towards the crowd. Three men climbed onto the stage, carrying a brazier between them, and set it down beside Peter. He pulled the poker from the fire. A dull orange heat smouldered in its tip, which I saw was forged in the sign of the cross. Two men took the woman by the arms, though she did not resist or even flinch, and turned her to face Peter.

'Receive the mark of Christ as a sign of your penitence. Let it live in your flesh, as He lives in your soul.'

Somewhere in the distance a rumbling began. Some in the crowd looked to the heavens; others glanced over their shoulders and made the sign of the cross. Peter paused.

A host of mounted knights broke into the clearing. Tents tottered and collapsed as flying hooves kicked over the stakes and pegs that held them. As they met the pilgrim throng the horsemen turned aside, riding around the fringe of the crowd like dogs herding sheep. Last of all, flanked by four knights in full armour, came Count Raymond. He lowered his lance and trotted forward, using the tip to prise a path between the pilgrims until he could look down at the blood-soaked figures cowering on the stage.

'Amanieu? Amanieu of Vienne? What have these peasants done to you?' He swung around towards Peter. 'How dare you touch a knight of mine, let alone inflict . . . *this*?' For all the vicious battles he had fought and the blood he had spilled, there was genuine shock in Raymond's voice.

Peter put the branding iron back in the brazier. Sparks flew up from the coals. 'This man was caught in adultery.

The laws of Moses and of Christ demand punishment.'

For all I would willingly have stabbed the branding iron through Peter's heart at that moment, a part of me marvelled at the transformation wrought in him. Not so long ago he had been a snivelling, pox-scarred wretch of no consequence, who might have died a hundred times over on the march from Constantinople and never been remembered. Now he stood on the dais in his spotless robe and serenely traded words with the greatest prince of the age. What could have changed a man like that?

Raymond pricked his horse with his spurs and pulled on its reins, so that it reared up. Its hooves flailed in the air, terrifyingly close to Peter Bartholomew's head.

'I am the authority,' Raymond snarled. 'I say who is guilty and what their punishment will be. As for you, even to touch one of my knights is death.'

'This was not my doing,' protested Peter. 'My disciple Amanieu, and the woman he lay with – they sinned, and they knew they must be punished. It is to save their own souls. Do you see any bonds restraining them?'

Raymond turned to the knight.

'Is this true, Amanieu?'

The knight, naked and streaked with blood, nodded. Raymond spat onto the stage.

'Then you are a fool. A fool for sleeping with that whore, and a thrice-cursed fool for submitting to this peasant's madness. As for you,' he hissed at Peter Bartholomew, 'I raised you from nothing and I can return you to nothing. Do not *dare* challenge me again.'

Through all this confrontation, the accused woman had stood at the edge of the stage, bleeding, shivering, naked and forgotten. Now, suddenly, she took three steps towards the brazier and snatched the branding iron from the fire. She held it with both hands, the burning cross pointed towards her, then plunged it into the soft flesh of her breast.

I never thought a noise alone could rupture a man's soul, but the woman's scream of terrible, euphoric agony hit me like poison. I leaned forward and retched, my body unable to stomach the evil. When the scream stopped, I looked up.

The woman lay sprawled unconscious on the platform, the smoke of burned flesh rising from her wound. Peter Bartholomew stood over her, a beatific smile adorning his face.

'Go,' he declared, 'and sin no more.'

ΚΣ

❧❧❧❧❧

Raymond gave his decision that night; the next morning, we struck our camp and headed west for the coast. The road led us down from the plateau where we had camped, into a green, steep-sided valley. To our left, the valley climbed away until it merged with the lower slopes of the distant mountain, while opposite it rose to a series of commanding bluffs and hilltops. We could only see them in snatches, though, for the warmer air in the valley brought a thick mist down over us. Ragged fingers drifted by, curling round as if beckoning us on. From behind, the low melody of the pilgrims' psalms droned in the fog.

'I hate that sound,' said Anna. 'Like a wasp, hovering over your shoulder and waiting to sting.'

Soft hoofbeats cantered down the line towards us. I

half-drew my sword, then let it slide back in its scabbard as I saw Aelfric emerge from the mist. He dropped down from the saddle to walk beside us, leading his horse by its reins.

'The scouts say there's a castle ahead.' He jerked a thumb to our right, to the northern side of the valley. 'High up on those bluffs.'

I groaned. The ordeal of the day before had drained me as much as any battle, and I could not countenance the thought of having to fight now. 'Will the castellan let us pass in peace?'

Aelfric shrugged. 'I don't think anyone asked him.'

'Will Raymond attack?'

'He's a fool if he does. The castle's perched up there like a crow's nest. Cliffs on three sides, high walls all around, and probably a garrison ready to roll us straight back down the hill with rocks and boiling pitch. They've had plenty of time to know we're coming.'

'Perhaps they won't see us in this mist,' said Sigurd hopefully. Though he untied the leather cover from his axe soon afterwards.

The fog seemed to lift higher as we moved down the valley. It did little to relieve my spirits. The crest of the ridge to our right was still obscured, and I was constantly glancing up to reassure myself there were not hordes of Saracens waiting to slaughter us. Gradually our pace slowed and our column squeezed up on itself, until even in the lingering mist I could see the clustered banners of Count Raymond's bodyguard close ahead of us.

'If we get any nearer those horses they'll be shitting on our heads,' said Sigurd.

Count Raymond must have thought the same; soon one of his knights came riding back to order us to slow down even more.

'You must not leave the pilgrims behind,' he chided, shooing us back like chickens. His horse danced skittishly in the road. 'If anything were to befall them—' He broke off as startled shouts rippled back from the men ahead. 'What?'

With a hiss and a blur of speed, something sharp and dark flew across the road and struck him square between his shoulders. The knight looked down, his hands grasping instinctively for the new limb that seemed to have sprouted from his chest. Blood dribbled out of the wound; then the weight of the shaft sticking from his back unbalanced him and he toppled from his saddle.

We did not stare for more than a moment. I flung myself at Helena and Zoe and dragged them to the ground, covering them with my body. Somewhere underneath me the baby squealed. I pulled my shield free and held it as a roof over us while I clambered to my feet. Sigurd was beside me, his shield in one hand and a small throwing axe in the other. His long battleaxe lay on the ground beside him. The other Varangians had formed a tight circle around us, crouching low as a ragged rain of arrows began thudding into the leather. When I had satisfied myself that Anna, my daughters and Nikephoros were safe, I edged my head around the side of the shield and peered out.

A loose cordon of Saracen archers had appeared on the northern side of the valley, a little way up the slope. They must have been lying in wait, for they could not have descended from the castle so quickly, but they did not seem to have come in strength. Not unless we had more unpleasant surprises awaiting us.

But the attack seemed to have been more a squall than a storm; it was already beginning to blow itself out. Either the Saracens had only intended to harass us or they had not expected the speed of our reaction: few armies ever can have matched the Army of God for discipline on the march. Ahead of us, Count Raymond's men had begun a furious counter-fire of arrows, pinning down the Saracen archers while dismounted knights advanced up the slope, shields held aloft. In the face of such an onslaught, most of the Saracens turned and began scrambling up the hill towards safety. Many were too slow to reach it.

A young knight came sprinting up the road and squatted beside Nikephoros.

'Count Raymond says we must climb this hill and capture the castle above.' The youth gulped a quick breath, glancing over our shield wall. 'He wants the Varangians to advance on his right flank.'

'Capture the castle?' Nikephoros echoed. 'The count will never be able to hold his men together on that hill, and who knows how many men the Saracens have up there? You cannot even see it in that cloud.'

It was true: although the mist had lifted from the road, it still cloaked the upper reaches of the valley. As the retreating Saracens reached its height, they vanished into cloud.

'It would be madness,' said Nikephoros, voicing all our thoughts.

'It is what Count Raymond requires.'

Nikephoros swore, looked up at the hillside once more, then turned to Sigurd. 'Take your men and protect the count's flank as best you can. Try not to get killed. And you,' he said, staring at me, 'find Count Raymond and persuade him to call off this lunacy.'

I looked down the road. The ordered ranks of the Provençal army had broken apart and were swarming up the hill like a flock of birds. Mounted on a bay horse among them, his body thrust forward in the saddle, was Raymond.

My heart sank. 'Can I take some of Sigurd's men?'

'Take Aelfric and Thomas. And make sure you reach Raymond before he gets himself killed.'

The slope grew rapidly steeper as we climbed, and the air around us thickened with fog. Soon we could see little more than shadows – or occasionally a ball of golden haze where a shaft of sunlight struck through. We could hear the clash of arms and the screams of battle close ahead, but the fog hid all sight of it from our eyes. It was as if we had stumbled into some ancient battlefield, where armies of ghosts still waged a forgotten war. I held up my shield, wary of stray arrows.

A dark shadow came stumbling out of the mist – a Frank, his helmet cut open and blood streaming down his face. He clutched his head, one hand trying to staunch the blood while the other tried to wipe it from his eyes.

'*Count Raymond!*' I shouted at him. 'Have you seen Count Raymond?'

He ran past us, stumbling down the hillside without answering.

We carried on, moving an arm's length apart so we had free hold of our weapons. The mist no longer formed an impenetrable wall but was breaking up, pulling apart in shreds and coils. Some drifted along a few feet off the ground; others settled over the bodies of the fallen like shrouds. Soon even those dissolved, blown apart by a rising breeze as we came over a crest and looked out on the hilltop.

It was a lonely place to die, a small stretch of rugged, broken ground rising and narrowing to a promontory. A grey castle stood at its tip, its walls built so close to the cliffs that it seemed to sit on the clouds that filled the surrounding valley. It reminded me of the monastery at Ravendan. One corner of its main tower was missing, and a breach in the stone curtain wall had been filled with wood. Perhaps the garrison relied on lofty isolation to protect themselves, but they had underestimated the Franks. Raymond's charge up the hill had overtaken many of the fleeing Saracens, and even as the last remnant squeezed through the open gate they had to turn to defend themselves from the Provençal vanguard. Archers tried to shoot from the walls, but the Franks repulsed them with a merciless bombardment.

'The count.' Aelfric pointed, though I had seen him too. He was still mounted, riding back and forth to avoid the darts and arrows that peppered the ground around him. He waved his spear in the air and urged his men on.

'Should we deliver Nikephoros' message?' said Thomas. It was easy to understand the doubt in his voice. In their hasty repairs to the castle wall, the Saracens had left a pile of rubble at its foot to form a natural ramp to the mended breach. A company of Frankish knights had climbed it, and were hacking at the crude repair with axes and mattocks. Hewn masonry and wood tumbled from the gap, building their platform still higher. The defenders had at least managed to close the gate, I saw, though there too the Franks were pressing hard.

'There's no gain risking our lives telling Raymond he should not have won his victory,' I decided. At the end of the promontory, I could see the mass of Frankish knights pulling the gates open. Raymond raised his spear and began to trot forward; cheers and cries of *Deus vult* – God wills it – rose in anticipation. And above all the shouts and artificial clangour of battle – stone, steel, leather and iron – I heard the bleating of sheep.

The gates swung out like two arms. The horde of knights drew back to let them open, spears and swords raised. Some men actually cast aside their shields to allow themselves free hands to kill or plunder.

The bleating I had heard seemed to grow louder, the murmur now punctuated by the bark of dogs. I could see a commotion by the gate: the knights had not delivered their killing blow but were milling about in confusion, some moving forward, some back, some spinning away as if parrying unseen enemies. Cracks appeared in their line; many of them seemed to be looking down around their feet instead of at their enemies.

A knight reeled away from the back of the throng, pursued – so it seemed – by a shaggy white dog bursting out from the hole he had left. But the dog galloped straight past him, and the knight, rather than returning to the attack, began chasing after it. Nor was it a dog, I saw, as it charged panic-stricken towards us – it was a sheep.

Aelfric saw it too and laughed out loud. 'Are these their best troops?' he marvelled. 'If so, we could be in Jerusalem in a fortnight.'

'Eating mutton,' added Thomas, a rare grin spreading over his face.

'We'll be sick of it by then. Look at them.'

A second animal had followed the first through the split in the Frankish army; two more came after it, widening the gap. Some of the knights ran after them, distracted on the brink of victory, but that left space for more panicked sheep to drive through the ranks. They split the Franks apart, surging through them like high water smashing through a dam. Many in the Frankish wall were carried away with them, either unable to resist the charging beasts or drawn along with them by greed. The castle was forgotten.

Raymond alone stood against the retreat, an island in the torrent of sheep and men, railing against them in impotent rage. 'This is not a foraging expedition,' he screamed. 'Come back! Come back and fight!'

But madness had seized them and they did not turn. They chased after the sheep like men who had not eaten in months, and more sheep followed after them. After the sheep came the dogs, snapping at their legs, and after the dogs, like shepherds, came the Saracens.

In little more than an instant, victory turned to rout. Many of the Franks had cast aside their weapons to grab onto the sheep with both hands; some were on their knees trying to hold the animals fast or slit their throats. They died first as the Saracens overtook them, slaughtered animals and slaughtered men tumbling indiscriminately over each other. I saw several of the stragglers brought down by dogs and mauled on the ground until the Saracens ended it.

It had happened so fast that I still stood immobile, hypnotised by the savage speed of fortune's reverse. Then an arrow clattered off a rock near by – the Saracen archers on the walls, driving on the Franks – and I saw our danger.

'We have to go.'

'Down the hill,' said Aelfric. A little way down, the sea of cloud still ebbed against the slope, thick and impenetrable. 'Into that. It's our best chance.'

As soon as I moved, all became chaos. Fleeing knights and soldiers were spilling off the hilltop and cascading down the slope around us, tripping and stumbling in their panic. The slope would have been dizzyingly steep in daylight, but in the mist it became a vertiginous world where every direction was down. We could not stand upright for fear of falling; we turned our backs to the mist and pressed ourselves against the crumbling earth, scuttling like ants on the face of the hill. Muted echoes of ghastly sounds filled the air: all around us men were screaming, falling, dying, but we could not see them. A helmet tumbled past, clanging like a church bell as it bounced from rock to rock.

Suddenly, I came over a hummock to see a standing shadow looming in the mist, its dark arm poised to strike me. I cried out in fear but my reactions were true: my shield came up, parrying his attack, while I scythed my sword at his knees to cut his legs from under him. He did not flinch, did not even make a sound, though my blade had cut so deep I could not pull it free. Terror overwhelmed me as I found myself suddenly defence-less – I tugged on my sword but it would not come. Instead, in my clumsy desperation I lost my footing and tumbled forwards, splayed out to receive the killing blow.

Another figure appeared in the fog. It stood over me, and I heard a familiar laugh.

'Well done, Father-in-law. You've killed a tree.'

His voice trembled on the brink of hysteria, but it was true what he said: the arm I had thrust aside with my shield was no more than a hanging branch, and the legs I had sliced into its trunk. White sap oozed onto the blade. I put my foot against the tree and pulled the sword free, cursing. As I tried to wipe the sticky sap on my tunic, I heard another sound in the fog near by. The shrieking, sawing braying of a horse in agony.

There was only one man I knew on that hillside on horseback. Praying Aelfric and Thomas would manage to keep close, I dashed towards the noise. It was not easy to follow – the cold screams sounded all around me, tangling with the fog and addling my senses, in my eyes and in my ears, until I could hardly tell if the fog was the sound incarnate, or the sound the howl of the fog.

Gradually, though, the noise grew louder. The closer I came the more unbearable was its anguish and the more I raced on, as if by finding the noise I might at last silence it. Damp earth and pebbles scattered under my feet; in my haste, I began to lose my footing. The only way to keep upright was to blunder on, faster and faster and ever more unbalanced, straight into the fog. A root snatched at my foot; I flung out my arms and threw myself back, but momentum carried me forward and down. I thumped into the ground with a bruising shock, slid a little way on my belly, then stopped abruptly, brought up against a warm, writhing mass blocking the path.

I screamed, thinking I must have come up against a corpse, though my screams vanished in the mad welter of sound around me. It was not a fallen soldier; it was a horse, crying out its distress like a newborn child. Sweat stained its flanks, foaming white in places, and I had no sooner raised my head than I had to duck to avoid a flailing hoof in the fog.

Somewhere in my fall I had dropped my sword, but

mercifully it had slid down after me, close enough that I could see it. I crawled away from the horse and reached for the weapon, feeling a flood of relief as my hand closed around the hilt. I stood, feeling the grazes and bruises where I had fallen.

I was not alone. As the horse's cries weakened, I heard another sound in the cloud: the sound of running feet. It might have been Thomas or Aelfric, both of whom I had lost in my descent, but it came from down the slope and I did not think they had passed me. I skirted around the dying horse and edged down the hill. I had barely moved a yard when I saw two men: one lay on the ground, hardly stirring, the other stood over him, his sword poised for the kill.

I could not see much of either man: a bulge in a helmet where a turban might have wrapped it, the curve of a sword, a half-seen device on a discarded shield. It was a poor basis to choose who would die – but if I did not, there would be no choice to make. I stepped forward, deliberately kicking a cluster of pebbles downhill to distract my opponent, and as he half turned I lunged forward with my sword. The slope added weight to my thrust: the point of my sword struck his breast, forced its way through the scale armour, and I felt the sudden rush as the blade sank into the vital flesh beneath. I straightened, planted my foot on his chest and pulled my sword free as he sank to the ground, heeled to one side and rolled a little way down the hill.

I turned to his opponent. He lay on his back, one hand

clutching his ribs and the other reaching helplessly for the shield that had fallen out of reach when the horse threw him. The single eye looked up at me from his grizzled face.

'Count Raymond?'

His eye never blinked, staring with such intensity that I thought for a terrible moment he must be dead, and I had killed a man over a corpse.

'My knights,' he croaked. His voice was old and brittle. 'Where are my knights?'

Where were his knights? How had the greatest lord in the Army of God come to lie abandoned on a hillside, facing a solitary death at the hands of a lone Saracen? It was not how men like him were supposed to die.

'What happened?' I asked at last.

Raymond shrugged. 'We were retreating. One minute, all my bodyguards were beside me, the next they had vanished in the fog. I was trying to find them when my horse fell. Then a Saracen found me – and then you.'

I heard the scrape and rustle of someone crashing down the hillside above. With weary arms I snatched up Raymond's shield and tensed myself for an attack, but it was only Aelfric, with Thomas behind him. As they descended into view, Aelfric took in the scene at a glance.

'We have to get down from here.'

Our progress was agonisingly slow. With Thomas in the lead we edged across the hillside, flinching each time one of us rustled a clump of grass or kicked a pebble. Every few paces Thomas would pause, his young eyes and ears straining for any sign of danger. Count Raymond still lagged behind. The fall from his horse had not injured him badly, but it had left him with a limp, which seemed to grow worse as we continued. Several times I froze with terror as I heard his foot drag across a patch of loose ground; if any Saracens had been nearby they would surely have found us. The fog that had caused us so much confusion was now our salvation, a blanket hiding us from danger, and I looked at it with new eyes, praying it would not lift.

Though we could barely see it, our way led gradually down into a cleft in the hillside where a thin stream trickled between boulders. We followed it, hoping it would lead to the valley floor and the road. We had not gone far, when suddenly I heard the tumble of rocks, a cry, a splash and a resounding clang. Three of us turned in horror. A little way up the gully Count Raymond lay sprawled in the stream. He must have stepped on a loose rock and upended himself.

We froze, listening for signs we had been heard. Even Count Raymond lay still and let the stream trickle over him. For long seconds there was nothing save the babbling water and a wounded horse braying in the distance. I began to relax, glancing down the stream and wondering if it was too treacherous to attempt. And then, just as we had convinced ourselves we were safe, a spear ripped through the fog and struck the soft earth of the stream bank. It stuck there, quivering with the impact, scant inches over Count Raymond's head.

We had not heard a sound; now, suddenly, it engulfed us, rushing down both sides of the gully as our enemies emerged from the mist. Aelfric moved fastest; he plucked the spear from the earth, reversed it, and, as the first Saracen appeared, drove it into his belly. The man's momentum carried him on, impaling him so deep that Aelfric had to let go the spear and leap clear before his enemy barrelled into him. The man fell writhing in the stream.

'Make a line,' shouted Raymond. He was on his feet, his sword in his hand, his armour dripping wet. Another Saracen stumbled down the slope with a spear, too fast to control himself; Raymond parried the thrust easily, kicked the man's feet from under him and plunged his sword into his neck. Blood bubbled into the stream.

'*Back!*' Aelfric stood shoulder to shoulder with Raymond, swinging his axe as more attackers poured in. He wielded it awkwardly, not with the usual scything cuts but with short, spasmodic darts. In our desperate defence he could not commit himself, for a single mistimed stroke would leave him mortally vulnerable. I prayed it was a lesson Thomas had learned, but I had no time to look, for I was under desperate siege myself. Two Saracens charged towards me along the stream bank; I punched one in the face with my shield and watched him skid on the slippery ground, exposing his neck to the kiss of Aelfric's axe. His companion paused, his sword hovering between us; I pounced on his indecision, swinging out my shield to check his sword while stabbing forward with my own. But he was too fast: he twisted away from the attack, at the same time grabbing on to my shield and tugging. I lost my footing on the slimy stream bed and was hurled onto my knees. Cold water rushed into my open mouth, choking off the scream; I tried to push myself up, but the water seemed to suck me down. In a second I would be dead.

Something splashed into the stream beside me, and a salt tang tainted the fresh water. For a moment I let it fill my mouth; then, realising what it was, I gagged in horror. The convulsion jerked my head up, out of the stream, and I looked around as the bloody water cascaded off my head. Thomas was standing over me, a bloodied axe in his hands. Just upstream from me, the Saracen lay unmoving. A great gash, from his collarbone to his navel, cleaved him almost in two.

'Come on,' said Thomas. Blood streaked his armour and his face was wild. In that instant, I barely recognised him. Half a dozen Saracens lay dead about his feet, though he could not have killed them all. They clogged the stream and added their blood to the reservoir filling up behind them. No more came to share their fate.

'Thank you.' My lungs burned from the water I had swallowed, and the words came out awkwardly.

Thomas scowled. 'You should be more careful next time.'

We clambered out of the stream and edged our way down the muddy bank. My feet were sodden and numb; I felt like some bedraggled animal as I hauled myself over rocks and around roots. The taste of blood and water fouled my mouth; I tried to spit it out but still it remained. Several times my weary legs gave way and my lumpen fingers could not seize a handhold: then I would slide or tumble a little way down the slope, smearing myself in mud, until at last a stone or hummock stopped me. Each time, getting up proved harder and harder, until at last I slithered my way into a small hollow where Aelfric and Raymond were waiting.

'Have we escaped them?'

As if in answer, Aelfric dropped to one knee, dragging Raymond down with him, and threw his shield over them. I thought he was joking; then, as I looked up, my heart almost died. The mist was thinning, and on the ridge above I could see a line of men, a company of dark shadows looking down on us.

I pulled my shield over me like a blanket, too weary to do more. A voice rang out from above, calling a challenge in some barbarous tongue.

Aelfric laughed, put down his shield and shouted back an answer. I waited to see what would come of it.

The voice from above sounded again, this time in Greek. It was accented, but wholly familiar.

'Let's get out of this bastard fog.'

ΚϚ

～～～～

Wounded and humbled, the Provençal army drifted back to the main column. By noon the sun had burned away the ceiling of fog, so that all could see the hillside strewn with bodies, and the proud castle triumphant on its promontory. Anna and Zoe ran to greet me as we returned, while Helena embraced Thomas without thought for the blood that stained her dress.

As soon as he had removed his armour, Raymond summoned his shamefaced army. Standing on a boulder, his arms spread apart in anger, he looked like nothing so much as Christ on Golgotha.

'I thought I had seen every piece of cowardice and treachery that men could devise.' He held his voice calm, but there was a throbbing tremor in the words which threatened to shake it apart. 'I thought there was nothing shameful on the battlefield that I had not seen. But today . . .' His shoulders slumped; his head dropped, before rising slowly to fix its hate-filled gaze on the watching army. 'Is this how the Army of God fights? If you were not creatures of lust we would be feasting in that castle this very moment, and I would be drinking to your valour. Now, we have nothing to feast on but our wounds.'

He paused and surveyed his host, daring them to disagree. No one spoke.

'Where are my bodyguard?'

Half a dozen men shuffled forward from the ranks. They had removed their armour and quilted jerkins, and wore only woollen tunics with crosses sewn on the sleeves.

'Two hours ago I was lying up there with a Saracen's sword at my throat. *All alone.*' The last two words resonated deep with anger, as if he had had to wrench them from his soul. 'If not for the grace of God, I would be one more corpse on the hillside.' He pointed up behind him, where flocks of crows wheeled above the ridge, then looked back at the six men standing before him. 'Where were you then?'

One of them, a stocky man with a ruddy face, looked up. 'We lost you in the fog and could not find you.'

'Really?' With a coiled energy far beneath his years, Raymond leaped down from his boulder and advanced towards the man. 'All six of you?'

Six faces stared back at him. Several flushed with some-thing like embarrassment, but none showed shame or begged forgiveness.

319

'Have you forgotten your oaths to me?' Raymond's voice was sharp as ice. 'I chose every one of you, to sleep by my bed, eat at my table and fight at my side. You—' He turned to one of them. 'Your father served me every day of his life; he fought beside me in seventeen battles, and when the eighteenth claimed him I was beside him. And now, in my greatest danger, you leave me blundering among my enemies like a blind man.'

The ruddy-faced man edged forward a little. 'My lord, we—'

'*Your* lord? Who is your lord? A knight who abandons his lord is no knight at all.' Without warning that he even considered it, he punched the man square in the face. Age may have lined his skin and stooped his back, but it had not corroded the strength in his arm. The knight stumbled backwards, blood trickling from his nose.

'Stand up,' Raymond ordered. 'Stand fast, if you have not forgotten how.'

The knight shook his head to clear it, licking away the blood that stained his lip. Swaying slightly, he stepped forward again and snapped his feet together.

'Where was your courage on the mountain?' Raymond jeered. 'Did you forget it?' He swung his fist straight into the knight's chin. His head spun away with a sickening crack, but still he stayed standing.

'Do you remember the oath you took to me? To fight as my sword and serve as my shield? To suffer my wounds?' Raymond clasped his hands on either side of the knight's bloodied face and held it inches from his own. 'Why did you betray me?'

The knight looked as if he wanted to clear the blood from his mouth, but Raymond held him so close and tight he could not have done so without spitting in his master's face. He swallowed, and mumbled, 'We did not mean to lose you.'

Raymond loosed his grip, running his hand over the knight's cheek almost lovingly. 'You did not lose me in the fog – you abandoned me. Admit it.'

The knight whispered something I could not hear. Raymond shook his head, cupped one hand around the back of the knight's head and smacked him hard with the other.

'*Liar*,' he shouted. Beneath the grey stubble his cheeks had flushed crimson. 'Who told you to betray me?' He let go the knight and wheeled round. 'Was it *him*? An upstart peasant who thinks himself touched by God? Raymond stepped back, but only to give himself more room to drive his next blow into the knight's stomach. The man gagged and stumbled forward; Raymond could have caught him, but instead stood aside so that the knight fell at his feet.

'Was he trying to warn me?' He lashed out with his boot, kicking the knight in the face. A gasp rose from the watching army, but no one moved. The other five guards stood in a row and stared straight ahead, stiff as corpses. 'Crawl back to him, *worm*, and tell him I have heard his message.' Another kick. 'Does he think he will usurp my power?' Another kick, this time so hard that it rolled the

321

knight over with its force. 'Does he think he will steal my army from me, even my own household?' A kick. 'My handpicked knights.' Kick. 'My dearest friends.'

He drew back his leg as if to kick the man in two, then instead pivoted away to face the army. No one moved to help the knight, who lay broken and whimpering in a pool of blood and mud.

'Is there anyone else who questions my authority?' Raymond demanded. He was breathing hard, spent with his violence. 'If so, let him see that I am in command here. I am in control.'

He paused, then repeated it more quietly, almost like a prayer.

'I am in control.'

Raymond's fury at the men who had deserted him was not matched by gratitude to those who had saved him. He said nothing to me, and I received precious little thanks from Nikephoros when I found him. 'You were supposed to stop the count ever going up that hill,' was all he said after I had told him the story. 'Now he will not leave here until that castle falls, even if he has to spend half his army taking it.'

Thankfully, it did not come to that. Late that night we crept up the hillside once again, clambering between the bodies of the fallen, and as the first smudge of light began to crease the horizon we climbed onto the ridge. Two companies ran forward, carrying their scaling ladders under a roof of shields against the expected onslaught, but it never came. No defenders rose from behind the battlements, and no arrows rained down on the tiled shields.

'Perhaps they're still asleep,' Aelfric suggested.

The assault parties planted the ladders in the ground and raised them to the ramparts. At a sign from Count Raymond, another company of knights ran to the rubble ramp that led to the breach they had attacked the day before. Behind them, our archers waited with arrows nocked and strings tensed. Their arms strained with the effort – too much for one, who lost his grip and sent his arrow aimlessly towards the castle. It clattered into the walls and provoked a furious rebuke from Raymond – but no answer from within.

The first knights climbed tentatively to the tops of their ladders, paused for a moment, then vaulted through the embrasures. More followed on their heels; others ran up the incline and burst through the breach. Still we heard no shouts, no challenge or sound of battle.

'Is it a trap?' I wondered aloud.

Raymond waved more companies forward. Their feet fell softly on the dewy ground, and they held their weapons carefully so as not to make a sound. Birds had begun to sing in the grass; a swallow flew up from a tower and wheeled above it, but otherwise the dawn stillness still gripped the hilltop, and men moved as if in a dream.

A rumble from the gatehouse dispelled that. The gates began to move and a ghostly, disjointed clangour rippled through our army. 'Here it comes,' men warned each other.

A crack of light opened between the gates, widening as they swung out. Every man among us strained forward to see what would emerge.

A single figure in Provençal armour stood framed in the gateway, silhouetted against the grey morning light. Behind him, I could see that the courtyard was empty, save for a single sheep tethered to a stake in the ground, grazing on the weeds that grew between the cobbles.

The knight pulled off his helmet. 'It's empty. There's nothing there but ghosts and the spoils of war.'

Sigurd spat on the ground, then deliberately began wrapping the deerskin cover over his axe head.

'Let's hope Jerusalem is as easy.'

It was a strange outcome – to have lost a battle we should have won, and won a battle we did not fight. Every man in the army, from Count Raymond to the humblest groom, seemed disoriented and frustrated. We had prepared ourselves for a great assault, our passions raised high with expectation; without a battle, the passions remained unspent, and curdled in our hearts. Many quarrels broke out that week, even among the Varangians, and a sullen disappointment clung to the army as we plundered the fertile valley for food.

Two slow weeks after the battle we came out between the arms of the mountains and looked down on the coastal plain. From early in the morning I could see the blue-glazed expanse of the sea ahead, with a river running eagerly to meet it, while to our left a walled town stood precariously on a narrow spur protruding from the mountain.

'Arqa,' said Nikephoros, riding beside me. 'From here, we can be at Tripoli by nightfall, and then only ten days' march to Jerusalem.'

A heaviness seemed to lift from my heart. Though it was only the middle of February, I thought I could feel spring welling up in the roots of the leafless trees and vines around me. The sea sparkled in the distance, offering its promise of infinite journeys, and the sun seemed warm on my face.

But we did not reach Tripoli that night. Instead, we made our camp below Arqa, the fortified town on the mountain. And there, Count Raymond decided, we would go no further.

κζ

〰〰〰

Another siege. Sometimes I thought there must only be one wall in all the world, spiralling around itself like a snake, and that however often we broke through, we would only advance to confront it again. I stood on a ridge in the shadow of the mountain and felt the warm February sun on my cheek. To my left, the foot of the mountain swept out to form the natural buttress on whose formidable heights the town was built. The only approach was by a thin neck of land little wider than a bridge, carved away by the fast river that flowed along its base. The Provençals had tried to force their assault across the promontory and failed, losing many men. Now, two weeks later, they had resigned themselves to the familiar toil of siege work.

A heavy crack sounded behind me, like rock breaking off the mountain. I did not bother to look. I heard the familiar whiplash of coiled rope unspooling, the whoosh of the sling and the creak of timbers. A flock of starlings squawked their protest, though even they must have grown used to it. A heavy stone flew close over my head and sailed over the deep ravine that divided us from the town, spinning and tumbling in the air.

It struck Arqa's wall with a thump and an eruption of dust. A few dislodged bricks fell into the bushes at the base; otherwise, there was no discernible effect. Behind me, I heard the Provençal engineers begin the laborious effort of winding back the catapult.

'Even if you make the breach, you'll never get your men up that slope.' Tancred sat on a black gelding and surveyed the town across the ravine. Beside him, Raymond and Nikephoros tried to calm their own steeds after the noise of the catapult. I stood attentively by Nikephoros' stirrup, more an ornament than an aide, and absent-mindedly stroked the horse's flank.

'We'll wear it down,' said Raymond shortly.

Tancred rolled his eyes. 'Not if we wear ourselves down first. What does Peter Bartholomew say to this delay?'

He pulled on his reins, turning his horse to face north. Beneath the heights of Arqa the road wound along the plain, lined with the tents and baggage of the Provençal army. Beyond, a little apart, more tents and makeshift shelters covered a rounded hill, enclosed by a low wall of wood, wattle and rubble. In its centre, on the crown of the hill, a large cross stood empty to the sky, almost as if waiting for something.

'Well?' pressed Tancred. 'What does the peasant messiah say?'

'Do not call him that,' Raymond snapped. 'And what he thinks does not matter.'

'Even when what he says is true?' Tancred looked to the south, where an ancient bridge carried the road towards the coast and Jerusalem. 'We should have kept moving.'

Nikephoros, who had learned to prefer silence during Tancred and Raymond's arguments, stirred. 'Not with this army. You would be walking into the lion's mouth. Better to wait until you are large enough that his jaws cannot devour you.'

Raymond slapped the pommel of his saddle impatiently. These were not new debates. 'Listen to what the Greek says. Your youth makes you impatient.'

'My poverty makes me impatient. I entered your service because you promised conquest and plunder – not to sit at the foot of a fortress of no consequence and throw stones at it.'

Another whip-crack from behind launched another boulder into the air. This one actually bounced off the wall, landing on the slope below and tumbling slowly down among the gorse and sagebrush until it came to rest at the foot of the spur. A cloud of dust rolled down the hillside after it. Above my head, I heard Nikephoros mutter something about Sisyphus.

'You entered my service because I paid you five thousand *sous*,' said Raymond to Tancred. 'What happened to those?'

'I spent them on my army. A good lord is bountiful to his vassals.'

The slight was not lost on Raymond. 'And so I will be. Arqa belongs to the emir of Tripoli. When we have made an example of it, he will see our might and offer a rich ransom to be spared.'

'I heard he had already offered gold to let us pass.'

'When we have taken Arqa, he will offer more.'

'And how much will he offer if we do not take it?'

A bang echoed across the ravine, and a white projectile flew up from within the town. At first it appeared to rise straight into the air; then, gathering pace, its trajectory became clear. It seemed to move much faster from the receiving end, I noticed: there was no thought of trying to avoid it. The three lords on horseback stood still as stone, trapped at the mercy of an unswerving destiny.

The rock rushed over our heads and struck the cliff behind us. The earth shivered under our feet; I heard a crack as the rock split in pieces, and a rain of stone fell to the ground. A surprised cry rang out among the clatter, then choked off suddenly. Looking back, I saw a knight lying on the ground amid the fallen rubble. A dent in his helmet was the only damage I could see, but he did not move. Others ran over to help him, though their efforts did not last long.

'Their catapult is stronger than yours,' said Nikephoros, stroking his agitated mount.

'Then we will break it,' snapped Raymond. His face was pale, his single eye roving over the chaos behind him. 'We will break this feeble town, and make such an example of it that every lord from here to Jerusalem will grovel in the dust as we pass by. Godfrey and Bohemond will see they have no choice but to hasten here and submit to my standard, and you' – he jabbed a finger at Tancred – 'will have your gold.'

Behind him, two knights began rolling another rock up the slope to load into the catapult's sling.

'Raymond is more visionary than Peter Bartholomew if he thinks besieging Arqa is the answer to his troubles.' Nikephoros strode across the carpeted floor of his tent. In the lamplight, monstrous shadows mimicked his movement on the wall behind. 'He does not know what he wants.'

It seemed to me that Raymond knew too much what he wanted: to be master of Antioch, unrivalled captain of the Army of God, impregnable warlord and conqueror of Jerusalem. I kept silent.

'And meanwhile, his gamble – our gamble – has failed. Bohemond, Godfrey and the others say they will follow Raymond south – but they do nothing. Bohemond is waiting for Raymond to overreach himself and tip into disaster, while Godfrey watches to see which way the dice will fall. Who can blame him? While they wait, Raymond can go no further. If they come, he will lose his cherished authority over the army. So he waits here, throwing stones at Arqa like a boy at a bird's nest.' He kicked the table in the corner of the room, shaking the candles on it. A shower of wax fell like snow. I had rarely seen his passion so unreined.

'If we are not careful, Raymond's army will wither at Arqa and Bohemond will have all the excuse he needs to stay at Antioch for ever. Do you know what the emperor would say to that? We have to break this stalemate.'

Nikephoros dropped into his ebony chair and slumped back, more like a soldier in a tavern than an imperial dignitary. 'You must speak to Peter Bartholomew.'

I had not expected it, though perhaps I should have. 'Raymond hates Peter Bartholomew now. He will not listen to him.'

'Raymond hates Peter Bartholomew,' Nikephoros agreed. 'But only because he fears his power. And because he fears him, he will do what Peter demands.'

Despite the heat of the bygone day, the night was cold as I crossed our small camp to my tent. Thomas and Helena were inside, Helena with the baby gurgling at her breast. I dropped my eyes: even after a month living and travelling together, I was still not used to the sight of her nursing. Thomas sat beside her, running a whetstone along the rim of his axe. He still concentrated hard at the task, I noticed, squinting and frowning, though his fellow Varangians could do it with no more thought than breathing. The weapon looked vast and ravenous beside the tiny child in Helena's arms.

'Where are Anna and Zoe?' I asked.

Helena lifted the baby away, flashing a view of shining raw-red skin before she pulled her dress closed.

'Anna took Zoe for a walk.'

'She shouldn't have.' Why did I always sound so humourless with my children? 'Not after dark. It's dangerous.'

'Aelfric went with them.' Thomas kept his head down as he spoke, rasping his axe and concentrating more studiously than ever.

That could be dangerous in different ways. 'I hope I won't have another daughter marrying a Varangian.' It was supposed to be a joke, but no one smiled. I reverted to the task at hand. 'Nikephoros has ordered me to visit Peter Bartholomew's camp.'

'*That* could be dangerous,' said Helena sternly. She wiped the baby's mouth.

'That's why I want Thomas to come with me.'

Thomas took two more long strokes with the stone before looking up. Even then, he did not look at me but instead glanced at Helena. She nodded, and he rose.

'Leave the axe,' I told him. 'I doubt the pilgrims will welcome it in their camp.'

Thomas scowled, but laid it back down on the blanket. Its blade winked as it caught the flame of the solitary candle in the tent.

We did not speak as we climbed the hill to the pilgrim camp. Thomas had always been quiet, but I felt a growing distance between us now and I did not have the words to bridge it. Perhaps there were none that could. He walked one step behind me, never complaining, but his very presence seemed a constant reproach.

A line of stakes marked the edge of Peter Bartholomew's domain. Crude axe blows had sharpened their tips to points, which seemed sharper still in the flickering light of the watch fire. A guard challenged us as we approached the opening in the fence: he wore no armour, but his spear was real enough. So was the laugh that answered my demand to speak to Peter Bartholomew.

'Do you want to speak with Saint Michael and all the angels as well? Peter Bartholomew' – the guard crossed himself with his free hand – 'does not receive visitors.'

As if to encourage us away, the guard stepped towards us, into the firelight. Thomas gasped, and I had to hold my face stiff to hide my shock. Even with the fire plain on his face, more than half of it remained dark – not in any shadow, but stained with bruises as if someone had tipped a bottle of ink over it. Scars and scabs rose among the bruises, and thick welts lay open on his cracked nose.

'Count Raymond did this to you?' I murmured, taking in the stocky figure and the matted hair that had once been fair.

The guard grimaced, making his face even more grotesque. 'It is better to suffer for doing good than evil. That is what Peter says.'

'Raymond has expelled you from his service?'

'He stripped me of my rank, my armour, my servants.

He says that when we return to Provence he will take away my lands as well.' He cracked a ghastly smile. More than half his teeth were missing, and blood still oozed from his gums. 'But that will not happen. Not once we reach Jerusalem.'

'*If* we reach Jerusalem.'

He leaned forward on his spear. 'We will reach Jerusalem. It has been prophesied.'

I stared him in the eyes – one swollen and half-shut, the other wide open. Perhaps Raymond had kicked out more than his teeth, for I saw no craft or machination behind them, just innocent faith. I leaned closer.

'If you want to reach Jerusalem, you will let me speak to Peter Bartholomew.'

He shook his head, though this time with some semblance of regret. 'I cannot. He will not be disturbed.'

'I will not disturb him,' I lied. 'But you can see that our path is faltering again.' I pointed up behind me, where the watch-fires of Arqa burned high on the mountain spur. 'Count Raymond will not give that up lightly. What I have to tell Peter Bartholomew could change his mind.'

The guard hesitated, but I could see the doubt I had sowed. He glanced at me and Thomas, then back to the encampment, then to us again.

'Peter Bartholomew will not see you,' he reiterated. 'But I will take you to him.'

He called another guard to take his place, and led us up the hill into the heart of the camp. Raymond's beating had broken more than his face: he walked with a heavy limp, dragging his foot and learning on his spear like an old man's staff.

'I have a friend who would make sure that mended properly,' I told him. But he only muttered something about the healing of Christ, and shuffled on through the camp. Though it must have been a camp of thousands, sprawled all down the slope, there was neither sound nor light save the flap of our footsteps, and a golden glow from the very top of the hill.

'Are all the pilgrims in their beds?' I wondered.

The guard touched a finger to his cracked lips. 'Peter Bartholomew has ordered it.'

The camp thinned as we neared the top of the hill. By some twist of the landscape the summit was hidden until we were almost upon it: then, suddenly, I could see three solitary tents set to form an open-sided square, with the vast cross I had seen from the mountain at its centre. The tents on either side flickered dimly with the light of lamps within, but the third shone like a beacon. A regal light burned through its delicately spun walls so that it appeared as a pyramid of light, celestial in its radiance. I could hear a soft song rising within, like a psalm or a lullaby – many overlapping voices, though no shadows darkened the golden walls save for the black silhouette of the cross.

'Is that Peter Bartholomew's tent?' Thomas's voice rang with suspicion and wonder.

The guard did not answer, but took me by the arm and pulled me towards the dim tent on the left. Even he seemed awestruck to be there: his grip was slack, and the light beamed on his shattered face to make it seem almost whole again. He lifted the flap of the tent, called something inside, then beckoned us in.

After the still beauty outside, the tent we entered was a mean and shabby place. Its lamps hissed and spat, filling the space with an oily smoke; the cloths that divided the apartments were stained yellow, and hung crooked from the ceiling. Tangled heaps of carpets and furs lay discarded on the floor, and at least half the furniture seemed to have been knocked over as if in a brawl. An unpleasant odour hung in the air, despite the oversweet perfumes that tried to mask it.

'Wait here,' said the guard. His ease had vanished, and he scuttled out of the tent before we could answer. Through the cloth partition I could hear rustles and a low grunting, like a pig rooting in the ground – and occasionally a high-pitched whimper. I did not dare look at Thomas.

The grunting stopped. I looked to the canvas flap, expectant and dreading, but there was no sign of anyone emerging. And then, suddenly, a voice from the tent door behind us.

'What do you want?'

Thomas and I spun around. He had arrived with startling silence, but he did not look like a quiet man. His pockmarked face was bloated and heavy, his belly likewise, though the rest of him was meagre enough. His eyes were too small for his face and his mouth too large. Something sticky seemed to be smeared on his chin. He wore a long camelskin robe tied with a leather belt: he hooked his thumbs in it, and puffed out his chest.

'I have a message for Peter Bartholomew,' I said. 'It will help the army reach Jerusalem.'

The man's eyes fixed on me. 'Peter Bartholomew, bless his holy name' – he tapped a perfunctory sign of the cross across his chest – 'is at prayer. He will not be disturbed.'

'He will want to hear my message.'

'Then you can tell it to me.' His voice was coarse, even by the standards of the Provençals. There was no poise in his manner, only blunt strength.

'It is for Peter Bartholomew alone,' I insisted.

'No one comes to Peter Bartholomew, bless his name, except through me.' He gave an ugly smile. 'I am his steward and his prophet.'

'I have seen him many times.' I spoke mildly. Despite his obvious dissolution, there was a menace in the man's face I did not want to provoke.

'That was in the past. Now that the time of trial is coming, he must gather his strength and devote himself to God. If he saw every disciple who sought his blessing he would never sleep.'

'I am not his disciple.'

The steward gave what was meant to be an indulgent look; it emerged more like a leer. 'We are all his disciples – though some do not know it yet.'

'Then will you tell him Demetrios Askiates has brought a message for him.'

He shook his fat head. 'Tell it to me.'

'It is for him only.'

My obstinacy was beginning to irritate this self-proclaimed prophet: his small eyes narrowed, his hands began to ball into fists by his side. Thomas saw it too and edged closer, but I flicked my head to keep him back.

'Raymond cannot advance to Jerusalem unless Bohemond and Godfrey come to reinforce him. But they will not come until Raymond asks – and his pride will not bend to that.'

The prophet folded his arms across his chest. 'So?'

'Peter Bartholomew—'

'Bless his name.'

'. . . has influence Raymond cannot ignore. If he commands Raymond to send for Bohemond and Godfrey, to ask for their help, Raymond will do it.'

The prophet stared at me. 'Is that all?'

'It is enough.' I hoped that was true. I had little faith that the fat prophet would relay what I had said, and less still that Peter Bartholomew would act on it.

But the next day, Aelfric reported he had seen a knight leave Count Raymond's camp and ride north to Antioch.

κη

~~~~~~

The boy stood between his mother's bare legs, his arms wrapped around them. His young face was screwed into a mask of concentration as he surveyed the ground in front of him. Worry furrowed his face like an old man's – though these furrows were plump and fertile, ripe for planting, not the arid, barren lines of age. With a hiccup of resolve, he suddenly unlatched himself from his mother and lurched forward, flailing his limbs like a newborn foal. One step, two, three – and the beginnings of a fourth before the momentum undid him. He sprawled face-first into the carpet of pine-needles, a plaintive bawl lamenting his failure. Helena ran forward and picked him up, dusting the pine needles off his blue tunic.

'Soon he'll walk better than his grandfather,' said Sigurd.

I picked up a pinecone and threw it at him, but he swatted it away with the palm of his hand. The boy – my grandson – stopped wailing as he watched it fly into a patch of tall grass.

'With an arm like that, you should be throwing rocks at Arqa,' Sigurd teased me. 'You'd do no worse than the catapults.'

I waved the insult away. We were sitting in a glade in the forest that covered the lower slopes of the mountain – Thomas and Helena with the baby Everard; Zoe, picking the scales off pinecones to get at the nuts within; Sigurd, and Anna sitting on a fallen log beside me. We had brought baskets of bread and fruit, for it was a rare escape from the grim confines of the camp.

'There was a full moon two nights ago,' said Sigurd. 'A whole month we've been here now.' He pointed to Everard, who had balanced himself against his mother and was teetering forward, summoning courage for his next advance. The anticipation and delight in his young face seemed to have forgotten all memory of ever having fallen, though his knees were black with earth.

'If that boy set out for Jerusalem now, he'd still be there before this army.'

Everard obliged Sigurd's pessimism by choosing that moment to launch himself into another doomed run. This time he only managed two steps before the inevitable collapse. Helena stepped forward and wrapped him in her skirt, hushing the cries.

I smiled, trying not to let Sigurd's pessimism sour the

mood in the glade. What he said was true enough. In the nine weeks since we had set out from Ma'arat we had come, by Sigurd's reckoning, less than a hundred miles. In the past month we had not moved at all. The Army of God's resolve, once a keen and indomitable blade, had been bent so far that it had snapped. It could not be remade, not with the same strength, and the men who had swung and slashed their way across Asia Minor now prodded forward like blind men. The first incarnation had been terrible, terrifying to witness. This agonising decrepitude was simply a slow, aimless death.

Everard was ready to try again. He pushed off from Helena and ran forward, flapping his arms like an injured bird. Four steps, five, and then – just as it seemed he could defy his limitations no longer, he reached the sanctuary of my knee. He clung on desperately, and I had to prise his little hands away to hoist him up on my lap. I ruffled his hair – fair like Thomas's, though already growing steadily darker – and pointed through a gap in the trees where the slope fell away to the plain, and the coast beyond.

'That is where you need to go,' I told him. 'To Jerusalem.'

He snatched hold of my outstretched finger and began pulling on it. Anna reached over and tickled his chin, while Helena seated herself on the ground, leaning against the fallen log and chewing on a crust of bread. She looked well, I thought. Her face, sallow during the winter, had begun to brown again in the spring sun, and there was new vigour in her arms when she picked up her son. Anna had told me that Helena had struggled for a long time with feeding the baby, unable to nourish his body without enfeebling her own. It had been worst during the lean weeks at Ma'arat, and our subsequent travels had allowed little chance for recovery.

'What's that?'

I craned forward so that I could see what Sigurd had seen from his vantage on the opposite side of the clearing. A disgruntled fist tugged on my finger, trying to recapture my attention, but I ignored it. Thomas was on his feet beside Sigurd and staring over the tops of the pine trees to the west.

'An army.'

I passed the baby onto Anna's knee and ran over. My eyes were not as sharp as Thomas's, but even so I could see the procession winding stiffly out of the valley and down towards our camp. Sunlight gleamed on their weapons like the scales of a snake, with two white banners like fangs at their head.

'Can you see the device?' I asked. In the camp below, men were running out of their tents and staring, but I could not tell if they were preparing for battle.

'The cross of the Army of God,' said Thomas. 'And beside that, the banner of the five wounds.'

Godfrey's standard. I looked at my family in the glade, trembling that he should have come so near them. 'And the Norman serpent banner? Is that there too?'

Thomas shrugged. 'Not that I can see.'

I pulled on my boots. 'I had better go. Nikephoros will want me.'

Anna hoisted Everard down from her lap and set him on the ground. He swayed, then dashed resolutely forward towards his mother – as if he had never fallen before, would never fall again. But of course he did.

I was summoned almost immediately. Duke Godfrey's arrival occasioned a council of the princes, and Nikephoros required me to be his mouth and ears. They met in Count Raymond's tent – not his great pavilion, with its silk curtains and rich furnishings, but a small, square tent erected in a field a little distance from the camp. The princes watched each other warily.

'But where is Bohemond?' asked Raymond. He said it lightly, as if referring to a well-renowned horse he had been curious to see. No one was deceived.

Godfrey looked up. Where the trials of the past two months had slowly twisted the roots of Raymond's soul, so that his whole body appeared crooked and misshapen, Godfrey seemed to have benefited from the interlude. His bearing was firm, his face bright, his blond hair thick as a lion's mane and his blue eyes unyielding with purpose.

'Bohemond set out with us from Antioch two weeks ago. Three days later, he turned back.'

Raymond breathed a slow sigh, like a warm summer wind. His hunched shoulders relaxed and his bearing straightened, so that he seemed taller, more noble again.

'He will not come,' he declared softly, almost to himself. 'He has shown himself at last.'

343

'He swore he would honour his oath to worship at the tomb of Christ,' said Godfrey.

'When better men have captured it.' Raymond laughed in savage triumph. 'Bohemond's part in this enterprise is over. Our names will ring in history as the conquerors of the holy city; Bohemond's will be forgotten, or remembered only in the annals of traitors and cowards. As soon as Arqa is taken we will fall on Jerusalem like wolves.'

'*As soon as Arqa is taken?* I did not bring my army here at a forced march to defend you against a few Saracen villagers marooned on a hilltop. We should go now.'

Several of the other princes nodded their agreement. Raymond stiffened, bending forward like a bow drawn tight.

'I have besieged this town for a month; I will not see all that effort wasted now.'

'Better than seeing it wasted two months from now,' said Tancred.

Raymond looked as if he might strike Tancred – and Tancred, equally, as if he would relish fighting the old man. Fortunately, at that moment the council was interrupted by a commotion among the guards. A small knot of men were trying to push through, their voices raised in indignant protest. The guards waved their spears and shouted them back; for a moment I feared this might be the moment that the entire army broke apart in open battle. But Raymond must have recognised one of them, for he angrily called the guards to let the newcomer in.

A short, pot-bellied man shrugged his way between them and marched across to the tent. The camelskin tunic flapped around his knees, bulging out over the leather belt that tied it, and his small eyes surveyed us from the ill-tempered face. He seemed different in daylight, smaller in every part except his belly, but I recognised him at once as the man I had seen in the pilgrim camp – Peter Bartholomew's self-styled prophet.

He did not have the air of a peasant approaching the great princes of the earth. He held his head high and sure, his fat lips pouting as if he had already detected some slight against his dignity. All the princes stayed seated, save Raymond who was already standing.

'What is happening here?' he demanded. He turned on Count Raymond. 'Why have you summoned secret councils without my lord Peter Bartholomew's presence, bless his name?'

In any other place, to speak as he did to a man of Raymond's station would have been death. Instead, Raymond choked back his obvious anger and said simply, 'This does not concern Peter Bartholomew.'

'That is for him to judge.' The prophet's eyes swept around the gathering, defying them to argue.

Godfrey ignored him. 'Who is he?' he asked Raymond. His face was a mask of distaste.

'I am John, disciple and prophet of Peter Bartholomew, bless his name.' He rounded on Godfrey, who somehow contrived to evade the accusing stare and fix his gaze just over the man's shoulder.

Godfrey stood. 'I thought this was to be a council for princes – not paupers and rabble.'

'Wait,' Raymond pleaded. 'At our councils at Antioch, we always had leaders from the pilgrim host present.'

'If Peter Bartholomew is their leader, why is he not here himself?'

Raymond was about to offer an excuse, but the prophet John spoke more quickly. 'The time is not yet ready for Peter Bartholomew to reveal himself. He is preparing for the time to come – the time foretold by the prophecy. The time when the last shall be first and the first last.' He spun around, fixing his small eyes on the princes. 'You know what is coming. *The King will ascend Golgotha. He will take his crown from his head and place it on the cross, and stretching out his hands to heaven he will hand over the kingdom of the Christians to God the Father.*'

Godfrey moved so quickly I did not see what he did. One moment the peasant was standing, the next he was writhing on the ground, squealing in outraged agony until Godfrey's boot on his throat choked off the sound.

'Who told you that?' he demanded. 'Where did you hear it?'

He half lifted his foot from John's neck so that the wretch could speak. 'Mercy,' he spluttered. 'It is what Peter Bartholomew preaches. It is written in his book.'

'*What book?*'

'The book of prophecy,' squealed John.

'*Liar!*' Godfrey's cheeks were flushed; I had never seen him lose his temper like this, not even on the mountaintop

346

at Ravendan. 'That is not his book.' He took his boot off John's throat and delivered a sharp kick to his ribs. 'You should keep your dogs better trained,' he hissed at Count Raymond, 'or they will pull you down and devour you. Bring Peter Bartholomew to me.'

Raymond squirmed. 'I cannot—'

'He will not come.' John had struggled to his feet. 'Not until the appointed hour.' He circled around like a cornered dog, keeping his eyes fixed on Godfrey. 'And then, Duke Godfrey, beware, for his revenge will be terrible. The good wheat he will gather into his granary, but the *chaff* – he almost spat out the word – 'he will burn with unquenchable fire.'

κθ

꜒꜒꜒꜒꜒

There were no councils after that. Godfrey's army crossed the bridge and made their camp to the south-east of the city, well away from the Provençals, while Tancred extricated his men from Raymond's camp and took them south on foraging raids. Peter Bartholomew and the pilgrim horde stayed aloof on their hilltop. On the twenty-fifth of March, the Feast of the Annunciation, the Franks celebrated the start of their new year. It seemed to bring new life to the world: wildflowers bloomed on the hillside among the pines, and in the valley green buds began to sprout from the skeletal boughs of fig trees. A white sun shone from cloudless skies, warming the earth to dust. Even the crack and thud of siege weapons was, for a time, drowned out by birdsong. But it did nothing to brighten the mood of the Army of God. You had only to look at their faces to see the thunderclouds that gathered over them, to feel the charge in the sultry calm that gripped them. Soon, I feared, the storm would break.

It came on Holy Wednesday, the Wednesday before Easter. That morning I ate the stale, presanctified bread and listened to the priest read the gospel. *The hour has come for the Son of Man to be glorified. Now is the judgement of this world; now the ruler of this world will be driven out. Walk while you have the light, so that the darkness does not overtake you.* Afterwards, I sat with my family in our camp, while Helena wove daisies into a crown for Everard.

'I don't like Holy Week,' Zoe declared. 'Everything is pain and death.' She had never been shy of speaking her mind, though her thoughts seemed more provocative now than they once had. I had learned to choose when to answer and when to ignore her; Helena, however, could not restrain herself.

'Without the passion there is no resurrection. The sufferings of holy week are the foundations on which the church is built.'

I said nothing; I had my own reasons for disliking Holy Week. It was then, eighteen years ago, when the emperor Alexios had captured the imperial throne while his troops sacked the city where my wife and newborn daughter lived, and it had been Holy Week too when, sixteen years later, the Franks had tried to seize Constantinople. Instead of humility and love, this festival of exalted suffering seemed

349

more likely to provoke violence and frenzy. I had seen too much of it.

'What's that?'

I looked where Helena was pointing. From the hill to the north, where Peter Bartholomew and the pilgrims had their colony, a long procession had emerged and was winding its way towards the main Provençal camp. There must have been thousands of them, and even at that distance I could hear the melody of the hymn they sang.

'What does it mean?' Zoe asked, tugging my sleeve. 'What are they doing?'

'I don't know.' It might have been nothing more than a rite for Holy Week, some Frankish custom we did not know, but I doubted it. Already, at the foot of the hill and in the valley, I could see knights and soldiers emerging from their tents to stare in surprise.

'They look so solemn,' said Helena. 'More like an army marching to war than a host of pilgrims.'

She was right: rigid discipline gripped the pilgrim line, and they walked as if moved by a single, solemn purpose. A terrible foreboding rose in my heart; I shook off Zoe's hand and broke into a run, threading my way first between the tents, and then through the thickening crowds who flocked towards the same place. Up on the mountain spur men abandoned their siege tools and descended to meet us, while others poured over the bridge from Duke Godfrey's camp.

The pilgrim column reached the north side of the camp, where the valley floor began to rise, and halted. The crowd of knights and soldiers gathered around. Raised above all, on a rocky outcropping, stood Peter Bartholomew. He wore a long robe of pure white wool, with only a rope belt for adornment. His hair and beard had been washed, combed and tied straight with bands of cloth, and his sallow skin had been embalmed with oils and perfumes. Only his misshapen nose broke the picture of perfection, and betrayed the man he had once been.

He lifted his arms. The long sleeves of his gown hung down like wings.

'Rejoice, my brothers. The Lord came to me last night in dreams. Our deliverance is at hand.'

The pilgrims erupted in cheers and jubilation, hosannas and amens. Many of the facing knights joined in, though at least half – mostly the men of Normandy and Lorraine – remained impassive.

'Bring out the relic, the holy lance that pierced our Saviour's side, so that I may swear the truth of my vision.'

Three priests brought the golden reliquary that contained the fragment of the holy lance. One knelt on the ground and held up the casket to Peter, who laid both hands on its lid. Waves of light rippled from the crystal and gold, bathing his face in celestial radiance. A sigh shivered through the crowd.

'I swear by the holy lance . . . No!'

He broke off, snatching his hands away as if they had been burned. The crowd gasped – could this be punishment for a false oath? – but before they could move Peter had unlatched the reliquary, thrown back the lid and

351

plunged in his hand. He pulled it out and held it in the air, his fist clenched around something too small to see.

'I swear *on* the holy lance.'

The crowd erupted in a turmoil of euphoria. The din must have carried all the way to the lofty walls of Arqa far above us on the mountain, perhaps even to heaven itself. No one could see the lance – it was only a fragment, after all, no longer than a nail – but no one doubted that he held it. Even I felt a trembling in my heart, as if by touching the relic Peter had plucked a string that resonated in all our souls.

The light on Peter's face burned brighter than ever. Still holding his fist aloft, he turned to survey his congregation. Wherever he looked, the noise seemed to redouble.

'The way of truth is a thorny path. Will you receive this vision? Will you hear the words the Lord spoke to me, and believe them?'

I thought I felt an edge to his words, a sharpness like the mouth of a trap. But my thoughts were drowned by the commotion around me, thousands of voices all crying out that they *would* hear Peter's vision.

Peter bowed his head. Behind him, for the first time, I noticed his lieutenant, the self-styled prophet John. I scanned his face for signs of what was to come, but could read nothing in it except pride.

'I saw the Lord,' Peter declared. 'Last night, while I prayed.'

Several in the crowd shouted 'Amen', though the majority stayed still and silent, their heads lowered and their hands clasped before them, as if they could not trust themselves to let go. Many of the women swayed with eyes closed, transported by mystic rapture.

'A black cross stood before me, its wood rough and ill fitted. I trembled to see it, but the Lord commanded me: "Look up on the cross you seek."'

His far-seeing eyes stared up as if he could look through the vault of the sky all the way into heaven itself.

'And suddenly, there upon the cross, I saw the Lord stretched out and crucified, just as in the gospel. He hung naked, save for a black and red linen cloth tied around his loins, bordered with bands of white, red and green. Saint Peter supported Him on the right, and Saint Andrew on the left.

'Then the Lord spoke to me in a voice as deep as thunder. "Why do the Franks fear to die for me, as I died for them? I went to Jerusalem; I did not fear swords, lances, clubs, sticks or even the cross. Why do they fear to follow me?"

'I had no answer to give.' Peter's voice was desolate; he stood stooped and hunched like an old man. 'But the Lord said, "The army is riven by doubters and unbelievers. The covetous, the jealous, the cowards and the wicked. They have forgotten their calling: pretending caution, they corrupt even the bold and tempt them away from the righteous battle."'

Peter raised his head defiantly, staring straight ahead at a point in the crowd. I could not see who stood there, but I could guess.

'"But these evil men infest the body of this army like maggots," I said. "How can we root them out?"

'Then the wounds of Christ reopened, and blood gushed out from his hands, his feet and his side.' Peter waved the hand that still clasped the fragment of the lance. 'He asked, "Do you see my wounds?" And by some divine power my hand was stretched forward so that my fingers penetrated the wound. My arm became sticky with blood; within I could feel the bones of his ribs and the soft flesh of his intestines.'

His face lit up with sickened wonder. At the back of the crowd, I heard someone retching.

'The Lord continued, "As you see these five wounds, you must command Count Raymond, Duke Godfrey and all the princes to order their army in five ranks, as if for battle. Then the heralds will shout the war cry, *Deus vult*, three times, and the Holy Spirit will move across the face of the army, dividing them. And in the first rank you will see the best men, those who do not fear swords or spears or the torments of battle. They reside in me, and I in them, and at their deaths they will take their rightful places by my side.

'"In the second row are the auxiliaries, a rear-guard to protect the front rank. They are the apostles, who followed me and ate at my table. Behind them come their servants, who bring food and weapons to the front line – they are like the ones who pitied me on the cross but did not have the courage to act. All these men, I tell you, are worthy to be saved."'

Peter surveyed his audience, breathing in their adoration. Then something changed: the beatific smile vanished, and anger clouded his face.

"'In the fourth rank are the cowards and hypocrites, those who shut themselves up when the war comes because they do not trust in my strength to bring victory. It was they who crucified me, who said I deserved death because I claimed to be king, the Son of God. I *am* the Son of God.'"

Peter seemed to rip those last words from the very depths of his soul, shouting with such adamant defiance that you might have forgotten he was merely recounting the words of a vision. He breathed hard as if pressed down by a great burden, and his face was wet with sweat. His whole body convulsed with a raging energy.

With a visible effort he calmed himself. "'At the back, in the last rank, you will find the worst of men. Men who are not content to flee the battle themselves, but who use their guile to seduce others, braver and better, to abandon their duty. They are snakes, poisoning the army against me. They are the true brothers of the traitor Iscariot, the heirs of Pilate, and I will show them no mercy.'"

Once again, Peter's burning gaze was trained on that place in the crowd to my left, where Duke Godfrey's knights were gathered thickest.

"'What shall we do with them?" I asked.'

Peter raked his eyes over the audience, revelling in their dread anticipation. He licked his lips – his throat must have been parched from the effort, but when he spoke again his voice was deep and vivid, a terrible sound that seemed to come not from within him but through him, like a great wind funnelled through a doorway.

"'Kill them all.'"

λ

〜〜〜〜〜

A shocked silence fell upon the crowd. Eyes downcast, they began to edge away from Peter like a receding tide, while the princes pushed their way forward and gathered in front of him for a council. I attached myself to Nikephoros and watched discreetly from the margin.

'Does God say that I should massacre the fifth part of my army?'

The Duke of Normandy, normally reserved, stamped his foot and pounded a fist into his palm. 'Have I mortgaged my birthright, left all I held dear behind, and come so far through such torments, only to be told that my men are not worthy?'

From high on his rock, Peter Bartholomew stared back implacably. 'Not the fifth part of your army – only those the Lord knows as traitors. He did not say there would be equal numbers in all the ranks.'

'I say there is only one traitor we need to be rid of – the sooner the better.' Tancred touched one hand to his sword hilt, while the other sliced a gruesome gesture across his throat.

'Why?' asked Peter. 'Are you afraid of justice? You will stand in the front row when the army assembles, but where will you find yourself when God has winnowed His field?'

'Enough!' Raymond stepped to the front of the princes and swung around to face them. 'God has already showed the high favour in which He holds Peter Bartholomew. It was through him that He revealed the holy lance.'

It was not the definitive argument he had hoped. Several of the princes sniggered audibly, and at the back I heard a voice that sounded like Tancred's muttering something about a roofer's nail. Raymond's single eye glared at them, but the insult was too much for Peter Bartholomew. He leaped down from his boulder, almost shouldering Raymond aside in his haste to confront his doubters.

'Does anyone dare question the sanctity of the holy lance? You all saw it – you witnessed these very hands dig it from the ground. If any man doubts me, let him say so to my face, so that I may know my enemies.'

'Nobody doubts the lance.' Raymond made to lay a soothing hand on Peter's arm, then thought better of it. 'We all saw the miracle it brought at Antioch, our God-given victory against the Turks.'

'Nobody denies that God granted us the victory at Antioch,' Duke Godfrey agreed.

'Through the lance,' Peter insisted.

Godfrey shrugged. 'He works in mysterious ways. I do not presume to read them.'

Another man, a priest with bright orange hair who stood beside Godfrey, spoke up: 'Even Bishop Adhemar, bless his memory, doubted the authenticity of your iron splinter.'

That was almost true: he had certainly doubted the authenticity of Peter Bartholomew. Perhaps Peter knew that, for the priest's charge only inflamed his temper further.

'It is not an iron splinter,' he raged. 'It is a fragment of the lance of Longinus. That *splinter* touched the living flesh of our lord Jesus Christ. It was there on Golgotha when the destiny of the world was remade with His blood, and it has come back to us now, after a thousand years buried in the mud of Antioch, to show that the consummation of that destiny is at hand.'

More than once, then and afterwards, I wondered if God – or some other power – truly did speak through Peter Bartholomew. How else to explain the transformations he underwent, the sudden energy that could illuminate his mean body like the sun coming from behind a cloud? One moment he was a braying peasant, the next a pillar of righteousness effortlessly dominating his audience.

'Did God strike you deaf when I preached my vision?

359

Were you so blind to its meaning? The Lord is not coming to winnow our army, but to reap the whole world. You know what is written: when the Son of Man comes in His glory, He will separate the people one from another as a shepherd divides the sheep from the goats. He will put the sheep at His right hand and tell them, "Come and inherit the kingdom prepared for you from the foundation of the world." But the goats He will send into the eternal fire.'

Such was the force and conviction of his words that it was impossible to tell if he was reciting the Gospels, recounting a past dream, or witnessing the horrors he foretold even as he spoke them. The priests and princes drew back, cowering from the assault of his vision. Raymond seemed bewildered; Godfrey looked shocked, while the other faces watched with doubt, fear, hope and guilt.

The red-haired priest stepped forward tentatively. 'I did not mean to question the truth of your vision.'

'Or of the lance?'

'Or of the lance.'

Peter's face still blazed with righteous fervour. 'Does any man?'

None did.

'Besides,' said the priest, 'you were not the only man to dream of the lance. There was a priest at Antioch named Stephen of Valence who also received a vision of it, before we uncovered it.'

'Stephen of Valence received a vision that promised deliverance to come,' Peter corrected him sternly. 'He did not see the lance. That was confided to me alone.'

'But it corroborated your story.'

Peter sniffed. The radiance had departed again, and he seemed diminished. 'For most men, my word was enough.'

'But none doubted Stephen. He was so sure of his truth that he willingly offered to undergo the ordeal of the air or the ordeal by fire to prove it.'

'I would have done the same if anyone had demanded it. Who says I would not?'

'Nobody,' said the priest. He spoke reasonably, earnestly. 'I only said that Stephen *volunteered* to suffer the ordeal.'

All the men in the crowd stood silent, watching Peter Bartholomew. A new fire pulsed in his face, different and angrier than the celestial glow when he prophesied. He moved towards us, his arms twitching.

'Is that what you want? To see me thrown down from a high tower or set on a pyre? Do you think you will see my body destroyed, broken on rocks and burned in flame? You seek to test me, as the scribes and Pharisees tested Christ once before. But I will have the victory. I will fly through the air and walk through fire – let any man who doubts me come and witness it. But let him be warned that when the trial is over, it will be visited on him tenfold for his disbelief.'

Raymond looked appalled. 'That is not necessary. No man doubts you. We have your word.'

'And soon you will have the word of God. You know what is written in the psalms: *He will command His angels to guard you in all your ways. They will bear you up on their hands so that you do not dash your foot against a stone.*'

361

'It is also written, in the same place: *Do not put the Lord your God to the test*,' said Raymond's chaplain severely.

'And you should heed those words. Any man who doubts me doubts the Lord himself. Anyone who tests me, tests God.'

Godfrey looked ready to hit him for his audacity. 'That is blasphemy.'

'Light the fires and we will see.'

'No!' said Raymond. Godfrey rounded on him.

'Do you have so little faith in your tame peasant that you fear to put him to the ordeal? Do you fear that your authority might die with him, when all men see that the lance was a hoax concocted by charlatans, connived at by princes who should have known better. If you truly wished to preserve your authority you would not be trying to protect this peasant from roasting himself on his own pride – you would lead your army from Arqa this very afternoon, and not halt until you were at the walls of Jerusalem.'

The corner of Raymond's dead eye-socket twitched, but before he could answer Peter had shouted, 'Count Raymond protect me? Why should I need it, when I am robed in the armour of God? Build your pyres, stoke them up as high as you can. Two days from now I will pass through the flames and not one hair on my head will be singed. The flames will burn away your lies. The heavens will part with thunder, every element will be dissolved with fire, and all things will be revealed.'

*   *   *

They built the fire in the valley, at the narrowest point where its slopes offered plenty of vantage for the curious. Olivewood boughs were stacked four feet high and doused with oil, laid in two parallel rows just far enough apart that a man could walk between them. It was full thirteen feet from one end to the other – more than enough time for God to prove his favour, as Sigurd observed.

Good Friday dawned clear and warm, though it was one of those days when the senses and the soul misalign themselves, and even sunshine feels overcast. A grim expectation gripped the camp – long before the appointed hour, the audience had gathered thick as crows, many thousands of them rising far up the slope like the crowds in the hippodrome. Like the hippodrome, the nobles had the choice places nearest the arena, while the mass of peasants thronged the heights above. A cordon of barefoot priests stood around the pyre and held back the onlookers, singing the psalms appointed for that holy day.

> *Be wise, O kings,*
> *Be warned, you rulers of the earth.*
> *Serve the Lord with fear,*
> *And trembling kiss His feet,*
> *Or He will be angry, and you will perish,*
> *For His wrath is quickly kindled.*

Many of the pilgrims joined in that verse with relish, while the lords touched their swords and looked anxiously around them.

363

There was no place of honour for me. I sat with my family about halfway up the hill, looking down into the cauldron of the valley. Up there the atmosphere was like a village festival or a fair. Peddlers picked their way through the crowd with trays and baskets of nuts, olives and water. Others offered less wholesome wares: one man carried nothing but an enormous tray of bones. I beckoned him over.

'What are those?' I asked.

The peddler, a ruddy-faced man whose rough features seemed set in simple, honest contentment, gave a gap-toothed smile. 'Relics.'

'Relics of whom?'

He nodded down to the waiting pyre. 'Of him. These bones' – he picked one out and offered it to me for inspection – 'come from the lepers and cripples who Peter Bartholomew, bless his name, healed with his touch.'

'Not very well if this is all that remains of them.'

Anna reached into the tray and took another bone, a tiny thing barely larger than a comb's tooth. 'Has Peter Bartholomew healed many squirrels?'

Rather than take offence, the peddler gave a broad, innocent grin. *'He knows all the birds of the air, and all that moves within the field is His.'*

Anna rummaged some more in the tray. 'And these?' She pointed to an assortment of half a dozen mismatched pebbles.

'Stones that Peter Bartholomew, bless his name, has himself touched. And here . . .' The peddler leaned forward confidentially and extracted a thin clay vial from inside his tunic. He uncorked it and held it to Anna's nose. 'A few drops of his most precious blood. I was walking behind him in the forest when he pricked himself on a briar; I gathered it fresh from the thorn myself.'

'I thought it was usual to wait for a saint's death before distributing his relics,' I said.

'Only because you have never been in the presence of a living saint. Although . . .' He knelt down, rearranging the bones and stones in his tray. 'I have an agreement with one of the chaplains. If Peter Bartholomew, Christ preserve him, does not survive his ordeal, I am to get a bone from his forearm – and possibly his left hand. A Narbonnese priest offered me ten ducats for the arm, but if you were interested . . .'

I shook my head, smiling to hide my disgust. 'I'm sure Peter Bartholomew will triumph in his ordeal.'

The relic-seller beamed. 'I pray he does.'

The sun climbed higher and hotter, so hot that I feared it might set the fire alight before the appointed hour. The still air was drenched with the stink of oil and sweat; flies swarmed all around us. The mood of the crowd grew impatient: some wondered when their saviour would appear, while others taunted them that he had run away rather than be revealed as an impostor. In the sweltering heat the arguments became angry, and several men had to be pulled apart from their quarrels. Others let their purses speak for them, and laid wagers as to whether Peter

Bartholomew would survive, how long it would take him to traverse the corridor of flame, and whether the angels who carried him up out of the blaze would be seen by the audience.

A little after noon we heard a shout go up from the camp. In an instant, every man was on his feet, watching the solemn procession climb the valley. A cohort of Provençal soldiers led the way, forcing a path through the throng. Behind them came Count Raymond and a bishop, then a knot of priests huddled around a figure I could not see. They proceeded slowly, in a cloud of foliage where the peasants showered them with olive leaves and wildflowers. The air sang with adoration and the valley echoed with hosannas like the highest sphere of heaven.

At last the procession reached the open space around the fire. The watching crowd fell silent, and the only sound came from the cordon of monks who still sang their psalms. *Wicked and deceitful mouths are open against me, speaking against me with lying tongues. They beset me with words of hatred, and attack me without cause.*

The priests separated. In their midst, revealed like the stamen of a flower, stood Peter Bartholomew. The shining white robe had gone, and he wore only a simple tunic, which barely hung to his knees. His beard had been shaved close to the cheek, no doubt so it did not catch fire, and he had cropped his hair short. I could not see his face, but there was no strut or defiance in his posture, only humble concentration. He did not acknowledge either the praise or the insults of the crowd, but kept his gaze fixed on the ground.

'For the love of Christ, call it off,' Anna murmured beside me. 'You cannot tempt God like this.'

The priests and soldiers who had escorted Peter fanned out, forming a loose circle a little way from the fire. Four men stood at its centre: Raymond; the harelipped priest who served as his chaplain; a robed bishop and Peter Bartholomew. Peter knelt before the bishop, while the chaplain announced solemnly, 'If Omnipotent God talked to this man in person, and Saint Andrew revealed the true holy lance to him in vigil, let him walk through the fire unharmed. But if he has lied, let Peter Bartholomew and the lance he carries be consumed by fire.'

The crowd bellowed out a resounding 'Amen'. The bishop snapped open the golden reliquary, and laid the invisible fragment of the lance in Peter Bartholomew's cupped hands. Impervious to the building tension, the monks still chanted their psalms.

Let all who take refuge in you rejoice;
Let them ever sing for joy.
Spread your protection over them,
So that those who love your name may exult in you.
You bless the righteous, O Lord;
You cover them with favour as with a shield.

Now it was Peter Bartholomew's turn to speak. On previous occasions before such vast crowds his voice had carried effortlessly, somehow amplified to reach the furthest corners of his congregation. Now, that brightness was gone. I could barely see him behind the monks and priests who circled him, and his mumbled words were inaudible to all save the closest bystanders. The passage between the logs loomed before him like a tunnel.

Search me, O God, and know my thoughts.
See if there is any wickedness in me,
And lead me in the way everlasting.

The chaplain had carried a clay lamp, its light invisible in the brightness of the day. Now he presented it to the bishop, who spoke a few words of prayer over it and hurled it against the waiting pyre. The vessel shattered; for a second I saw twin tongues of flame racing along the tops of the corded wood, then the entire edifice erupted. A pillar of fire rose up, devouring the birds who had circled too low over it, and black smoke choked the sky. The crackle of wood was like the gnashing of great teeth.

A gust of wind blew smoke in my face, stinging my eyes. I squinted through the tears, so that Peter became little more than a dark blur at the foot of the flames. He must have been touched by God, for how else could he have stood so close to that blaze. Though I heard many things afterwards from those who had stood closer, I did not see him throw out his arms to embrace his fate; I did not see his eyebrows catch fire or his tunic start to smoulder, and I did not hear the last words he said before entering the inferno. *Forgive them, Father, for they know not what they do.*

I do not know how long Peter Bartholomew stayed in that fire. Afterwards, some claimed they could see his shadow through the flames, striding serenely forward and laughing, as if the fire and coals did little more than tickle him. Others swore that he had not passed through the ordeal alone: they had seen dim figures walking beside Peter, holding his hand or leading him on. For myself, I saw nothing but a glowing curtain of flame.

> *My hands and feet have shrivelled;*
> *I can count all my bones.*
> *They stare and gloat over me,*
> *And divide my clothes among themselves.*

Had the monks resumed their chant, or did I merely hear the words in my heart? I no longer knew: everything was ash. I was vaguely aware of Anna's hands gripping my arm – I saw the bruises later – and a murmur swelling around me as the crowd began to voice their doubts. Where was Peter Bartholomew? Surely he could not have survived in there so long. Had all his boasts been in vain? Had the lance failed him? Some men dropped to their knees and prayed for his survival; others sat in the grass and wept. Why had God forsaken them?

With a cloud of sparks and a shriek of unutterable pain, a black figure stumbled from the fire. He was naked as a child, his hair and clothes burned away, his skin turned

369

to cinders. He could barely stand; as he stepped away from the flames, he flung out his arms for balance as if he had never stood on his own before.

'*God help us!*' he screamed.

The crowd of pilgrims howled with triumph. As one, they rose up, poured down the hillside and engulfed him.

λα

〰〰〰

A pall of smoke from the smouldering fire covered our camp for the rest of the afternoon, shrouding the sky and bathing us in a sickly twilight. That did not deter the pilgrims, who flocked around the dying fire in their thousands. As the heat retreated they would run in and snatch at the coals or charred branches, holding them aloft like trophies, even as the embers burned into their skin. Afterwards, they showed these scars like wounds won in battle. I thought they were trying to find the fragment of the lance, which Peter must have dropped in the flames; Thomas explained that they were taking the ashes as relics of the holy ordeal, fragments of Peter Bartholomew's own cross. They stripped the fire bare, until by evening all that remained was a black scar on the earth.

'But he failed the ordeal,' Sigurd objected as we sat by our tents that night. 'Who would want a relic of that?'

'Sometimes the battles you lose are more glorious,' said Anna – mocking him, for she had never in her life thought any battle glorious.

Thomas did not laugh. 'Peter Bartholomew did not lose his battle, and he did not fail the ordeal.' He spoke very deliberately, straining to check his obvious emotion. 'We saw him emerge from the flames. *If he has lied, let Peter Bartholomew and the lance he carries be consumed by fire* – that was the test. The flames burned him, yes, but they could not overcome him.'

I sighed. The ordeal was supposed to have been a test, absolute proof one way or the other, yet now it seemed it had only added new layers of doubt and confusion. Was that an admonition that I should have more faith – or a warning against credulity? *Show me your way, O Lord,* I prayed, *and grant me wisdom to see.* Once I had styled myself an unveiler of mysteries, a seer of truths that other men were too obtuse or blind to see. Now I could not even be sure what had happened before my own eyes.

Anna laid a hand on Thomas's shoulder. 'Time will tell. If Peter—'

She broke off. All evening the camp had murmured with the songs of lamentation for Good Friday. Priests and pilgrims had gathered in their congregations, as the disciples must have gathered in their homes one evening long ago, after they had come down from Golgotha. The music filled the air with melancholy; they wept for themselves, as much for Peter. But now one sound grew louder, a solemn chant swelling above the rest. I jumped to my feet. A train of lights was snaking its way down from the valley and I ran to the road to watch them pass.

It reminded me of a funeral, of that procession I had seen in Antioch half a lifetime ago when they laid Bishop Adhemar in the ground. Barefoot priests led the way with veiled crosses, and acolytes carried long candles beside them. Behind came Peter's prophet John, his camelskin coat covered with a black gown that had been artfully torn in many places; after him a dozen men I did not recognise, and then the mass of pilgrims. Not just pilgrims, I saw – many knights and soldiers walked among them too. Candlelight flickered on their faces, windows in the darkness revealing their grief: cheeks smudged with soot, eyes shining with tears, hearts stricken with disbelief. They carried a bier, and for a shocked moment I thought it must be Peter Bartholomew's corpse. Then it came past me, and I saw it was only an effigy of Christ's tomb, with a high crucifix towering above it. They had garlanded the crucifix with flowers – poppies, narcissi, dandelions and roses; the flowers shivered and swayed as the bier moved, so that with the colours of their petals it appeared that the cross was wreathed in flame.

'*The dead shall live,*' they sang, '*their corpses shall rise. Awake, you who dwell in dust, and sing with joy.*'

Peter Bartholomew was not dead, but he barely lived. According to rumour he lay in his tent on the hill, a burned-out ember of a man, and awaited God's judgement. That was not enough for Anna, who insisted on going to him to see if she could ease his suffering. 'He was my patient once before,' she reminded me. But the crowds about his tent were so great we could not get within two hundred paces of it – and anyway, we were told, he had refused all salves and ointments, saying that the Lord alone would decide his fate.

'If he spurns medicines, he has made Christ's decision for Him,' Anna complained. But every hour on Easter Saturday the crowds around his tent grew, so many that the pilgrim camp could barely contain them. The surrounding tents were stripped back to make room, first from the top of the hill, then ever further down the slopes, until Peter's tent stood in solitude on the bald summit.

Unexpectedly – for he had not even attended the ordeal – it was Nikephoros who showed the greatest interest in Peter's fate. He summoned me to his quarters on the Saturday morning and questioned me at length; he even asked what Anna thought, which was extraordinary, for until then I had not realised he knew she existed.

'She is certain that without a doctor's attention he will die of his wounds?' he pressed me.

'Even if he did accept it he would hardly have much hope. Any other man would have died already of those wounds. That he has survived until now is . . . fortunate.' I could not bring myself to say *miraculous*.

Nikephoros seemed satisfied. 'The sooner the better.'

'But if Peter Bartholomew dies, and the lance is discredited, Raymond will be much weakened.'

Nikephoros dripped wax on the dispatch he had just written. 'Raymond is weakened anyway. He built his house on shifting sands, and now they have swallowed him. No doubt he will salvage what he can by claiming that the peasant in fact survived the ordeal, but few will believe him once they see Peter Bartholomew laid out in his tomb.'

'But then—'

'Peter Bartholomew's death will weaken Raymond. As he is the only barbarian who even pretends to support the emperor, that would be a setback. But if Peter Bartholomew survives, if tomorrow he appears to his peasant congregation resurrected . . .' Nikephoros pressed his seal into the soft wax. 'What do you think will happen then?'

I rose early on the Sabbath just as the day was dawning. Helena wanted some herbs for the Easter lamb, and I had said I would find them. I slipped out of our tent alone and walked quickly towards the mountain. I told myself that I remembered seeing some wild rosemary growing in the forest there, though I might not have remembered it so well if the path had not led close to the pilgrim camp. Though I had heard Anna's diagnosis, a deep and unanswerable part of me still whispered that the Lord made all things possible. I scanned the hilltop, seeking a sign: thousands of pilgrims still kept their vigil on its slopes, many of them prostrate with prayer or exhaustion, and the faint melodies of hymns drifted down to me in the dawn stillness. But the songs were scattered and tentative, their message nothing more than fading hope.

Disappointed, and disgusted with myself for it, I turned away towards the place where I thought I had seen the rosemary. I was not alone. As Easter dawned without its Messiah, men and women had begun to trickle down from the hill and return to their camps. I tried not to look at them – the disappointment in their faces was too painful to see – but one caught my eye. Despite the warmth of the April morning he wore a cloak that hung to his ankles, its hood raised to cover his face. As I watched, his course seemed to drift imperceptibly towards the forest on the mountain ridge to the north-east, gradually taking him away from the army.

Perhaps he was no more than a pilgrim looking to relieve himself in private; perhaps he wanted to pick herbs too. But there was something surreptitious about him, something deliberately evasive that I had seen before in men who had had good reason to avoid discovery – the same reason, most often, as I had had for finding them. And so, more from habit than anything else, I followed him into the forest.

It was not difficult. The trees were thick enough that he could not see me, and my footsteps were silent on the thick carpet of pine needles. Thin columns of sunlight filtered through the foliage; if I had not been so intent on my pursuit, I might have paused to marvel at the simple beauty of a spring morning. But I pressed on, pausing twice when the fluttering of birds in the branches above temporarily frightened me – and a third time when I came to a bend in the path and heard voices ahead.

'He hasn't recovered?' As the voice spoke, I heard the

abrupt bite of a shovel breaking earth, and then the rasp of iron on loose stone.

'There'll be no resurrection for him.' The shovel dug into the stony ground again, harder this time. 'If I could have tied a rope on him and dangled him in front of the crowds like a puppet, I would have. That would have been enough. But he won't get up from that bed again, except to fall into his grave.'

The second voice sounded familiar, though I could not place it. I crouched low and moved off the path into the undergrowth, trying to find a place to see. Every branch I touched or leaf I brushed caused a stab of fear, but the sounds of digging drowned out any noise I made. I came closer, and eventually found a place where if I lay on my belly I could just see through the gap beneath a squat bush. I had brought a knife with me to cut the herbs; I pulled it from my belt, and watched.

Two men stood in the clearing with their backs to me, one in a brown tunic and the other in blue. They had already dug out a sizeable pile of earth. As I watched, one of them knelt and reached into the hole with both hands, pulling out a bulging sackcloth bag. Its contents shifted and clinked as he set it on the ground and brushed the dirt from it.

'Where will you go?' asked the man in the blue. He drew a knife and sliced through the cords that tied the neck of the bag.

'North to Tortosa. I can find a boat there to take me home. I've had enough of this adventure.'

The man in the brown tunic pulled out an empty sack

he had kept looped over his belt. He held it open while the other shared out the contents of the buried bag. I heard the trickle of a stream of a coins.

The man wrapped a rope around the neck of the bag and tied it fast. 'It may not be eternal life, but at least we have some inheritance from Peter Bartholomew.'

'Bless his name,' added his companion instinctively.

'Curse his name! He would have ruined us – and might still, if anyone thinks to look for us. He may have convinced us he was the one foretold in scripture and the prophecy; he may even have convinced himself. But he did not convince God.' He lifted the two sackcloth bags in his hands. 'Thank Christ he convinced men with deeper pockets.'

He tested the weight of the bags. 'This is fair.'

'Then we should go. Before the others think to look for us.'

The two men embraced. 'God go with you.'

'And with you.'

They spoke the farewells quickly, mechanically. Then, without a second glance, they parted and left the clearing, one taking a path to the north and the other heading east. I counted towards twenty under my breath, wondering which to follow. I had only reached eighteen when I heard a sound from ahead. Dropping down on my stomach again, I saw the man in the brown tunic re-emerge from the path he had taken. He looked around cautiously, then hurried over to where the shovel still lay on the ground. As he bent down to take it I saw his face for the first time: only for a second, framed between branches, but I knew it at once. The prophet John. He had lost his camelskin robe and cut his hair much shorter than before, but the puffy face was as unpleasant as ever. It was his voice I had remembered.

He walked across to another place in the clearing, a few yards away from the first hole, and began digging. I edged around through the undergrowth so that I was behind him again, trying to time my movements to the strokes of the shovel, and waited until he had finished his hole. It did not take him long – whatever he was excavating was not buried deep. He put the shovel aside, glanced over his shoulder, then dropped to his knees and scrabbled in the earth.

I only needed four strides to cover the distance between us. Distracted by his buried treasure he barely heard me coming: the first he properly knew was when he felt my weight pinning him down, one hand on the back of his head and the other holding a knife to his throat.

'Did you forget something?'

'Thaddaeus?' His voice was frightened, pathetic – not the voice of a man who had presumed to lecture princes. 'I forgot about this bag, Thaddeus; I would have come after you to give you your share, I swear to you.'

'I do not want your gold.'

Through his terror, he must have realised I was not his cheated companion returning for vengeance. 'Who are you?'

I didn't answer. 'You were Peter Bartholomew's self-annointed prophet.'

'No,' he squealed. 'No!'

I twisted the knife so that the flat of the blade was against his throat, and pressed hard. 'Liar. I saw you with him.'

I loosed the pressure a little so he could breathe to answer. 'I never knew him.'

'You stood in his tent and told me that no one came to Peter except through you.'

I doubt he remembered me from that, but it was enough to puncture his feeble resistance. All energy left him and his body sagged forward, so limp that I had to pull the knife away lest he slit his own throat.

'Why were you stealing away so fast?' I demanded. 'Shouldn't you be at your master's side, in the hour of his greatest suffering?'

'Peter Bartholomew is dead!' He cried out the words like a wounded animal.

'When I left the camp, Peter Bartholomew still lived.'

'Yes – if you can say a man lives because his heart beats and his lungs breathe. He will cling to life as long as he can, and who can blame him? He knows what awaits him in the world to come.'

'Angels and seraphs hymning his praise, and a seat at the right hand of the Father? Or is he bound for the dark places where false prophets and deceivers languish?'

John mumbled something I could not hear. I made him repeat it.

'For what he has done, he will be cast in the deepest pit of hell.'

Even for one bent on apostasy, it was a terrible thing to say – and spoken with savage hurt.

'Why? What lies did he tell you?'

John writhed and whimpered in my grasp but did not answer.

'Was it the lance?'

He nodded eagerly. 'Yes – the lance.'

'What else? Did he claim he was a saint? A prophet?'

'At first he said he was only a messenger sent to proclaim the things to come. But the more the Lord spoke to him, the greater his claims grew. First that he was a saint – then that he had been possessed by the spirit of Elijah to prepare the world for its tribulations.'

'Did he tell this widely?'

John shook his head. 'Only to us, his closest disciples. He said the time to reveal himself had not yet come.'

He spilled out his words, unburdening himself with the eager gratitude of the penitent. But I had heard enough confessions to know when a heart had given up all its secrets – and when it had not.

'Elijah was not the limit of Peter Bartholomew's ambition,' I guessed. 'He went further.'

I twisted John around so that he lay on his back. I wanted to look in his eyes. I took the knife from his throat and stepped back, though not so far that he could hope to escape me.

'He told us he was the one foretold by the prophecy.' John whispered the words, as if afraid to hear himself saying them. 'The last and greatest of all kings, who will come at the end of days to capture Jerusalem.'

'The son of God?' Even I was whispering now.

John did not answer directly. *'When the Son of Perdition has risen, the King will ascend Golgotha. He will take his crown from his head and place it on the cross, and stretching out his hands to heaven he will hand over the kingdom of the Christians to God the Father. This will be the end and the consummation of the Roman and Christian Empires, when every power and principality shall be destroyed.'*

His gaze was distant, and he recited it with the familiarity of well-worn verses of scripture. But I had spent my youth in a monastery, had heard every word of the Bible so many times it was as familiar as my own name – and I had never heard that passage.

'What is that?'

John's eyes refocused on me. 'The prophecy,' he said simply.

'Whose prophecy? Peter Bartholomew's? Was it another thing revealed in his dreams?'

He thought for a moment, as if he had never questioned its provenance before. 'No. It was written down in a book – and Peter could not write.'

'But he could read.'

John gave a sly smile. 'He pretended he could not, but I often saw him alone in his tent poring over the book. And how else would he have known what it said?'

'Did he show it to you?'

'Only once.' John shrugged. 'It made no difference – I do not have to pretend to be illiterate. But I saw the images that illuminated it. Terrible things. Monsters with the heads of Saracens and the bodies of lions ripping women's bellies

382

with their claws and devouring the unborn children. Locusts with tails like scorpions; a red dragon with seven heads and ten horns. Men dressed as women lying unnaturally with each other in pools of blood, even as the carrion birds picked out their entrails.' He trembled with the memory. 'And at the bottom of the page, a radiant king on a white horse. He wore two crowns; his left hand wielded a lance with which he dispatched the Saracens and Ethiopians who assailed him, while his right stretched out to the cross on Golgotha.'

I knew what they illustrated. 'The last days. And how did Peter Bartholomew come by this manuscript?'

'He said he found it in a cave after a dream.' Again that sly, slightly rueful smile. 'But I also heard that he stole it from one of the princes.'

I remembered Godfrey's sudden fury when John had quoted a passage of the prophecy at him in Raymond's council. 'Do you know who he stole it from?'

'No.'

'But he came to believe that he was the king foretold.'

'Perhaps.' John sat up, raising his hands in ignorance. 'By the end, I do not know what he believed. The way he walked into that fire, he might have thought he was Christ himself reborn. He fooled us all – even me, who knew better than most what he was.'

His voice faltered. It might merely have been self-pity, a lament for the power he had lost, but I thought I detected grief as well for the visionary betrayed by his own dreams. For a moment I almost felt sorry for him.

Then I remembered that this was the man who half an hour earlier had spoken of stringing up Peter like a puppet to preserve his authority. I remembered the woman caught in adultery, so bewitched and brutalised that she had plunged the hot brand into her breast; the knights from Count Raymond's bodyguard who had broken their oaths and abandoned their lord in the fog. There had been no pity in the faith Peter Bartholomew preached.

I jerked my knife at the fallen prophet. 'Go.'

He scrambled to his feet. One hand reached for the sack of coins he had taken, then paused as he caught my eye. He contrived a pitiable, beseeching gaze.

'Take it.' I would have liked to count out thirty pieces of silver for him, but at that moment I only wanted to be rid of him. He snatched up the bag, took a last look around the clearing, then crossed quickly to its edge. Just before he disappeared into the trees, he looked back.

'The prophecy says that the king will come when we wrest Jerusalem from the forces of Babylon.'

'So?'

His fat face twisted in an unpleasant smile. 'Don't you wonder? If Peter Bartholomew was not the promised king, who is?'

λβ
~~~~~~

As Peter's condition worsened, so too did Raymond's spirits. He kept to his tent and let it be known he was praying for Peter Bartholomew. Up on the mountain our siege engines stood silent, while down in the valley the army held its breath and waited.

At dusk on the Thursday after Easter, Nikephoros lost patience and demanded an audience. As we walked through the camp I could not help looking up the northern hill where Peter Bartholomew still clung to life. There was nothing to see: his tent was dark, and none of the surrounding pilgrims had lit fires. It was said that even the least wisp of smoke sent Peter into paroxysmal fits, clawing at his skin and screaming like a demon.

Raymond's tent, by contrast, was ablaze with light –

golden candlesticks inscribed with the sharp-figured script of the Arabs, looted from their churches; wrought ivory lamps that must have been gifts from the emperor Alexios; and a host of other vessels burning oil, wax, tallow and coals, banishing the shadows from every corner of the room.

He would not have admitted us; indeed, his stewards tried to turn us away three times, but Nikephoros was more than a match for Frankish functionaries and harangued them into submission. We found Raymond alone in his chamber: if he had been praying, he had not coupled it with fasting, for the furniture and carpets were strewn with plates and bowls, half-finished meals congealing within them. Red wine stained Raymond's tunic and blushed his lips like a harlot's.

'Is there any news of Peter Bartholomew?' His voice was dull and empty, his words slurred.

Nikephoros shrugged. 'He is only delaying the inevitable. Not for much longer, I think.' He swept a plate of gawping fish-heads from the chair where it rested and sat down opposite Raymond. I stood behind him.

'But there is still hope?' The desperation in Raymond's voice was pitiful.

'No!' Nikephoros slammed a fist on the arm of his chair, rattling the cups on the floor beside it. 'Forget Peter Bartholomew. If you never spoke his name or thought of him again, it would be a great blessing to you.'

Raymond staggered out of his chair. Nikephoros rose to meet him, and for a moment they stood facing each other, one face blazing bitter fury, the other cold with contempt.

'I am the lord of thirteen counties and captain of the Army of God.' Raymond invoked the titles without strength, as if they had become no more than the hollow shell of a lost faith. 'You cannot speak to me—'

'I am speaking to you as a friend,' Nikephoros insisted. He raised a hand, and though he did not touch the count he shrank away, dropping back into his chair. Nikephoros remained standing.

'Peter Bartholomew betrayed you,' he said, more softly now. 'He tricked you, as he tricked so many others. Forget him.'

Raymond sank his face into his hands. 'Why did he insist on that ordeal? He did not have to, and he should not have let himself be goaded into it. What of it if some of the princes were jealous of his power? The pilgrims trusted him. That was all that mattered. Who will guide them now that Peter Bartholomew has gone?'

'Who cares? They are just peasants – a rabble.'

'But put enough peasants together and they will become a power to be reckoned with. They have nothing to offer save their faith – but that can be a mighty weapon when you are fighting for God. Peter understood that. While he lived, the pilgrims put their faith in him, and through him in me. They paid me no tribute and added no spears to my army, but their loyalty proved my greatness to the other princes.'

'Then send one of your priests to minister to them.

They may have abundant faith to give, but it is easily won. If you do not, someone else will.'

Raymond looked up in hope. 'And there is still the lance. Peter carried it intact from the flames; I have it in my chapel.'

'Forget the lance!' Nikephoros kicked out at a cup that stood on the floor: it flew against the side of the tent and spattered a dark stain down its wall. 'Forget Peter Bartholomew. Forget the lance. Forget Arqa. They are only distractions, poisoning the army with false hopes and lies. All that matters is Jerusalem. That is where you should be looking.'

'But without Peter Bartholomew—'

'Without Peter Bartholomew you are free of a treacherous ally. If he did one good thing in his life, it was to walk into that fire and rid us of his madness.'

Nikephoros looked around wildly, seeking something else to kick. Finding nothing, he strode towards the door. Just before he reached it he turned. His cheeks were flushed in the lamplight, and his breath was faster than it could ever have been in the courtyards of the imperial palace. With great effort, he tried to check his anger.

'You are still the greatest lord in this army. You still command more men, and more honour, than any of your rivals. If you lead them to Jerusalem now, everything that has happened here will be forgotten.'

He turned to go, and almost walked straight into a servant hurrying in through the door. Nikephoros cursed the unfortunate and cuffed him aside, while Raymond fixed him with a weary glare.

'I told you to leave me alone.'

The servant bowed, rubbing his ear where Nikephoros had hit it. 'Mercy, Lord. There are men outside you must see.'

'What men? If it is Godfrey or Tancred come to gloat, I will not give them that satisfaction. If they have come to pity me, I do not need it.'

'Forgive me, Lord, but these men are not from Duke Godfrey's camp – or Tancred's or Duke Robert's.' He swallowed. 'They say they have come from Egypt.'

The Egyptians were waiting for us outside the tent, on a makeshift parade ground illuminated by many torches. I could see at once why the servant had trembled with such wide-eyed awe: even to me, who had sailed up the Nile and walked in the shadows of the pharaohs' glory, there was something savage and exotic in their appearance. Some were still mounted on the camels they had ridden, perhaps all the way from Egypt; others had dismounted and stood proudly in front of their animals. As for their masters, their silver armour moved like dragon scales, their swords were curved like lions' teeth, and their solemn faces were black as the depths of Sheol. One of them carried the black banner of the Fatimids, though the fabric disappeared in the darkness so that the white writing seemed to flutter over their heads as if by witchcraft. If they had announced they came not from Egypt but from the deepest reaches of hell, and not on an embassy but to reap the earth, few would have disbelieved them.

But three men stood among them who did not look like spectres of the apocalypse. Two of them, indeed, wore thick wooden crosses over their tunics to prove their true faith. Their faces were pale, like moons against the darkness, and pitted by hardship. One in particular seemed to have suffered terribly. His left arm had been reduced to a stump, not even reaching the elbow, and his once-powerful frame was now stooped and skewed. Some tufts of his hair still grew russet-brown, but the greater part was white, like dust. Worst of all were the eyes, bulging out of his face and interrogating the world with a terrible, candid bitterness.

'Achard?'

I spoke tentatively, hardly believing what my own eyes told me. In my mind I was suddenly transported many hundreds of miles away, to a moonless night and a river, a desperate battle and monsters from the deep feasting on the dead. Achard had called on me to save him.

I looked away, ashamed by the memory. As I did, I saw another face I knew. He had been watching me, waiting for me, and his white teeth smiled broadly in the darkness.

Two hours later I sat by my fire with Anna, Thomas, Sigurd and Bilal. Sigurd eyed him warily, and made a great display of oiling and polishing his axe-blade while we talked – though in truth, despite the extremes of their skin, the two men had much in common. Both were built like warriors, and held themselves with the easy confidence of strong men. Anna, who had always maintained that God made all men the same beneath their skins – Christian or Ishmaelite, orthodox or heretic – covered herself modestly and watched. Only Thomas seemed troubled: he stared at the ground, fidgeted with whatever came to hand, and said almost nothing.

'You escaped, God be praised,' said Bilal, and I remembered that the last time he saw me I had been going to my death. 'I knew that you never reached the other side of the river; and I heard that a detachment of the caliph's horsemen had been massacred by *Nizariyya* bandits in the eastern desert. But there was no way of knowing . . .' He gave a tight smile. 'Many men get lost in the desert.'

I thought back to those terrible days: the thirst, the heat, the emptiness that flayed away the layers of my soul until the hollow core was stripped bare. In the deepest places of my heart I still bore the scars.

'Bilal saved us,' I told Anna. 'I owe him my life.'

Bilal shrugged off the compliment with a graceful lift of his shoulders. 'With the vizier away the caliph had lost his senses. Al-Afdal approved what I had done when he returned. Though not before the Franks had suffered cruelly in the caliph's dungeon.'

I shivered as I remembered the sight of Achard's tormented body. 'What did the caliph want from them?'

'Revenge for those who had escaped. To win the love of his people by persecuting Christians. To show his independence of the vizier.' Bilal flicked his hand at the empty air. 'Who can say?'

'What happened to Achard?'

391

'They dragged him half-dead from the river. The crocodiles had torn off one of his hands, and part of his leg as well. They healed him as best they could but the arm became infected. They had to amputate three times to cut off the poison. When that was done they sent him to the caliph's torturers.' Even Bilal, hardened to suffering by a lifetime on the battlefield, did not hide his pity. 'His body may have been broken, but his will did not suffer. If anything, his ordeal only strengthened his faith. And not through any mercy of the torturers.'

Thomas picked up a stick and began scoring the earth by his feet.

'How long was he in there?'

'Only a week. It was long enough. Then the vizier returned and freed them. He was furious with the caliph for making enemies where we did not need them.'

'Then perhaps he should have arranged it so that Achard never returned.'

'He considered it,' Bilal admitted. 'Achard's anger is like a tumour inside him, feeding on itself and consuming him. I have known violent men, and good men driven to anger, but never such a hate-filled man as that. The world offers him nothing but revenge. He is not a man I would want to face in battle.'

He leaned forward, locking his gaze on mine. 'And you should fear him too, Demetrios. He has not forgotten that you escaped and he did not.'

λγ

~~~~~~

News of the Fatimids' arrival spread quickly through the camp – and even beyond. At first light next morning, the garrison of Arqa – which had not troubled us for almost a fortnight while we broke off the siege work to celebrate Easter – began a furious bombardment of rocks and arrows.

'They are afraid we have come to make an alliance with you to steal their lands, Christians and Fatimids against the Arabs,' said Bilal.

'Have you?'

'Wait and see.'

Count Raymond had his men erect a new tent to receive the ambassadors, on the northern ridge well beyond the main camp. He claimed it was sited to be safe from attack, though I suspected he was more worried about what the pilgrims would think if they saw their leaders sitting down with Ishmaelites.

Though it was hardly a private affair. Jealousy and distrust had fractured the army: no man was willing to come alone, or to appear with the smallest retinue. The princes brought their guards, their secretaries, their bishops, priests and chaplains, their knights and standard-bearers. It did not help the atmosphere in the room: by the time we had climbed the slope, and then crowded ourselves into the confines of the tent, the air was sweltering and ill-tempered. What must the Fatimid ambassador have thought of us? I wondered. He sat on a cushion near the door, a round-faced man with a soft beard and hard eyes.

'In the name of the one God, the almighty and merciful, greetings,' he said. An aide relayed his words in translation. 'And greetings from my master, the caliph al-Mustali, and his faithful servant the vizier al-Afdal.'

Each of the princes introduced himself in turn. Even that took almost half an hour, for none was inclined to brevity. Expressions of welcome quickly meandered into self-aggrandising bravado, mixed with clumsy innuendo at the backward errors of the Muslims. The Fatimid ambassador listened more courteously than they deserved, giving the appearance of attending every word, though it seemed from his eyes that he already knew exactly who they all were.

'My master has followed your progress with interest,' he said, when at last it was his turn to speak again. He did not say that his master had been amazed at how faltering and shambolic that progress had been, though he somehow managed to insinuate it in his face. 'From here, you are only forty miles from his border.'

'All we desire is to reach Jerusalem.'

The ambassador nodded. 'And Jerusalem is in my master's possession.'

'For the moment.'

There was an awkward pause.

'There does not need to be a war between us,' the ambassador tried again. 'We have many enemies in common. Far better to destroy them than each other.'

'If the caliph hands over Jerusalem, we will gladly make an alliance and fight beside him,' Godfrey offered.

The ambassador replied with a smile of totally insincere regret. 'The caliph cannot do that. Jerusalem is one of the holiest cities of Islam. The heir of the prophet, peace be upon him, would dishonour both Allah and his people if he surrendered it. Even to worthy men like you.'

'He will be dishonoured a great deal more when we cast him out of it in ruin,' Tancred warned.

'We pray that will not be necessary,' Raymond added quickly. 'But if the caliph has followed our progress, he knows how far we have come and what trials we have suffered. We did not come for riches or glory or conquest.' He tapped the white cross sewn onto his robe. 'We came for this: for the love of Christ, and the humble desire to worship where he died. We cannot turn away now, so close to our goal.'

'Not as close as you think. You cannot measure the distance to Jerusalem in miles alone.' The Fatimid leaned forward on his cushion. 'Even if you take Arqa, there are a dozen cities just as strong between here and Jerusalem. Will you reduce them all? Then there are the natural obstacles. You have heard of the *Raz-ez-Chekka*, the Face of God? It is two days' march from here, a place where the coastal road runs so close between the cliffs and the sea that you can only pass in single file. Twenty men there could block your passage for ever. And even if you did reach Jerusalem, you would find yourselves in a desolate land, dying of thirst before impregnable walls.' He shook his head, as if he could not comprehend the hardships he described. 'You have come a long way through extraordinary dangers, yes. But that does not mean the worst is behind you.'

'All the more reason to hurry on then,' said Tancred, staring at Raymond. Many in the tent muttered their agreement.

'You would only hurry on to your doom. And you would make enemies where you do not need them. When I spoke of the hardships you have suffered, it was not to belittle them. My master the vizier' – I noticed he had dropped the pretence of serving the caliph – 'has seen how you long to pray at your shrines in Jerusalem. He can see it would be neither just nor prudent to deny you your goal after you have come so far.'

'It is not for him to deny or grant. Only God has that power,' said Godfrey.

'God is truly strongest and most mighty,' the envoy agreed. 'But, *mashallah*, al-Afdal controls Jerusalem and its approaches.'

'Not for long,' Tancred interrupted.

The envoy's face hardened, and he lifted his hands as if calming a misbehaved child. 'Please. I did not come here to swap boasts and insults. I have come, at the command of the vizier, to make you this offer – if you will hear it.'

Tancred smirked. 'What could an Ishmaelite have to say that was worth hearing – except his death cry?'

'*Silence!*' Raymond swept his stern eye around the room, before returning his gaze to the envoy. 'What does your master propose?'

The envoy sat very still for a moment, so that only his eyes moved, darting about the tent like a snake sizing up its prey.

'If you will swear peace with the Fatimid caliphate, al-Afdal will give safe conduct and protection to any man who wishes to see Jerusalem. All he asks is that you leave all weapons, except what is prudent for a traveller to carry, at the borders of his lands; and that you come in small numbers, no more than twelve at a time.'

He pressed his fingers together and leaned forward earnestly. 'You have won many victories, but you have also suffered many losses. How many men have died already so that you can see Jerusalem? How many more will die if you insist on fighting your way to the end?' All trace of

397

impatience was gone from his voice; his eyes pleaded with us to accept his offer. 'You call the prophet Jesus Christ the Prince of Peace. What better way to honour him, and yourselves, than if you come to Jerusalem in peace?'

'Christ may have been the Prince of Peace, but he also said, "I bring not peace but the sword."'

The Fatimid ambassador had been sent out while the princes considered his proposal. But instead of the princes it was a humble priest who had spoken first – Arnulf, the red-headed priest who had challenged Peter Bartholomew's claims to divine authority. He had never spoken in a council before; I wondered who had given him permission to do so now.

Worry creased the Duke of Normandy's brow. 'We swore an oath to pray at the Holy Sepulchre. How will God judge us if we choose to fight, and lose, when the Egyptian offered us a way to fulfil our oath.'

'You cannot honour an oath by dishonouring yourself,' Tancred jeered. 'Do you remember what this signifies?' He tapped the cross sewn on his tabard. 'We swore to liberate the holy city from the vile race who possessed it – not to go and gawp as sightseers.'

'The question is: do we have the strength to fight our way to Jerusalem, and then into the city itself?' said Godfrey.

'And even if we do, how many will be left when we have finished?' asked Raymond.

The red-haired priest, who showed not the least awe at being in such exalted company, sniffed. 'We should count each of the fallen as nothing less than a blessing from God. You know Pope Urban's promise: all who die in battle against the Ishmaelites shall have remission of sins, and will feast on the fruits of the kingdom of heaven.'

'Even if we did want to accept the Egyptians' offer,' said Godfrey, 'how are we to know it is honest? "Come to Jerusalem unarmed, in small groups," he says. But what if when we step into the holy city we find a host of Ishmaelites waiting to cut us down?'

There were murmurs of agreement around the tent.

'What do we know of the way the Fatimids honour their oaths? A year ago we sent four of our most trusted knights to negotiate with them. Only three have returned. Why not ask them if the caliph's offer is sincere?'

The others nodded. Achard pushed through to the front and stood before the princes, his bulbous eyes staring at them. He had not washed or changed since his journey: he stood before them in the same dusty tunic, the same dirty bandage tied over the stump of his arm, his face still unshaven. Every man watched him, yet none would meet his gaze.

'I will tell you how much you can trust the king of the Egyptians.' He twitched his stump. 'He is the enemy: he was born in Babylon and he has come to Jerusalem to take his seat in the temple of God. I have seen it.'

For a moment a stunned silence overtook the crowded tent; then it erupted in an incredulous clamour.

'You have seen Jerusalem?' Godfrey asked, when the noise had subsided.

The scars on Achard's face were set hard with pride. 'I have. We passed through it on our way here.'

'Praise be to God,' the Duke of Normandy murmured, touching the cross he wore. 'Then you have walked the holy way, and knelt by the tomb of Christ.'

Achard lifted his head with disdain. 'I have not. I refused to set foot in the city while it lay captive to the pagans. When I enter it, I will come as a conqueror fulfilling the destiny of Christ – not as a hostage.'

'Then you would reject the Egyptians' offer?' Godfrey asked gently.

Achard answered with a horrible, sneering laugh. 'Their presence in the city is an abomination before God: and the city will not be cleaned or made new until it has been washed in their blood.'

The chamber erupted in approval. Men stamped their feet on the ground and clapped their hands together; they shouted amens and cried to the Lord to bring them swiftly to Jerusalem.

'You should go at once,' Achard agreed, when he could be heard again. 'God has opened the way.'

'Has He?' asked Raymond. Through all the cheering he had barely made a sound, tapping one hand half-heartedly on the arm of his chair.

'Yes.' The tumult seemed to have fired Achard's soul: he stood straighter, his shoulders stiff and his face burnished with colour. 'Do you think the Egyptians would have allowed us to return, or sent you this offer now, if they were as strong as they pretend? I did not set foot inside

Jerusalem, but I saw the garrison there. The walls are fear-some, yes, but not impregnable. The Ishmaelites took the city after a siege of only forty days. Surely God would deliver it to us even faster.'

'And the road from here to Jerusalem?' pressed Raymond. 'What of that?'

Achard shrugged. 'The Fatimids say they have mastered all of Palestine. But when we came here from Jerusalem, we travelled by night and camped in hidden places. I do not think the coastal cities are loyal to Egypt. If we arrived at their gates and said we had come to overthrow the Egyptian invaders, I think they would welcome us with food and speed us on our way.'

The tent was suddenly alive with optimism, babbling with questions and hope. Several of the princes declared that they would march on Jerusalem that very night. Achard shook off their enthusiasm, lifting his one arm like a gallows to recapture their attention.

'I have not reported everything I learned on my travels.' His voice was severe; the colour had drained from his face, so that the scars stood out in a livid web against the skin. 'While I was held captive in Egypt, a delegation of Greeks arrived to treat with the caliph. Two of them are in this room now.'

He swung around to fix his bulging stare on Nikephoros, and me behind him. The men around us seemed to shrink away: others craned their heads to stare.

'We went to Egypt for the same reason as you,' said Nikephoros. 'Because we thought the Egyptians might join us against the Turks, when the Turks still held Jerusalem.'

'So you said. But I learned differently. Your real purpose was to make an alliance with the Ishmaelites against *us*, to annihilate our army and divide the lands we had conquered between you.' As shock and anger hissed around the room, he stepped forward and stabbed a finger towards us. 'Do you deny it?'

Standing behind Nikephoros I could not see his face, but I saw him stiffen as though an arrow had ripped through his heart. Before he could answer, Raymond said uncertainly, 'This is a solemn charge against our closest allies. How could you know it?'

'Because their treachery was too much even for the Fatimid vizier to stomach. When he granted the Greek an audience, he hid me in a secret room behind his chamber so that I could see and hear it for myself.'

A silence of condemnation gripped the crowded tent. Nikephoros held himself still, swaying slightly like a man on a high wall trying to keep his balance.

'Yes, there was treachery in Egypt.'

A hiss, confirmation of every wickedness and evil the Franks had ever imputed to the Greeks.

'But it was not mine. The viper king of the Egyptians, the high priest of their heresy, has tried to confound us at every turn. He has dangled alliances or threatened war as his whim permits. And now that he fears his black hands are about to be prised off the holy city, he has tricked this poor broken knight into thinking he saw something he did not. He has tried to break apart the holy union at the heart of this army, the alliance of all Christians from east and west.' He looked around at the assembled princes, knights and bishops. 'I trust you will have the wisdom to recognise the lies of the devil when they creep into your councils.'

'*The lies of the devil?*' screeched Achard. 'These are not lies. These are things I saw and heard with my own eyes and ears. Does anyone say I have been possessed by the devil?'

'You have been in his power – as we all were in Egypt. The devil is the prince of illusions. In his palace, how could you be sure of anything you saw? Was there a fire burning in the room?'

'It was October.'

'And there was a sweet smell in its smoke – as if spices or incense had been sprinkled on the flames?'

'There was. But—'

'And candles burning?'

'You seem to know a great deal about the scene,' said Godfrey.

'I know how the devil works his snares – the better to resist them. I am not ashamed of it. The emperor Alexios made sure that I did not go to the arch-fiend's palace unprepared.'

'Or perhaps you went to meet one of your own,' snapped Achard.

Nikephoros looked around. 'Everyone can see that Achard has suffered terribly at the hands of the Fatimids. Perhaps he blames the Greeks, because God ordained that some of us should escape while he did not. Perhaps he was enchanted by demons, or perhaps his tormented mind conjured memories of things that never happened. But you do not have to choose his word or mine against each other. Look around you: use reason. If the emperor had turned against you, would his grain ships be crowding the seas between here and Cyprus to bring the food you rely on to support your armies? Would he be sending you subsidies of gold, fresh arms and horses?'

He dropped his voice. 'You can believe the word of an addled knight who has spent too long in the bosom of the enemy, or you can believe the word of a lord of Byzantium. For the sake of our great undertaking, I hope you see clearly when you choose the truth.'

A fresh silence descended on the tent as the princes considered his words. Raymond looked eager to speak, even opened his mouth to do so, then retreated as he realised his word would carry less weight than others'.

'No one can question the emperor's generosity to us,' said Godfrey. 'It has sustained us through many hardships, and – God willing – will help speed us to Jerusalem. Achard must have been mistaken.'

The others nodded, though without enthusiasm. Achard, however, looked mortified. The stump of his arm tensed and quivered, as if he were shaking an invisible fist; his eyes bulged so far out that it seemed only the veins around their edges held them in.

'I was not enchanted,' he screamed. 'I walked freely into the heart of Babylon, into the palace of the damned. I suffered torments you can barely imagine and I did it willingly, for the glory of Christ. And now you tell me that I did not see what I saw?' He slammed the palm of his hand against the stub of his truncated arm, never wincing. 'What about this? Will you say that there is a healthy arm here, that my leg does not ache each time I step on it, that the burns and scars that the caliph's torturers carved into my body are figments of my imagination? Did I *dream* it?'

'No one questions what you endured,' said Raymond hurriedly. 'The ancient martyrs themselves would stand in awe of your strength. You will be honoured with gold, with lands, with men – I will give you a company of my own knights to command.' He stood and walked forward, embraced Achard and offered him the kiss of peace. 'But the Greeks are vital allies. Loyal allies. What you say about them cannot be true.'

He retook his seat, so that Achard stood alone in the ring of princes. I could see two attendants hovering behind him, waiting to take him away, though they did not dare approach. He looked around wildly, his staring eyes accusing every man in the room. No one met his gaze. Tears ran down his cheeks; out of habit he lifted his left arm to wipe them away, then realised he could not. He turned, and ran out of the tent.

'God go with him,' said Godfrey softly. 'This was not his fault.'

λδ

∽∽∽∽∽

The Fatimid envoys departed that afternoon: it was not safe for them to stay longer in the camp. Count Raymond sent a troop of cavalry to escort them to a safe distance and I rode with them – though Nikephoros berated me for it afterwards. It was not good for Byzantines and Fatimids to be seen in company, he warned me.

'Will you return to Egypt?' I asked Bilal. We rode together, he on his camel and I on the dirty-grey palfrey I had commandeered at Saint Simeon and ridden ever since.

'No.' He did not look at me as he spoke; his eyes were forever scanning the road ahead, the undergrowth by the wayside, the slopes above, always searching for danger. 'I will join the army at Jerusalem.'

'Then we may meet again.'

'I hope not. Not there.'

We rode on. 'If only Christ had gone to die on a rock somewhere out at sea,' I said.

'And if the prophet had been taken up to heaven from some scrap of sand in the desert.'

I gave a sad laugh. 'Then men would have built shrines and castles over those places, and found some reason to fight each other for them.'

'Truly.' Bilal's gaze wandered over the trees to our left. Suddenly, he stiffened. 'What is that?'

'Where?'

Without answering, Bilal swung himself out of his saddle and leaped down. His sword seemed to be in his hand before he had even touched the ground. He ran into the forest but did not go far – I could see his yellow cloak bright between the branches. With a great rustling and squawks of protest, a startled flock of crows rose up into the air.

'Well done,' I called. 'You've saved us from an ambush by birds.'

'It wasn't the birds,' he shouted back, and the grimness in his voice silenced my humour utterly. 'Come and see.'

I dismounted and followed cautiously through the gap he had entered. The air was cooler in the forest, and darker: I needed a moment before my eyes could adjust. Though even before I could see, I could smell what was coming.

Bilal pointed into the air, his other hand holding his cloak over his mouth to block out the stench. A few feet

407

off the ground, a foul object hung from the branch of an oak tree. I could not call him a man: the crows and carrion-eaters had seen to that. His skin was blackened, his belly bloated and his toes eaten away. A brown tunic, sprayed with blood and soaked with his bile, hung in tatters from his shoulders – it seemed the only things holding the body together were the noose around his neck and the belt about his waist.

Driving back my horror, I looked closer at the belt. It was made of black leather, finely made and with the design of an eagle worked into it. A belt that I had seen before, clasped around a camelskin robe.

'I knew this . . . man. He was . . .' It was too hard to explain. 'He assisted a holy man in our camp.'

'Did he owe you money?'

Bilal pointed to the ground. A little distance from the body, a small pool of silver trickled from the mouth of an open sack.

'Whoever did this, it was not thieves.' Bilal turned to me. 'You said you knew him. When did he go missing?'

I thought back to our encounter in the clearing. 'About a week ago.'

'Then he must have come here soon afterwards.'

'He had plenty of reasons to flee. He must have hanged himself in remorse.'

'Perhaps.' Bilal pointed to the corpse, twisting this way and that with the flex of the rope. 'But did he tie his hands behind his back first?'

An impatient voice called from the road in Arabic.

'I must go,' said Bilal. 'We have many miles to travel, and I should not be seen with the body. You will bury him?'

I nodded.

Bilal sheathed his sword and walked back to the road. 'This is a bad omen at the start of a journey.'

'I will pray you arrive safely.'

'And I will pray to God that you travel safely too.' Bilal clapped me on the shoulder. 'But not to Jerusalem.'

Sigurd and I buried what remained of John in the forest. I hesitated as to whether to put a cross over his grave, for I was not sure he had been true to Christ either in life or in death, but in the end I decided it was not for me to judge. I tied a branch across the trunk of a tree and let that stand for a marker, though the only rope I had to use was the one that had hanged him. Then I returned to the camp, and went up the hill to pay a last visit to Peter Bartholomew.

It had been a full week since his ordeal. A few of his followers still held vigils outside the tent, but it was easy enough to thread my way through them. The three tents still stood in their rough horseshoe, though the ground around them was churned to dust like a battlefield. Eight knights from Count Raymond's household guarded the door.

'I want to pray a while with Peter Bartholomew,' I told them. A thick spear-point swung down to discourage me.

'Peter Bartholomew is close to God. No one is allowed in his presence.'

'I would pay for the privilege.' I held up the purse and the guard felt it, pleased and surprised by the weight. He did not even trouble to haggle. 'You are only buying a few moments with Peter Bartholomew,' he warned me. 'And no souvenirs.'

I ducked into the tent. The guard watched from the door, though I could hardly have stolen anything. By the light coming in through the open flap I could see that the room was as bare as a monk's cell. Peter Bartholomew lay on a low bed, covered in a linen sheet that would surely become his shroud. Only his face protruded, swaddled in bandages, which left only his eyes and nose exposed. Even that hardly seemed necessary, for his eyes were shut and his breathing faint.

I looked around, then back at the guard.

'Where are his possessions?'

The guard stiffened. 'I told you: no relics.'

'I don't want relics. But I heard he had a manuscript, a sacred text that foretold many things to come. I hoped to see it.' I glanced down at Peter to see if he had heard me, but he had not moved.

'The priest took all Peter Bartholomew's belongings for safe-keeping – to protect them from thieves and relic-hunters. You said you came to pray,' he added pointedly.

I knelt beside Peter's bed, careful not to touch him, and offered a silent prayer for his soul. He had raised himself up like Lucifer to dizzying heights of pride, until he vied with God Himself. But I wondered if that was truly the cause of his demise – or if it had been brought on not by his threat to God, but to men.

I leaned forward, stifling my nose against the stench of burned and rotting flesh, and kissed him on his bandaged cheek.

'God forgive you, and bring you to His peace at last,' I whispered.

Five days later, Peter Bartholomew died. They buried him in the high valley, beneath the scorched earth where he had suffered his passion. Many in the army scoffed and said that death had proved him a fraud, but for every man who disbelieved there was another who held that Peter had survived the fire, that he only died from being trampled by his disciples when he emerged. And every day that we were in Arqa, and for years afterwards, pilgrims would gather at his grave and wait, praying for a miracle that never came.

But by then, I had other concerns.

λε

∞∞∞∞

The siege of Arqa was failing: everyone knew it. Everyone, at least, except Count Raymond. He had suffered the death of Peter Bartholomew as an almost personal affront, and would not countenance leaving Arqa until he had restored his reputation by its capture. And so his reputation only suffered more.

One evening, three weeks after Peter Bartholomew had been laid in the earth, Raymond summoned Nikephoros and me to his quarters. There was still light in the sky, but in Raymond's tents all the lamps were lit. His melancholy seemed to have subsided: his eye was bright, and he moved with more energy than I had seen in months. He held a thick piece of paper, with cut strings and broken seals dangling off it like cobwebs.

'A rider has just delivered this.' He held it out; Nikephoros reached for it, but instead Raymond passed it to his chaplain who cleared his throat and began reading.

'*From his most serene holy majesty, the* basileus *and* autokrator, *the emperor of the Romans Alexios Komnenos; to his brothers in Christ, the princes and captains of the Army of God: blessings and greetings.*'

'Greetings,' Raymond muttered, waving him on.

'*Though we have been absent from your campaign, not a day has passed when the great deeds you have worked to the glory of God have not been present in our heart. All our empire rejoices at your victories. And now that we have heard your army is poised on the borders of the holy land, ready to strike towards Jerusalem itself, piety and duty command us to leave the comforts of our city and join you in the holy task appointed. Wherefore we ask you to remain in your camp, to gather your strength, and await our arrival on the feast of Saint John the Baptist, the twenty-fourth day of June. Then Greeks and Romans shall be united in one host, the kingdom of Babylon will tremble, and the arch-enemy's forces will be scattered and destroyed.*'

The priest looked up. 'That is all.'

'May I see the letter?'

Nikephoros took the paper from the chaplain's hands and read it silently, fingering the seals between thumb and forefinger. 'You said the messenger who brought it was Greek. Where is he now?'

'He said he could not delay. He galloped away the moment I had taken the package from him.'

'Did he?' There was a dangerous edge in Nikephoros' voice, but Raymond did not appear to notice it.

'This is the best news we could have had. How long have I pleaded with Alexios to come to our aid, to prove his loyalty and to silence those who question his friendship? This gives the lie to Achard's false accusations. At last the emperor's authority will bring unity to our fractured host.'

'The other princes will not wait for the emperor,' said Nikephoros. He strode beside me as we walked back to our tent. 'Even if they cared about Arqa – or Raymond – they would crawl over coals to reach Jerusalem before the emperor arrived.' He gave a dry laugh.

'Strange that a messenger who had ridden all the way from Constantinople should deliver the message to Raymond's door, and then gallop away at dusk without even looking in on the Byzantine camp,' I said noncommittally. I had an unpleasant idea that I knew who had written the letter – and it was not the emperor whose seal adorned it.

'Stranger still that it was sealed with wax. The emperor seals his correspondence with gold. But the seals were genuine. Not the emperor's personal seal, but one used by the palace.' He lifted his hand so I could see the gold signet ring gleaming on his finger. 'I have one. So did my predecessor, Tatikios.'

'The ring Duke Godfrey stole from me,' I murmured. Was this why? Surely that could not have been his purpose

414

when he lured me to Ravendan all those months ago.

Nikephoros walked on in silence, so long that I wondered if he blamed me for what had happened. 'The letter was a forgery,' he said at last. 'So obvious I am surprised even the Franks did not see it. There were half a dozen mistakes in the grammar alone.'

'But if you saw it was a forgery, why not say so to Count Raymond?'

Nikephoros swung around. 'Because it served my purposes. Do you think I want to spend the next six months rotting outside Arqa because an old man is too stubborn and too blind to give up a lost cause, and because none of his companions has the strength or will to defy him?'

'But if Duke Godfrey forged the letter, aren't you curious as to why?'

He shrugged the question away. 'Probably because he's as sick as I am of waiting.' His voice dropped. 'The emperor did not send me here as a mark of favour. It was an exile, a diplomatic way to remove me from his court for as long as possible. I think it appealed to his humour to send me to Jerusalem as penance.'

Unconsciously, he played with the embroidered hem of his sleeve. 'Perhaps I deserved it. But I have served my sentence, and I would like to return to Constantinople. So if a letter appears that will force the barbarians to act, however mysterious and fraudulent it may be, I will not question it.' He touched me on the shoulder, perhaps the most sincere gesture I ever had from him. 'We have both been away from home too long.'

415

I could not argue with that, but it did not soothe my worries.

Sigurd threw a handful of dry grass on the embers of the last night's fire and poked at it with a stick. Even in the dim half-light before dawn, the coals barely glowed.

'In England, in my father's time, the kings could only raise their army for forty days in a year. That concentrated their minds wonderfully on the business of making war.'

'Do you still miss it?' I asked.

'England?' Sigurd sounded surprised by the question. 'Of course. In the same way that a one-armed man misses his limb.'

'When you left, did you know you would never see it again?'

'I . . .' Sigurd paused. 'I don't remember. There was too much confusion, and I was too young. But I must have thought I would see it again, or I would never have left.' He grimaced. 'Even so, I clung to a tree that grew beside the water when it was time to leave. My uncle thought he would need to chop it down I held on so tight.'

'I would have done the same to Constantine's column in the forum if I had known it would be so long before I saw it again. I thought I wanted to see my family – but now they are here, I think it was the city I wanted really.'

Sigurd balled his fingers into a fist and stared at it.

'Don't worry yourself too much with your family. They don't know where they are and they're frightened. Even if we were all in Constantinople, it would not be

416

perfect. Helena would still be struggling to understand where her allegiance to her husband ends and to her father begins.'

'I would have been happy for her to abandon me for her husband completely, if only he'd kept her safe in Constantinople.'

'You should watch Thomas. He is too eager for battle.'

'Whereas you, of course, have harnessed your axe to an ox and made it a plough.'

Sigurd looked serious. 'I have been in enough battles that I know what to do – and even, though you may not believe it, when to step back. If Thomas charges into his next battle thinking he can avenge his wounds with every sweep of his axe, he will make an easy kill for some Ishmaelite.'

'He saved my life,' I said, ducking away from Sigurd's warning.

'And you saved his. But it will mean precious little if you and he don't live long enough to make the debt worthwhile.'

I made a final attempt to reinvigorate the fire, then stood and wiped the ash from my face. Down the slope, I saw Zoe returning from the river where she had been sent to fetch water.

'Your daughter will be strong enough to join the Varangians soon,' said Sigurd. 'Look at the way she carries that water jar – almost as if it was empty.'

It was true: she held the jar one-handed, and it bounced freely as she ran towards us though no water spilled out.

Forgetting the fire, I ran to meet her, instinctively checking for any sign of injury.

'Are you all right?' I called. 'Are you in danger?'

She shook her head, her loose hair flying across her face. 'The camp across the river – Duke Godfrey's camp.' She gulped a deep breath. 'It's gone.'

Duke Godfrey's camp, which for the last two months had stood on the southern side of the mountain spur, was a ruin. A film of smoke hung over the ground like a dawn mist: through it I could see scraps of charred cloth hanging from the ribs of tents, beds of ash still smouldering, bare patches in the earth where tents had once stood. I rubbed my eyes.

'Did the Saracens creep down from the city and burn the camp in the night?' I wondered. 'Why didn't we see any flames?'

Sigurd gestured to the bulk of the spur behind us. 'That would have hidden it.'

'But we would still have heard the battle.'

'If there was a battle.' Sigurd stepped forward and walked a little way forward. 'Do you see anything strange about this battlefield?'

I looked closer. Though the embers still smouldered and the ash was fresh, the carcass of the battle had already been picked impossibly clean. There were no bodies.

'What's that?'

I looked up. A man in a white cassock was walking towards us between the rows of ruined tents, striding the battlefield like the angel of death – though I did not think the hem of an angel's robe would have been soiled grey by the ash he kicked up as he walked. Nor, in my image, would he have been old and balding, with a pronounced wart on his left cheek.

He reached us and made the sign of the cross. 'Good morning, brothers.'

'What happened here?' I asked.

He looked around, as if seeing the wreckage for the first time. 'Praise God, the Holy Spirit moved in the hearts of the faithful last night and roused them like a great wind. As one, they rose from their camp and set out on the road to Jerusalem.'

'And this?' I gestured to the ruin.

'Whatever they could not take they burned. They will not be coming back.'

'So Duke Godfrey has gone . . .'

'And the Duke of Normandy, and the Count of Flanders, and Tancred—'

'Tancred was in Count Raymond's service,' I interrupted.

'He left it – they all left. I was the only one who stayed behind, to tell you what has happened. And now that I have done so . . .' He put his fingers in his mouth and whistled. A grey horse, which had been grazing on the sweet grass by the river, trotted over. The priest lifted himself into the saddle, with surprising ease for a holyman, and took the reins. As his cassock rode up over his boots, I saw the glint of spurs on his heels.

He offered a crooked smile. 'Tell Count Raymond this: the time for vanity and hesitation has passed. If any man from his army, knight or peasant, wishes to see Jerusalem, let him hasten after us: the other princes will welcome his service. But there will be no more delays now. They must come quickly, before the whole world falls away to ash.'

He turned his horse and kicked its flanks. Dust and cinders billowed up behind him as he left, so that the pale horse and its pale rider vanished in the cloud. By the time it had settled again he was gone, though the drum of his hoofbeats seemed to echo for a long time afterwards in the valley. Not only echo, but grow louder, swelling out until they sounded all around me.

I looked around, and saw the reason. It was not the departing priest I had heard, but Count Raymond, galloping down towards us with a score of his knights and nobles behind. They thundered over the bridge, then reined themselves in.

'What has happened here?' Raymond demanded. His face was white, glistening with sweat. He gestured up to the promontory behind us. 'Have the Saracens done this?'

I told him what I had heard, though he barely seemed to listen. He paced his horse around me, this way and that, glancing distractedly at the remains of Duke Godfrey's camp. His knights kept their distance and watched.

Only when I had finished did Raymond go still, though he would not look at me.

'Tancred went?' he said bleakly.

I nodded.

'*He took an oath to me!*' A terrible groan, like the cry of a wounded boar, tore the air. Raymond doubled over in his saddle, clutching his arms to his stomach, then suddenly jerked upright and threw out his hands as if grasping at the air for balance. The men around him drew back.

'They have abandoned me,' he whispered.

One of his knights edged tentatively forward. 'They have only been gone a few hours. If we march quickly we could overtake them by sunset and join our armies for the final charge.'

'And what about Arqa?' Raymond looked up at the walled town on its promontory above us, as inviolable as ever; then at the road winding away towards the coast and Jerusalem. A solitary tear seemed to trickle from his eye – though perhaps it was just sweat, for the sun was already hot.

'Give orders to strike the camp.'

λς

〰〰〰〰

We caught up with the other princes the following day. The Flemings, Normans and Lotharingians embraced the Provençals gladly, rejoicing to see the army reunited, but Count Raymond rode in the midst of his bodyguard and remained unseen. That evening the princes concluded a peace with the emir of Tripoli, and the next day we proceeded on to the coast. This was the place the Fatimid envoy had warned us against, a treacherous spot where the rampart of the mountain met the sea in a dizzying cascade of fractured cliffs and crevices. A stiff onshore wind drove waves against the rocks, filling the air with spray, while sea birds called mournful cries from above. Here the road seemed to disappear into the rock: even standing at the foot of the mountain, we could not see where it went until our guide showed us a path, which the breaking waves had carved out of the cliff. It was little more than a ledge, barely two feet above the surging sea and scarcely wide enough for two men to walk even in single file. The stronger gusts of wind whipped the waves so high that they overflowed onto the path, so that boiling white water foamed about our feet, snatching and sucking at our ankles as it tried to drag us into the sea. When a few men lost their balance and fell screaming into the water, no one dared leap in to save them; we could only watch them drown.

Yet even that was not the limit of its defences. At the very tip of the headland, where the path dwindled almost to a sword's width, our Roman ancestors had built a gate-house to command the road. Its ancient stones were wet and black with age; one wall seemed to grow out of the cliff itself, the other plunged straight into the sea.

'*Raz-ez-Chekka*,' said our guide, pointing to it. He giggled. 'The Face of God. Only the worthy will pass.'

Duke Godfrey crossed himself. 'The gates is narrow and the way is hard,' he murmured.

I shivered, and I was not alone. In that lonely, perilous place I could almost feel the terrifying weight of God's gaze on me, searching my soul for its infinitesimal worth. The dark gates in the tower opened before me like ravening jaws, and the small windows above watched like eyes. Water bubbled around my feet; gulls called their plaintive song and the waves roared in my ears. Dizziness broke over me, so that even as I stood still the tower seemed to rush closer. Helpless, I stared into its eyes. They were not cruel, nor angry, nor even sad: only unfathomably empty. Then – I swear – one of them winked. I gasped; the world spun away and the sea rushed up to swallow me.

A Varangian hand grabbed my shoulder, and stout arms hauled me back. I blinked, rubbing the salt from my eyes. In front of me, the tower stood where it always had, and a white gull perched on the sill of one of the windows.

'The Egyptian was right,' said Sigurd. 'Six men could hold that tower until Judgement Day.'

But the tower was empty, and the rotten bar that held the gates gave easily under a few blows. Worthy or not, we passed through unhindered.

Perhaps the Franks had been right: perhaps God did will them on. Certainly it felt so during those last weeks of May: after the twenty months we had taken to crawl the hundred miles between Antioch and Arqa, we managed twice that distance in only twenty days. Every obstacle suddenly seemed to fall away from our path, so much that I began to wonder what had ever held us back. Narrow passes through the mountains, which a hundred Saracens could have held against the entire human race, stood undefended; fresh springs flowed with such abundance that the whole army could not exhaust their supply. Even the seasons seemed altered: though it was only the middle of May, the harvest had already ripened. In the orchards, boughs yielded up their fruits, while the wheat in the fields seemed to bow down before our approach, each stalk willingly offering its neck to our sickles. We hardly needed the emperor's grain ships, whose white sails kept pace with us on the western horizon as we marched down the coast.

I do not mean to give the impression that it was easy – of course there were hardships. The same sun that fattened the wheat burned our skins and parched our throats. The bountiful land could also be treacherous. One evening we made our camp by a stony river bank: in the night, a host of fiery snakes slithered out from the stones and bit many of the army. They died horribly, bloated out so far you could hear the joints snapping inside them. At Sidon, the Saracen garrison sallied out unexpectedly and massacred a company of pilgrims as they foraged. And our holy road was no defence against the usual trials of life. Horses went lame, milk soured, men quarrelled. But against the storms that had ravaged us before, these were nothing: spring squalls forgotten almost before they had passed. They could not stem the confidence and expectation that grew in the army every day.

For, like the Israelites of old, we had come at last into the promised land, a country that had already been ancient when Romulus laid the first stone of the first Rome. Every town we passed resounded with history: Tyre, whose cedarwood Solomon used to build the temple in Jerusalem, and Byblos, whose parchment gave its name to the scripture written on it; Accaron, where the Philistines took the Ark of the Covenant, and Caesarea, city of King Herod. Phoenicians, Babylonians, Persians, Greeks,

Romans and Saracens – all had possessed this land, or parts of it. Their monuments remained, a palimpsest of the past, though the men themselves had long since rotted to dust.

We celebrated Pentecost and rested a few days. Then, we left the coast and headed inland, towards the spine of mountains that had loomed on our eastern flank every day for the past fortnight.

'And somewhere in those mountains is Jerusalem,' said Thomas. It was early June; we sat around the dying embers of our campfire and lay back, looking up at the stars. Anna's head rested on my chest, while Helena and Thomas cradled the child – no longer a baby – between them.

'I wonder if it will appear as it does in the Bible,' mused Helena. 'Jewelled walls and golden gates and . . . everything else.'

'It will probably look like any other town we've passed,' I told her, trying to douse the hopes that flared in my own heart. 'Stone walls, dusty streets, square houses.'

'It won't,' Zoe protested. 'We can't have come so far just for that.'

'We'll see.'

'If we make it to Jerusalem.' Even there, sitting under the same sky that Christ must have seen a thousand years earlier, Sigurd's pessimism remained unshaken. 'Why haven't the Fatimids attacked us yet?'

'Only you could grumble about that,' Anna teased him.

'Either they have some ambush planned or they are drawing us on to Jerusalem deliberately.'

'Or they're too weak to oppose us.' Thomas propped himself up on one arm, using the other to tousle his son's hair. 'We've descended too swiftly, before they can gather their forces.'

I shook my head. 'They don't have to gather their forces – they're already there, behind Jerusalem's walls. Why should they confront us in open battle? They know that we will come to them.'

'And no doubt they'll be ready for us.'

Later, after the others had gone to bed, Anna found me still lying by the fire. She lay down beside me and burrowed into the crook of my arm, pressing herself against me in a way she had not done in an age. Perhaps I should have shied away from such sinful touch so close to the holy city, but the warmth of her body awoke a craving I had almost forgotten how to feel. I turned her towards me and kissed her eagerly, running my hands over her dress with the awe of fresh discovery.

'Not here,' she whispered. She stood, took my hand and led me to a small gully. The night was hot but we did not remove our clothes, nor dare lie on the ground for fear of scorpions and adders. Anna leaned against a boulder, arching backwards as I pressed my kisses against her lips, her throat, her cheeks and her hair. She moaned when I entered her, as hungry for me as I was for her.

Lust made us impatient, and our hasty coupling was

over too soon. After we had finished I held her in my arms, still joined with her, breathing in the smoky texture of her hair. Though when I pulled back to look her in the face, her cheeks were wet.

'Are you crying?' In the moonlight I could not tell if it was sweat or tears.

'No,' she said quietly. Then, after a moment, 'Yes.'

I touched her dress, dark with sweat where I had pressed against her. 'Did I hurt you?'

'No.'

'Is it guilt?'

'*No.*' She turned away and wiped her cheek with her sleeve.

I wrapped my arms closer around her and pulled her into me, cradling her head against my chest. 'Soon,' I promised her. 'In four days, five at the most, we will reach Jerusalem.' I marvelled that I could say that, and that it could be true.

'Yes.' She sniffed. 'I don't know . . . perhaps that's why I feel so tired, suddenly. It's so close, the hope is almost too much to bear.'

'Hope of seeing the holy city?'

'Hope of going home.' Fresh tears sprang from her eyes, but she ignored them, stroking a finger through my beard. 'I'm ready.'

'So am I.'

'And Helena should hurry home too. Has she told you?'

I started. 'Told me what?'

Anna pressed a hand over my groin. The smile had

428

returned to her face, and her eyes gleamed with mischief. 'You and I are not the only ones who have been sneaking away from the camp. Helena is expecting another child.'

I drew back in amazement. 'When?'

'Six months from now.'

I counted in my head. 'How long has she known without telling me?'

'Two months – and she did not tell me either. But I recognised the signs.'

'I saw that she looked healthier, that she had grown again,' I defended myself. 'I thought it was the abundance of food.'

Anna laughed. 'She did not tell you because she was afraid it would worry you on the march.'

'It would have.' I had to pull away from Anna and lean against the wall of the gully, so bewildered was I by the emotions Anna's news had unleashed in me.

'It's lucky we're almost ready to go home.'

The next day we came to Aramathea, a prosperous town in the foothills of the mountain range. We approached with caution, for if the Fatimids wished to mount a defence before we reached Jerusalem this was their final opportunity. But when we reached the gates we found the town abandoned, not just by its garrison but by every single inhabitant. They had left behind a great store of grain and provisions, and full cisterns from which we gratefully filled our waterskins. We knew there would be scant water in the mountains ahead.

Of all those days marching, I remember the last one the best. The whole army was awake before dawn, like children at Easter, and before the cool morning could grow stale we were well on our way. We were now deep in the mountains, the first places God made, and the weight of ages was everywhere in the wizened landscape around us. Deep clefts furrowed the faces of barren hills, and desiccated veins of white rock were all that remained of the rivers that had once brought life to the soil. It did not seem like the promised land flowing with milk and honey, but we did not care. Our songs resounded off the crumbling valleys: pious hymns of thanksgiving; proud songs of war; and sometimes more poignant songs of the countries we had left so far behind. Happiness, wonder and laughter bubbled up from the army like fresh springs, and the faces around me seemed to glow with joy.

By midday, the still air had grown thick and heavy. On another day we might have rested through the worst of the heat, but that afternoon there was no thought of delay. I walked between my daughters, Helena on my left and Zoe on my right, glancing at Helena's belly so often that she scolded me for my unseemly impatience.

'You won't see him growing as you watch.'

'Him? She may be a girl.' Though I would not tell Helena so, I wanted a girl. Her mother would have wanted a granddaughter, I thought.

A shadow of worry drifted over me, and I looked at the steep valleys around us for any hint of an enemy. It would have been an easy place for the Ishmaelites to ambush us, but once again they chose not to.

I squeezed Helena's hand – and then, so she would not feel left out, Zoe's. Of all of us, I think the journey had been hardest for her. Anna had come for me, and Helena for Thomas, but Zoe had come because she had to. Looking at her now, I could see how it had changed her. At home in Constantinople she had been much the livelier of my daughters, teasing Helena and me to distraction, but ever able to defuse our anger with a grin and a hug. Now the mischief and vitality had gone; she spoke rarely and laughed less. Often in our camps she seemed to disappear into the background, not absent in person but not present in spirit. Though her body had grown in the past two years – even the past few months – her face seemed thinner, as if age and experience had somehow pinched it shut.

I smiled at her, trying to prompt the smile I remembered so well. 'Soon,' I promised. 'Soon this will be over.'

The sun waned, breathing its dying light into the dust that surrounded us so we seemed to walk in a golden cloud. I stared forward obsessively; with every turn in the road I expected to see Jerusalem before us, shining on its hilltop, but it did not appear. Then scouts who had ridden forward came back, and announced it was still ten miles to Jerusalem. Many wanted to press on through the night, but the princes would not allow it. Haste was peril, they said: the road was too dangerous, our enemies' intentions unknown. We made our camp near a village, though few pitched their tents. One word hung on everybody's lips – spoken with excitement, with awe, with reverence and with fear. *Tomorrow.*

'Anyone would think we're to find Jerusalem as empty as Aramathea,' Sigurd grumbled. We had built our fire in a rocky circle near the road and sat on the surrounding boulders. Thomas had caught two pigeons, which we roasted on spits over the coals. 'The journey doesn't end just because we arrive.'

'Ours does.'

I looked around. Nikephoros was standing behind us, dim against the twilight. Perhaps because I was in mind of endings, I remembered the first time I had seen him: the magnificence, the power and the arrogance of his presence. The new beard he had worn had grown full; the cushions and gilded furniture that had decorated his quarters then had long since been lost or abandoned on the road. That evening he had not even pitched his tent, but laid out his blankets on the ground like the rest of us. In the soft haze, dressed only in a plain linen tunic, he almost looked humble.

'Our journey ends here,' he said again, perhaps thinking we had not heard him. He looked at Sigurd. 'Have your men formed up to march at dawn. We will make for the coast and find a ship there. Perhaps we will find the grain fleet; otherwise there are English ships in the emperor's service still patrolling these waters. One of them will take us home.'

For a moment his only answer was the sound of boiling fat sizzling on the coals.

'But . . . Jerusalem.' I pointed foolishly, as if it stood not fifty yards up the road. 'What about Jerusalem?'

'Jerusalem was not my destination. My orders were to see that the Franks reached it and now, praise God, I have. Even they should be able to find it from here.'

'And what will they do then?' asked Sigurd. 'They have not won any victory yet.'

Nikephoros shrugged. 'Thirty Varangians more or less will not decide the battle. To fight it would be a waste – it does not even matter who wins now. Be ready to march at dawn.'

I hardly knew what to feel. For two years and more I had longed to see Jerusalem and go home, until the two desires, once contradictory, wound themselves so tight around me that they became inseparable. It had become my purpose: to be denied it now felt almost as though Nikephoros had ripped out part of my soul. Looking at the others, I saw the same disbelief reflected on all their faces – Thomas's most of all.

Yet in my shock, one part of me still saw clearly. *It does not even matter who wins now.* Even Nikephoros' diplomatic guile could not hide the true emotion beneath the words: not indifference, nor resignation, but savage glee.

I ran after Nikephoros, away from the campfire, and halted him.

'Achard told the truth,' I said slowly. 'You did go to Egypt to make an alliance with the Fatimids. What was the bargain? That we would bring the Franks to the altar at Jerusalem if the Fatimids would wield the sacrificial knife?'

Darkness shrouded Nikephoros' face, but his voice was clear and unrepentant. 'The emperor was a fool ever to consider taking the Franks as allies. Wise counsellors warned him against it, but he was too weak.'

'So you took it upon yourself to break the emperor's alliance, to finish what your wise counsellors failed to do at Constantinople.'

Nikephoros laughed, and the contempt in his laughter told me I was wrong again. 'I took nothing upon myself. I am the emperor's obedient servant. There is nothing I have done that he did not order me to do.'

I felt as if I had been dropped into a void without bounds or depth. 'The emperor?'

'When the barbarians refused to surrender Antioch, he saw his mistake at last. You can hunt with wild dogs, but you cannot be surprised if they take your quarry for themselves. And when they do, there is only one solution.'

I shook my head, trying to clear the confusion within. Nikephoros thought I was contradicting him.

'Jerusalem is nothing – a bauble to dangle before barbarians. Alexios thought it would bring them to his aid, but it has served just as well to lead them to their destruction. Now the Fatimids will finish it, and those grain ships you saw by the coast will sail to Alexandria as their reward.'

'But the Fatimids rejected our bargain – they drove us into the desert. Or was that part of the deception too?'

434

'The caliph did not want to make an alliance with Christians. While his vizier was away he tried to sabotage it.'

'But the vizier had revealed your bargain to Achard.'

'He thought his interests were best served by discord among the Christians. He would rather have kept us quarrelling far away from his borders. But now the barbarians are here, he will do what he must. He has no choice. That is the simple perfection of the emperor's scheme.'

He moved closer to me, a pale blur in the gathering darkness.

'Did you really ever style yourself the unveiler of mysteries?'

A rumble sounded like thunder, and the earth trembled beneath my feet. I stepped back, just as the noise resolved itself into the pounding of many hooves. A column of horsemen swept around the turn in the road. A fiery aura surrounded them from the torches they carried, though I could see little inside it save a host of spears and helmets, flying manes and churning hooves.

'What is happening?' I shouted up. 'Are we under attack?'

One of the knights reined in his horse and drew aside to let the others pass. 'We are going to Bethlehem.' He shook his head in wonder at what he had just said. 'The Christians there have sent messengers: the Fatimids have abandoned it. Come with us and see.'

I glanced at Nikephoros, revealed now in the flaring torches. He shrugged.

'Go with them, if you like. Stay here and fight for Jerusalem, if that is what you believe in. I give you my permission. Or you can come home with me.'

'Be quick,' warned the knight. Most of the column had already passed by, and the light they had brought was fading. 'I cannot wait.'

I stared at the ground. My cheeks burned with shame; my eyes ached to cry, but no tears would come.

'I . . .' I could hardly speak. My only solace was darkness. 'I will go home.'

λζ

∾∾∾∾∾

No one slept that night. Like ice after winter, the army had already begun to break up. Some followed Tancred's men to Bethlehem; others, unable to endure one more hour of waiting, rose from their beds in the middle of the night and hurried on along the dark road to Jerusalem. I lay on my blanket, unsleeping, and heard them go – first dribbling away in their twos and threes, then growing to a trickle which eventually became a flood. I stayed in my bed.

As with all sleepless nights, the darkness seemed to last for ever – and still be over too soon. After so many hours of wretched waiting, no sooner had my thoughts finally quieted into sleep than a dirty light began to spread from the east, and Sigurd was shaking my shoulder, urging me up. Well before the dawn Nikephoros had appointed for our departure, we were ready to leave.

We did not delay; we might have lost our nerve. As we marched through the camp many called that we were going the wrong way, that Jerusalem was behind us. When they realised our purpose their shouts became angrier. They lined the road to watch us go, hurling abuse: we were traitors, cowards who did not dare look upon Jerusalem for fear of God's judgement. He would find us, they warned. One or two of them threw rocks, and I feared for a moment that in their fervour they might stone us to death, but a few glares from the Varangians cowed them enough and they soon lost interest. They had better things to do that day.

By mid-morning we had gone several miles down our road, unpicking the threads of the previous day's journey. Nikephoros rode at the head of our little column; the rest of us walked, for I had sold my horse the night before to a Provençal knight who had lost his. The Franks would have reached Jerusalem by now, I thought. I wondered what they had found there.

'Twenty-thousand Egyptians waiting to massacre them,' said Sigurd, when I voiced my question aloud.

A fresh stab of betrayal lanced through me and I glanced ahead to Nikephoros. I had not repeated what he had revealed to me, not even to Sigurd. He loved the emperor he served and he loved his honour: I could not imagine how he would accept the ignoble truth of our mission. As for the others, how could I tell them that everything they had suffered for had been a lie? Thomas had not spoken a word since Nikephoros announced we were going home; his face was hard and still as stone. White knuckles clenched the haft of his axe, and several times I saw him angrily kick out at pebbles in the road. I think he would have deserted in an instant if it had not been for Everard, Helena and her unborn baby.

Just before lunch, the road turned into a steep-sided valley. A stream-bed meandered along the bottom of the embankment, though nothing but dust flowed there now, and on the far bank the flat ground was planted with many fruit trees. It seemed an arid sort of garden, but water must have lingered somewhere in the recesses of the earth, for many of the trees had blossomed. Some already even bore fruit. We called a halt and scrambled across the stream, into the welcome shade of the orchard.

Once again, I saw what secret miracles lingered in this land. June was only a week old, but the fruits had swollen so ripe you could not tell if they would break free of their branches or burst from their skins. Anna plucked a pomegranate from a gnarled tree and cut it open. The seeds glistened inside like a cupful of rubies; she scooped them out and fed them to me, and afterwards I licked the red juice from her fingers. Zoe and Helena gathered dates and apples in their skirts, while the Varangians laughed and shied rotten figs at each other.

I could have stayed all afternoon in that drowsy orchard. Leaning against a tree, Anna's head cradled in my lap, I realised that what I really longed for was not to go home, nor to Jerusalem, but simply to not go anywhere:

to lie down and rest and be still. I swatted away a wasp that was buzzing around my ear and closed my eyes, wishing I could stay there for ever.

Anna lifted her head. 'Did you hear that?'

'What?' I stroked the skin on the back of her neck, still smooth and pale where her hair had covered it against the sun. 'I can't hear anything.'

She shook my hand away. 'Listen.'

I listened. The wasp buzzed as it hovered over a fallen apple; further off, I could hear Sigurd's men laughing, and the enthusiastic babble as Everard chattered away beside Helena. And further still, from up the road, I heard a low rumble, like wind gusting through a rocky cleft. But the day was still, and there was no wind.

I clambered to my feet and stepped out from under the tree, shading my eyes. To my right, Nikephoros had stood up in his stirrups and was waving impatiently, signalling we should be on the march again. Despite the heat, he had chosen to wear his full imperial regalia: the heavy dalmatic embroidered with gold, and the jewelled *lorum* sparkling in the sun. A few of the Varangians had already answered his summons; others were slowly drifting back through the trees. To my left, Thomas was walking with Helena and Zoe: Everard sat on his shoulders and snatched at butterflies. And beyond him, where the road came around a turn in the valley, a plume of dust was rising into the blue June sky.

'Demetrios.' Sigurd's voice called me from somewhere to my right. '*Get down!*'

Wrapped in the dust they churned beneath their hooves, a company of horsemen swept around the bend in the road. I could hardly see them at all through the cloud – little more than flashes of spears and armour in the billowing dust – but there was something terrible and hungry in their speed, like an eagle hastening on to devour its prey. I crouched low, frantically waving Thomas and the girls to do likewise.

Perhaps, in their haste, the horsemen might have missed us if not for Nikephoros. He sat on his mount beyond the cover of the orchard, tall in his saddle and shining like a beacon. Even the most casual traveller would have seen him and gawped – these men were looking for him. They reined in on the far bank of the dry stream and pulled around into a loose line opposite us. I counted about twenty of them, and as the dust settled I saw that every one was dressed for battle. They seemed to be Franks, though they carried no standard.

'Who are you?' Nikephoros' challenge echoed out – imperious and aloof, but strangely dead in the arid valley. No one answered. At the end of the line, the knight who had led them drew his sword and lifted it over his head. Instinctively, I looked to his shield to see if it bore any tell-tale device.

He did not carry a shield – could not have, for his left arm ended in a grotesque stump barely inches from his shoulder. That told me more than any insignia. His eyes were hidden in the shadow of his helmet, but in my mind I could almost see their bulging stare looking down on us in triumph, the veins livid with the joy of revenge.

'Traitors!' he shouted, and the valley walls chorused his words so that wherever I turned the accusation bombarded my ears. 'You abandoned me to the Ishmaelites once before. You will not do it to the Army of God.'

He waved his sword forward. The row of spears swung down. Opposite them, Nikephoros raised a single arm as if he could somehow hold them back. And, for a moment, it seemed that he did – on either side of the dusty stream, not a man moved.

The dark note of a horn blasted through the silence, but not from the Franks. It sounded from high on the hillside opposite, behind us. I turned to look. At the top of the northern slope, facing the noon sun, a new line of horsemen had appeared. The spikes on their helmets and the bosses on their shields glittered like knives. One of them angled forward a spear, and the black banner of the Fatimids unfurled before him.

The horn sounded again.

'Christ preserve us,' murmured one of the Varangians beside me.

Perhaps this was the battle we deserved. For so many months Nikephoros had schemed to bring the Franks and the Fatimids into the same place, to destroy each other for his benefit. Now, in that dry valley, they would meet at last – and we would be nothing more than dust to soak up their blood. A cloud of arrows flew up into the June sky and dipped into the valley, gathering deadly speed as they fell. The Egyptians plunged after them, leaning far back in their saddles as they spurred their horses through the gorse and scree, nimble as goats. They might have managed to surprise us, but the Franks were no strangers to ambush. With shouts of '*Deus vult*' they kicked forward, down the embankment and across the dry stream to the orchard.

'To me!' shouted Sigurd. He stood between two trees with his legs apart, his axe swaying in his hands, and for a moment I was not sure if he was calling for help or summoning his enemies. 'To me!'

I could not help him – I had to get to my family, and I had no weapon except my knife. I held Anna's hand and dragged her after me as I ran through the orchard, desperately calling for Helena and Zoe. Horsemen closed from both sides. The ground was hard and flat, perfect for them; they came gliding through the trees like snakes, their spears stabbing like forked tongues. There was no time for the Varangians to form a line to resist them – they were scattered through the orchard, mostly unarmed, and could do nothing.

A flash of blue in the yellow grass ahead caught my eye – Helena's dress – but before I could reach her a rider galloped out between the trees in front of me. It was a Fatimid – not an Ethiopian like Bilal, but lighter skinned, a Turk or an Armenian. He hauled on his reins and swung the horse around, raising his spear over his shoulder like a javelin. I pushed Anna away, hoping the horseman would ignore her, then turned and started running. My heart screamed that I was going the wrong way, away from my daughters, but I had little choice. The sound of charging hooves rose up like a wave behind me, climbing higher until I was sure I must feel the life-ending blow of a hoof smashing open my skull, bone to bone. Still I ran. I shuddered with the tremors rising up from the earth; at the very last moment, when I was sure I had left it too late, I flung myself to my right, tumbling away into the shade of a fruit tree. The horse thundered past me; the Turk gave a howl of anger and tried to reverse his spear for a thrust, but too late – his momentum carried him on. As he tried to turn, another rider rode out of the fray. A sword flashed and the Turk's head flew from his shoulders, rolling several yards before it finally came to rest among the fallen fruit beneath a tree.

I scrambled to my feet. *Damn Nikephoros*, I cursed. *Damn the emperor and his treachery*. This was the world he had wished into being, a world without friends or allegiance, faith or honour. Two horsemen, one a Turk and one a Frank, charged down a fleeing Varangian, riding so close their knees almost touched. The Turk loosed an arrow and the man fell; as they rode over him, the Frank plunged his spear into his back and I saw the two hunters share a look of exultation before galloping after their next quarry. Through the trees a Varangian and a Frank pulled a Turk from his horse and butchered him, then turned their bloody blades on each other. Everywhere I looked the world was spiralling into the chaos from which God called it – and somewhere inside it were Anna and my children.

'Here.'

The voice spoke behind me and I whipped around, almost plunging my knife into him before I saw who he was. Aelfric stood there, his axe in one hand and a bloodied sword in the other. He offered it to me.

'I have to find my daughters.' I had to shout to be heard over the roar of hooves and the hiss of arrows. 'And Thomas and Anna.'

'Thomas was in the trees over there.' Aelfric jerked a thumb behind him. 'With Beric and Sigurd.'

'But Helena and Zoe were . . .' I looked around, disoriented. Where had they been?

The ground rumbled again as another horse cantered by. His rider must have been following some other prey for he did not see us under the tree. Without so much as a glance, Aelfric swung his axe in a low scything arc, straight into the horse's fetlock. It ploughed into the ground in a spray of blood and braying screams.

Aelfric pressed the sword into my hand. 'Make sure he's dead. Both of them,' he added, as the wounded horse screamed its agony to the sky.

He ducked out under the branches and ran across to where one of his comrades was trying to fend off two dismounted Franks. Too numb to do otherwise, I ran over to the fallen horse. Its master had been a Turk – not that it mattered now. He was trapped in his saddle, his left leg crushed under the horse's weight. His brown eyes stared up at me, imploring. I raised my sword to finish him, but found I did not have the will. I killed the horse instead.

445

'*Helena!*' I shouted. '*Zoe! Anna!*' The only answer was clashing steel and the shouts of men. Somewhere through the din I thought I heard a child crying, and I stumbled towards it. But in the dizzying cacophony of battle I could not follow any sound for long – soon it was gone, leaving me more desperate than ever. *Where were they?*

Dazed and anguished I wandered through the orchard, slipping on grass that had become slick with blood. Men were dying all around me but I barely noticed – the world was dark to my eyes. *Where were my family?* My sword hung limp in my hand, unused. *Where were they?* Two knights chased each other straight across my meandering path, barely a foot away. Though I was an enemy to them both, they did not even look at me. Was I invisible? Had I died and become a ghost?

I had not. I came around a pomegranate tree, and there was Achard staring at me. A broad grin split open the lower half of his face; he looked down, and it seemed all the contempt, resentment, envy and anger that the Franks harboured towards Byzantium was distilled into that triumphant sneer. He pulled back his spear a little, testing his grip. There was nothing I could do.

And then several things happened at once. From somewhere ahead of me, not too far, a girl screamed. Almost simultaneously, a horn sounded from up the valley. And just afterwards, an apple flew out of the sky, arced through the air and struck Achard on the side of the helmet where it covered his ear.

It was not a heavy blow. Even bareheaded it would

barely have bruised him. But he felt it – and, not knowing what it was, turned instinctively to see. It was all the time I needed. I lunged forward and grabbed hold of the spear, trying to wrest it from his grasp. Even before he realised what was happening his fingers had clenched around it; for a moment we pulled against each other. But I had two hands to his one, and I was pulling down. With a cry of triumph I felt it slip out of his hand; I stepped back, swung the spear around and lunged for his throat. Blood showered over me, blinding me. I let go the spear, and as I wiped the blood from my eyes I saw his horse cantering away, the one-armed corpse still bouncing in its saddle.

The horn sounded again. Something had changed – I could hear it all around me. The clash of arms had faded almost to nothing, drowned out by the rising drumming of hooves. Through the trees I could see dark shapes rushing by, like a shoal of fish seen from a boat. Then they were gone; the sound faded up the valley, and an unbearable stillness settled on the orchard.

I looked around. Sigurd was standing a little to my right, his axe leaning against his side and an apple in his hand. He waved it at me, then took a large bite.

Through the fog of my thoughts I vaguely understood he must have saved me, but that was of little consequence. I ran over and gripped his arm like a madman, staring in his eyes. 'Where are they? Where are Anna and the girls?'

All triumph vanished from his face. 'I thought they were with you.'

'I couldn't reach them. I thought Thomas—'

I broke off as I heard footsteps running through the trees. My heart kicked twice – once in fear of some new enemy, once in hope it might be my daughters. It was Thomas. His face was flushed; he had a cut on his cheek and another on his arm, but they were not what troubled him.

'Helena?' he gasped. 'Have you seen her? My son?'

Our eyes met in a moment of shared torment. Then, by spontaneous accord, we turned away and began sprinting through the orchard, shouting their names.

'Wait,' called Sigurd anxiously. 'You don't know if it's safe.'

Safe – what was that? All around me, the dappled sunlight shone on the wreckage of the battle: a Frankish knight sliced almost in two by a gaping axe-wound; another crushed under his horse; two Varangians impaled on a single spear, and others still wet with the wounds that had killed them. Panic rose in my soul – now I moved not like a ghost but like a fury, overturning corpses indiscriminately, spilling guts from gaping holes and inflicting fresh wounds on men who had suffered enough. I shouted their names over and over, until the words ran together, lost all form and became meaningless. I shouted them anyway – and did not realise Sigurd had been calling me until he sent one of his men to fetch me.

'Over here,' was all the Varangian said. His face was grim. He led me through the orchard to the eastern end, where a low wall divided it from the uncultivated wilderness beyond. Just inside, a thorn tree grew against the

448

stones – and even in my madness I could see there was something different about it. Amid all the gnarled and curling branches, one stuck out longer and straighter than the others. As I came closer I saw it was no branch but a spear, driven into the tree with such force that it had stuck cleanly even after passing through the body it pinned against the bark. The sun shone through the branches and picked out some of the jewels and gold on his robe, but only a few: many of the jewels had been cut away, and the golden threads were soaked with blood. The spear had gone straight through his belly into the tree; it still quivered there, rising and falling each time he breathed.

'We found this on the ground beside him.' Sigurd passed me a silk cord, such as a woman might use to tie her dress. Anna's belt. I snatched it with a cry and pressed it to my face, then knelt beside Nikephoros. His face was almost white, his eyes closed against the sun. With every breath, air and blood bubbled up from around the protruding spear shaft.

'Anna. My daughters. What happened to them?' I murmured in his ear. 'Did you see?'

The eyes blinked open and I held up my hand to shade them. A milky film had begun to cloud his sight; of the raking scorn with which he had watched both princes and pilgrims, almost nothing remained.

'Hostages,' he whispered.

My guts clenched within me. 'They were alive? Who took them? Franks?' I could not bear to imagine what revenge they might wreak on Anna and my daughters.

449

But I had asked too many questions – and Nikephoros had neither strength nor breath to answer them. His head lolled to one side; he half raised it again, then let it slump back. I realised he was trying to shake it.

'Not Franks.' The dying eyes widened in affirmation. 'The Egyptians? Where did they take them?'

Afterwards, I wished I had not made Nikephoros waste his last breath saying it. There could only ever have been one answer to that question. Coughing blood into my face, he twisted his head around and – agonisingly slow – lifted his left arm so that it pointed east, back up the valley. A vile soup of blood, bile, air and water slurped out of his wound; I thought I would vomit again, but I could not drop his gaze. He was grasping for breath, his chest heaving as he tried to snatch enough air for one final word.

'Jerusalem.'

Then his arm dropped, his eyes closed, and the spirit left him for ever. We buried him under one of the fruit trees, then turned back to Jerusalem.

III

Zion's Gate

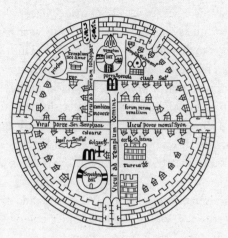

June – July 1099

λη

⟨∘⟩⟨∘⟩⟨∘⟩

'Behold Jerusalem, the navel of the world. The royal city that Christ the Redeemer exalted by his coming, beautified in his life, consecrated with his death and glorified by his resurrection. All the lands about it give forth their fruits like a paradise of heavenly delights. Behold it now.'

I sat on the blessed soil of the Mount of Olives and gazed down on the holy city.

Mere reality had not inspired the priests to change their sermons. Perhaps the land around Jerusalem had once been a fertile paradise of delights; now it was barren. From the heights of the Mount of Olives I could see the treeless, lifeless summits of the mountain range stretching far into the distance, rising and falling like waves. The broken ground was parched a dirty white, stippled with scrub and bushes, which produced nothing but thorns and poison. And there in its midst sat Jerusalem.

It was smaller than I had expected – a fraction of the size of Antioch. It spread over two hilltops, Mount Zion to the west and Mount Moriah to the east, lower than the surrounding ridges but divided from them on three sides by deep ravines, so that it stood proud on its promontory, a jewel in the crown of mountains. Just within its walls, on the eastern side nearest where I sat, I could see a vast open courtyard, built so high that its floor was equal with the height of the walls. An octagonal church surmounted by a bulging dome stood in its centre, sheathed in tiles that shone blue and green like the sea. With the still expanse of the courtyard setting it apart, lifting it above the jumbled dwellings in the city beyond, it was the most magnificent structure to be seen; I had assumed at once that it must be the church of the Holy Sepulchre. In fact, I learned, from men who had been to Jerusalem before on pilgrimage, it was the Temple of the Lord, built on the place where the great temple of Solomon had once stood. Now the Ishmaelites had taken it for their own. Beyond the great courtyard the city dipped into a shallow valley, then rose again in the slopes of Mount Zion. A stone bridge spanned the divide between the two mountains.

The holy slopes of Mount Zion had long since disappeared under the city; the buildings were packed so close together that from a distance I could not even tell if there were any streets between them. Christ's tomb must lie somewhere in that warren – buried, like the cave it had once been. And somewhere near by, amid all the marvels, relics and incense-soaked churches, was my family.

It had been the middle of the night, four days earlier, when we finally reached Jerusalem. Despite the late hour I went straight to Count Raymond's tent. I had expected to have to wake him – in my grief I would have woken the dead if necessary – but when I got there I found the lamps inside were lit. The guard who admitted me told me the count was with someone, and as I waited in the antechamber, I could hear muffled voices through the curtain that divided the tent into its different quarters.

Despite my surroundings, I found myself suddenly shivering from head to toe. Tears ran down my cheeks and I hugged my arms to my chest, hoping Raymond would not hear. The numbness that had gripped me since the battle in the orchard was wearing off, and the black wave of emotions it had held off now reared over me. Exhausted as I was, I tried to hold it back.

A sound from the next room snatched my attention back. Count Raymond's voice was suddenly raised, and in the midnight silence his words carried clear through the flimsy curtain which hid him.

'Have you come this far just to sit on the doorstep? The holy city is over there, barely a bowshot away. Everything we have fought for. Are you now suggesting we should balk at taking it?'

The reply came more quietly. Drawn by instinct, I

455

moved closer to the curtain to hear. It sounded like Duke Godfrey's voice. A shard of ice froze in my soul to hear it.

'I want to get inside that city as much as you or any man. But I will not throw away the prize just as my hand is closing around it. Have you forgotten why it took us two years to get here? We needed eight months to reduce Antioch, almost two months to take Nicaea. Even Ma'arat needed two weeks. As for Arqa—'

'That was different – they were merely waymarks on the holy road. Now we are at Jerusalem, God will surely win the victory for us. Besides . . .' Raymond lowered his voice. 'Every man in this army, pilgrim and soldier alike, has waited years for this moment. Many are almost sick with longing. They cannot wait – if we do not lead them, they will take matters into their own hands.'

'When God made us princes it was so that our wisdom would govern lesser men's passions,' said Godfrey scornfully. 'Wait a few days. Once your men get used to the miraculous fact that they have come to Jerusalem, they will be less impatient. Then we can invest the city properly, prepare siege engines and ballistas—'

'*Siege engines and ballistas?*' Raymond mocked him. 'And what will we build them out of – dust? There was a reason King Solomon sent all the way to Mount Lebanon for cedarwood when he wanted to build his temple. You will not find timber within twenty miles of this place.'

'Then we will go further – all the way back to Antioch, if we have to. But we will not risk everything in a premature assault. Patience is the companion of wisdom.'

'And faith is more important still. God is so powerful that if He desires it, we will scale the walls with a single ladder. He will help us.'

'Only if we help ourselves.'

I heard a movement and quickly scurried away from the curtain. A second later it pulled back, and Duke Godfrey stepped through. His eyes narrowed with suspicion when he saw me, then widened in surprise.

'I heard you had gone to Byzantium.'

'I came back.'

He shrugged, as if to show it was no concern of his. 'And Nikephoros? Has he returned?'

'He has not.'

You did this, I wanted to scream at him. My arms ached to strike him, to pound him and kick him until his bones were like wax and his flesh like water, until he screamed for forgiveness for the evil he had done me. But I could not – not there. He left the tent, while by the opening in the curtain I saw Raymond watching me carefully.

'What happened to Nikephoros?'

He must have guessed from my expression. He brought me into his private chamber and sat me on his couch, calling his servants to bring wine. I held the cup in my hand but barely drank as I told him everything that had happened. Almost everything.

The lines on Raymond's face deepened as I told my story. When I described how my family had been taken hostage, he rose and stepped towards me as if to comfort me, then turned aside and poured himself another cup of wine instead.

'That's all they have in this country,' he muttered. 'No water, only vines.'

I carried on. When I had finished, he fixed me with his good eye.

'But why would Achard have done such a thing?'

'Because Duke Godfrey ordered him to.' I blurted it out, my words burning hot with anger. I cursed Duke Godfrey. I cursed Nikephoros, who had refused to confront him after the ambush at Ravendan and had now paid the price. Most of all, I cursed myself. I had known the danger Godfrey threatened, and I had led my family into its shadow.

Raymond started. 'Why would he do that?'

'Because he hates the Greeks. He tried to seize Constantinople from the emperor. When that failed, he tried to kill me at Ravendan. Now he has murdered Nikephoros and sent my family into slavery. *I will kill him,*' I raged.

Raymond was watching me closely, and not only with sympathy. 'But why were you on the road away from Jerusalem? Where was Nikephoros going?'

I could only hope my distraught face hid any guilt. *What sort of man have you become*, I wondered, *using your grief for deception?*

'Nikephoros needed to speak to the supply ships from Cyprus. He thought you would want them to bring siege equipment – timbers for building,' I added, remembering what Godfrey had said.

Raymond looked at his hand, scraping dirt from under his fingernails. 'Then he died on a wasted errand. By God's grace, we will have taken the city by the end of the week.' He pulled me to my feet and clamped his hands on my shoulders, staring me straight in the eye. 'I know Achard has done a terrible thing to you, but you cannot lay it at Duke Godfrey's door, not before the city is taken. We rely too much on his strength. And the sooner Jerusalem falls, the sooner you will be reunited with your family.'

Back on the Mount of Olives, the priest had finished his sermon. His congregation – ten thousand knights and men-at-arms – muttered 'Amen', then broke into an excited chatter as they saw a small party walking up to the outcropping knoll that served as a pulpit. The red-headed priest, Arnulf, led them, a golden cross radiant over him; the princes followed and arrayed themselves in a semi-circle on the outcrop. Arnulf stood in their centre, turning the cross this way and that so that golden rays flickered over the front ranks of the watching army. An acolyte knelt before him and held up an open Bible.

'Blow the trumpet in Zion, and sound the alarm on the holy mountain! Let its inhabitants tremble, for the day of the Lord is near. A great and powerful army has come: their like has never been seen before, nor will be again in the ages to come.' He looked around, taking in all the assembled warriors. 'From the head of His army the Lord shouts out His battle-cry – how vast is His host. Truly, the day of the Lord will be great – and terrible.'

With a heavy slam, Arnulf let the book fall shut. The acolyte scurried away, and Raymond stepped forward. His cheeks were flushed, and an ungainly smile played over his face, as if he wanted to show humility but did not have the patience for it.

'Three years ago we left our homes, our fields and our families to seek Jerusalem. Here we are. Tomorrow, praise God, it will be ours.'

The congregation cheered and stamped their feet on the ground. A low cloud of dust rose up around their knees.

'We will attack at dawn. By noon, the city will have fallen.'

Chain mail shifted and clanged as ten thousand armoured heads rose from prayer. In the grim light before sunrise I could make out little more than the coned helmets and spear-shafts that rose around me like a forest – though in the east, a dark shadow was slowly resolving itself into the silhouette of a mountain as the dawn spread behind its peak. Horses galloped up and down our lines, their stirrups jangling as their riders barked the orders they brought. For the third time that morning I checked that my shield was buckled tight, then half-drew my sword and touched my thumb against its edge. I had promised myself that if – *when* – I ever rescued my family, I would throw it away, or give it to a smith to hammer into impotence.

One of the heralds cantered up to us. 'Be ready. The front ranks have begun the assault. God wills it.'

'God wills it,' the knight who commanded our line replied. After the losses the Varangians had suffered in the orchard, there were no longer enough of us to make our own company: we had had to submit ourselves to a Frankish command. It had almost destroyed Sigurd's pride – and worse was to follow when we discovered that none of the leading knights would accept our service. The glory to be won by being first into Jerusalem was not a prize they would share lightly, least of all with our tattered band. At last we found a knight from Flanders who had lost half his company in the siege of Ma'arat and did not have the wealth to attract others: he took us happily enough. But he was old, and most of his knights were men he had fought with since boyhood. He was happy enough to bide his time near the back of the army.

'The vanguard will have marched clear through Jerusalem and on into Egypt by the time we reach the walls,' I fretted. I could only hope that reverence for the holy city would keep the Franks from the sort of pillage they had inflicted on Antioch. The thought of my daughters and Anna escaping the Ishmaelites only to be slaughtered – or worse – by Franks was like a noose around my heart.

'And what will we do when *we* enter the city?' Sigurd asked. It was the fifth time he had asked that question, and I had no good answer. All I had were Nikephoros' dying words – and I did not even know how accurate they might be. The Fatimids could have taken their captives to another fortress, or to a cave in the hills, or . . .

461

I shook my head to clear it of evil thoughts. 'We will do what we can, and trust to God for the rest.'

On my right, Thomas was staring forward with desperate intensity, his axe ready in his hands. When I touched his arm, he jerked as if I had cut it open.

'Keep loose,' I warned him. 'You won't be able to swing your axe if your arms are so tense.'

Without a word, he turned back to look at Jerusalem. Not a muscle in his face moved. All his life was in that city: his dead parents, his captive wife, his son – perhaps even his God. I hoped he would find at least some of them beyond the walls that now loomed ahead of us in the blue dawn.

Another herald galloped up the line towards us. 'The front ranks have reached the outer walls. Prepare to advance.'

I had spent two years and a thousand miles trying to reach Jerusalem. Now, as the sun's molten rays crept over the ridge and began to touch Mount Zion, I began to march the last few hundred yards. The faces around me were wide-eyed, like men awakening into a dream; many crossed themselves, and some wept openly. The battle-hymn of the Army of God resounded in my ears like clashing cymbals.

'God wills it!'

λθ

'It would have been better if God had willed them to bring ladders.'

Sigurd spat on the ground. All his weapons were laid out around him, silver in the moonlight – his great battleaxe, a pair of small throwing axes, a sword and two knives. One by one he polished them with a cloth, rubbed them with oil, then wiped them clean. It was an exercise in futility: I knew for a fact that not one of those blades had touched so much as the beard of an enemy that day.

'Perhaps our faith was not strong enough,' said Thomas. He sat on a rock a little distance away from us, resting his chin in his hands. They were almost the first words he had spoken since we returned from the battle.

Sigurd, who had one of the throwing axes in his hand,

looked as though he might willingly put it into Thomas's skull. 'The only thing that was too weak was the sense of those shit-cursed princes.'

For the Army of God, which had cracked open the greatest fortresses of antiquity and defied the combined hordes of the Ishmaelites, the assault on Jerusalem had been a disaster. Ten thousand men had tried to climb into the city with a single ladder between them. After some hours of fighting they had breached the low outer wall and charged through, only to pass into the dead ground between the curtain wall and the great rampart. Buttresses between the two walls hemmed in their flanks, so that the defenders could rain down missiles from three sides. When the Franks had tried to make a tortoise roof with their shields, the Egyptians had simply broken it apart with rocks and then poured arrows into the gaps. Meanwhile, thinking the city must have fallen, more men flooded through the breaches so that those in the front were crushed against the main wall or trampled underfoot. They had filled the ground between the walls like lambs in a pen, and like lambs they had been slaughtered.

Yet despite all this, they had managed to raise their ladder to the main walls. A Norman knight had started to climb it. The air around him was dark with arrows; the ladder swayed and shuddered as stones ricocheted off it. Still he climbed, somehow untouched by the cloud of missiles. The defenders brought vats of boiling water and tried to pour it over him, but in their haste they tipped it too quickly and it fell on the men at the foot of the ladder instead. No one heard their screams: the entire army was holding its breath, waiting to see if the knight could reach the top. That he had not been plucked from it already seemed nothing short of a miracle – proof, for those who sought it, that God had ordained their victory. The further he went the more they allowed themselves to hope. Weighed down by his armour, his progress was agonisingly slow; once he seemed to slip, and the whole army gasped, but he regained his footing and continued inexorably up. *God is so powerful that if He desires it, we will scale the walls with a single ladder*, I remembered Raymond had said. Now, before the eyes of all men, his words were becoming manifest, and the army trembled with fearful expectation.

The knight gained the final rung, reached out his arm and fastened his hand on the embrasure between the battlements. For a moment, he must have looked down to see the holy city framed in stone. A great cheer rose up from the army; more men started climbing the ladder, while the rest surged forward. The knight on the ladder glanced back down, and though I could not see his face I could imagine the triumph on it. He waved his sword to rally the army and screamed, '*Deus vult!*'

From the ramparts before him, a heavy sword flashed down. The knight cringed back, flailing his arm, and we saw in horror that the hand that clasped Jerusalem had been severed from his body. He flung away his sword and scrabbled for a grip, but he had no chance. An arrow pierced his side, another his shoulder; he lost his balance and crashed down onto the crowds below, spinning as he fell.

On the walls around us, the Fatimid archers resumed their bombardment. Scores of the Franks had lowered their shields to watch the ascent; now they paid for their carelessness. Mercifully I was too far back to trouble the bowmen: they did not want for targets. From up on the walls, a pair of hands reached through the embrasure and pushed away the ladder. It pivoted back, then toppled down into the fray. Within seconds it had been ground to splinters as the Franks rushed to escape.

'The only miracle was that the Norman did not die,' said Sigurd.

Thomas looked at him with the sure contempt of youth. 'There were no miracles today.' His voice was hollow, heartbroken. 'The Norman survived because three corpses broke his fall. There were enough bodies between those walls to clog the gates of heaven.'

I said nothing. I knew some of the anguish he must feel – I felt enough of it myself. But he seemed to have taken the defeat so much to his heart that it consumed him. At the height of the battle, when the Franks were fleeing back through the breaches, he had even tried to rush forward, though it was certain death. Sigurd had held him back, almost breaking his arm to do it. I prayed it had only been the madness of war – not the weight of his sorrows becoming unbearable.

'I've heard that Count Raymond will move his camp

around to the south,' said Sigurd, breaking the awkward silence.

'I wonder how many will go with him?'

'Twelve of us, at least.' Sigurd gestured to the Varangians, all that remained of his company. 'No one else will have us.'

'We may be the only ones.' I knew that several of Raymond's captains had transferred their allegiance to other princes in the aftermath of the battle. 'No wonder he wants to move his camp away from the others.'

Sigurd held up his throwing axe to the moonlight, squinting down the blade. He grunted with grudging approval – then looked up in surprise as a shadow fell over him. A youth in a yellow tunic had emerged from the darkness, blocking out the moon. His skin was smooth, his dark hair curly: he might easily have been taken for a Saracen. Perhaps that was why he wore an outsize wooden cross on a cord around his neck. It seemed to cause him some discomfort.

'Who is Demetrios Askiates?' he asked, in heavily accented Greek.

'Who are you?' I retorted.

He would not say, but reached into the folds of his tunic. Sigurd tensed his arm, the oiled axe gleaming in his hand, but there was no danger. Instead, the boy pulled out a brooch and tossed it across to me. I examined it. The gold was leaden in the moonlight, but the design was clear enough. A tree wrought in enamel – reds, blues and greens – and two birds flanking it.

'You know whose it is?'

I nodded, dumbstruck. It had been a gift from the imperial treasury to Anna, after she saved the emperor from a spear-wound.

'Then come with me.'

I wanted to bring Sigurd, but then I would have had to take Thomas, and I did not trust him in his evil mood. So I went alone. The youth walked behind me through the camp, letting me meet the challenges and give the watchwords, then took the lead. Ten minutes brought us to the north-eastern corner of the city: we rounded it, then dropped away from the walls as the ground descended into the steep valley that divided the Mount of Olives from the city. The night deepened as we went down – I clutched the brooch so tight its pin pierced my hand, but I carried on until suddenly I saw a faint light winking in the darkness.

The light drew closer as we reached the bottom of the valley. The ground was broken here, strewn with rocks, though it was only when I stubbed my toe on one and looked down that I saw they were not boulders, but fragments of a shattered building. The remains of toppled columns, tumbledown walls and fallen arches littered the landscape like bones on a battlefield. The destruction must have happened some time ago, for grass and bushes had grown tall around the ruins. Where a solitary piece of wall still stood, a fig tree had twined itself through the empty window.

But the corpse of the building remained, buried in the ground. A flight of open stairs brought us down into an oblong pit lined with stone. Two rows of stumps marked where the columns had once stood, and though most of the ground was covered in earth, in a few places you could still make out the tiles of the mosaic floor. It must have been a church, I thought. And despite its desolation, it still seemed to be in use. At the far end, unhidden by any altar screen, two black-robed priests with long, white beards bowed before a long-vanished altar. It was their light I had seen, a lone oil-lamp resting on a fallen capital. The flame illuminated the face of a high stone mausoleum – the only structure to have survived the destruction.

'Do you know where you are?'

I swung around. With all my attention on the ghostly scene in the sanctuary I had not noticed the man sitting on the stub of a column to my right. He stood, his cloak rustling around his legs.

'Bilal.' I stepped towards him, then checked myself, suddenly overtaken by confusion, fear. I opened my palm to reveal the brooch. 'Did you send this?'

'Yes.'

'Are they . . . ?' I could not bring myself to finish the question.

He offered a tired smile. 'They are safe.'

Relief flooded through me. So much tension had knotted itself around me that week that, in the end, it was all that had held me together. Now it washed away and I dropped to my knees. The poison bile that had filled my body rose in my throat and I let it pour out onto the once-holy ground, praying God to forgive me. In the chancel, the priests continued their low chanting.

Bilal took my arm and pulled me to my feet. I would have embraced him, almost fallen upon him with thanks, but something held me away. There was a distance in his manner that I had not seen before.

'A squadron of our cavalry surprised a column of Frankish knights,' he said. 'There was a battle.'

'I was there.'

'But not with your wife and children. They found them with the ambassador, Nikephoros.'

There was no rebuke in his words, but I felt it anyway like a hammer. 'They fell upon us so quickly there was nothing I could do. I was separated from them. I—'

Bilal held up his hand to still my babble. 'God is the All-Hearing and the All-Seeing. Perhaps He did not mean you to be with them. Nikephoros fought to protect your family – bravely, they said – and died for it. If you had stood beside them, the same might have happened to you.'

I remembered Thomas's desperate longing to charge into the battle that morning. You could not escape guilt by dying.

'As it was, they assumed the women must be Nikephoros' wife and daughters, and therefore worthy of ransom.'

So Nikephoros' pride had served a purpose in the end. I remembered the golden robe he had worn that day, the jewelled *lorum* wrapped around his neck. Perhaps he had

470

already imagined himself back in the perfumed halls of Constantinople, returned from his exile. And he had fought to protect my family. Suddenly, for all his deceits, I found I no longer hated him.

'But I have no money to ransom them,' I said, trying to comprehend all this unexpected news. 'And the Franks will not waste their gold on Greeks.'

'My masters would not offer them to the Franks. All Muslims may seem the same to the Franks, but we understand the differences between the Christians well enough. When the vizier needs to buy favour with your emperor, then he will offer him the women as part of some bargain.'

'But the emperor will know they cannot belong to Nikephoros.' Hope rose within me. 'Can you help them escape?'

Bilal sighed, and I could see that he wished I had not asked it. 'I cannot.'

The euphoria that had lifted me subsided. I sank down on one of the stone stubs. Bilal stayed standing, silhouetted against the priests' lamp at the far end of the nave.

'At least I know they're safe,' I said, when I could control my voice again. 'Thank you for that.'

'It is the least I can do. And the most. But for as long as my people control the city, no harm will come to them.'

'A long time if our attack this morning was any omen. Did you see it?'

'I was there.' Bilal looked away, unwilling to talk more of it. Perhaps he was embarrassed by the wanton ease with which the Franks had given themselves up to be slaughtered.

471

A thought struck me. 'The vizier must be confident of victory if he is already able to think of bargaining with the emperor.' No answer. 'Is the vizier here now?'

Bilal shifted uneasily.

'Come,' I urged him. 'Do you think I'm trying to pry secrets out of you? I want to know, in innocence, if I will ever see my family again. Nothing else.'

'In innocence?' Bilal repeated the words with heavy irony. 'Can there be such a thing? When we fought beside each other in the pyramid, when the Turkish troops tried to harm that boy, we did it because we hated evil, nothing else. When the caliph in his madness threatened to kill you, I warned you for the same reason. But we are in Jerusalem now, and the next time your army charges at those walls you will be on one side and I will be on the other. It will be a battle to the end. So how can you and I speak to each other in innocence?'

Bilal looked away, to the light in the sanctuary of the church. The two priests must know we were there, must have heard us, but they continued with their ritual as if we did not exist.

'Do you know where you are?' Bilal repeated the question he had asked when I first arrived. I looked around, then up. Far above us, the fires on the city walls burned bright against the sky from the great courtyard of the Temple Mount.

'You are in Gethsemane. This was the church of Mary, the mother of Jesus and that tomb' – he pointed to the stone mausoleum – 'is hers.'

You could hardly breathe in this place for the weight of history. 'But Mary was taken up to heaven. When Saint Thomas came to her tomb three days after she fell asleep, her body was gone.'

'Then the tomb must be empty. But your priests still offer their prayers here.'

I looked up at the walls again, thinking of the other, greater sepulchre within. If we ever reached it, we would find that lying empty too. A desolation swept over me, a feeling of terrible absence. I suddenly knew in my heart that God had departed this place, that these half-buried tombs were nothing more than fossils, footprints left in the clay where He had once walked. 'So many deserted tombs.'

'Even the dead cannot bear to stay here,' said Bilal. I could not tell if he was joking.

'If your cavalry had not kidnapped my family, I would never have come.' It was an unfair thing to say, perhaps, but it seemed to pierce the curtain that had descended between us again. Bilal thought for a moment.

'We cannot speak to each other in innocence, but I will tell you this. If you ever have cause to use it, I will be in God's hands. You have seen the Noble Sanctuary on the mountain top?'

'The great courtyard with the octagonal church?'

'It is a shrine, not a church,' said Bilal irritably. 'It was built by the caliph to mark the place where the Prophet, peace be upon him, ascended to heaven.'

'It is a church, built by Byzantines to mark the place

where Solomon's temple stood and where Abraham went to sacrifice Isaac,' I retorted, repeating what I had heard from pilgrims. 'It is called the Temple of the Lord.'

'For the moment it is called the Dome of the Rock. God willing, it will be for ever. But if the day comes when it is not, then your family will be in as much danger as me. So listen. Beyond the Noble Sanctuary lies a valley that divides the two hills, Mount Moriah and Mount Zion. A stone bridge crosses over it. On the far side of the bridge the street runs west, to a corner where two tamarisk trees grow. If you go right, there is a house with an iron amulet in the shape of a hand nailed to its door.' He held up his own hand, palm out. 'That is where you will find your family – if you take the city.'

'Do you really think it so unlikely?'

Bilal shook his head – though whether to answer my question or to deny it I could not tell.

'*I will send for the king of Babylon,*' Bilal murmured. '*I will bring him against this land and its people and I will destroy them utterly. The whole land shall become a ruin, a waste, and its people will be his slaves.*'

'Where did you hear that?'

'I heard Achard say it, when we came here on our way north from Egypt. He said it was an ancient prophecy.'

'It comes from the prophet Jeremiah.'

'Then perhaps it is true.' Bilal turned away. 'I must go – I have already been away too long. Malchus will take you back to your camp.' He whistled, and the youth emerged from the darkness where he had waited.

474

'Goodbye, Demetrios. I would say I hope we meet again, but I fear it will be a terrible day if ever we do.' He considered this for a moment, then shrugged. '*Allahu a'alam.* God knows all things best.'

He climbed the cracked steps out of the sunken church and vanished into the night. There were no Franks watching this part of the city – the ground was too steep, their numbers too few – and I supposed he would slip in through one of the gates easily enough. Even so, I delayed a few minutes lest anybody see us together. While I waited, I lowered myself to my knees and offered a few, heartfelt prayers – thanks that my family were safe, and intercessions for those who had died that day. Above all, I prayed that all those I loved would escape that place where God had gathered them. Those were the prayers that tested my faith the hardest.

The night was warm, and I had been awake since well before dawn. I must have prayed longer than I thought, for eventually I felt an arm shaking my shoulder and opened my eyes with a start. The youth was looking down on me.

'You fell asleep,' he chided me. 'Come. You must go back.'

Keeping to the shadows once again, we clambered up the valley and followed the walls towards the camp. Behind us, two priests stood in the pit and offered their prayers to an empty tomb.

μ

⬚⬚⬚⬚⬚

The next day Count Raymond moved his camp to the south, to a narrow tongue of land in front of the walls on Mount Zion. It was perilously exposed, within easy bowshot of the archers who manned the Zion Gate: the other princes condemned his decision, and many of his knights refused to accompany him. He went anyway and we followed. The failure of the assault had dissolved whatever ties of fealty and honour he still held over his men. He could no longer even garrison his camp, but had to send envoys to his rivals to buy their knights' service with gold. Each day, I heard, the price went up.

Two days after the battle, the princes held a council and agreed they would not risk another assault without siege engines.

'If we can find the wood to build them,' Raymond complained. He had called me to his tent next to a small church on Mount Zion. The air inside was stifling, and flies buzzed about our heads. 'There's barely enough wood here to build a campfire. It's a miracle the Romans found enough to crucify Jesus.' He stopped, blushing furiously. 'Christ forgive me, I did not mean that. But we must have wood if we are to get into Jerusalem.'

I could guess why he was telling me this.

'I want you to take your men west towards the coast and search for wood.' He swatted at one of the flies. 'It will do you good to be away from this place for a few days.'

'Did he say if he wanted us to come back?' Sigurd enquired.

It was a fair question: for two days our search had taken us ever further from Jerusalem, with nothing except stunted olive trees and shrubs to reward us. The sun burned down on us, parching our throats, and all the time we felt the heavy threat of the Ishmaelites all around us. Several times we came around turns in the road to find dust still lingering in the air where departing hooves had kicked it up; twice we saw their riders silhouetted on distant hilltops, watching us from afar. Though they never came near, their presence stirred a poison in my belly: the fear that I might die in one of these forgotten valleys and leave my family condemned to perpetual slavery. I often walked with my sword drawn from its scabbard; at night I lay awake long after the others had fallen asleep, staring at the darkness and trembling at every sound it made.

Two mornings after leaving Jerusalem, the rugged hills dipped towards the coastal plain. I was worn down to exhaustion; I had hardly had anything to drink, and my tongue had swollen so fat in my mouth I thought it might split my skull open. Sharp pains spiked through my head with every step – steps that only took me further from Jerusalem. The loathsome city had wrapped itself tight around my soul, and the further I went from it the more strongly I felt it pulling me back.

We had just descended into yet another valley when Aelfric, who had gone ahead, came running back to meet us.

'Three riders coming towards us,' he said breathlessly.

'Did they see you?'

'I don't think so. But the sun was in my eyes – it was hard to be sure.'

We scrambled up the hillside, hiding ourselves behind boulders and trees. I found a small depression in the slope masked by a bush and lay there. Thomas crouched down beside me, stroking the blade of his axe. In a matter of seconds, all the Varangians had vanished.

We waited. For what seemed an age we heard nothing but bird song and the chatter of insects; once, there was a clatter as one of the Varangians dislodged a pebble, but otherwise no one made a sound. I could almost hear the sweat sliding down my face and dripping onto the stones beneath me. And then, rising slowly beneath the other sounds, the regular clop of horses' hooves. The noise grew louder, echoing around the valley – and with it came voices.

I edged forward to the lip of the depression, keeping low behind the foliage, and peered out between the branches. The three riders had come level with me. They wore neither helmets nor armour, and if they sat uneasily in their saddles it was only from lack of habit. Otherwise, they talked and laughed like men on holiday; as I watched, one even broke into a song.

> Hwær cwom mearg? Hwær cwom mago? Hwær
>   cwom maþþumgyfa?
> Hwær cwom symbla gesetu? Hwær sindon sele-
>   dreamas?

To my astonishment, another voice answered – not among the riders but from the hillside. It picked up the melody and carried it on. Four more voices joined in, and suddenly the valley was awash with the weird sounds of a song it had never heard before.

> Eala beorht bune! Eala byrnwiga!
> Eala þeodnes þrym! Hu seo þrag gewat,
> genap under nihthelm, swa heo no wære!

Sigurd stepped out onto the road, still singing. It was he who had first answered the song, I realised, and its foreign sound was his native tongue. He stood in front of the riders, and at last I saw what should have been obvious from the start. The men on the horses were almost indistinguishable from the Varangians who swarmed down the hillside to greet them. All had the same rough red skin that came when pale white skin had been alloyed by the sun, and each face was covered by hair the colour of metal: gold, copper and bronze. Some wore it in braids and some tied with twine; some had beards and others were clean-shaven. Otherwise, they could have been brothers.

The lead rider sang the last verse of the song in unison with Sigurd, their eyes locked on each other. A sardonic grin had spread over the rider's face, while Sigurd's remained cool and distrustful. When the song was done, they eyed each other cautiously.

'You should be more careful, riding alone and unarmed in these mountains,' said Sigurd.

The rider glanced around at the Varangians. 'Careful of what?' he asked insouciantly. 'I heard there was nothing in these hills except peasants and goatherds. And wood-cutters,' he added, looking at the axes we carried. 'Have you come to sell us firewood?'

'Or to cut you down to size,' Sigurd growled. 'Who are you and what are you doing here? Have you come from Byzantium?'

I could not understand his attitude. If I had been in their far-flung country and met a fellow Greek on the road, I would have rejoiced. Sigurd, by contrast, seemed to take his countryman's presence as a personal affront. Perhaps it was the way of their people – certainly the riders seemed unworried by it.

'Varangians?' He shook his head. 'We're just humble sailors with a cargo to sell.'

'What cargo?' Apart from a few panniers and blankets tied to their saddles, the Englishmen carried nothing.

The rider crossed his hands in his lap and stared up at the sky, as if trying to remember. 'Nails. Ropes. Grease and oil. Saws, planes, adzes and augers. Timber.'

Sigurd flushed and lifted his axe angrily. 'Do not mock me,' he warned.

The rider remained infuriatingly calm. 'Everything I described – and more – is sitting on the docks at Jaffa, waiting for someone to buy it. Come and see for yourself.' He laughed. 'Saewulf will be happy to see you.'

On a knuckle of land that pressed out into the Mediterranean, flanked by sandy beaches, we found the port of Jaffa. Its western face descended steeply to the sea, so that from below the houses built on it seemed to blend into a single construct of golden stone, red pantiles and wooden balconies. Only when you looked closer did you see that the picture was imperfect. Many of the buildings were missing their roofs; no washing hung from the houses, no children played in the alleys between them, and no guards paced the badly ruined walls. Even the fortress which should have guarded the town was reduced to a single tower.

'The city is abandoned,' said Thomas, as we stepped over a fallen arch into the town's main street.

Sigurd grunted. 'There are always rats who'll move in.'

At the foot of the hill, a dock crooked its protective embrace around a small harbour. White foam ruffled the water at its mouth where a thick hawser had been stretched across it, but it had not kept out the six ships that lay moored against the wharf. Stout masts rose from their decks, and their high prows were carved in the likeness of fantastic beasts. One was shaped like a dragon, another like a monstrous fish, while the largest took the form of a ravening wolf.

I knew that ship, had spent long weeks enduring a difficult winter voyage aboard it, cursing its heaving deck and leaky seams. Bobbing at anchor, bathed in June sunshine, she was almost unrecognisable now. As to what she was doing there, I could no more guess than when I had first seen her drawn up on a beach on the dusky Egyptian coast.

We descended to the harbour. A great quantity of crates, sacks and barrels had been piled on the dock, together with some long timbers. In the corner where the harbour walls turned across the bay, an unused sail had been draped over a frame of lashed-together oars to make a rough awning. As we reached the bottom of the hill and stepped out onto the hot stone of the wharf, the figure resting in its shade rose; he did not approach, but stood there waiting, watching while we crossed towards him. The ships' crews lounged among the cargo, and the smells of salt and alcohol were thick in the air.

Saewulf had not changed much in the six months since we parted on a freezing January day near Antioch. The leather band was still bound across his forehead, tying back his long brown hair; he had shaved off his beard, though perhaps that had to do with the fresh scar that ran livid down his right cheek. Many men would have been disfigured by the wound, or would have hidden it in self-conscious shame. With Saewulf, it was simply one more line among many. He stood with the same cocky posture, his hands thumbed into his belt and his shoulders thrust back, and still watched the world with the same amused detachment I had seen on that beach in Egypt.

In contrast to his easy confidence, we must have seemed an awkward and ill-tempered group. Gathered behind Sigurd, we shuffled to a stop in front of the awning and waited nervously, our gazes darting about our surroundings, while the two captains stood and stared each other in the eye in some sort of unspoken contest. All around, the sailors put down their tools and cups to watch us.

'I thought I'd got rid of you twenty years ago, when you deserted Byzantium to go back to the ruin of England.' Sigurd's words were slow and clear, carrying to every corner of the harbour.

Saewulf shrugged. 'If you had stayed in Byzantium, you would have kept rid of me.' His eyes played across the group of Varangians behind Sigurd; he saw me and Aelfric and smiled.

'At least two of your men already have reason to be grateful to me. And now perhaps I can help you again – unless you came to Jaffa for fish.' He swept a hand around the harbour. 'All the fishermen have gone, I'm afraid. But perhaps I can interest you in my cargo.'

'Why are you here?' Sigurd stepped closer, looming over his countryman. The Varangians around me put their hands on their axes. 'Why has a coward like you happened upon this port, five hundred miles from any friendly harbour, with enough supplies to besiege Constantinople? Are you still working for the Normans – or have you whored yourself to someone else since then?'

Saewulf let Sigurd's outburst break over him like spray from the bow.

'I work for myself – as I always have.'

'I'm sure you're very good at it.' Sigurd had not backed away.

'Good enough to see that when a desperate army besieges a city without any trees, they'll pay well for wood. Unless, as I said, you came for the fish.' He squinted at us. 'What did you do with the men I sent to Jerusalem?'

'We sent them on to Jerusalem to fetch men to carry back your supplies.'

'If they can carry the gold to pay for this, they'll have enough men to carry back what they buy.' He saw Sigurd's scowl of disdain. 'I'm offering them the keys to Jerusalem. They should pay well enough for that. Besides, it wasn't easy to bring it here. There are Fatimid ships swarming all over these waters. Three nights ago they would have sunk us, if the wind hadn't turned.' He patted one of the nearby casks. 'If God does want the Franks to have this, then He surely wants them to pay for it.'

Saewulf glanced out of a narrow window in the seaward wall. It had taken us most of the day to reach Jaffa and the sun was setting, a golden bowl pouring out its rays on the burnished water.

'The Franks won't be here before tomorrow morning. Stay with us tonight, and I'll tell you about England.'

Whatever quarrels he and Sigurd might have had, Saewulf feasted us royally. His men had been out in the hills that day and brought back two boars and a small deer, which they roasted over a fire at the end of the dock. There was no lack of wood here. Waves lapped against the stone piers, fat sizzled in the flames and wine poured freely into cups, spilling as they clashed in toasts, then draining into thirsty throats. For all their captains' hostility, Saewulf's crew and Sigurd's Varangians met each other with the joy of long-lost friends, proving their delight in the quantities they drank. Many of the sailors, like Saewulf, had served in the Varangian guard at one time or another, and the rest all seemed to share cousins, half-sisters or friends in common.

'To England,' Saewulf toasted, raising his glance and then emptying it. 'You should come back, Sigurd – see what a green country looks like. Escape all this dust and rock.'

'Not while there's a Norman sitting on the throne,' said Sigurd. He emptied his own cup and poured another, splashing the wine in his haste.

'You would never see him. You would walk in English

fields, eat and drink English bread and beer, and see your grandchildren grow up where they belong. What does it matter who sits in the castles?'

The wine had infused passion into Saewulf's usual detachment. His face was flushed, and he waved his hands earnestly as he spoke.

'The Normans stole our country,' Sigurd insisted.

'England is still there. The white cliffs still stood when I sailed away. The only person who is keeping you out of your home is *you*, sitting here and sulking over injustices you suffered more than thirty years ago.'

'What should I have done? Surrendered to them like you did?'

'Surrendered?' Saewulf laughed, the cup swaying in his hand. 'Do you think I got down on my knees in front of King William and swore him allegiance? I have never seen him in my life. If I sailed you back to England tonight, do you think he would be standing on Pevensey beach to meet you – to fight you in single combat for the crown of the realm?' Sigurd made to interrupt, but Saewulf carried on over him. 'You're no more to him than the mud on the sole of his boot. The only person who cares about your righteous exile is you. And when you're on your deathbed, what will you tell your grandchildren? That you wasted your life because you could not bear to let go of your hatred? That your pride would rather you served a foreign king in a foreign land than live in your own?'

'I would rather serve the man I choose, than the man

who tore away my country, who killed my father and raped my family.'

'That man died twelve years ago. One of his sons rules England now – and another, as I hear it, is a prince in your Army of God. Have you noticed that the emperor you adopted to escape the Normans has now sent you to fight beside them?'

'The emperor takes his allies as he needs them,' said Sigurd tightly.

'And he abandons them when they're no more use to him.' Saewulf rose, swaying, though whether that was the effect of wine or his habit of being at sea I could not tell. 'I know what you think of me – that you stand fast and defend your oaths while I go where the wind blows.'

'And where the money calls.'

'And where the money calls,' Saewulf agreed. He was slurring his words now, slopping wine over the rim of his cup as he waved his arms. 'But there's nothing noble clinging to a rock when the tide is rising. Especially if the rock turns out to be nothing but sand.'

Sigurd lumbered to his feet, his face red in the firelight. 'I came to Byzantium as an orphan: without family, without a home, without even a country. Now I am a captain of the guard in an empire that was young when our ancestors hadn't even learned to build boats.'

'An empire that has only survived so long by buying barbarians like you in the dark times – then throwing you out with the night soil the moment they see the dawn.'

'Liar!' bellowed Sigurd. 'The emperor has never

betrayed me. I stood beside him at the battle of Paradunavum, when almost every other man in his army had deserted or been slaughtered, and when we took our revenge four years later at Lebunium, I was at his side again. Are you telling me that instead of that, I should have spent those years scratching at soil that the Normans had left barren, grovelling in the dust each time a Norman rode by and praying his eye wouldn't fall on my daughter?'

'I'm telling you that when you're among your own people, you know who your enemies are.' Saewulf reached out and grabbed the golden ring on Sigurd's arm, pulling him forward like a bull. 'The emperor you love so much may have thrown you some crumbs when he was in trouble, but now he has betrayed you. Do you know why I have arrived here with a ship full of siege equipment?'

They were standing almost chest to chest now, Saewulf's fingers still tight on Sigurd's arm. I was amazed at his boldness. Sigurd towered over him; for a moment I thought he might slam his forehead against Saewulf's skull in rage. But the sea-captain's question had surprised him.

'Did the emperor send you?'

Saewulf laughed. 'The emperor sent the siege weapons – but not to Jerusalem, and not on my ship. I took them off a Cypriot convoy we surprised two weeks ago at sea.'

'Piracy.' Sigurd almost spat the word in Saewulf's face. Saewulf shrugged it off.

'Where do you suppose the Cypriot captain told me he was going with his cargo? To Jaffa, to help the poor Franks? No. He was going to Alexandria, to deliver these supplies to the Fatimid caliph to use against the Franks when he brings his army up to Jerusalem.'

Sigurd tried to pull away, but Saewulf kept a tight hold on his armband. 'The emperor you love so much has betrayed the Franks – and you. You can hardly move on the seas out there for all the imperial grain ships hurrying to Egypt. The emperor has found new allies; now he will cast his old ones into the fire.' He laughed again, a taunting, harrowing laugh. 'At least he has betrayed the Franks because he wants to get Antioch back from them. You, who served him so faithfully, have been discarded simply because he cannot be bothered to save you.'

With a roar of anger, Sigurd tore himself from Saewulf's grip, picked him up and hurled him against a pile of barrels. They tumbled over and rolled around the wharf like pigs on their backs. Sigurd bounded towards his opponent, but this was not the first dockside brawl Saewulf had fought. He was already on his feet, crouching low; he ducked aside as Sigurd sprang past him, kicking the Varangian's feet from under him so that he sprawled on the stones.

I looked around. Dozens of ruddy faces were watching the fight, but none moved.

Sigurd got up, brushing dirt from his tunic. 'Liar,' he shouted again at Saewulf. 'Why should I believe the word of a pirate and a traitor?' He looked around, defying anyone in the crowd to defend Saewulf. 'Would we be here if the emperor had betrayed us? Would we have spent the last two years fighting beside the Franks, crawling through deserts and over mountains?' He was staring straight at me, and my face must have revealed the truth for he took a step towards me and demanded again, more loudly, 'Would we?'

I had never told him what Nikephoros revealed to me the night before he died. I couldn't have. How can you knock down the pillar of a man's world? But my silence told him enough. All I could do was shake my head in misery.

Howling like a wounded ox, like Samson chained in the temple, Sigurd raised his arms and charged. Saewulf tried to sidestep him again but was too slow; Sigurd thumped into him and together, grappling and struggling, gouging and biting, they lurched across the dock. The men about them leaped to their feet, but none moved to help. They knew this was not their fight. I stood with them, watching, numb with desolation. How had it come to this?

Sigurd and Saewulf staggered to the edge of the dock. Ripples of light reflected on the water below, as if the sea itself had turned into a pool of fire. For a moment I saw them silhouetted against it, two dark shapes locked in inexorable combat. Then, with a cry and an almighty splash, they toppled off the edge of the wharf and fell into the water.

We rushed to the side and looked down. Two heads bobbed in the harbour, their arms flailing around them to keep afloat. The shock of the water and the risk of drowning had finally driven them apart, each more concerned with saving himself than destroying his opponent. With much splashing and spluttering, they paddled across to the harbour stairs and hauled themselves out.

'Drowning me won't change the truth,' said Saewulf. 'Nor will drowning yourself.'

Sigurd shook himself like a dog, and stalked away.

There were no more songs that night. The sailors and Varangians scattered around the harbour, making their beds wherever they could or wherever the wine overtook them. Sigurd found himself a niche in the wall and collapsed there alone, cursing away any man who came near him. As for me, the fire had burned low before I got to sleep. But once I did, I found to my surprise that I slept more peacefully than I had in weeks. Perhaps it was the wine; perhaps I had simply reached a place beyond hope or fear. Either way, I lay on the deck of one of the ships, letting it rock me like a cradle, and slept without dreams until the sun had climbed over the knuckle of the hill and started to warm my face.

But perhaps it was just another trick of the fates. For if I had slept less, and listened more closely to the darkness, maybe it would not have been so late before I discovered our new danger.

μα

〰〰〰

'How badly do you want my cargo?'

I opened my eyes. Saewulf was crouching over me, the dawn light soft on his scarred face. Red weals and bruises bore witness to his struggle with Sigurd the night before.

'How badly do you want your siege equipment?' he asked again.

I lifted myself on one elbow. My mouth was dry, my head uneasy from too much wine the night before. 'What do you mean?' A horrible thought struck me. 'Do you want money?' I looked to see if he had a knife in his hands. He did not, but the fish-handled dagger was still tucked in his belt within easy reach. Had Sigurd been right about him?

He bared his teeth at me. 'This isn't about money. Come.'

He dragged me to my feet and led me onto the dock, up a crumbling flight of stairs to the rampart atop the harbour walls. He pointed out to sea.

'That is what I mean.'

It was a scene the ancient poets could well have recognised. The rose-fingered dawn reached down to the water, her caresses stirring rippling waves. The sea shone with a blinding light, and a fresh wind blew in from the west. Birds soared in the cloudless sky, then swooped down in search of fish, barely disturbing the waves as they dived beneath them. And there, black as flies against the shimmering water, a fleet of ships sailed towards the harbour.

'Are they . . . ours?'

Saewulf shook his head soberly. 'Egyptian.'

I counted them – eight, against six of Saewulf's ships in the harbour behind me. Glancing back, I could see his crew still sprawled around the docks, slowly beginning to stir as word of their danger spread.

'Can we fight them?'

'Not at sea – not with an onshore wind.' He turned to me. 'So, how badly do you want that cargo?'

If it would help me get inside Jerusalem and reach my family, more than life. But I could not carry it back single-handed – nor stand alone against the Fatimids.

'How badly do you want your gold?'

Saewulf grinned, though there was no humour behind it. 'That cargo cost me nothing. I could as easily have thrown it overboard as bring it here.'

'But you did bring it here.'

'And now I'm trapped.' Saewulf looked around, his eyes ever calculating. 'Each one of those Egyptian ships carries more men than my entire crew. They're armed with catapults and naphtha throwers. If they get into the harbour' – he gestured to the hawser, which sagged across the harbour mouth – 'they'll burn us down like haystacks.' He brushed his hand over the rampart. A trickle of mortar and rubble crumbled away at his touch. 'We won't get much defence out of these walls. If you value your life, you'll run inland as fast as you can. They won't risk straying too far from their ships – unless they've got allies on shore on the way.'

'But we have allies coming too. If your men reached Jerusalem, then the Franks should have sent men to collect the cargo. They might even come this morning.'

'And if they don't?'

I shrugged, helplessly. Looking out to sea, I could see the Fatimid ships roving towards us, ever closer. 'I would not count on them to save us.'

'Then we'd better fight hard.'

I stared at him. 'You'll stay?'

Saewulf shrugged. 'I'm a sailor – I'll stay with my ships. And hope your reinforcements come quickly.'

As if to mock his words, a crack echoed from the deck of the foremost Egyptian ship. A clay canister, pink like the sun, sailed through the air over our heads. We spun about to follow its arc, watching it drop into the harbour just past the hull of Saewulf's flagship. It seemed to bounce

494

on the surface of the water, then slowly sank. Steam blew from its spout as the water met the burning oil inside.

'Christ's shit.' Saewulf looked down at the docks, at the drowsy sailors stirring themselves from sleep. The cargo lay stacked all about them; suddenly all the timber, sacking and barrels looked like nothing so much as piles of kindling waiting for the match.

'We're sitting on top of our own pyre,' Saewulf muttered. 'We need to clear it off the docks.'

I hardly cared for myself, but the siege materials were our last, best chance of breaking into Jerusalem. If they turned to ash, so did all our hopes. Even as I watched, another oil canister shot out from the Fatimid fleet. This one carried all the way over the harbour and smashed against one of the warehouses that lined the shore. There was a flash as the pottery vessel exploded into shards, and then a burst of oily smoke. Liquid fire slithered down the stone wall. Over my shoulder, out to sea, three splashes rose as a ranging flight of arrows dipped into the water. With the white feathers on their tails, they almost looked like the diving gulls.

Saewulf turned and hurried down the steps two at a time. 'Have your men move the cargo up the hill, near the gate. It'll be easier to grab it there when we have to retreat.'

I followed him, trying not to lose my footing on the crumbling stairs. 'What will you do?'

Saewulf gestured to the warehouse opposite. The naphtha had burned out, leaving scorched tentacles trailing down the wall. 'I'll start a fire.'

Down on the docks, Saewulf's men had already shaken off their slumbers and were hurrying about. Despite the suddenness of our desperate plight, they seemed calm enough, moving to some purpose they evidently understood. I could not guess it – nor, apparently, could the Varangians. I found them clustered in a knot in the lee of the walls, watching unhappily. Facing an enemy on land they would be fiercer than any man; confront them with a battle at sea, even one contained in the confines of the harbour, and they did not know what to do.

Sigurd had woken and was standing among them, squinting against the light. A black bruise ringed his left eye and his matted hair sprawled untidily over his shoulders. At the sight of me approaching, his face screwed up in disgust. The last night's quarrel had left us with too many things to say to each other.

I said none of them. As quickly as I could, I relayed Saewulf's instructions. I thought Sigurd would object, but he simply sneered his approval, then picked up the nearest sack and threw it over his shoulder. It must have held almost twice his weight in iron, but he did not flinch.

'Where do you want it?'

It was hard work that wanted many men; instead, the twelve of us laboured to carry the sacks and barrels through the deserted streets of Jaffa, up the slope to the fallen arch where the gate had once stood. Each time we reached the gate and deposited another load, we looked out to the east in search of an approaching army. Each time we turned back towards the harbour we looked west, over the harbour walls to the sea beyond. The Egyptian ships had dropped their sails for battle and had their oars out, prowling the water like wolves. For some reason, they did not seem to have fired any more naphtha canisters at us.

'Why don't they attack?' I wondered.

'Perhaps they're waiting for reinforcements,' said Aelfric.

I looked back to the east but there was nothing. Meanwhile, down in the harbour, Saewulf's men seemed to have started doing the Fatimids' work for them. On all but one of the ships they had stripped away the rigging and felled the masts; I could see the long trunks lying on the wharf, the sails still wrapped around the yards. Perhaps Saewulf meant to deny the Egyptians a target – though if so, he had forgotten his own flagship, whose green banner still flapped defiantly from its masthead. By the time I had brought my next load up to the gate, the ship had slipped its moorings and was creeping out towards the harbour's mouth, its banks of oars rising and falling. I could see its crew manning the benches, and Saewulf standing by the tiller in the stern, a coat of chain mail pulled over his green tunic and a helmet gleaming in the sun.

'But he said he wouldn't attack.' I did not understand. The Fatimids would surely burn Saewulf into the water, as he had predicted – or crush him head-on. Their lead ship had neared the harbour mouth and was closing rapidly. Two more followed close behind on its flanks.

'Perhaps Saewulf found his balls after all.' Sigurd dropped a sack of trenails with an angry thud. 'Thirty years too late.'

'Or perhaps he's lost his mind.' No other ships were moving to support Saewulf's lone charge – in fact, so far as I could see, their crews seemed to be busy dismantling them. One was already at least a foot nearer the water, and I could hear the urgent sounds of saws and hammers reducing it ever further. What was Saewulf doing? I looked at Sigurd, wondering if he understood his countryman's madness any better than I did. He gave no sign of it.

It looked as though Saewulf meant to ram the Fatimid ship bow to bow. Watching, I felt a memory stir in me, of an October afternoon without a trace of autumn, when Bilal had taken me to see the caliph's shipyards. Was this one of the boats I had seen drawn up on that island in the middle of the Nile, then a skeleton, now clothed in its full war-like flesh? Had fate been drawing back the curtain that day, offering me an unwitting glimpse of my future?

The two ships were barely a spear's throw apart now, their collision inevitable. The Egyptian ship was broader, heavier and stronger: with the carved lion's head on her prow, and the banks of oars like wings, she looked like nothing so much as a griffin in flight. With her copper ram she would overwhelm her adversary in an instant, then overrun the harbour and the cargo. We would save none of it – we would barely have time to save ourselves.

And then something extraordinary happened: a new madness, which made everything else seem almost rational. A cluster of sailors on Saewulf's deck let go the ropes they held. The square sail they had bound tumbled loose from the yard and was immediately hauled taut. With the onshore breeze almost straight ahead, the effect was dramatic: the ship shuddered to a halt; then, pushed by an invisible hand, began to drift backwards.

Next to me, Sigurd turned away in disgust. 'Coward,' he hissed.

Whether a desperate tactic or a sudden loss of nerve, Saewulf's trick would not save him. The Egyptian ship was too close, the carved lion's outstretched arms almost ready to maul the retreating wolf. One more heave on their oars would surely bring the two together.

The lion-headed prow passed between the two ruined watchtowers. Saewulf had placed archers in the ruins: they loosed a few arrows, but they were mere pinpricks, fleas against the lion's side. They would not stop the ship. It ploughed forward, its bow wave intersecting the line of surf across the harbour mouth. The line, I realised, where the water rippled over the submerged hawser that lay there.

The Egyptian ship blundered head first into the snare Saewulf had prepared. The hawser caught in the elbow where the copper ram joined the prow: the ship shook and cracked. Caught off balance and unable to move forward, its momentum instead carried it along the length of the rope, spinning it around. The mouth of the harbour was not wide: before the crew could react, the sliding bow had careered into the end of the pier. Splinters exploded as the bow shattered; the copper ram must have snapped off, or else been driven back into its own ship. With a great tearing of canvas and cordage, the mast broke free of its holding, tottered for a moment like a drunkard, then crashed to the deck. I saw several of the crew crushed beneath it, or floundering in the tangle of rigging it had brought down.

This was what Saewulf had planned, and he was ready for it. Without need for a signal, his men rushed along the docks to the points nearest the stricken ship. The archers in the watch towers – suddenly far more numerous – rose up and began a new, furious assault. This time they had dipped their arrows in burning pitch, bringing a squall of fire rushing down on the stricken ship. The water around it blistered and spat as wayward arrows dropped wide of the mark, but many more struck home. With her loose sail sprawled across the deck where the mast had fallen, it was a matter of moments before she caught light, and her battered crew had neither time nor discipline to quench the flames. Some flung themselves in the water, where Saewulf's waiting crew speared them like fish; others tried to scramble onto the pier where the ship had run aground, but men were waiting for them there with axes. None escaped.

A column of black smoke rose into the air as fire took hold of the ship, and the water around it began to boil. Beside me, watching up on the hillside by the fallen gate, I heard Sigurd sigh. He had once told me that, in the legends of his people, the bodies of fallen heroes and kings had been sent to their pagan afterlife in burning ships. I

500

wondered if the sight now stirred some deep ancestral memory in him.

But it was too soon to celebrate a victory. Flames and smoke streamed from the dying ship's hull, her crew were all slaughtered or burned, but still – against all reason – she did not give up. Incredibly, she seemed to be moving again. At first I could not see how; then I realised that the fire at her bow must also have burned through the hawser that held her. Freed of that restraint, she was drifting ever closer into the harbour. A few of the English sailors on the pier thrust out their spears in a vain attempt to catch her, but if they touched her at all they only succeeded in prodding her further away.

Whatever his cunning, this was not something Saewulf had expected. His ship sat in the water barely a boat length away, beam on, and his men had deserted their oars to take up their spears and bows. The wind that pressed the ship towards them also blew its smoke into their faces; by the time they realised the fire was moving towards them, it was too late.

The triumphant cheers that had sounded around the harbour fell silent. I saw Saewulf and his crew stare in confusion at the looming fireship for a moment, then turn and run for the side. The two boats came together, wrapped in smoke; I heard the hollow knock of two hulls embracing, and saw the shower of sparks erupt where they had struck. Flames licked up through the smoke, hungry for the fresh tinder of Saewulf's ship. The last thing I saw was the green banner at the masthead, billowing out in the hot wind that gusted from the fire below. Tongues of flame reached up to tear it down, shrivelling it black.

'We won't escape that easily.' Sigurd pointed to the harbour mouth. Another Fatimid ship was already nosing through the entrance, no longer barred by the hawser. Another followed close behind it. From the watchtowers and wharves, Saewulf's men tried desperately to stop them with stones and arrows, but the Fatimid ships rowed stubbornly on. Some of their oarsmen fell, but most did not, while from the wooden turrets amidships their archers were able to direct their fire down onto the men on the docks.

Sigurd threw aside the sack he had been carrying and picked up his axe from where it leaned against the remains of the gatehouse. 'We'd better get down there.'

It was not a moment too soon. In the few minutes it took us to get down the hill to the harbour, the battle had changed again. Saewulf's ship had burned almost to the water, but its smoke still clung to the air. Another one of the Fatimid ships had caught fire too, adding to the fog, but that was no victory for it had already managed to dock; its men had spilled out and were fighting their way forward. The English sailors tried to beat them back, but they were heavily outnumbered.

We ran along the dock, making short, darting runs and then ducking behind the crates and sacks that still littered the ground. In places, the stones were slick with blood; in others, pools of oil burned where the naphtha canisters had exploded. I saw Thomas hike up his tunic to try to piss the fire out and dragged him back behind the barrels.

'That's sea-fire,' I warned him, shouting to make myself heard over the roar of battle. 'Water makes it burn more. You need vinegar' Sword drawn, I swung out from behind the sheltering barrels and charged forward again. Sigurd was on my left, the harbour's edge to my right. Glancing down, I saw splintered wood and bodies floating in the water – some were splashing for the harbour stairs, but most lay still. I wondered what had happened to Saewulf – had he escaped his burning ship? I had no time to think about it. An arrow hissed past my head, and I slithered to the ground behind a pile of stones. But my run had taken me too far forward, to the blind chaos where the armies contended. Even as I rolled over on my side, a curved blade swung out of the smoke before me, striking sparks on the quay-stones. I leaped to my feet, staggering back to avoid the swinging cut that followed. I had no shield; all I could do was parry the blow with my own sword and feel the shudder as the heavy blade took the impact. Then it was forward into the smoke, hewing and slicing. At least I did not have to worry about arrows, for we were too close to our enemies for the Fatimid archers to risk shooting into the fray. Everything was confusion: there were too many obstacles scattered across the dock for either side to form a line, and so we battled in our ones and twos between the naphtha pools, shattered crates and corpses. More by necessity than any plan, we found ourselves fighting in pairs, shoulder to shoulder, one man acting as the other's shield. I fought with Sigurd. At first we tried to shout

503

instructions to each other, or warnings, but the sounds of the battle – the burning ships, the spitting oil, the war-cries of both armies and the clash of arms – engulfed us. All we could do was keep our eyes open against the stinging smoke and trust each other.

Perhaps we should have been grateful to the smoke: at least it served to hide our meagre numbers from the Egyptians. Even so, there was little disguising it. Soon our enemies were coming at us from the sides rather than the front; sometimes a few of Saewulf's men pushed forward to help, but they could not hold their ground. Our only advantage was that with the wall on one side and the water on the other, the dock was narrow enough that even our small force was enough to keep the Egyptians from tearing through us. But still we were ground remorselessly back.

Walking backwards, I did not see the tall pile of sacks until I almost stepped into it. I twisted around to get past it, trying to keep my gaze ahead; unfortunately, Sigurd went the other way and in an instant, we were separated. I looked frantically about to find him again, but at that moment a new wave of Fatimid soldiers charged out from the smoke. Howling like a ghost, one of them lunged his sword at me. I parried it and stepped back, but as I did so I tripped on an iron ring set in the quay. With my hand already numb from the ringing clash of our blades, I let go my sword completely as I lost my balance and sprawled backwards. I rolled over and sprang to my feet as the Fatimid advanced towards me. I could not see the sword, but a broken barrel lay on the ground nearby, its staves spread open like the petals of a flower. A few of them had fallen into a pool of naphtha and started to burn; unthinking, I picked one up and thrust it in my enemy's face. His eyes widened in horror as his thick beard caught fire; for a moment I saw his face and helmet wreathed in flames – bathed in light, as the apostles must have appeared at Pentecost. He dropped his sword and clutched at his face, then swung away and threw himself over the edge of the quay into the water. I saw him floundering there, clinging to his shield like a raft while the weight of his armour tried to suck him down.

There was no time to savour my victory. By the time I had found my fallen sword and retrieved it I was being forced back again. Even to be armed was a rare advantage now: the sailors around me were having to fight with whatever they could lay their hands on. I saw one pulling iron shackles from a sack and flinging them at the Fatimids using a sling made from his shirt; others wielded ship-building tools as weapons. One had even made a rudimentary flail from a plank with three nails hammered through the end. He had stripped to the waist, his tunic folded back over his belt, and his fair skin glistened with beads of water. Despite his crude weapon, he moved with a breathtaking grace, whirling about like cinders floating on currents of air. His wet hair swung behind him, as if to counterbalance the flail in his hands, which clawed and gouged any who came near. Even in battle I had rarely seen such pure, animal ferocity.

As he turned to counter some new attack, I glimpsed

505

Saewulf's face beneath the whirling hair. The careless detachment had vanished; the cautious man who acclaimed profit and disdained all else had become a warrior in the mould of his ancestors. And beside him, even more remarkable, stood Sigurd, rolling his axe and bellowing defiance at the Egyptians. Watching them, knowing Sigurd's loathing of Saewulf, you might almost have thought they did not realise the other was there. They stood, half-turned away from each other, ignoring each other completely: it was only after I had watched for a few moments that I realised the unspoken intricacy of their movement. If Sigurd knocked an adversary off balance, he pushed him left so that Saewulf could club him; if Saewulf forced a man backwards, Sigurd's axe was waiting to sever his neck. It was an awesome pairing.

With Sigurd and Saewulf to anchor us, we had at last managed to regroup behind a makeshift barricade of planks and barrels. The Egyptian attack seemed to be weakening. A few of their soldiers still struggled against the English sailors, but most seemed to have retreated back along the dock, into the swirling smoke. I did not doubt they would return in greater numbers – even Sigurd and Saewulf at the peak of their rage could not defy them all.

Sigurd sent a Fatimid swordsman sprawling backwards with a well-aimed kick, then turned. His face and arms were drenched in blood, but he seemed unharmed. He screamed something unintelligible in his native tongue and swept his arm forward. I did not need to know the words to understand the meaning: desperate though it was, we had to close with the Fatimids before they started to bombard us with their missiles again.

A dangerous lightness overtook me – not light-headedness, but a lightness of spirit, which, at the last, accepted the inevitability of defeat and embraced it. I vaulted over the box that had protected me and charged forward. The weariness of battle seemed to fall away; I was sprinting along the dock, among the rubble and jetsam that the shifting tides of battle had left behind. Sigurd was in front of me and Saewulf beside him, with English sailors and Varangians all around. I saw Thomas to my left and breathed a prayer of thanks that he had survived this long. Still no one opposed us. In the distance, I heard a trumpet sound.

The euphoria that had carried me forward drained as quickly as it had come. I had a cramp in my side, my knuckles were bleeding where I had grazed them on the quay, and my arms were suddenly barely able to hold the sword upright. Seeing no danger, I stopped short, bending double to gather my breath. Only then did I look around.

We had almost reached the end of the harbour where the Fatimid ship had docked, yet we stood there unopposed. Inside the harbour, I could see the dying embers of a ship disappearing beneath the water, hissing and fizzling. Another ship remained afloat and undamaged, but it was not coming towards us: with every stroke of its oars it pulled further away. Fatimid soldiers crowded its deck, while in the water I could see others who had discarded their weapons and armour swimming desperately after the retreating ship.

'Did we win?' I wondered aloud.

No one answered. Sigurd, still in the grip of battle, stood on the harbour's edge and shouted abuse after the fleeing Egyptians. When that did nothing, he picked up a smouldering piece of wood from the dock beside him and hurled it towards the ship. It fell well short, though it did provoke one of the archers on the ship's stern to retaliate with an arrow. That flew wide, but it was enough to drain the battle lust from Sigurd. He fell silent and stepped into the shelter of the wall, while the Fatimid ship disappeared out of the harbour.

The trumpet I had heard during our charge sounded again. At the time I had thought it must be my imagination, or perhaps a flight of angels come to take me to heaven, but this was different – too clear to be my imagination, too strident for the hosts of heaven. I turned around.

We were not the only men on the docks. At the far end of the harbour, where three of Saewulf's ships still lay moored, a troop of horsemen had ridden out onto the quay and dismounted. More men were spilling down from the town after them. All were armed and mailed, though even from that distance I could see many were limping or leaning on their comrades for support, as if they too had been in a battle. Their banners were frayed and stained, but there was no mistaking the design on them: a blood-red cross.

'Thank God.'

The leader of the new arrivals handed his bridle to a companion and came towards us, striding between the host of small fires that still burned around him. The Varangians and sailors around me turned to face him, arms crossed, watching impassively.

He halted in front of Saewulf and removed his helmet, shaking free a mane of tawny hair. I recognised him: he was Geldemar Carpinel, one of the lesser captains in Duke Godfrey's army.

'If you came for the battle, you're too late.' Saewulf gestured to the debris all about, as if the Frank might not have noticed it. 'We won.'

Geldemar stiffened. 'We fought our own battle. Four hundred Arab troops and two hundred Turks. We found them on the plain near Aramathea – coming this way.'

'I hope you saw them off.' Geldemar gave a smug nod. 'You don't want to run into them again when you leave.'

'Leave?' Geldemar sounded peeved. 'We've only just come here.'

As if by way of answer, another naphtha canister sailed over the wall and exploded against the watchtower in a cloud of fire. A fig tree that had grown out of a crack in the wall burst into flame.

'I thought you said you won your battle,' said Geldemar suspiciously.

'There are always more enemies. Unless you want to meet them, we had best get on. Have you brought pack animals?'

*   *   *

509

They had, though it was the devil's own job to load them while the Egyptian ships beyond the harbour bombarded us with fire. We scavenged what we could from the cargo on the dock, while Saewulf's men methodically dismantled the ships that survived. When they had broken them down to the waterline, they towed them to the harbour mouth and scuttled them. Soon all that remained were bundles of planks and timbers tied to the mules.

By the time we had loaded up the last of the animals, the harbour swirled and glowed with the reflected flames. The wind had carried the fire into the town on the hillside, and that too had begun to burn. In the places where the sea-fire had spread over it, even the water burned.

In my determination to see that we saved every scrap that might help make our siege engines, I was one of the last to leave. Sigurd and I hoisted the last batch of planks onto the mule's back and tied it tight, then turned to go. I cast a last look at the harbour. Ash and oily scum covered its surface, but the water still drew my drawn and bleary eyes. Soot and dust had mingled with sweat and blood to coat my skin, my hair, my clothes: I could almost feel it cracking when I moved. I longed to be clean – but there was no time for that.

Saewulf slapped the laden mule on the rump, and it trotted obediently away towards the gate. Now there were only three of us left on the dock.

'There goes your last ship,' I said to Saewulf. 'What will you do now?'

He shrugged. 'A captain should stay with his ship – even

if it's in pieces. Besides, you'll need someone who knows how to use those tools, if you ever want to build your siege engines.'

μβ

∿∿∿∿∿

Our return to Jerusalem found the army in grim spirits, which even the arrival of our cargo did little to improve. The streams of living water promised in scripture no longer flowed: the land was parched, and the few wells that lay around the city had been poisoned or stopped up by the garrison. Worse, while we had been away the Franks had intercepted messengers from the Fatimid vizier, al-Afdal. He was coming from Egypt with a great army, he said: he would be there in a month. If the garrison could only hold out until then, the Army of God would be ground into dust. The Franks gritted their teeth and swore it would make no difference: this was exactly what had happened at Antioch, they said, and they had prevailed then. By God's grace, they would take Jerusalem and then march out to destroy al-Afdal as well. But they spoke too loudly when they said it, and the hands that clutched their crosses trembled.

All our hopes now rested on God – and on the materials we had brought from Jaffa. The masts from Saewulf's ships were raised again, far from the sea, the cornerposts of the two vast siege engines the Franks had designed. The towers reached higher than the walls themselves, and every day they grew. The wheelwrights gave them feet; the carpenters built platforms and ladders within while the women wove wattle screens to cover them. Finally, the tanners nailed on skins of mottled hides so that fire could not burn them. It gave the machines a monstrous appearance. On each, the drawbridge at the summit gaped like an open jaw, while the arrow slits above seemed like blundering, half-blind eyes. The Franks named them Gog and Magog, the beasts who would come at the end of time to besiege Jerusalem.

A strange mood overtook the army in those last few weeks. They stood on the brink of an impossible victory, and equally on the threshold of destruction, yet to look at their faces you would not have seen much trace of either hope or fear. Even the threat of al-Afdal's army did little to stir their passions. They had suffered the journey for too long: now that they had arrived, it meant nothing. You could see it in their eyes – the numb awareness that these should be days of passion and drama, of triumph or terror, and the quiet, reproachful despair that they felt nothing. Each day they toiled with willing, dead hands:

they lay on their bellies to drink from stagnant pools where animals wallowed; they wandered carelessly within bowshot of the walls and barely murmured when the arrows struck them.

Yet life stirred among the waste and wreckage of our hopes, if you looked carefully. But it was not the fresh, clean life that drives out winter; this was the sort that crawls out of holes and feeds on rot. It did not show itself, but I became aware of it, shadows moving at the fringes of my perception. I saw it in the groups of pilgrims who huddled together, whispering; in sly glances that sidled away when I looked at them; in the mysterious slogans that appeared scrawled on boulders overnight: unsettling verses from the Revelation of Saint John speaking of tortures and trials ahead. I felt it in the brooding presence of the towers, ever-present and stark against the skyline. More insidiously, I heard it from the mouths of the priests. When they opened their Bibles, it was always to Daniel or Ezekiel. *I will strew your flesh on the mountains, and fill the valleys with your carcass; I will drench the land so that your flowing blood laps the mountain tops, and drowns the streams and rivers.* When they preached, they spoke of the kingdom to come with rare urgency, as if they could glimpse the holy city through a tear in the clouds. Though few of them were gifted preachers, their words seemed to touch their audiences like tongues of fire. Dull faces flared with passionate intensity; in those moments, I began to suspect that the army was not exhausted, simply nursing its meagre strength. It improved my hopes of taking the city, but it filled me with foreboding.

Unsurprisingly, in that atmosphere, men started to see visions again. Some saw winged creatures swooping down from heaven; some saw saints in shimmering raiment; some saw magical beasts – griffins, basilisks and unicorns – and no doubt others saw worse visions that afterwards they did not dare voice, but tried to forget in their hearts.

Among these visions, one came with particular authority. A Provençal pilgrim announced that he had seen Bishop Adhemar, who had ordered a penitential procession around the four walls of Jerusalem to free the army from the filth of the world. So, on a Friday afternoon in early July, we marched around the city.

Looking back, it was a miracle we were not all massacred. By Adhemar's command, given in the vision, every man in the army had removed his boots and walked barefoot. If the Fatimids had sallied out from the city, they could have ridden through us like a field of wheat. Perhaps they could not believe our temerity and assumed it must be a trap; perhaps they simply laughed to themselves and left us to our folly, seeing it as the last throes of an army dying of thirst and madness. Perhaps they pitied us. Whatever their reasons, they stayed within the walls.

And if they thought we were mad, who could argue? We knew the risks, and still we marched blithely on. Fear of death did not deter us; instead, the army seemed to drink it in. The whole procession had the air of a macabre carnival. Seven priests walked at the front of the column with ram's horns, blasting out a cacophony that filled the valley, from the walls to the surrounding hills. Men and women danced in rapture; they held their weapons aloft and waved them to heaven – spears and swords, but also billhooks, cudgels, even pilgrim staves. The trumpets blasted, and the pilgrims sang so hard they almost screamed. Each time we came near one of the gates the noise rose to a fevered crescendo as we waited to see if it would open for an attack; each time we passed safely, the air shivered with the sound of delight. Drunk on its own daring, the army tottered forward; they had abandoned caution, thrown off the chains of fear that had bound them so long, and every step that they did not fall only convinced them of their invincibility.

'I once knew a herder who grazed his oxen where wild onions grew,' said Sigurd. He had to bellow in my ear to be heard. 'It made them swell up like melons. When they let it go . . .' He waved his hand in front of his nose. 'It sounded like those trumpets.'

'Perhaps they think the walls will fall down if they blow hard enough.'

'Then there'll be nothing to stop the Egyptians running out and slaughtering us.'

I shrugged. 'It worked for Joshua.'

At least Joshua had been allowed to wear his boots. The ground beneath my feet might be holy, but it was merciless. The stones were so hot they raised blisters even through a thousand miles' worth of callouses, and when once I did not look where I trod I quickly felt the pain of a stubbed toe.

I stepped out of the procession and knelt to rub my toe. The procession flowed past. Seen from below, with the blazing sun above, the pilgrims became little more than barefoot shadows, a jabbering confusion of limbs and blades that writhed like tendrils of smoke over a fire. Or perhaps they were like a thicket of walking trees, their branches rippling as if in a breeze. The spikes of their spears looked more like palm fronds, and the sunlight was so strong the metal seemed to wilt in its glare.

I blinked. Thirst and heat had not made me delusional. The men and women passing by no longer carried weapons, not even the crude tools of the peasants, but palm fronds. They were dressed in white, and they seemed to come from all the tribes of the barbarians – Normans and Provençals, Lotharingians and Flemings – but they all sang the same song.

Salvation belongs to God on His throne, and to the Lamb who is his son.

I stood up. The crowd's momentum had carried Sigurd on well past me and for the moment I was on my own. I stepped back into the procession, feeling dark and dirty among so much white. Immediately, I found myself in the shade of a broad palm frond, which an old man held aloft with frail but unyielding arms. He turned to greet me, smiling in welcome.

I gestured around. 'Who are all these people?'

His skin was dark and mottled with liver spots, but his teeth were as white as his robe. '*We are those who have come out of the great ordeal. We have washed our robes and made them white in the blood of the Lamb.*' His brown eyes stared at me.

It was the last answer I had expected. Stranger still, I found I knew the words to continue it. '*They shall hunger and thirst no more; the sun will not strike them, nor any scorching heat.*'

He nodded approvingly. '*The Lamb on His throne will be our shepherd, and He will guide us to the springs of the water of life.*'

'I'd be glad to find any spring in this foul heat.'

The pilgrim frowned. 'The earth's water is stagnant and stale. Soon we will all taste the sweet water of life.'

Dazed by sweltering heat and sound, stifled by the dust our army kicked up, I almost let myself ignore him. But there was a firmness in the way he spoke that was almost like a promise. *Soon we will all taste the sweet water of life.* I had heard such sentiments before, but hearing them now, with the walls of Jerusalem looming over me, I could feel their power anew.

The pilgrim looked at me cautiously, as if noticing for the first time the shabby colour of my tunic among the sea of white. 'Things that were prophesied are now stirring to life. Have you heard?'

My mouth was dry, but once again I found I knew the words he wanted. I loosened a brick in the wall of my memories and reached into the dark crevice within – to a clearing in the woods, and the fat, frightened peasant who had styled himself a prophet.

'*When the Son of Perdition has risen, the king will ascend Golgotha.*'

I could not remember any more, but it was enough. The pilgrim recited the rest. '*He will take his crown from his head and place it on the cross, and stretching out his hands to heaven he will hand over the kingdom of the Christians to God the Father.*'

'But the man who brought that prophecy died a terrible death, forsaken by God. I thought his prophecy died with him.'

'It was not Peter Bartholomew's prophecy,' said the pilgrim. His eyes were hidden in the dappled shade of the palm frond, but his face was angry. 'In his pride, he confused the prophet and that which was prophesied. He thought he was the promised king.'

'*The last and greatest of all kings, who will come at the end of days to capture Jerusalem.*'

'As if that grasping peasant could have been a king. The first time Christ came, He came in humility. When He comes again, it will be with all the majesty He can command.'

My scepticism must have showed. 'Do you doubt it?' the pilgrim challenged me.

'*Of the hour of Christ's coming, no man knows,*' I quoted him.

'Until He does come.' He grabbed me by my sleeve and

spun me around, staring hard into my eyes. 'The consummation of the world has already begun. The last and greatest king is here. I have seen him.'

I stared at him. There was no hint of a lie on his aged face. 'You have seen the risen Christ?'

'As clearly as you see me now.'

'But . . .' I struggled to think, let alone to speak. 'But . . . why hasn't the world ended?'

'Even after He returns, the day of judgement does not come straight away. There is to be an interlude of forty days, so that sinners may repent. But there is not much time. He appeared to us the night we reached Jerusalem, and that was thirty-three days ago.'

This was impossible. Of course I believed that Christ would come again in glory, as the creed proclaimed, to judge the living and the dead – but I had never thought it could come in my lifetime. It was an idea, an abstraction out of time, as far in the future as the creation of the world lay in the past. It was not something I was born to experience.

'You should not be surprised when God's promises are honoured,' the pilgrim reproved me. 'It has all been written in the prophecy.'

The prophecy. I had only heard it in snatches but I could feel its danger, a dark serpent coiled in the heart of the army. It had poisoned Peter Bartholomew when he touched it, thinking it was meant for him. Who else would it claim? Worse, what if it were true?

'There is still time to prepare yourself – God is merciful.

Meet me an hour after dusk at the church of Saint Abraham, near Saint Stephen's gate, tomorrow night.'

'Will the redeemer be revealed there?'

He put a finger to his lips. 'Be patient. You will meet him soon enough.'

μγ

⚬⚬⚬⚬⚬

Did we have seven days to live? It was hard to believe. The following day, Saturday, was almost stifling in its predictability. I rose at dawn and spent the morning carrying wood as we continued the slow business of preparing the siege engine. The sun climbed over us, then began to sink back. The sounds of war echoed off the ancient hills – blacksmiths beating out blades on their anvils, farriers exercising horses, the clatter of rocks as labourers gathered stones for the catapults – but I barely heard them. Even the noise of my own hammer was dull to my ears, a metronomic beat tapping out the hours in the still air.

When dusk began to chase the sun from the sky, I put down my tools and made my way to the church of Saint

Abraham: a small church with a cracked dome, barely a stone's throw from the city walls. I did not tell Sigurd or Thomas I was going. I half expected – and half hoped – that the pilgrim would have forgotten me, or thought better of his offer, but as I approached the church he stepped out of the shadow of the doorway and beckoned me to follow.

'Where are we going?' I asked.

'Not far.' He looked at my tunic, then threw me a white blanket. 'Wrap this around you.'

The blanket was grubby and smelled of straw, but I did as he told me and followed him. My misgivings grew the further we moved away from the camp, up towards the brow of the ridge that dominated Jerusalem to the north. We were not the only ones on this road: pale figures flitted through the night all around, though I could not make them out. When I looked back, I could see the city laid out beneath me, a chain of watch-fires surrounding the lamplit streets and churches. To my left, on the eastern side, a smaller cordon of light marked out the dimensions of the Temple Mount. From there, I traced the line of the stone bridge, which spanned the valley to the western city. *On the far side of the bridge the street runs west, to a corner where two tamarisk trees grow. If you go right, there is a house with an iron amulet in the shape of a hand nailed to its door.* I stared at the flickering lights. Did one of those lamps burn in the window of the room that held my family? Was Anna looking out of it even now, staring up at the night and thinking of me? My heart beat faster, and

I felt the familiar pain tighten in my chest.

'Hurry,' hissed the pilgrim. 'There is not much time.'

I turned back up the slope, leaving the lights behind. But the darkness ahead was not complete: the more I looked, the more I could see an orange glow tempering the air, until suddenly we came over the crest of the ridge and looked down into the hollow beyond.

On the far side of the ridge, the land formed a natural bowl, a steeply sloping amphitheatre of dry earth and grass. It occurred to me that these were the same hills where a thousand years earlier the blessed shepherds must have waited with their flocks and heard the angels' tidings. A second later, I realised why I had thought of it, for it seemed as though all the intervening ages had collapsed and a parliament of angels had gathered once again. Dim white figures filled the valley, seated on its sloping banks in rows or wandering around its rim. There seemed to be hundreds of them, perhaps thousands. They were singing, a soft and beautiful hymn that barely disturbed the night but seemed to flow like water into the amphitheatre. *To Him who is seated on the throne, and to the Lamb: blessing and honour and glory and power.* Two fires burned in its centre forming the boundaries of an implicit stage, and though they were far enough apart that a man could stand between them and barely break sweat, it reminded me uncomfortably of the twin fires of Peter Bartholomew's ordeal.

My pilgrim guide found us a space to sit on the hillside. No sooner had we settled, though, than the hymn died away and the entire congregation rose to its feet. In the bowl of the valley, a procession wound its way past the fires and stopped behind them, a shadowy line just out of reach of the light. There were seven of them, all dressed in white and all holding dark objects clutched to their chests.

One stepped forward into the pool of firelight. The flames rippled on his cheeks, misshaping them, though his eyes and mouth remained in shadow. He must have been a priest, for he wore a stole around his neck with a heavy cross hanging over his chest. He took the bundle he held and raised it so all could see – a parchment scroll, fastened with a round wax seal the size of a medallion. Holding it aloft, he snapped the wax like bread at the Eucharist. Crumbs of wax fell to the ground. In a deep, rolling voice he declaimed: 'Come.'

A sigh went through the crowd like a wind – a wind that seemed to bring with it the chime and jangle of metal. It grew louder; then, from the right of the hollow, I saw the source. A white horse trotted out of the darkness. It seemed to glide through the night: its hooves disappeared in the shadow over the ground, and if they made any noise the dust silenced it instantly. Mounted in its saddle sat a knight, or perhaps a king, for he wore a silver crown. He rode stiff and erect, ignoring the gaze of a thousand silent eyes on him, and on his shoulder he carried a long bow. As he passed behind each fire he seemed to melt into its light and disappear, then reappear as a dim radiance in the darkness beyond.

As he vanished into the more complete darkness on the margins of the valley, a second priest stepped forward to stand beside the first. He too held a scroll; he broke the seal and again said, 'Come.'

A second horse came out of the night, following in the tracks of the first. This one seemed darker, though when he came close to the fire I could see he was a chestnut colt, his glossy coat so deep it was almost red. Its rider did not wear a crown, but held up a great sword so large I wondered if any man could wield it.

'*He came to take all peace from the earth, so that men would fall on each other in slaughter,*' whispered the pilgrim in my ear. I nodded; I knew. All around me, the standing crowd watched in awe. Did they believe that the horses and their riders were spirits from realms beyond imagining? It hardly mattered. Like icons, the vision it offered transcended any thought for its substance.

One by one, the priests stepped forward to snap the seals on their scrolls and call forth the riders. A huge stallion came, so black it was barely visible but fluttered like a veil against the night. Its rider carried a pair of scales. After him, a pale grey mare whose rider carried a long scythe over his shoulder. It should have been green – but that thought was driven out by the sudden baying of dogs, as a pack of hounds came bounding after the horse across the valley, hunting an invisible quarry. Firelight gleamed on their open jaws.

Those were the last of the animals, for the fifth seal brought not a horse but a company of men and women.

Unlike the solemn procession of their predecessors, they staggered like drunkards; their clothes were ripped open to expose their naked bodies beneath, their hair torn, their white faces streaked with blood. They wailed with loud voices, and their plea was at once pitiable and terrible. '*Sovereign Lord, holy and true, how long before you judge the earth and avenge our blood on its people?*' They too vanished into the night.

The fires had sunk low, and the darkness squeezed closer around the seven priests. It should have made the stars shine brighter, but when I looked up the sky had disappeared. A rising wind blew over the valley, worming its way among the stones and setting up a low, mournful moan that swept around us. The priests were now barely shadows against the red orb of the firelight. I thought I saw one shuffle forward; I did not hear the snapping of the seal, but I knew he must have opened it when a host of tiny fires rose above our heads, arcing up from the rim of the valley like a constellation of artificial stars. They seemed to hang in the sky for a moment, then tumbled towards the earth like a fig tree dropping its fruit. They burned very white, tracing lines of light in the dark air as they fell. The crowd gasped – but before the ground could quench the stars a new light rose in the valley. The two fires had been rekindled: they blazed up like beacons, and in the light I saw that the seventh and last of the priests had stepped forward. The fires banished all shadows and illuminated him like daylight, so I could see his face plainly: Arnulf, the red-headed Norman priest who had

527

denounced Peter Bartholomew. Exultant triumph glowed in his eyes as he surveyed the watching crowd; when he raised his arms the entire congregation sank to its knees. On that steep hillside the effect was giddying, tipping us forward so that we seemed on the brink of falling into darkness.

In one hand Arnulf held a swinging censer, spilling out incense like brimstone; in the other, he clasped a sealed scroll. For the moment, he did not break it. Instead, an acolyte came forward, knelt in front of him and opened a book. It was too dark and distant for me to see its pages, but I could imagine the images that decorated its pages. Monsters with the heads of Saracens and the bodies of lions; locusts with tails like scorpions; a red dragon with seven heads and ten horns. *And at the bottom of the page, a radiant king on a white horse.* The book that Peter Bartholomew had found or stolen, which Arnulf had reclaimed from his quarters after the ordeal. The book in which the prophecy was written.

'Hear the prophecy of our Lord God,' said Arnulf solemnly. His voice was far off, too small to fill the cavernous bowl, but it was carried back to me in an instant by the whispered repetition of the crowd. Their voices rippled and rustled like the flutter of wings. 'Given in secret, in ancient times, and revealed now to His elect at the dawn of His coming. Listen.'

The kneeling pilgrims rocked back on their haunches and bowed their heads.

'When the thousand years are ended, Satan will be

released from his prison. The sun will grow dark and the moon's light will fade; the stars will fall from their orbits and the powers of heaven will be shaken. False prophets will arise; they will come in Christ's name, saying, "I am the Messiah," and they will lead many astray. The land of promise will be filled with men from the four winds under heaven.'

Arnulf paused. Looking around, I could see the congregation drinking in his words with the delight of familiarity: they had heard it before. Perhaps I had too, but not like this. It was as if all the things I had known formerly had been cut into pieces, then sewn together to give new form, new meanings.

'Two great prophets, Enoch and Elijah, will be sent into the world. They will defend God's faithful against the attack of the Antichrist and prepare the elect for the coming storm.'

The whispering in the crowd grew more agitated, like the shivering of leaves.

'Then the Gates of the North will be opened and the demons will fly forth: Anog and Ageg, Gog and Magog, Achenaz, Dephar and Amarzarthae. They will eat the flesh of men and drink the blood of beasts like water. The Antichrist will gather up the nations for battle, as numerous as the sands of the sea, and they will march from Babylon to the camp of the saints at the beloved city.

'Then a king of the Franks will again possess the Roman Empire. He will unite the crowns of west and east; he will be the greatest and the last of all kings. When the Son of

Perdition has risen, the King will ascend Golgotha. He will take his crown from his head and place it on the cross, and stretching out his hands to heaven he will hand over the kingdom of the Christians to God the Father. This will be the end and the consummation of the Roman and Christian Empires, when every power and principality shall be destroyed.'

All I could hear now were the whispers of the crowd, and the flex of chain as the smoking censer in Arnulf's hand swung back and forth, a pendulum beating out the rhythm of his words.

'An angel will appear in the sun, calling to all the birds that fly beneath heaven: "Come and gather for the great supper of God, to eat the flesh of kings, the flesh of captains, the flesh of the mighty, of horses and their riders." The King will capture the Beast, together with the prophet who deceived with false miracles, and cast them into the lake of fire. All the rest will die by the sword, and the birds will be gorged with their flesh. Not one will survive.

'Then death shall be no more – nor sorrow nor pain – for all the former things shall have passed away. The holy city, the new Jerusalem, will come down out of heaven, and the Lord will dwell with his people. The kingdom of the world will become the kingdom of our Messiah, and he will reign for ever.'

Arnulf looked up, letting the censer come to rest. Around me, the whispered repetitions rolled away into silence. The acolyte who held the book closed it and shuffled back out of the light.

'As for the one who reveals these things,' Arnulf declared, 'he says: "I am coming soon."'

The crowd took up his words, repeating them over and again so that the call seemed to whirl in the air like a flock of crows. *I am coming.* Arnulf let it build, standing in the crux of the valley with his arms spread apart. The six priests behind him seemed to have melted away so that he stood there alone and exultant. Still the chant grew. *I am coming.*

With a deft movement Arnulf suddenly took a step back, upended the censer and dashed it to the ground. A cascade of glowing coals spilled out. They should have lain there dying; instead, like sparks on tinder, they seemed to ignite the earth. A huge fire erupted from the ground where they had fallen, so vast I thought it must have consumed Arnulf. Even on the heights where I knelt, men cowered back from the blaze. After the darkness before, I felt as if a hole had been burned through my eyes. But still the chant went on. *I am coming.*

Squinting through the pain and tears, I saw Arnulf on the far side of the blaze. Wreathed in fire, he held aloft his scroll, snapped the seal and threw the parchment on the flames. It disappeared, one more cinder in the inferno. Smoke drifted up to envelop me, choke me; the crackle of flames filled my ears, and with it the blast of trumpets, the ripple of harp strings. The earth trembled beneath me and my flesh seemed turned to water. *Woe, woe to the inhabitants of the earth.* The slope fell away, plunging into a bottomless pit; I tottered on my knees, swayed and fell forward.

531

Thankfully, I had just enough wit or instinct left to throw out my hands. They fell on the stony ground, jarring me to my senses. Crouched on all fours like an animal, I looked down into the pit of the valley. The fire still burned high, and I could still see a figure through the flames. But it was not Arnulf. He wore a dark riding cloak with the hood pulled up, shading his face, but I could see that he stood both taller and broader than the priest. Even in shadow, he radiated power.

Above the trumpets, the harps, the roaring flames, I heard three words echo around the deep bowl of the valley, spoken with the sound of a thousand voices.

'Here I am.'

I could bear it no more. Stumbling to my feet, I fled.

μδ

∽∽∽∽∽

I ran back to the camp, scrambling and staggering as if all the forces of hell had already burst their gates to pursue me. I barely knew where I was going until Count Raymond's pickets challenged me; then, calmed by the feel of familiar ground, I wandered until at last I managed to find my tent. In my madness I almost tripped over Sigurd, lying sprawled in front of the door of the tent.

'Where in hell have you been?' he demanded.

'Closer to hell than you know.'

The tremors in my voice stayed his anger. He stood, and led me to the rocky escarpment on the edge of the camp. The night was warm, but my experience had left me so cold I could not keep from shivering. When Sigurd saw this he left me, and presently returned with a blanket, which he draped around my shoulders, and a flask of strong wine. He would not let me speak until I had taken three large gulps: then, as gently as he knew how, he pressed me for my story.

When I had finished, he grunted. 'If strife in the world meant the end of it, the world would never have begun. Men have been prophesying its doom ever since they realised it was created.'

I took another draught of the wine, relishing its acid taste on my tongue. That at least felt real. 'It would almost be better if the prophecy was true. At least Anna and the children would be out of danger.'

I had hoped Sigurd would say something to reassure me against my pessimism. Instead, he stared into the darkness and said nothing. I hugged my knees to my chest. My panic was subsiding, but reason brought a chill clarity that was unrelenting in its grip.

'It doesn't matter if the prophecy's true or not.'

'It'll matter if it does come true,' Sigurd objected.

'No.' My voice was thin and hollow. 'What matters is that there are men in this army who believe that it's true. There were hundreds there tonight, maybe more.'

'They'll have a surprise when they wake up the morning after we capture the city and discover it's still there.'

'No!' I banged my fist on the stony ground. Sharp fragments of rock dug into the side of my hand. 'They believe that the consummation of the world is at hand. If they capture Jerusalem they will destroy it, fill it so deep with blood that it drowns.' I pulled the blanket tighter around me: I was shaking so hard I thought my bones might break from their sockets. 'They will kill every man, woman and child in that city in order to fulfil the prophecy and bring on the apocalypse. *Not one will survive.*'

Sigurd was quiet. For a moment I wished he would put his arms around me and hug me like a woman, anchor my desolation. But he was captive to his own thoughts and did not move.

'Then we'll have to reach Anna and your daughters before the Franks do.' He looked over his shoulder and pointed at the siege tower, a hulking silhouette against the glow of the city beyond. 'We need to be the first men onto the walls.'

'The first men to die with a faceful of Saracen arrows.'

'Perhaps.' Sigurd picked up a stone and tossed it down the embankment. 'What else can we do? If the Franks want to drown the city in blood, all we can do is run before the wave.'

At another time, the thought of putting myself in the front rank of the battle of the ages would have terrified me. Now I accepted it with meek dread. I had never wanted to see Jerusalem; now I would be the first on its walls or, more likely, die in the attempt. Once again, the veil between the worlds drew back and I almost heard the fates laughing. And, in their laughter, I heard a new threat that left me far colder than any thoughts of Saracen arrows and fire.

'What if Count Raymond doesn't take the city?'

Sigurd shrugged. 'Then the world won't end – and Anna and the others will be safe.'

I shook my head. 'That was not what I meant. Raymond has lost more than half his army in the last month, and when he launches that siege monster at the walls, he'll have to push it uphill over broken ground. Meanwhile, Duke Godfrey will be attacking from the north with twice his numbers.'

'So . . .'

'So the first men off Raymond's tower may not be the first men into the city.'

The white stallion reared up on its hind legs, its front hooves clubbing at the air. The groom who held the halter leaped back, hauling on the rope to bring the horse down. He barely managed to stay on his feet; I was surprised he did not get his head kicked in.

Across the paddock, Duke Godfrey stood by the wattle enclosure and watched, his arms folded across his chest. Four knights stood around him in a wary circle. If any man had benefited from Raymond's decline, it was Godfrey, and though he had professed indifference it had obviously affected him. He seemed to stand taller, his shoulders broader. There was an authority about him – and, more than that, a knowledge of it – such as I had seen in few other men. Bohemond had been one, but with him power had always been a spectacle. Chasing it, wrestling it, relishing it – he hid nothing, but made a theatre of his ambitions. Some men shrank from their power and others, like Raymond, believed they possessed more than they did, but none seemed so effortlessly comfortable with it as Duke Godfrey.

536

His guards stiffened as I approached, and moved to bar my way, but Godfrey murmured that I should pass. I walked the few paces across the dusty ground and stood beside him at the fence.

'I did not send Achard to kill you.' He did not look at me, but kept his gaze fixed on the stallion in the paddock. 'He went of his own will, because he hated you for what you did to him in Egypt.'

'It can be hard to forgive the men who betray you,' I said coldly.

'But if you cannot do that, you end up as Achard did: destroyed.' Godfrey flicked his head. 'I told you once before that you should leave behind those things that do not concern you.'

'You told me to go home to my family. And now I cannot, because they are in that city.' I gestured to the walls a few hundred yards distant. 'Because of what Achard did.'

At last Godfrey turned to me. 'Did you come here to hurl your bitterness at me, Demetrios Askiates? What do you want?'

I swallowed, trying to calm myself. 'I want to be the first man in the city.'

'Many men want that honour,' he rebuked me. 'Many men have begged me for it. But it is not my gift to give. Only God can decide it – if He means us to capture the city at all.'

I nodded, and crossed myself. One thing about Godfrey had not changed: his pedantic piety.

'Many men have lost their families – I cannot give you my army for that.'

'I don't want your army.' I tried desperately to fight back my temper. 'I want to join it.' I had raised my voice, and the guards had noticed. They began to close on me, but Godfrey raised his head a fraction to nod them back.

'I will submit my men to your authority. Varangian guards, from the emperor's palace at Constantinople. There is not a king in Christendom who would not want them in his army.'

'Except perhaps the Norman king of England,' said Godfrey drily.

'They will fight to the death for you.'

Godfrey stared out at the paddock. The white stallion had been calmed, and was now allowing the groom to lead him around the ring.

'Will you be riding him in the assault?' I asked.

Godfrey laughed dismissively. 'I would not risk him. He is too good to be felled by an Egyptian arrow.'

'Then risk me,' I pleaded. 'Put me in the vanguard of the battle. When they hurl rocks and arrows and fire at us, put me on the top of your tower.'

'I think you have spent too long with your Englishmen. I have heard they fight every battle as if they want to die in it.' He laughed again, the same short laugh as when I had asked about the horse. 'Perhaps that is a good thing.'

I waited. Godfrey drummed his fingers on the wattle fence. His horse was skittish, tossing its mane and kicking

538

out its hooves as if the meagre business of walking around a ring demeaned it.

At last, without looking at me, Godfrey said, 'You can go with the tower, if that is your wish. But first you must submit to me and swear your allegiance.'

I dropped to my knees in front of Godfrey and repeated the few words he told me, forgetting them almost as I spoke them. When I had finished, he held out his hand like a bishop so I could kiss his ring. Loathing myself, I pressed my lips to the cracked, black stone that bulged from the worn gold. His ancestors' ring, I remembered: I had seen it before, in his tent before the council at Rugia. I wondered what had happened to the other ring, the gold seal that had been taken from me at Ravendan. He had wanted me dead, then; now, I feared I would grant him his wish. Fate is inescapable.

I got up, brushing the dust from my knees.

'All those who will be with me at the top of the tower are already chosen,' he announced. 'So are those who will be on the second level, ready to charge over the draw-bridge when we lower it.'

'But—'

'You and your men will go at the bottom of the tower. We will need strong arms to push it.'

There was nothing I could say. Godfrey knew it.

'You may go. I suppose you will have to tell Count Raymond how you have changed your loyalties.' Again that tight smile. 'No doubt he is used to hearing it by now.'

*   *   *

I found Raymond in his tent, alone, as he often was in those days. He must have just finished paying his knights and labourers their wages: a broad table laid with a chequered cloth had been set in the middle of the room, piled with small stacks of coins, and a pair of scales sat at rest in its centre. I remembered the scales the third horseman had carried in the ceremony the night before, and shuddered.

'What do you want?' He sounded impossibly tired, an old man whose life had become a dispiriting ordeal. Barely looking at me, he dropped a succession of coins into one of the pans of the scale until it sank into balance.

The July sun had turned the tent into an oven. The cloth walls seemed to throb with the light outside and stifle the air, but that was not why I felt ill.

'It is about the assault . . .'

Raymond swept the coins into his palm and arranged them on one of the cloth squares. 'The towers are almost ready. The English captain says we should be able to launch our attack on Wednesday, Thursday at the latest, if the priests agree.' Absent-mindedly, he began arranging the coins in a pattern like a flower. 'I am glad that you came. I wanted to talk to you.'

The sickness in my stomach seemed to grow. I tried to speak to pre-empt whatever he would say, but my mouth was suddenly too dry.

'The princes have already begun to discuss who will rule Jerusalem when we conquer it. The kingship of Jerusalem should only be given to the mightiest and worthiest of princes, and I wanted your assurance that the emperor has not wavered from his commitment to me. That when the victory is won and the city liberated, I will have his support for my claim.'

I stared at him, not knowing whether to feel pity or scorn. Even after all his humiliations, his disastrous entanglement with Peter Bartholomew, his stubborn pursuit of the siege of Arqa, the loss of half his army, he had not learned humility. He stood on the diminished rock of his own dignity while the tide washed out, and railed at the waves for going the wrong way. It was so childish as to be ludicrous.

Something of my astonishment must have shown on my face, and perhaps Raymond felt it himself, for he added softly: 'I was lord of thirteen counties, and I left them all behind to pursue this vision of Christ that the Pope conjured before me. My court at Toulouse was the greatest court west of the Alps – now my court is a tent that smells of horse shit. I am a realist, Demetrios. I know I am nearer the end of my life than the beginning, and I came here knowing I would not go back. But that does not mean I should die without dignity. What are Bohemond and Godfrey? Second sons and bastard sons of worthless lines. Did you know that Godfrey only inherited his dukedom because his hunchback uncle was sterile as a mule? What did they give up to come here? What sacrifices did they ever make?'

Even if there had been an answer, he would not have wanted to hear it – least of all from me. I shrugged, and looked at the floor.

Raymond sat back and fiddled with his coins again, sliding them across the chequered cloth to form the shape of a cross. 'After all I have suffered, this ordeal will not have been for nothing. You understand.'

A silence fell between us, in which the only noise was the clink of coins as Raymond's hands knocked them together.

'I will not be fighting in your army when we attack Jerusalem.' I rushed the words out, stumbling and mumbling. Only when I had finished the sentence did I dare to look at Raymond. He sat very still: the only thing that moved was the corner of his empty eye socket, which twitched rapidly.

'Why not?' The words rasped out like a knife being dragged across a stone. 'Is it money?' He scooped a big fistful of coins off the table and shook them at me. 'I thought you of all men, Demetrios Askiates, were above mere greed.'

You of all men. It was a clumsy attempt at intimacy, no doubt meant to shame me. Instead, it only hardened me against him. If he had known me at all, he would have known how false his flattery was, how often I had fought for money. The fact that for once I cared nothing for money, that I would have given all the gold in his treasury to not have to do this thing, only added to the insult.

'I have given my allegiance to Duke Godfrey,' I said shortly.

With a hiss of rage, Raymond rose to his feet and hurled the coins at me. I felt them rain against my face as I threw up my hands to cover myself, as they bounced away to fall on the ground. On the soft carpet that covered the floor they hardly made a sound.

'*Traitor!*' screamed Raymond. 'You have betrayed me, sold yourself like a whore to my enemies.' He scrabbled on the table for more coins, pelting me with his pieces of silver. 'Take them! I took you into my camp and put you under my protection, and this is how you repay me? I stood by your emperor when no one else would. I was his staunchest ally, and all the while Godfrey plotted against him in secret. Have you forgotten that when he was at Constantinople he even tried to wage war on your emperor, he hated him so much?'

'My family are in Jerusalem,' I said simply. 'I have to reach them before they get lost in the slaughter. For that, I must follow whoever will lead me inside those walls soonest.'

'And you think that I will not?' Raymond pounded his fists on the table, so that the remaining coins leapt in the air. The scales toppled over with a crash. 'I will prove you wrong, Greek. I will be over those walls before Godfrey, before Tancred, before all the liars and cowards who have betrayed me. I will seize its strongholds and towers and make myself lord of Jerusalem, though the devil himself come to take it from me. And you will beg me to release your family, Greekling, as I begged you to stand with me now.'

If there had not been a table between us, I think he would have knocked me to the ground. Instead, he hissed between his teeth, '*Go!*'

I went. The last I saw of him, he was kneeling on the floor, gathering up the coins he had hurled at me and weeping.

That was Sunday. On Monday I spent the day trying to avoid Sigurd's fury: he had not reacted well when he heard I had volunteered us as mules to drive Godfrey's siege tower. On Tuesday his temper had cooled, at least to the point where it simmered rather than boiled. By Wednesday it was forgotten. Word went through the army that the final assault would begin next morning, and suddenly there was no time for anything. The hours seemed to slip by like water, and still we had blades to sharpen, armour to oil and dents to hammer out of our shields. A troop of women left the camp at dawn and did not reappear until sundown, returning with skins and buckets of water that they had filled from springs many miles away. The priests recited masses and prayers throughout the day for the endless procession of knights and pilgrims who flocked to them seeking communion, confession and blessing. I wondered how many of those gulping down the transubstantiated bread believed their next meal would be in the celestial city in the presence of Christ. Even Sigurd, who had never entirely let go the pagan gods of his ancestors, disappeared that afternoon to make his confession. Thomas went for much longer and returned with a fiery determination filling his eyes.

That evening we gathered around our camp fire for the last time. A red sun flamed in the west; the hot urgency of the day had cooled into stillness, and now we sat and tried to replenish our strength before the onslaught. Sigurd wiped a rag over an axe that was already sharp enough to split a hair in two, while Thomas wound a fresh strip of hide around the grip of his shield. I took two twigs I had rescued from the kindling pile and methodically cut the thorns away with my knife, stripping them smooth. When that was done I laid them across each other at right angles and wound a piece of twine over the join to form a crude cross.

'Have thoughts of the battle brought you back to God?' Sigurd asked.

I kept my eyes on my work and did not answer. The truth was that I needed a cross to wear in the battle, to mark myself as a Christian if we succeeded in getting inside the city. Once I had believed in its power to save my soul; now I only saw its power to protect me from the violence of men.

Sigurd took my silence for assent. 'It's as well. We'll need all the help He can give us tomorrow, if He doesn't damn the Franks for being so stupid as to attack the strongest corner of the city.'

I shrugged. The open ground that divided the armies, barely a bowshot wide, ended in a shallow ditch that then rose into the outer wall, a low barrier designed more to impede an attack than withstand it. The Egyptians would not defend that for long. They would retreat up onto the main ramparts and rain death down on us from there, fully fifty feet high, and guarded on the corner by a vast tower. The tower of Goliath, they called it, and I feared it was with good reason.

'You won't topple that with a sling and a stone,' said Sigurd, following my gaze to the tower. 'It's madness to attack there.'

It was, and the Fatimids had had almost a month to prepare for it. They had spent every day of the last four weeks repairing those walls and strengthening them, filling them with arms and men and supplies. They had not even tried to hide it. When we attacked there the next day, it would be against the strongest, best-defended corner of the city. Not for the first time, a shiver of doubt ran through me as I wondered if I had chosen the right path by abandoning Raymond.

I looked at Thomas. Ever since he had returned from the mass he had barely spoken a word. There had always been a distance between us, ever since I first hauled him out of a fountain in Constantinople. His marrying Helena had narrowed it, for a time, but in the past month I had felt it stretch wider than ever.

'Tomorrow, God willing, we'll be standing beside the tomb where Christ himself lay.'

'Or lying in our own graves,' Sigurd added.

Thomas laid his shield against his legs so that it covered them like a skirt. 'Better to be dead in the next world than alive in this,' he said softly.

I stared at him across the fire. The hot haze that rose from the coals seemed to melt his features like wax, so I could barely recognise him. How deeply had the wound of Helena and Everard's capture struck him that he could say such things? With a crush of shame I saw how little I had noticed him this past month, how superficial my care had been. With my own wounds so raw, it had been too easy.

I crossed myself, more out of habit than belief, and saw Thomas sneer at my false piety. 'You cannot give up on this world – not while your wife and son are held captive. There is no other.'

'Lift your eyes higher, old man. Of course there is another world. And it is a better place than this.' He tossed a leaf onto the coals and watched it curl and shrivel to ash. 'Our world is a dying ember; that world is the sun.'

'But there is no point trying to get from here to there.'

'No!' Thomas banged his fist on the rim of his shield, like a warrior before battle. 'The point is not to get from our world to that one. The point is to bring that world here, to remake it on earth.'

I shook my head in disgust. 'You sound like Peter Bartholomew.'

For a moment Thomas did not reply. In the ever-changing firelight, his face seemed to churn with indecision. I could see part of him wanting to abandon the argument, but another part – a stronger part – could not let go.

'Why did we come here – why did any of us come here – if not to try and make the world more perfect?'

'You cannot perfect the world with bloodshed,' I said sharply.

'No? Then how do you plan to rescue your daughters?'

I shook my head in frustration, trying to sift the

547

sediment that clouded my thoughts. 'Arnulf and his followers don't want to perfect this world. They want to throw it all out and start anew, remake it entirely.'

'And what is wrong with that? That is the inheritance promised in the Gospels. Why not seize it? Why struggle day by day to mend this sick and broken world, when in one glorious moment we could cure it?'

'You don't cure something by killing it.'

'Perhaps the sickness has spread so far there is no alternative.'

'No!' I stamped my foot, lifting a cloud of dust. 'And if it has, it is not for us to decide. Arnulf preaches that we should kill every man, woman and child inside that city in our impatience to bring on the kingdom of heaven. *Every one* – including your wife and son, my children and grandchildren. Can that be right?'

Thomas looked uncertain. 'Perhaps that is the price of the kingdom of heaven.'

'I do not believe that. But even if it was, there is no man alive who could demand payment.' I tried to calm myself. Speaking more surely than I felt, I said, 'God made the kingdom of heaven as an ideal, an example for men to dream of. It is not a place that we can reach except when He calls us there. It is certainly not a place we can call into being.'

A tear trickled down Thomas's face, though I could not tell if it was of rage or sorrow. 'Then why does He tempt us with it?'

'Maybe to see if we resist.'

με

~~~~~

'Wake up.'

I couldn't wake – I had not been asleep. I opened my eyes to see a Frankish sergeant with a long moustache looking down on me.

'Is it dawn already?' It seemed only minutes since I had gone to bed. Around me, all was dark.

'Barely midnight. Get your armour on and follow me.'

He led us swiftly down the hill to the place where the great siege tower, Magog, stood in its pomp. It disappeared into the darkness, ready to lay siege to the stars themselves for all I could see. Or perhaps that was wrong. As my eyes balanced with the night, it seemed that the tower was shorter than I remembered it. Perhaps it was the night playing tricks on me.

I heard the grate of wood rubbing together, a slither and a thud. And then, in a dialect I did not understand, a succession of short, hard words that sounded like curses.

'I almost broke my toe,' complained an aggrieved voice.

'I'll break your leprous arm if you're not more careful,' retorted the first man. Belatedly, I realised that I knew his voice – it was Saewulf's. I found him standing at the foot of the tower, while eight Frankish men-at-arms laboured to lift a massive slab of wood.

'What are you doing?' I whispered. 'Did this come off the tower? Have the Fatimids struck it with their stone-throwers?'

'Not yet.' Saewulf turned away to hiss instructions to another team of men, who seemed to be manhandling one of the wattle screens down from the summit of the tower.

'What then? Are you dismantling it? Have we abandoned the siege?' Every possibility was dreadful, but that was too much to contemplate.

Saewulf grinned, his teeth white in the darkness. '*I will tear it down, and rebuild it in three days.* That's what Christ said. But this shouldn't take more than a night. We're taking it apart and rebuilding it over there.' He pointed to the east.

I gaped. 'In one night?'

'That's what we built it for.' Even as he spoke, another piece of siding slid down from the tower, like a snake shedding its skin.

'Is Count Raymond doing the same?'

Saewulf shook his head. 'The stubborn bastard built his tower where there was nowhere else to go. Now he'll just have to push it up exactly where the Fatimids expect.' He slapped the side of his tower affectionately, like the rump of a horse. 'And so will we, if we don't hurry. Take that, and follow where the others lead you.'

It was an exhausting, eerie night. Hour after hour, we trudged back and forth over the ridge above Jerusalem, ferrying the dismembered machine to its new site. We were forbidden from carrying lights lest we betray our secret, while a choir of priests kept up a chorus of hymns and anthems to mask the clatter of our work from the watchers on the walls.

The night seemed unending – as if day had been abolished, and all nights ran together unbroken. I prayed for it to end, and then prayed for it to last as I watched the achingly slow progress of the tower's reassembly. My hands grew chafed and numb from manhandling the pieces of the siege tower, my legs were weary and my head ached from lack of sleep. But just as Saewulf's carpenters were hammering the last few trenails into the uppermost storey of the tower, and the wheelwrights oiling its axles, a bloody smear of red trickled over the Mount of Olives in the east. I thought of Arnulf's prophecy, and wondered if this would be the last of all days – and even if it was not, whether I would see another.

Dawn brought fresh urgency to the world. Birdsong was drowned out by the blast of horns and trumpets as

551

the Franks summoned their armies to battle. They assembled on the spur that dropped towards the city, their banners limp above them in the still morning. On the high walls in front of them the sentries from the Fatimid garrison looked out in disbelief. To them it must have appeared as though the land itself had shifted in the night, a mountain erupted and a forest of spears grown in the arid soil.

Once all the army had assembled, the princes rode out. Godfrey came last of all, riding the white horse I had seen in the paddock. He had braided its mane with silver ribbons so that it shone in the morning like dew. Just in front of him, on foot, Arnulf carried a golden cross with fragments of the True Cross embedded in it. I wondered if relics could hold memories, and if so if those few splinters of wood felt the stir of being so close to the place where they had lifted a man to his willing death, a thousand and more years ago.

The princes reined in, turned to face the army and dismounted. There would be no place for horses in the coming battle. Grooms led the animals away, while Godfrey and Arnulf walked towards the hulking tower. Its back was open and undefended, so we could see them slowly climbing the ladders inside all the way to the roof of the machine, as high as the towers that guarded Jerusalem behind them. There Godfrey turned around to face the watching army.

A murmur of awe shivered through the crowd. At that height he was high enough to catch the first rays of the sun coming over the Mount of Olives, and in its pure light he dazzled like a god. His fair hair glowed like a nimbus of pale gold; he wore a white tabard sparkling with five golden crosses for the five wounds of Christ, and a white cloak hung from his shoulders. Even the mail hauberk beneath seemed to have been brushed with silver, and polished so bright it shone white in the dawn. He gazed out on the army and lifted his arms wide. The gold cross gleamed above him like a sign from heaven.

He drew a breath, as if to make a speech, but there were only two words he needed to say that morning and he shouted them with all his voice: two words that had propelled the army all the way to the gates of Jerusalem. *Deus vult*. The army cheered. They hammered their sword pommels against their shields; they stamped their feet and the butts of their spears on the ground until the dust rose in clouds to their waists. Most of all, they shouted. They roared out the cry until it filled the valleys like the ocean, rolling from the Mount of Olives across Mount Moriah and Mount Zion all the way to the western ridge. They roared until the earth trembled with their noise, until it seemed they might shake down Jerusalem into dust.

Three boulders rose into the air and hurtled towards the walls, flung by the mangonels we had brought up in the night. They struck home against the ramparts, and the rhythmic chant of *Deus vult* swelled into a chaotic roar of triumph. And so the battle for Jerusalem began.

As Godfrey clambered down from the roof of the wooden tower, Arnulf removed the golden cross from its staff and fastened it to an iron spike that protruded from the top of the tower. It gleamed like a crown. Perhaps it seemed right to him that men would die under fragments of the same wood that had crucified Christ, but I did not think that the man who died on that cross had intended it to be stained with blood again. All around me, men were running about to prepare the assault, while the bombardment from the mangonels flew overhead. I had just started moving towards the tower when I heard a voice calling my name. I turned, to see a Frankish knight looking at me commandingly. His name was Grimbauld, one of Godfrey's lieutenants. He had lost the lower part of his left arm in the battle for Antioch, but had adapted the slings on his shield so that he could bind it on to what remained. Too unbalanced to wield a sword with skill, he now carried a club-headed mace in its stead.

'You!' he barked. 'Get to the ram.'

I stared at him, my eyes dry and hollow. 'Duke Godfrey told me my place was on the tower.'

'I tells you where you go, and that's where I tell you.' He took a half-step forward, and one glance into his bull-brown eyes convinced me he would not hesitate to wield his mace on me if I defied him. Cursing my bargain with Godfrey, I led Sigurd and the others towards the ram.

It was a squat, brute thing, built low like an animal crouched to pounce. Because they could not find a tree big enough for their purpose, they had taken three trunks and bound them together into a giant arm, then capped its fist with iron. They had mounted this horrendous weight on a ten-wheeled carriage whose axles were themselves almost as thick as tree-trunks. Wicker canopies covered it from above, protruding like wings, while wooden stakes bristled from its side like arms for men to push it. Ropes had been fastened to it as well, so that the whole machine took on the appeareance of a monstrous beetle, or a scorpion caught in a snare. They called it Apollyon, the angel of hell whose name is Destruction. Now, men flocked to it, lining its sides and taking up the ropes like draught animals. Sigurd and I were lucky: we found spaces by the side of the beast, pushing on its staves rather than hauling on the ropes. That put us under the canopy, which shielded us from the sun and would presently shield us from hotter things, though it also meant we were blind to everything except the stooped backs of the men in front of us. Glancing around, I saw Thomas and Aelfric two rows behind us. I could still hear the crack of the mangonels, the rush as the stones flew overhead and the thud as they collided unseen with the walls. Mercifully, I did not hear any response: as yet, the Fatimids did not seem to have managed to bring their own battery to bear on our new, unexpected position.

Grimbauld lifted his mace. The men on the ropes pulled them taut, while those on the wooden bars tensed their arms against them. Now I could not look at anything except the rough wood beneath my fingers, and the ground below. If I lost my footing here I would be trampled by the men behind me in an instant – or, worse, ground under the wheels.

I did not see Grimbauld's mace drop, but I heard the command that accompanied it.

'Begin.'

With a groan that seemed torn from the wood itself, we heaved on the ram. It rocked forward an inch, and for a moment the sum strength of three hundred men held it there. Then it rolled back. A dispirited moan shuddered through us. My arms, already sore from the night's labours, burned anew.

From the corner of my eye I saw Grimbauld walking back. He disappeared from my sight, but he must have taken up a position at the rear of the machine for a moment later I heard the cry of 'Ready', and then the beat as he rapped his mace on the end of the tree-trunks. We hauled again. The ram edged forward, tottering, but fear of failing must have given us new strength, for this time it rolled forward. An inch, no more, before it shuddered to a standstill.

'I'd like to find whoever made these wheels and tie him to the rim,' muttered Sigurd grimly.

I had neither breath nor time to answer. The mace struck its beat again, and again we pushed forward with all our strength.

It was not how I had hoped it would be – a headlong charge, a terrifying scramble up the walls, and then victory. It was not even the dense, desperate mêlée of hand-to-hand combat I had feared – not yet, at least. Instead, the battle for Jerusalem was nothing more than drudgery. For what seemed like hours we heaved, hauled and cursed the machine forward, inch by terrible inch. Some men fainted with exhaustion and had to be dragged away, but I stayed in my place, refusing to let go. I was tiring badly, but if ever I failed to move forward with the others I immediately felt the harsh touch of the bar behind striking me across my shoulders. The wheels barely seemed to move – as often as not, we had to drag the ram forward rather than roll it, leaving two great welts in the earth where we had passed. When I looked back, it was pitiful to see what little distance we had come.

Meanwhile, the sparks of battle began to take hold and burst into flame around us. Alone among the Franks, Tancred's company had kept their horses: they rode in a loose screen on either side of us, shielding us from any counter-attack and peppering the ramparts with arrows. They had to be nimble, for although the Fatimids still did not seem to have brought up their heavy siege weapons, they had by now managed to deploy smaller slings and rock-throwers, which lashed us with well-aimed stones. To all that I had already lost or diminished on that pilgrimage – my family, my strength, my faith – I now added my humanity. I saw the men on the ropes dying, their faces smashed in or their necks broken, and all I felt was relief. When rocks hit the wattle roof above me and bounced away, I did not just feel gratitude for my protection, but jealous pleasure that I had what others did not. And when I saw the arrows begin to fall around me, cutting men down, I was glad, for it meant we must at last be nearing the walls.

The end, when it came, was sudden. We were stooped like slaves, pressing our bleeding hands against the staves to drive the beast forward, except that this time the ram did not stop when we did. It rolled on. Those who held on to the handles were dragged forward, while those who had let go found themselves knocked down by the men behind. Standing at the end of the bar, and far enough forward, I just had time to see what was happening. I jumped clear, pulling Sigurd after me as we stumbled into the fevered mass of men around us.

The Franks had chosen the line of their attack well. The ground here sloped quite steeply to the outer walls: as soon as the ram crossed the rim its head went down, and the full power of its dead weight was unleashed. The men who had given every ounce of their strength to move it that far suddenly found themselves left behind or – unable to move themselves fast enough – trapped beneath it.

It struck home with a thunderclap, shattering the wall like glass and blasting it into a thousand fragments. Through the dust cloud that engulfed it, I saw the ram lumbering on. With a second crash, deeper and more profound than the first, it slammed against the inner wall. Deep cracks exploded through the stone, but it did not break. Only then did the ram come to rest.

The break in the battle lasted a heartbeat longer, while bricks and dust slowly settled. Then, in an instant, the fighting erupted again, fiercer than ever, and this time I had no roof to shield me. Through the choked air I saw Grimbauld standing defiant, his shield held over his head and his mace pointing towards the walls. '*Forward!*'

'*Forward!*' Another voice echoed it in my ear. Sigurd. He ran forward and I followed, craning around to see if Thomas was with us. In the dust, we must have been all but invisible to the defenders on the walls, but they poured their missiles down on us like rain. Several fell near me; one arrow planted itself right between my feet, but I ran on. The ruins of the wall loomed before me. I slid to a halt behind it and huddled close so that the missiles could not strike. Sigurd was with me; a second later, Thomas dived into the shelter as well. A scratch on his face was bleeding, but otherwise he seemed unharmed. Nearby, I heard Grimbauld still bellowing us to advance.

'We won't get through that gap,' said Sigurd. He pointed to our left. A little way along the wall, I could make out the rear end of the ram protruding through the hole it had smashed. The inner and outer ramparts were so close here, and the ram so long, that it could not pass all the way through but plugged the very opening it had made.

Grimbauld had seen it too. '*Back to the ram!* Bend yourselves onto those ropes and pull, curse you.'

It seemed almost impossible that anyone could have survived in that storm of arrows, but men came running through the fog and tried to pick up the traces that lay splayed out behind the ram. The dust was settling, but the air was not growing any clearer. If anything, it seemed thicker. And from somewhere beyond the wall, I smelled burning.

'The ram,' shouted a voice. 'The ram is on fire.'

Holding up my arm as a makeshift shield – better to take an arrow in the hand than in the face – I risked a glance over my barricade. With the ram stuck beneath the walls, the Fatimids could drop burning straw and oil on it at will. Flames already licked up from the wattle roof, and a column of black smoke poured into the sky, though it would take an age for the great trees beneath to burn.

'*Get it out of there!*' Ten teams of oxen could hardly have hauled the ram up that slope, yet men still tried, running in to harness themselves to the beast Apollyon. If more did not die, it was only because the smoke from the fire blinded those who had set it. But the ram would be ashes before we dragged it free. Instead of trying to move it, men now clambered around it into the narrow space between the walls. There they tried to smother the fire with dust and earth – but the ground was stony, and there was little they could use. Beside me, Thomas made to follow them, and I had to grab the collar of his hauberk to haul him back.

'No.' With the roar of battle in my ears, I put my face an inch from his merely to be understood. 'Think of Helena and Everard. You will not help them by dying now.'

He shrugged off my hand, but did not go further.

Now a new and terrible thing happened: women began to appear in the battle. They staggered out of the smoke, bent double under the weight of the burdens they carried – vessels of water to quench the burning ram. The sight of the water made my parched throat ache for a sip, even a single drop, but there was none for me. Each vessel was solemnly handed forward to the men at the front, then poured on the tongues of flame that licked the ram. Each time the water touched the fire it vapourised in an instant, hissing up in terrible gouts of steam. It was torment to witness.

At length, a knight came running back to Grimbauld, crouched near us in the lee of the wall, and shouted that the fire had been put out. All around, the bodies of women – girls, some of them – lay strewn with the men, promiscuous in death.

Grimbauld glanced over his shoulder. 'Go back to Count Godfrey,' he told the knight. 'Tell him to bring up the siege tower. We'll never get close without men on the tower to cover us.'

The knight saluted and ran off, weaving his way through the maze of corpses at his feet. After what seemed an age – though on a battlefield, time stretches as long as a man's life – I saw him return. Instead of a sword he carried two shields; he scuttled forward like a crab, creating an impenetrable wall against the arrows that swarmed about him. He crawled down the embankment to where Grimbauld waited and raised the two shields as a roof over them.

'Duke Godfrey says he cannot bring up the tower while the ram is blocking the breach,' he stammered. 'He orders you to drag it back – or, if that is impossible, to burn it out of there.'

Grimbauld stared at him with wild eyes. 'Burn it out?'

The knight nodded glumly. Even as he did so, another

column appeared at the top of the slope and began shuffling towards us. These men carried bales of hay and armfuls of firewood, piled so high they almost bent double with the weight. At the sight of them, a trumpet whooped from the walls, and a fresh burst of arrows showered down on them. Many fell clutching their burdens like children, but some managed to reach the ram and stack their kindling around it. When there was enough, Grimbauld lobbed a burning brand onto the makeshift pyre. Flames swept up around the great tree-trunks at the heart of the ram, and we cheered it, even as we stood on the corpses of those who had given their lives to prevent such a thing.

Cheers turned to disbelief as a torrent of water gushed from the sky, drowning out the fire in an instant. Gleeful shouts of triumph erupted from the wall; I looked up, and saw the Fatimids hauling back a great cauldron they had poured out. Some of them waved; I even saw one jump into an embrasure, pull up his tunic and – to the cheers of his companions – send a contemptuous stream of piss spattering down on the ram. An outraged volley of arrows pricked him back, but was immediately answered in kind as the Fatimids unleashed a new onslaught on the despairing Franks.

Grimbauld turned to the pilgrims. 'What are you waiting for?' he screamed. 'Bring more wood!'

The battle raged all afternoon. Each time we piled on fresh kindling, the Fatimids retaliated with a new torrent of water. With each subsequent attempt, the pile of wood and straw around the ram grew higher, until its vast bulk was almost buried, but even then it could not overcome the Fatimids' defence. There seemed no limit to the water they had in that city – and that, too, drove us to despair. The air was thick with smoke and hot steam that scalded my lungs; I felt that I must have fallen inside a vast black cauldron and be boiling inside it. Only when we managed to bring up jars of oil and soak the wood with that did we at last make a fire that the Fatimids could not quench. The flames licked up high over the wall: I doubt there was a man in the garrison who could have endured the heat and smoke, but though the wall sat undefended we could not go near it. The fire for which we had fought so hard, first to quench and then to light, had become our enemies' best defence. As the shadows lengthened and darkness fell, we left the walls behind and limped back to our camp.

μς

∽∽∽∽∽

Another day dawned – Friday. This time there was no great rallying of the army, no processions or speeches. We crawled up from the places where we had fallen asleep and massed around the base of the tower. I did not even need to get dressed, for I had slept in my armour on the ground where I collapsed, dead to the world until the trumpets summoned me. Pain racked my body: my limbs felt as though they had been disjointed and then hammered together with iron nails, and my hands were still bloody and raw from pushing the ram. Worse than that was the thirst: my mouth felt as though it had been swabbed with quicklime, but there was no water to slake it. We had spent all our supplies putting out the fire on the ram.

'Friday in Jerusalem. I suppose it's a good day to die,'

muttered Aelfric as we mustered at the tower.

'Or to defeat death,' Thomas reproved him. His cheeks had sunk in and his beard was ragged, so that he looked like a prophet stumbling out of the wilderness, far older than his years.

'Better to defeat the Egyptians,' said Sigurd. 'It has to be today. The army won't stand any more.'

'Has anybody heard how the battle went for Count Raymond yesterday, in the south?' I asked.

'Badly. Saewulf told me. He tried to bring his tower up to the walls but had to withdraw it. The defenders knew exactly where he was coming – they had ten mangonels waiting to bombard it with stones and fire. They say that afterwards the count could not persuade any of his knights to enter it again.'

In the mean, shrivelled husk that had become my heart, I thanked God for that.

A quarter of an hour after dawn, Duke Godfrey and his retinue mounted to their positions within the tower. I watched them jealously, wishing myself in their place. As well as his regular arms, Godfrey carried a broad crossbow to use from the top deck of the tower, and the sight of it reminded me of a similar weapon, many years and miles ago, that had first coaxed me onto the road to Jerusalem. I looked at Thomas to see if he remembered, but his eyes were dull and fixed elsewhere.

When Godfrey and his knights were in place, and the priests had mumbled a quick prayer, we took up the strain on the hawsers fixed to the base of the tower. My hands were still too sore to grasp it; I knotted the rope around my chest, harnessing myself to the beast behind and making myself its slave.

As heavy as the ram had been, this was worse. The tower stood almost ten times taller, so that every time we hauled I felt that we might pull the entire edifice crashing down on us. The halter around me dug into my chest, and there was no roof over my head to protect me from the sun or the rain of missiles. Whereas the previous day we had at least been able to make the first part of our approach in safety, this time we had no relief. The advantage of surprise we had gained two nights earlier was gone, and no sooner had the tower started to stagger forward than a volley of stones rose up from behind the walls. They spun slowly in the air, seeming to float so gently that I thought they might never land. And then suddenly they were almost upon us, dropping down with ravenous speed, rushing towards us. Watching in horror, I could see that these were not the pebbles and rocks that had harried us the day before, but full-sized boulders, heavy as a man, flung from mangonels. The defenders must have moved them up in the night – and ranged them with deadly accuracy. All three of the missiles in that first wave struck within a dozen yards of the tower, tearing into the lines of men who drew it. One struck a man's head and pulped it like a melon; another toppled five men in a row before it came to rest. Men ran to move the boulder out of the path of the tower, while the bodies of the fallen were left to be crushed under its wheels.

Now it became a war among giants, a *titanomachia* between the tower stumbling forward like a blinded Cyclops, and the invisible arms behind the walls, which hurled out boulders as children skip stones on a pond. From our own lines, the Franks' mangonels answered with fire of their own. I was merely a beetle scuttling about at their feet, while flights of rocks raced across the sky above. Death was sudden and everpresent. Several stones struck glancing blows on the sides of the tower, ripping away the skin. Another actually passed clear through one of these holes, plucked one of the knights inside from his perch and dashed him to the ground. But it was we on the ground who suffered most — crushed, shattered, torn apart or simply bowled over. Some of the soldiers who followed tried to help us: they brought up wooden hurdles covered with wicker and skins and held them in front of us. But those were designed to stop arrows, not rocks; they added nothing but debris to the battle. The soldiers' bodies made better shields.

All I could do was keep my head down and pray for mercy. Even if I could have picked out the boulders flying towards me, I could not have done anything to avoid them. The taut rope that tied me to the tower also tied me to whatever fate God granted me. Perhaps I grew numb to the fear, or perhaps the mere fact of survival when so many around me were dying gave me courage, but gradually — against all reason — it seemed that the bombardment was lessening. I could still hear boulders hurtling through the air — could even hear the snap of the mangonels behind the walls now – but they did not seem to be striking us with such frequency or ferocity.

I risked a glance up. The bombardment still went on, but now the missiles sailed over our heads – almost over the tower itself. We had come through the onslaught, and were now so close to the walls that the missiles could not strike us. The Fatimids had not moved their catapults to adjust for the change: perhaps they could not.

A ragged cheer went up from our ranks – and died as swiftly. Our progress had not made us safe, merely exposed us to new danger. Now we were in range of the walls, and the defenders unleashed a storm of small stones and arrows against us. They filled the air like locusts, preying on the men who strained to pull the tower forward. Our auxiliaries ran forward with the hurdles again and tried to shield us, though they could not guard every man. More useful to us was the tower. It stood a good six feet higher than the walls, offering the men on its top storey a commanding platform from which they could rake the ramparts with their arrows.

A horn sounded from its height. 'Into the breach!' bellowed Grimbauld. An arrow stuck from his shoulder, another from his leg, but they had not felled him. While those of us on the ropes strained to pull the tower closer, a tide of pilgrims swept around us and poured through the gap in the outer wall that the ram had made the day before. I could see its charred remains, still breathing wisps of smoke, beneath the inner walls. The pilgrims swarmed over it with hatchets and axes, pulling apart the burned wood and scattering the ashes. I heard several screams of pain as men grabbed pieces where the fire had not yet cooled – and more screams as the Fatimids on the wall tipped down stones and boiling water. At least the water must have doused what remained of the fire. The wreckage of the ram was pulled free, and the way lay open for the tower.

'This is it,' said Sigurd next to me. He had not bound himself to the tower as I had; he carried his rope over his shoulder, his vast arms bulging with the strain. His shield and his axe were slung over his back, ready for the moment when we could put down this terrible burden. 'Stay beside me.'

I nodded, unable to speak. We had reached the place where the incline steepened, where the ram had run away from us the day before, and I wondered how we would ever get the tower down it. If we let it go here, it would surely either topple over or career into the walls and shatter. But once again, the land had changed. A company of masons had come out in the night with picks and hammers to level the path, which now led gently down to the breach in the outer wall. We rolled the tower down the incline. A firestorm of arrows, balls of blazing pitch, hammers wrapped in burning rags and jars of flaming oil engulfed it, but the great beast Magog rolled on impervious as they slid or bounced off the skins that covered it. It passed through the breach, and came to rest at last in the space between the walls, a few yards from the inner rampart. For an instant, an awestruck silence gripped the battlefield as the men on the tower and the men on the walls stared at each other, almost face to face.

'*Deus vult!*'

The silence broke; the battle resumed. With the tower so close to the walls we could no longer pull it from the front, only get behind it and heave. But having been near the vanguard, I could not now get around the scrum of men who surrounded the tower. For a terrible moment, I found myself exposed in that lethal enclosure. A firm hand grabbed me and tried to pull me away – but I stayed rooted to the spot.

'*For Christ' sake, let go of that rope.*'

I still had the hawser tied around my waist. Fumbling, I drew my sword and managed to slice through the strands. Before I had finished, two hands had reached in and ripped the remainder apart.

'*Get down.*'

The same hands pushed me to the ground, knocking the breath out of me. Aelfric crouched beside me, covering me while I twisted my shield around and pulled it off my back. Only when I had it in place did I have a chance to look around.

'Where's Sigurd?'

He jerked his head to his right. Peering out from behind my shield, I saw Sigurd on one knee with his shield raised, while Thomas squatted behind him and hurled stones at the battlements with a sling he had torn from a dead man's tunic. To my left, the tower still crawled forward. Now that I saw it from a distance I could see it had suffered terrible punishment in the approach. Several of the wicker panels had been torn off, and one of its corner-posts actually seemed to have splintered in two, so that the upper levels sagged alarmingly. Miraculously – there was no other word – the golden cross at its peak remained unharmed, gleaming in the sun that now shone almost directly above.

Inch by inch, hair's breadth by hair's breadth, it ground forward. Up on the walls, the defence seemed to waver. Fewer arrows filled the air: I thought perhaps the Fatimids had lost heart at the sight of our progress. But they had prepared for this moment. They seemed to be lifting some massive object up over the battlements, hauling it out on pulleys that hung from the adjacent towers. At first I could not see what it was; then, as it swung free of the ramparts, it became clear. It was a long tree-trunk, suspended by chains and bristling with iron. Swords and knives, sickles and spikes, nails and hooks all sprouted from its sides like branches, while the wood itself was covered in a black coat of oily slime. It fell to the ground as the men above let go the chains, bounced once, then slid down the slope until its iron claws dug into the front of the siege tower. In an instant, a volley of burning arrows flew into it. A wall of flame rose up in front of the tower, engulfing it, and I groaned. No one could survive that inferno. Nor could they extinguish it with water, for when a nearby knight tried to throw some on the fire it merely exploded back at him in a massive gout of flame. This was a diabolic fire that could turn even opposing elements to its purpose. At the top of the tower I could see Duke Godfrey and his knights frantically pulling open the walls and looking down in terror, while at the bottom the men inside found they could not get out through the crowd of men who were still trying in vain to push the tower forward.

But Godfrey was not trying to escape. Instead, so far as I could see through the smoke, his men were manhandling some heavy object to the opening they had made in the side of the tower. Had they not noticed that this was a fire that could not be drowned?

A torrent of water cascaded down the front of the tower and the barrel tumbled after it, one more morsel for the fire. I closed my eyes. There was a hiss, as if all the waters of the earth boiled, and a wall of heat blasted over me. It seared my mouth, my hands, even my closed eyes. And yet – I lived. My hair had not caught fire, nor was my skin peeled away. I opened my eyes and peered out through my fingers. Incredibly, though the spiked tree-trunk still burned, it had not erupted into the pillar of flame I had expected. Nor had the fire taken hold of the siege tower. And the hot, moist air was saturated with the tart smell of vinegar.

The men on the tower pushed another barrel to the edge of the platform and tipped it over. Now that the flames were lower it did not evaporate in an instant but splashed around the wood. Some of it settled in a small pool in a hollow in the gound. Without thinking, I ran there and knelt beside it, scooping up the vinegar into my mouth before it could melt into the earth. It burned my tongue like acid, but it was the first moisture I had tasted in hours. Meanwhile, a team of Franks picked up the chain that had held the tree-trunk and dragged it away. The spikes and blades ploughed sharp furrows in the ground.

Now the battle took on a new, more dreadful intensity. The Fatimids had tried to break the tower with rocks and burn it with fire, and none of it had worked. Now they had nothing to rely on but their desperation. It might still be enough: they knew what vengeance the Franks would take on them in defeat, and they fought as only condemned men can. I thought of Bilal, and – even in the fury of battle – hoped he was not on those walls.

The siege tower was so close that the men at the top could almost stab their enemies with their spears, but they were still too far out to bridge the gap. The Fatimids redoubled their efforts, hurling fire against the tower even as they bombarded those of us on the ground with arrows, while we tried to shield ourselves from the onslaught and retaliate in kind to force them back off the rampart. With no more firepots to hurl, they fashioned crude balls of hair and wax, doused them in oil and set them alight. Most of them slid off the slick hides that dressed the tower and bounced down into the crowd at its base. One fell on the back of my hand, scorching a livid blister into the skin; I screamed, but did not drop my sword. I was lucky: some men found that the fire fell into the folds of their tabards or lodged in the gap between helmet and hauberk, setting them ablaze.

There were fewer arrows falling on us now, but more stones. One struck my shield and deflected harmlessly away; when I glanced at it, I saw in surprise that it had the crisp edges and smooth face of a brick. In their desperation, the Fatimids seemed to be tearing down the very walls that defended them in order to hurl them at us. But we were hardly better off: we could do little more than pick up the pieces and hurl them back. Glancing over my shoulder, I saw Thomas whirling his sling at the battlements. I wished he would take cover, for he made a tempting target.

Another rock struck me, this time on my shoulder, and my arm went numb. I could not stay out there. To my left, a hole gaped in the side of the tower where one of the panels had been torn off. Shouting over my shoulder to Aelfric, I ran to it, ducked underneath the splintered lintel and stepped inside. Instantly I was in darkness – a sweaty, heaving crush of men all pushing blindly forward, trying to drive the tower those precious final feet to the wall. Unthinkingly, I threw myself into the effort. Other men piled in behind me, but through the open hole in the side I could see the battle still raging. For all the Fatimids' frantic defence, the tide seemed to be turning against them. The ditch between the walls was filling with men, and though the Fatimids killed many, they could not turn back the inexorable swell. Ladders came forward and were lifted to the battlements; the defenders were quick to shatter their rungs with rocks before any man could climb them, but the Franks had learned their lesson from the first assault and had more in reserve. In perhaps the most unnatural sight of all that day, I saw a column of priests, all dressed in white, marching forward with a ladder held above their heads as they sang the words of the psalm:

> *You will not fear the terror of the night,*
> *or the arrow that flies by day,*
> *or the pestilence that stalks in darkness,*
> *or the destruction that wastes it at noon.*

Not one of them lived to see the ladder touch the wall.

Inside the siege tower, the crush was greater than ever. It was impossible to reach the front of the tower; instead, we pushed each other forward and hoped that would be enough. In the darkness, it was impossible to tell how much progress we made, though it felt as if we heaved hard enough to push down the wall and roll the tower over it.

And then, suddenly the press around me melted away. I looked up. From the corner of my eye I could see half a dozen ladders leaning against the wall, bowing in under the weight of the Franks racing up them like flames. The walls themselves now seemed to have caught light: as each man reached the top of his ladder, he passed into a shroud of black smoke and vanished.

I shook my head and looked around. The noise of battle seemed to be fading, and the press of men who had driven the tower forward had vanished. Only half a dozen remained, most of them rubbing their eyes like me. Two others who had been at the front, who must have absorbed the full weight of the crush behind, had slumped to the ground unconscious, their ribs broken and their chests staved in.

After so many years of suffering, so many months of longing, the last seconds were the most forgettable of all. I was climbing the ladder inside the tower. I had reached the first floor, past the gaping holes torn in its sides, past the corpses piled in the corners, onto another ladder. The rungs were slick with blood; I slipped, and might have broken my neck if my hauberk had not caught on the rung below and given me just enough time to steady myself.

I clambered onto the second level. After the gloom below it seemed almost impossibly bright, for the front wall had been lowered to form a crude bridge to the ramparts beyond. The noon sun shone in my eyes, making the pools of blood that soaked the bridge shine like glass. It loomed before me like a bridge to another world.

I stepped out. For a brief, dizzying moment, I looked down and saw the deep space yawning beneath. Then I passed between the battlements and was on solid stone once again.

I stood there on the rampart, inside the wall, and looked down into Jerusalem.

μζ

~~~~~

For a moment, I saw the city spread out before me – a tapestry of narrow streets, flat roofs, awnings, courtyards and turrets. Straight ahead of me, the great dome of the temple rose on the table-top of Mount Moriah; from there the city dipped into a steep valley, then rose again on my right to the heights of Mount Zion. A stone bridge spanned the valley about half a mile distant and I committed its position to heart, for that was where I would find my family. Far in the distance, I could see smoke rising from the southern walls where Count Raymond had attacked.

Then the view was gone. A hot wind fanned my face and a curtain of black smoke drew over the city. My eyes watered as I coughed to clear the fumes from my lungs. To my right, one of the guard towers was burning. The

Fatimids had tied bales of cotton and straw around it to protect it from the blows of our catapults, but these had caught fire and the whole tower blazed like a candle. The heat and smoke must have driven the defenders back long enough for us to gain a foothold – and once the flow had started, there was no staunching it. The garrison who had defended these walls so doggedly for a day and a half had been swept away by the Franks, who still poured over the battlements and rushed down into the city below.

A hand grabbed my shoulder and spun me about. Sigurd was standing there, his shield discarded but his axe in his hands. It was already smeared with blood. Thomas and Aelfric stood behind him, a poor remnant of the dozen Varangians who had gathered that morning.

'Where are the others?'

'Gone,' said Sigurd. 'And we'll wish we were with them if we don't move quickly. Come on.'

We followed the crowds along the rampart to the nearest tower, where a stair led down to the street. The press of men was almost inexorable, but by the door to the tower, the flow halted for a moment. One man was trying to push his way back. Knights shouted angrily and told him he was going the wrong way, but he persisted, forging through against the tide. The throng on the rampart was so thick that I could barely see him until he was in front of me; then he brushed past and was gone before I had even registered that it was Duke Godfrey. His white tabard was soaked with sweat, his golden hair matted with blood, and he stank of the vinegar he had

578

poured over the Fatimids' fire. Craning back, I saw him run across the gangway and disappear down into the siege tower.

'Maybe he needs to take a shit,' said Sigurd. 'Come on.'

All resistance had vanished. The Fatimids fled, and the space they left only sucked the Franks in faster. By the time we had barged down the stairs and gained the street we had slipped well behind the vanguard. Five mangonels lay abandoned behind the walls, one already burning.

I looked around, dizzied by the speed with which the battle had turned. In the back of my mind I tried to comprehend where I was, that I actually stood on the holy soil of Jerusalem. But it was too much to understand – and I had more pressing concerns.

'Which way now?' At ground level, with the narrow streets tight around us, I could not even see the dome of the Temple Mount any more. I had a general idea of its direction, but there were half a dozen streets and alleys leading into the city and it could have been any one.

'That way.' Before I could stop him, Thomas had decided. He pushed through the crowd and struck out down an alley.

'Wait,' I called, but I doubt he heard me in the uproar. Even if he had, he could hardly have stopped, for the flow of the crowd was relentless. Fearful of losing him entirely, we plunged after him, as the first screams began to rise from the buildings around us.

* * *

Whether chance or God or simply the instincts of the crowd guided us, we had chosen well. The road carried us quickly down the slope, and ended in a massive wall at the edge of the Temple Mount. Here euphoria ended and danger returned, for the remnant of the Fatimid garrison had chosen the vast bastions of the temple to make their last stand. They hurled down rocks and arrows – and also pots and pans, chairs and candlesticks, anything they could grab. But it was a desperate hope. They had trusted all their lives to defending the outer walls, and now that those were gone there was no time to erect new defences. Bodies began to fall among the makeshift missiles as the first of the Franks scaled the heights of the temple.

But that was not our battle. We turned right, and skirted the wall to its corner. The city that had hemmed us in suddenly opened out into the valley and there, barely two hundred yards distant, stood the bridge. Terrible shouts and the clash of arms echoed down from the courtyard above us, but I barely heard them. I ran along the base of the great rampart, trying to keep sight of Thomas ahead. The sun glared in my eyes and beat down on me; sweat poured down my face from under my helmet. I wiped it with my hand and tried to lick it off, desperate for water, but it only made me thirstier. All I could taste in my mouth was vinegar.

We came to the foot of the bridge. There was no way onto it from this side of the valley, for it projected straight out from the summit of the Temple Mount above us, but

I could see a flight of stairs climbing to join it on the far side. We stumbled down the valley, through the weeds and wildflowers that grew around the piers of the bridge. For an unreal moment I could almost believe I had left the city, that I was wandering through a pleasant meadow on a sun-baked hillside. Then I heard the clash of devastation rising ahead, and the illusion broke. The Franks had spread through the city like wildfire. Shouts and screams rose from the quarter in front of me; smoke began to taint the air. They could not be far from the house where Anna and the girls were kept, and I did not have to imagine what the Franks would do if they seized them before I got there. I was beyond exhaustion; I could barely lift my sword, let alone carry the great weight of my armour, but still I tried to increase my pace.

We staggered up the slope of Mount Zion, found the stair and clambered to its summit. To our left, the bridge ran back above the valley to the gate in the Temple enclosure; to our right, a dusty avenue led further into the city. I could barely see it for the great crowds that swarmed down it, men and women all fleeing across the bridge to the Temple Mount. *The Noble Sanctuary*, I remembered Bilal calling it, but they would not find sanctuary there.

On the far side of the bridge the street runs west, to a corner where two tamarisk trees grow. We turned right, against the flow of the crowd. Aelfric battered through with his shield, while Sigurd and I followed in his path. Though the Ishmaelites on that road must have outnumbered us a hundred to one, they ignored us. All they could think of now was saving themselves.

Thomas was still out in front of us, twisting and weaving through the crowd. Looking ahead, across the sea of oncoming faces, I saw he had reached a crossroads. More crowds poured in from the side-streets, pushing and screaming to get through, but that was not what I saw. On the corner of the streets two spindly trees protruded above the mob, their silver-green leaves preternaturally still in the uproar around them.

If you go right, there is a house with an iron amulet in the shape of a hand nailed to its door. That is where you will find your family.

The force of the crowd was so great we could barely move against it. Several times, even the combined weight of Aelfric and Sigurd could not keep us from being pushed back. My heart tightened, and a trembling seized my limbs: every passing second seemed to spell my family's doom. Thomas, meanwhile, had vanished from sight completely – all I could do was hope that he had reached the house in time.

At last, with a final heave, we broke through to the crossroads and turned the corner. The crowds were thinner here and we could move more easily. I stared around, desperately searching for the door with the iron amulet.

'Over here.'

Halfway up the street, Sigurd had stopped outside a square, two-storey house. A wooden balcony veiled the door in shadow, too dark to see from where I stood. I ran there, urging my floundering limbs into one last effort. There was the door, as Bilal had said, with an iron hand nailed neatly to its centre. An unblinking eye stared out of the palm, surrounded by an inscription in Arabic. I barely noticed it. The door was open: the frame was splintered where it had been kicked in, and one hinge hung loose from its post.

'Are we too late?' I croaked the question, barely able to move my cracked lips.

An anguished cry echoed from the darkness inside the house. Before I dared to look, I heard swift footsteps running towards the door. Thomas tore it open, pulling it so hard that it broke free and fell to the ground with a shattering bang. He stepped over it into the light.

'*It's empty.*'

The desolation as he howled his discovery cut open my soul like a knife. He shook like a wild animal; tears rolled down his cheeks. He tore his helmet from his head and dashed it to the ground, whirled around and lashed out at the wall with his boot. The ground itself seemed to tremble with the impact. '*Where are they?*' He turned to me in fury. '*You promised they would be here.*'

The power of his rage drove me back. I lifted my sword, fearing he might spring on me, and he might well have done if something else had not happened then. Most of the Ishmaelites had fled that street, though we could still see others hurrying past the crossroads towards the bridge; now, suddenly, two more came running towards us from the far end of the road. They were soldiers, the first I had seen since entering the city. Their scale armour was badly torn, and their faces were black with soot. With a howl of rage, Thomas took up his axe and ran towards them.

They were barely a dozen yards from me when they met: close enough that I could see it all, far enough that I could do nothing to stop it. One of the Fatimids, the taller of the two, raised an arm to ward off Thomas's assault. For a strange moment it almost looked as if he was offering a salute or a greeting, as if he had seen something he recognised. He did not even lift his sword.

Thomas bore down on him. Still neither man tried to protect himself. Surprise cut through my exhausted anguish and compelled me to see more clearly. It was not just soot that blackened their faces – it was the very skin itself. And there was something wrenchingly familiar in the figure of the taller man – the pride in his stance, even through battle-weariness and defeat.

There might have been hundreds – thousands – of the caliph's African soldiers in Jerusalem that day, but only one who would have come to that house. I staggered towards them; I tried to call out but my mouth was too dry. I told myself afterwards that Thomas would not have heard me anyway. He was screaming like a demon, a wild gibbering that only rage could interpret. Despair made the axe light in his hands. It flashed in the sun as it swept down against Bilal's neck, slicing through the collarbone and cleaving so deep it must have touched his heart. Even at the last, Bilal did not try to defend himself. He collapsed without a sound, the axe still embedded in him.

I ran towards them, too slow and too late. Thomas put his boot against Bilal's side and hauled on the axe haft, his rage not yet satisfied. But he had cut too deep, and it would not come loose. He tugged again, screaming at it to come free as he kicked Bilal's lifeless corpse. I doubt he saw anything else. Certainly he did not see the soldier who had accompanied Bilal. If he did not understand why his captain had died, he understood enough to avenge him. He lifted his short stabbing spear and lunged. With no shield, no axe, not even a helmet to protect him, Thomas never had a chance. The spear entered under his chin, drove through his skull and erupted through the top of his head with a burst of blood. His screaming choked off and he fell instantly.

The man who had killed him whipped around, saw he was outnumbered and fled down the street. I would have let him go, but before I could speak a small curved axe had flown from Sigurd's hand, overtaken the unfortunate Egyptian and planted itself in the base of his neck. He stumbled, fell, but did not die. Like a butterfly without wings he tried to pull himself forward, wriggling on his belly as the life gushed out of him. Then, mercifully, Aelfric ran to him and ended it with a blow of his axe. For a moment, silence descended on the street.

I reached Thomas and crouched beside him, though one glance was enough to tell I was too late. He must have died instantly. His blue eyes were wide, defiant to the last, but his face seemed strangely tranquil. Perhaps it was a trick of my disordered mind, but what I saw most in those last moments was his youth, as if his beard had receded and the angry furrows softened to give a glimpse of the boy he had been when I dragged him from a fountain in Constantinople. I had saved his life then; now it was gone.

I reached out two fingers and pulled his eyelids closed. *At least he lived to see Jerusalem*, I thought, and wondered if that was enough.

A gurgling moan intruded on my grief, and I turned. Bilal lay behind me – not dead, but dying rapidly. The axe was still stuck in his shoulder, its haft standing erect and casting a long shadow. I twisted around to kneel at his side. There were so many things I wanted to say to him – my guilt, my gratitude, my bitter anguish that I had failed his kindness – but need beat back all care with one overwhelming question.

'My daughters,' I whispered. 'Anna. Where are they?'

Blood dribbled from Bilal's mouth and seeped from his wound. I would have pulled the axe free but I did not dare: I feared it was all that wedged open the door between life and death. Reaching under him, I tried to lift his shoulders to make it easier to speak, but that only twisted the blade in his body and brought fresh screams of agony. I whispered in his ear again. 'Is my family safe?'

Bubbles rose from the crack where iron and flesh met. Bilal convulsed as he tried to gulp more air, but it was escaping far faster than he could regain it.

'*Where are they?*' I hissed, and for all my compassion I would have shaken him if I did not think it would have killed him.

He closed his eyes. And then, just before he gave up his spirit, he whispered a single word: '*Sanctuary.*'

'What sanctuary?' In this city of churches there must have been a hundred sanctuaries. But even as I saw that my question was useless, that Bilal would never speak to me or any other again, I saw the answer. For him, there could only be one sanctuary in the city.

'Mount Moriah,' I said. 'The Temple Mount – the Noble Sanctuary. That was where the Fatimids would have made their last defence.'

'Then let's hope they're still making it,' said Sigurd. He had retrieved his throwing axe from the corpse of Bilal's companion and wiped it on the quilted tunic he wore beneath his armour.

I leaned over and kissed Bilal on the cheek. Laid out in the sun, his flesh was still deceptively warm – as warm as life – but I could feel the death creeping through beneath.

'What shall we do with the bodies?' asked Aelfric.

'Leave them.' I made the sign of the cross over Thomas and offered the briefest prayer. I did not know what to do for Bilal, so in the end I did nothing. I hoped God would take pity on him.

We left the dead to bury themselves, and went in search of the living.

μη

We turned back towards the bridge, but we had barely gone ten paces when a great uproar stopped us. At first it sounded like waves surging over rocks; a second later it resolved into the shouts and cries of a great host. They came into sight at the end of the street and poured through the crossroads, the fleeing remnant of a routed army. Count Raymond must have broken through on the southern walls at last.

'We won't get through there,' said Aelfric. Indeed, while most of the army seemed to be retreating to the Temple Mount, several men had broken away and were streaming towards us. There was no thought of resisting them.

'This way.'

We turned north and ran. Shouts rose as the Fatimids

saw us and followed. Perhaps they thought they could still save the city, or that they might yet blunt our triumph; maybe they just wanted to die with honour. We fled from them, up the street, down an alley, through a gate that turned out simply to be a house built over the road, and into the heart of Jerusalem.

If I learned one thing that day, it was that Peter Bartholomew, Arnulf, even Saint John the Divine had all been wrong. The world did not have to end with ten-horned beasts and dragons, angels and fantastical monsters. The prophets who foretold those things had succumbed to the extravagance of their imaginations, and it had played them false. Nothing on earth could be so terrible as men. The whole city shook to the sounds of pain and torture as the Franks wrote their triumph in the blood of its people. They did not just murder the populace: they destroyed them. They tore them apart, child from mother, husband from wife, limb from limb until not one morsel of humanity remained. Not content with mere slaughter, they made games of their cruelty; they inflicted pain and studied it, then marvelled at their own ingenuity until even the most savage degradation bored them. Then, when there was no one left to kill, they fought each other for the division of the spoils.

Perhaps it would be kindness to say that they did not know what they did – that a madness had seized them, or blood-lust overwhelmed them, or that the many terrors of their pilgrimage had warped their souls. I do not believe it. They entered Jerusalem in full knowledge of what they would do. They came to end the world, impatient with the world allotted them, and if, in fact, it did not end that day it was not for want of their trying. They came in Christ's name, every one of them marked with the cross, but they had forgotten the sacrifice He offered and made a new god for themselves – one who could only be satisfied with blood. Like the rebel angels in the first age of heaven, they reached for a thing they could not possess, and in doing so forsook it utterly.

Through all these horrors, Sigurd and Aelfric and I tried to find a path back to the Temple Mount. Frenzied crowds of Franks and Saracens filled the streets; in some places we could barely get through for the great heaps of corpses that choked the way. In one place, I saw a group of men and women who had stacked pillaged furniture and timbers around a tall basilica. They danced around it, singing obscene songs about Jews, while the fire they had set billowed up through the house. A child was wailing inside, and I could hear his mother singing to comfort him even as the flames reached in through the windows. The sound made me think of Helena and Everard: for a moment, I wanted to rush in to the house and snatch the child and his mother away. But as soon as I stepped towards it, the joyous faces in the firelight became threatening, turning angrily towards me. I hurried on my way, though not so quickly that I did not hear the screaming as the first people began to burn.

But in all the slaughter, there was one man who did

not take part. We met him by chance, in a narrow street that descended what I thought must be the western side of the valley we had crossed earlier. The pitch of destruction here ran high as ever: blood sluiced through the gutters like rain in a storm, spilling out over the road whenever a body or a severed limb clogged its path. With my eyes to the ground, as much to pick my way over the human debris as to avoid seeing the abominations around me, the whiteness of the horse as it made its way through the stream of blood was almost unnatural. Blood had splashed over its hooves and fetlocks, staining the white hair red, but its flanks and mane remained ghostly white, untouched by the massacre. It was the colt I had seen Duke Godfrey training in his camp. Now, in the hour of his triumph, he rode it along the same road that Christ had walked with his cross to Calvary. He had abandoned his hauberk and his linen battle tunic, replacing them with a robe of shimmering white silk. His eyes were fixed ahead, impervious to the atrocities that surrounded him, his face set with furious concentration. On the hand that held the bridle I saw that he wore two rings: the ancient black gemstone of his ancestor Charlemagne, and a brighter, gold ring with the seal of the emperor Alexios engraved on its face.

Men paused in their labours as he went by, watching the strange procession wend its way up the bloody street. He had few attendants – only three knights, and Arnulf the priest carrying the gold cross, which he must have rescued from the siege tower. He wore a white cassock, though blood spattered it almost up to his knees.

They passed out of sight and we hurried on down the road. At the foot of the hill I could see the great ramparts of the Temple Mount rising up to the sky. We came through a devastated market and arrived in an open court-yard at its base. There must have been a cistern beneath the square, for the paving was riddled with dozens of open holes where the people could draw water. The plaintive moan of drowning souls echoed up through the well holes. On one side of the square a flight of steps led down into the cavern, where laughing Franks forced their victims into the water at spear-point. It was one of the myriad small cruelties of that day that some drowned while others burned.

On the far side of the square, a flight of steps led up into the heart of the Temple Mount. The gates that held it had been smashed in, and the only men who guarded it now were corpses littered on the stairs. We ran up, and emerged at last in the great courtyard of King Solomon's palace.

The first thing that struck me, even then, was its size. It must have been a full quarter of a mile long, and wide in proportion. Broad arcades lined its sides, hiding the rest of the city from us, while the courtyard itself was dominated by the octagonal Temple of the Lord, and the Temple of Solomon beyond. After the narrow maze of streets below, it was like coming out into a high valley among mountains – like ascending to the court of heaven from the confines of the world. But this was a heaven to make men weep to reach it. It had been overthrown: the Franks had broken in and, at last, brought their impieties back to the place where the first foundation of the world was laid. Mutilated corpses strewed the sacred ground, and the gentle arcades echoed with screams.

'There's no sanctuary here,' murmured Aelfric.

I found one of the Franks, a Norman knight trying to drag away a golden lamp half as high as he was himself. 'Where are they?' I shouted. 'Are there any left alive?'

He started like thief; if he had not been burdened with the lamp he might have drawn his knife and run me through. 'I'm alive,' he answered proudly. 'Praise God.'

Sigurd stepped forward and grabbed the knight's shoulders. He dropped the lamp, howling to see a crack appear in its crystal window. I glanced around nervously, hoping none of his companions would come to his aid, but they were too busy with their own treasures to notice or care.

'What about the prisoners?'

The knight laughed, careless of his danger. 'Prisoners? Look around you.' The sneer died on his lips as Sigurd's axe caressed his throat. 'Some took refuge on the roof of the Temple of Solomon. Tancred gave them his banner for protection.'

I stared at him. 'Tancred offered to protect them?'

'He thought they might fetch a ransom.'

I ran. It was like running in a dream, every stride falling short of where I stretched it, while the pursuing terror grew ever closer behind me. The Temple of Solomon was at the furthest end of the great courtyard, on its southern side – though near to the bridge, I saw with hope. If Anna and the girls had managed to cross it, they might have found their way to safety. But for how long? The Franks had been too perfect in their slaughter: I could not see any Saracens left alive in the courtyard now, and groups of knights were milling about in angry confusion. It would not be long before they went in search of new violence.

Seven arches loomed before me as I reached the Temple of Solomon at last. Compared with the intricacies and beauty of the Temple of the Lord, the Temple of Solomon was a squat and solid building, with nothing but a single dome at the far end to ornament it. I barely noticed it. A ladder at the side led up to the roof, from where a host of terrified faces peered down. Three Norman knights guarded the ladder, but they did not hinder us when they saw we wanted to go up. They waved us on with mock bows and false smiles. 'You can go up if you like,' they told us. 'It's the coming down that's hard.'

'That's what Jesus said,' said one of them, and his companions laughed wickedly.

We climbed the ladder, and came out at last on the roof of the temple. It felt like standing on the roof of the world. We were above the enclosure now, so I could see the entire city below rising to the western summit of Mount Zion. Screams filled the air, and the thick smoke from a thousand fires rose overhead so that – though it was only afternoon – darkness seemed to cover the earth. I wondered that there should be any light at all, but there was: a red, sickly glow that could only come from a withered sun. A warm breeze blew smoke and ash in my eyes, and I wept.

I turned away from the scene and looked behind me. Hundreds of cowering faces stared back. What must they expect from us? I began pushing through them, frantically calling for Anna, for Helena and Zoe, for Everard. To my right and left, I heard Sigurd and Aelfric calling the same. No one hindered us, but no one answered. Though they packed that rooftop so tight that many were piled on top of each other, they still contrived to part before me like lilies in water. All I saw was a sea of unknown faces, the last citizens of a dying world awaiting their judgement.

'Demetrios!'

From the far side of the roof, Sigurd called me. I stumbled over to him, tripping and kicking my way through the crowd, too impatient to wait for them to move. Agonising hope burned in my heart, but I saw quickly that there was no one with him. Instead, he was staring down into the courtyard.

'We don't have much longer.'

Looking down, I could see a crowd of Norman knights beginning to gather at the base of the temple, pointing and laughing. Behind them others were bringing up more ladders. Many had their swords out; others carried slings and bows.

The crowd on the roof had seen them too. One of their number, a statuesque woman with a baby still suckling at her breast, stood and began to remonstrate with them. No one could understand what she said, but the passion in her voice was such that at last two of the knights did run

595

back towards the Temple of the Lord. I saw them accost Tancred in the middle of the courtyard; I did not hear what they said, but I saw him shrug and open his arms wide in abdication.

The woman with the child continued her pleading. She got down on her knees and shook her hands imploringly at the men below; she pulled a gold coin from her dress and threw it down, begging them to save her. The knights rushed forward to where the coin had fallen and scuffled for it like dogs. Others shouted back at the woman, beckoning to her, calling that if she only leaped down they would catch her in their arms. 'Save yourself,' they urged her, but she would not go. They grew angry; they said that she must jump to see if her god would save her, and if He did not then she was a heretic and would be put to death. Of course she did not understand a word, but she could see the cruelty building around her. Her pleas grew more frantic. She pulled down her dress and offered her naked body to them, any degradation simply to live. That only drove the Franks to new heights of mockery. They whistled and demanded to see more, shouting obscene suggestions.

At length, one of them must have tired of the sport. I did not hear the bow loose, but I saw the arrow strike. It pierced straight through the child at her breast and pinned it to her heart. With a slow scream, she toppled forward and plunged to the ground.

Her death unleashed the frenzy that had been simmering among the Franks. Those who had bows shot them high in the air so that the arrows would rain down from above, while the men with ladders rushed to lay them against the temple. Some of the men on the roof tried to push them back but the Franks were too strong. They swarmed up the ladders and began the killing, stabbing and hacking or simply pulling their enemies off the roof to break on the stones. Such was the thirst for slaughter that some died in the hail of stones and arrows that their companions still launched from the courtyard below.

For one more moment, I searched the crowd for my daughters, praying that if I had to die I might at least die with my family. Then something hard struck me on the side of my head, and I sank into oblivion.

μθ

Perhaps the world did end. How else to explain the place where I woke? If it was not hell, then there are worse places of which even the Bible does not speak. A dull light filled the air, and carrion birds wheeled overhead. The dead were all around me. Heaps of broken bodies, broken limbs, broken faces. Their eyes stared at me in unceasing reproach but thankfully they did not speak.

'*Anna.*' I pushed myself to my feet and staggered to the nearest corpses, rummaging through them like a pile of old clothes. '*Helena. Zoe.*' The bodies were stiff; their blood had flowed together and hardened into a bond that seemed impossible to pull apart. Their faces stared up at me, frozen into the moment of their death: in anger, in despair, even in hope – pleading with me, even now, to rescue them.

'They're not here.'

I heard the voice but I ignored it, still clawing frantic-ally through the dead, until a gentle hand on my shoulder pulled me away. Sigurd stood over me, a dark silhouette against the amber sky.

'They're not here,' he said again. He had removed his helmet so that his copper hair hung loose over his shoul-ders. Blood streaked his face and beard, and stained his arms all the way to the elbows.

'Helena, Zoe, Anna, Everard – they're not here.'

A great wave of emptiness broke over me and I slumped back. I did not *feel* empty, for I could not feel. I did not understand it, for I was past understanding. Instead, as some men know pain and others know God, I *knew* – nothing. Sigurd crouched beside me and put his arm around me.

'They weren't on the roof?' Twisting around, I could see the squat bulk of the Temple of Solomon across the courtyard. The ladders still leaned against it, while workers on the roof rolled down the bodies of the slain. Memories of that last battle suddenly flashed in my mind. 'How did we escape?'

Sigurd did not answer, but pointed to my chest. The crude wooden cross I had carved beside the campfire on the eve of the assault still hung there, two small twigs bound together with twine. The mere sight of it filled me with revulsion; I snatched at it, ready to tear it off. But the habits of a lifetime are hard to dislodge, and a prick of faith stayed my hand. It had saved me, after all, even if

599

the men it saved me from wore the same emblem. I left it, for now.

'What about Aelfric?'

Sigurd shook his head. 'You and I were the only ones.'

I brushed my hand against the cross and whispered a prayer for Aelfric. Even in the midst of so much death I felt his loss.

'But the girls, Anna – they weren't up there?'

'Not that I saw.' He jerked his head, as if trying to dislodge something from his thoughts. 'It was hard . . . to tell.'

We sat there in silence for a moment, two living souls dwarfed by the death around us.

'What do we do now?'

Sigurd stood. 'We should find Thomas. At least we know where he is. He wanted so much to see Jerusalem – the least we can do is bury him here properly.'

It did not take long to find our way to the street where Thomas had died. We left the great enclosure of the Temple Mount and walked across the valley on the high bridge, staring down into the city. The slaughter had finished. The Franks had done everything in their power to bring paradise to Jerusalem and they had failed. They had washed the city in the blood of its people, but that had not cleansed it. It stank. Now they were faced with the wreckage and ruination of their efforts. I could see small groups of them below slowly beginning the wretched business of clearing the city.

'What time is it?' I asked. The bronze light made it feel like dusk, or perhaps dawn, but I could not see any sign of the sun. It was the smoke in the air, I realised, clouding the sky so that only dark light bled through.

'Saturday morning. You were unconscious all night.'

I rubbed my temple, flinching to feel the bruise where the stone had struck. 'Did it hit me that hard?'

Sigurd shrugged. 'There are some times when it's better to be asleep.'

Just for a moment, I glimpsed the torments Sigurd must have suffered during that lonely night, the horrors he must have witnessed as he stood watch over me. I did not ask; I did not have the strength for pity.

We crossed the bridge and walked west, to the cross-roads where the two tamarisk trees grew. The flies were thick on the ground, rising up in clouds as we passed. The heat and the stench were almost too much to bear. At the crossroads, I shed my armour and my quilted coat and abandoned them in the street, keeping only the thin linen tunic I had worn underneath, and the dagger tucked in my boot. It was a relief to be free of the burden. My whole body felt lighter, freer; I moved so easily I thought I might float away into the hazy sky.

I turned right, ran up the street and stopped. There was the house with its shaded balcony, its splintered door-frame and the door lying flat on the ground. There was the helmet Thomas had torn off in his fury, a round dent showing where he had hurled it against the wall. There were the two dark stains in the dusty road where Thomas

601

and Bilal had died, with a third a little further off where Thomas's killer had met his end. But the bodies were gone.

At another time, in another world, I should have dropped to my knees and wept that of all my family, not one could be found even to bury. On that day, overwhelmed by death, I just stood and stared.

'He's not here,' I mumbled to myself. Then, to Sigurd, 'Could he have lived?'

'No.' Sigurd spoke brusquely, refusing any compromise with hope. 'I saw him as well as you. He was dead.'

My chin sank against my chest in despair. Looking down, I saw the wooden cross still hanging there, jerking like a marionette as I moved. Its impossible promise of the miraculous dangled before me, taunting me. I hated it.

I heard a sound from the road and looked up. Two Frankish knights had come around the corner, wheeling a creaking barrow between them. A tangle of arms and legs dangled over its sides, the corpses piled so high they threatened to topple out. I stared at them, sucking back the bile in my throat, but I could not see Thomas's body among them.

The barrow stopped in front of us and one of the knights stepped out from behind it. His face was scarlet with sunburn, his moustache shaved short for battle. He was sweating.

'What are you doing?' he shouted at us. 'Who told you to linger around with so much work to be done?'

I stared at him vacantly. 'We . . . We were looking for a body.'

'And you couldn't find one in this shambles?' The knight turned to the barrow and tugged on a loose-hanging arm. Two bodies tumbled off and fell on the ground with a flat thud. A man and a woman, both Ishmaelites, both horribly ravaged by the wounds that had killed them. They fell one on top of the other, a casual piece of innuendo that seemed almost more horrible than the wounds themselves.

'There you go,' said the soldier. 'There's bodies for you. Take them away.' Still I stared at him. 'Left at the end of the road. Follow the others.'

Without another word, he and his companion lifted up the cart handles and pushed it on down the street. Sigurd and I stared at each other, each as confused as the other. Then, because there was nothing else to do, we picked up the two corpses and dragged them in the direction the knight had ordered.

We were not alone. At the top of the road we found many others – Provençals, Normans, Lotharingians and Flemings, as well as Ishmaelite prisoners, even Jews – working to dispossess the city of its dead. Carnage and devastation were everywhere; to look on it was to taint your soul for ever. We followed the procession across Mount Zion to the western gate, where the high citadel rose above the ramparts. No sign of siege or sack marked its massive walls, but it had fallen nonetheless: I could see the blue banner of Provence fluttering from the topmost tower, and Provençal archers patrolling its walls. Jerusalem was taken, but Count Raymond's jealous eyes still saw enemies everywhere.

We passed through the gate onto the bare mountain beyond. The ground fell away steeply into the valley, with a great crowd of knights and pilgrims milling about at its rim. A soldier shouted at us to bring our burdens there and, numbly, we obeyed. We hauled them to the edge and stared down.

For a moment I thought I truly had witnessed the resurrection. Looking into that ravine was like looking into the bowels of the earth, as if the jaws of hell had opened to disgorge the legions of the dead. The hillside was thick with bodies, their stiff arms outstretched as if trying to haul themselves out. At the bottom, still more corpses were piled up in vast mounds, like fallen leaves ready for the burning. There must have been thousands of them, ten thousands. Small groups of Franks clambered over them, piling cords of wood and dousing them in oil. I could not believe we had killed so many.

A group of pilgrims hauled a cart to the edge and upended it. More corpses tipped out like rubbish, tumbling and sliding down the rocky slope. I stared at them, trying to make out anything that could be Thomas, but it was no use.

'Come on!' shouted a soldier impatiently. 'Plenty more to come.'

We lifted the bodies we had brought and hurled them into the pit. When they had gone I said a brief prayer for Thomas, trying to imagine him lying lost among the naked, unnumbered dead. Then I went to find what we had come for.

After all our struggles, all that time, it was not hard to find. We followed the pilgrims who streamed back into Jerusalem from that open grave – down a sloping street, through the wreckage of what had once been a market or a bazaar, and then along a narrow, twisting alley.

'Are you sure this is the right way?' Sigurd asked doubtfully.

I was not sure, but I carried on. Around a corner, through a narrow door in a wall – and suddenly we were there. A shady, colonnaded courtyard, with lofty porticoes to our right and our left opening into dim chambers beyond. The waiting crowds within almost overflowed it, and the red-tiled roofs around the courtyard sagged under the weight of the pilgrims who had climbed up on them. It seemed to take an age to worm our way through the throng; several times our rough manners would have provoked violence if there had only been room to swing a fist. I drew the knife I had kept in my boot and balled my tunic around it. The closer we came the more slowly we progressed until suddenly, at last, there was nothing in front of us except the sweet smell of incense wafting out of the chamber within. We peered over the threshold, into the shrine of the Holy Sepulchre.

It had been an image in my mind so long, but – like so many things – it was not as I had expected it. From my childhood, I had always imagined the sepulchre as a great

stone cave, rugged and primal, yawning open in the middle
of the church. Perhaps it had been, once, but that had long
since been hidden by the artifice of men. It stood in the
middle of a broad, semicircular hall, under a lofty rotunda
whose centre had been cut out to allow a pillar of light
to plunge through. The shrine stood at its foot, so that
you could not tell if the tomb was the object or the source
of the brilliance. Tendrils of smoke writhed in the blood-
red light like souls in torment.

Of the tomb itself I could see very little. The bricks that
made its walls were scarred and pocked with holes, while
the lead cupola on top was badly scratched and dented.
It looked more like a roadside chapel than the tomb of
God. But even that I could hardly see, for the inside of
the church was as crowded as the courtyard beyond. A
phalanx of priests in golden robes circled the tomb, singing
a psalm of thanksgiving. In their centre, raised above all
of them at the door of the tomb, stood Arnulf. A radiant
triumph smirked on his face as he sang:

> *The Lord rejoices in his people,*
> *and adorns the humble with victory.*
> *Let the faithful exult in their glory;*
> *Let the high praises of God be in their throats,*
> *And sharp swords in their hands.*

An acolyte held the golden cross beside him, the fragments of the true cross erected once again on the hill of
Calvary. The princes stood in front of him, facing the

sepulchre, and their knights packed the chamber around them. Some had their heads bowed, but others stared around in wide-eyed astonishment, unable to believe where they stood. They seemed to have come straight from the battle: many still wore their armour, their tabards soaked with blood like butchers' aprons. Some were bloodied up to their elbows; others bore open wounds, which wept and bled as they sang the psalm.

> *Let the faithful wreak vengeance on the nations*
> *And punishment on their peoples;*
> *Let them bind the kings of the earth with chains*
> *And their princes with iron shackles,*
> *To execute on them the judgement of God –*
> *This is the glory of the faithful.*

'Praise the Lord!' shouted the crowd. The priests had stopped singing but the crowd carried on, repeating the antiphon again and again with such noise and fervour that I feared the dome might crack apart and collapse on them in the moment of their triumph. '*Praise the Lord.*' It was an awesome sound. Its monolithic unison seemed to ring with everything that was most mighty and terrible in the Army of God. The more often they repeated it, the louder they sang. Confidence became stridence, unison began to shake with disharmony. Looking at the fervent faces that thronged the sanctuary, breathless mouths straining to build the sound ever louder, it suddenly seemed to me that they were not gripped by glory or love of God, but by desperation. The moment of victory had passed and they knew it. They had come to find heaven, to capture God, but the tomb was empty. Soon they would have to leave that sanctuary and venture into the world they had made, a dark and terrible place, but for a little while yet they could delay it. So they sang on, not in joy but in dread of what was to come.

Voices grew hoarse, lungs tired. One by one, the knights at the back of the church fell silent and began to slip away. They pushed past me through the door, but I held my ground, keeping the knife hidden in the fold of my tunic. As the last sighs of the song died away, a troop of knights emerged and forged a way through the courtyard, penning us back with the hafts of their spears. But the crowds had suffered the torments of hell to reach this sacred place – they would not be turned away so easily. They pushed back against the soldiers, squeezing the way shut. Those who had begun to leave the church found themselves suddenly stuck in the midst of the crowd. And there, standing on the threshold not six inches away from me, was Duke Godfrey.

'Was it all you expected?' I murmured in his ear. Keeping my arm low, I turned the knife so that the point aimed at his side. I wondered if the blade was long enough to reach his heart.

He was trapped between the men trying to get out of the church and those trying to push in. He could not even turn to face me, but I saw his shoulders stiffen and his head go still as the blade pricked him. I looked down at his hand, at the two rings – one black and ancient, one gold and shining – that gleamed on his fingers.

'The ring of Charlemagne and the seal of Byzantium. Was that how you thought you would unite the crowns of east and west, as the prophecy foretold? Was that why you contrived to steal the ring from me, after you had failed to conquer Constantinople itself?'

Godfrey's chin lifted and he stared straight ahead. 'Make way,' he shouted. 'Make way for your princes, damn you.'

'If you move, the last thing you feel will be my dagger in your heart.' I would have to be quick: his guards would cut me down in an instant. But that did not matter, for they would only speed me to my family. 'Did you think that you were the one? That you would ascend Golgotha, take the crown from your head and place it on the cross, and hand over the kingdom of the Christians to God the Father? Is that why you destroyed Peter Bartholomew, not because he vied with God but because he vied with *you*?'

Ahead of Godfrey, the soldiers had at last begun to impose themselves on the crowd. A passage was opening.

'You thought you could remake the world by destroying it. You envied heaven so much you tried to wrest it from God. What will you say when you see Him now?'

But even as I spoke, the knife wavered in my hand. What did I want from Godfrey? Revenge? There was no revenge in the world that could punish the weight of his sin. Remorse? If he truly comprehended what he had done, he would have snatched the knife from my hand and plunged it in himself. My words would not stir him. As for repentance, that was not mine to demand.

I lowered the knife and let it drop to the ground. In the tumult of the crowd, no one even heard it fall. All that remained now was curiosity.

'Was it worth it?'

A path opened in front of Godfrey, but he did not move forward. He turned to look at me, and I stared into his eyes. For the merest instant, I looked through them to the soul within. There was no sorrow there, nor guilt: only, for the first time, a thin blade of doubt.

Then his body stiffened, his face hardened and the shutters closed over his eyes. I knew what he would say before he spoke.

'*Deus voluit.*'

God willed it.

V

〜〜〜

Sigurd and I stood at the edge of the street in the shade, the last two survivors. Amid all the ruin, Sigurd had found an orange, and his strong fingers dug away the peel to reveal the fruit within. When he had stripped it he pulled it in two and gave me half; I tore the segments off with my teeth, devouring them almost as fast as I could swallow. Juice trickled down my fingers and over my chin, glistening in the sun, but I made sure I licked off every drop. It was almost the first thing I had had to eat or drink since the assault, and it was like the waters of heaven in my parched mouth.

'What do we do now?' Sigurd asked.

'Go home, I suppose.'

I winced, remembering how much I had once desired

that. Now fate had made a mockery of that hope, too. What did I have to return to?

'Will you go back to the palace guard?'

Sigurd frowned and looked away. He was about to answer when something behind me caught his eye, driving the thought from his head. I turned to see. I could not help the spark of hope that flared in me, but I damped it instantly. All it would do was burn me.

We were not the only survivors. A few paces away, looking for all the world as if he had expected to find us, stood Saewulf. One arm was held in a sling, and there was a gash on his cheek that would no doubt harden into one more scar, but he still wore the same crooked smile. It did not entirely disguise the weariness in his eyes.

'How did you get here?' Sigurd asked.

'I followed Count Raymond. He still owes me money for his siege tower – though he was less inclined to pay after the Egyptians destroyed it.' He gave a small shrug of his shoulders, the acquiescence of a man well used to the whims of fate. 'He has taken the citadel, the tower of David. Did you know that?'

'We saw his banner there,' I answered. There was something in Saewulf's words that I did not understand, something that he was withholding. 'How did he take it so quickly?'

'He promised the captain of the garrison and his men safe passage out of Jerusalem if they surrendered immediately. It was a good bargain – on both sides. I was with him when he made it, and I was there when he entered the citadel. We found something there you should see.'

I looked into his eyes for a hint, but saw only the fathomless blue of the sea.

The convoys of the dead still flowed to the vast grave in the valley beyond the walls. Soon smoke from those pyres would choke the air once more, but for the moment the sky had begun to clear. The rust-red glow that had suffused the city all day hardened to a sharper, whiter light. We came quickly to the great bulwarks of the citadel, its walls laced with lead so that fire and chisels could not penetrate the cracks between the stones. Companies of Provençal knights guarded every gate, but they waved us through without challenge when they saw Saewulf. He led us into a courtyard among high towers, filled with men and horses. For the first time since I entered Jerusalem, I was in a place that did not stink of blood.

'Over there.'

I blinked, my eyes still struggling with the brightness after so long in the gloom. On the far side of the courtyard, forgotten amid the bustle, three figures sat in the shade of an arched colonnade. With the brilliant sun on my face I could barely see them, but there are some things that can be recognised without sight.

'Your Egyptian friend brought them here for sanctuary when he saw the city was lost,' said Saewulf. 'He went to find you, to tell you, but they said he did not return.'

I barely heard him; I was running across the courtyard, springing forward like a newborn lamb, each stride longer than the last. They saw me coming; they rose and rushed to meet me, their skirts swirling in the dust. They were dressed in strange clothes that I had not seen before, bright garments that seemed alive with the light they reflected. In her haste, the scarf Anna wore over her head blew away and her black hair streamed out behind her. Zoe ran beside her, taller than I remembered, and behind them came Helena with Everard in her arms. He had grown too heavy for Helena; she put him down and let him run free with her. I could hear them shouting; I was shouting too, though I did not know what I was saying. Then we were all in each other's arms, crying and laughing and repeating each other's names as if we had never spoken them before. The soldiers in the courtyard stared, disturbed from their grim business, but I did not care.

Everything that had to be said – about Thomas, about Bilal, about Godfrey and Raymond, about ourselves – could be said later. For now, I was ready to go home.

Lux Aeterna

࿐࿐࿐

Three weeks after they captured the city, the Army of God took to the field for the last time. At Ascalon, forty miles west of Jerusalem, they met the relief army that al-Afdal had brought from Egypt and, though outnumbered once more, routed it utterly. Many of the Egyptians were driven into the sea and drowned; al-Afdal himself only escaped by fleeing into the harbour and taking ship for Egypt. He never returned. I heard, some years afterwards, that he was eventually murdered by a caliph who had grown tired of his tutelage.

When Jerusalem had been conquered, the princes met in the church of the Holy Sepulchre and elected Godfrey king. But – faithful to his prophecy to the last – he put aside his crown and did not take the title of king, preferring

615

instead to style himself the Defender of the Holy Sepulchre. A few days afterwards, the red-headed priest, Arnulf of Rohes, was appointed Patriarch of Jerusalem. Raymond got nothing: but true to his vow he never returned to Provence. He died a few years later, once more pursuing a fruitless siege.

Despite the victory, Godfrey's reign was neither long nor happy. One by one, the other princes abandoned him, either to return to their homes or to make new conquests of their own. The borders of his new realm were weak and fragile; no sooner had one area been secured than another demanded his attention. Almost a year to the day after he marched through the golden gate and processed to Christ's tomb, Godfrey died in Jerusalem. Some said he had been poisoned, others that he had succumbed to fever; others still said that his heart had simply given up. When I heard that, I remembered the doubt I had seen in his eyes that morning in the Holy Sepulchre. It had seemed then like something sharp and dangerous; I wondered if it had not twisted in his soul until it cut a wound that could not heal.

Many assumed that Godfrey's successor should be Bohemond; he was summoned from Antioch, but he was away campaigning. Before he could return, he was captured by Turks and carried away deep into their kingdom where he spent four years rotting in captivity. In his absence, the lordship of Jerusalem passed to Baldwin, Godfrey's younger brother, who had left the Army of God before it even reached Antioch to carve out his own dominion in the east. He had none of his brother's pious scruples. On Christmas Day in the first year of the new century, at the Church of the Nativity in Bethlehem, he was crowned king of Jerusalem. And so the man who had abandoned the pilgrimage at the earliest opportunity, who never suffered its torments or fought its terrible battles, became its eventual victor.

I did not see any of it. Before Ascalon, before Godfrey had taken his throne, even before the embers from the funeral pyres had cooled, I began the long journey home. Before we left, I visited the Holy Sepulchre. After waiting almost three hours in a line of weeping pilgrims, I stepped inside the cupola, past the stone where the angel had announced the resurrection to the two Marys, and ducked into the small chamber beyond.

It was empty, of course.

We travelled in easy stages back to the coast, walking at dawn and at dusk, resting during the heat of the day. At Jaffa, we found the last ship from Saewulf's fleet, which had been away on patrol when the Fatimids burned the harbour. As August winds furrowed the sea, it slowly nosed its way west. The sun shone, and I spent the hours reaccustoming myself to food and water, nursing strength back into my limbs. I had not realised how far my body had withered until I tried to heal it. There were days when my joints were so stiff I could barely move; other days when my stomach rebelled against even water. Through all this,

Anna was at my side: preparing my food, teasing the knots out of my sinews, or just sitting in the shade of a canvas awning watching dolphins play in the water. We did not speak much. The ordeals we had endured loomed too large, mountains in our minds that we could neither conquer nor comprehend. Only by skirting around them, chiselling away small pieces each day, could we gradually reduce them and build the fragments into the houses of memory. It was as well we had Everard to distract us. If ever thoughts of the past grew too melancholy, there was always the sight of him running up and down the sloping deck chasing after gulls to lift our spirits. Amid thoughts of death and despair, his energy provided a necessary reminder of life.

We put into Cyprus and Rhodes, then turned north. One day we sailed past Patmos, the island where Saint John the Divine received his revelation of the world's end. I stared at it, a rocky outcrop barely distinguishable from the mainland behind, and wondered how much evil had come from the visions he saw in that cave. I was glad to see it slide into the distance behind us. The days were getting shorter now, the winds fresher: the sea was crowded with ships all hurrying to their harbours before the onset of autumn. The urgency affected all of us, and instead of watching the wake or the waves we began to gather in the bow, staring at the sea ahead.

At the beginning of October, we reached the port of Tenedos. According to some authorities, it was where the

Greeks had hidden their fleet during the siege of Troy, but there were few ships there now – only a gaggle of merchantmen waiting for the wind to change so they could navigate through the Hellespont and up to Constantinople. Here, Saewulf announced, he would leave us.

'I could spend a month waiting for the wind to change,' he explained. 'And another month waiting to get out again. You can get a boat to the mainland and be home in half that time.'

I looked at the grey sky and the white wavecaps beyond the harbour. 'But you can't take to the seas again now. I thought they were closed in winter.'

He grinned. 'The seas are never closed to an Englishman. And I've been away from home too long. Even if it's cold and wet and stinks of Normans.'

His was not the only farewell we had to make on Tenedos – nor the hardest. On the night before we parted, I was sitting by the mast with Everard on my knee, pointing out the constellations to him, when Sigurd and Saewulf came on deck. In a few short words, Sigurd told me his plans.

'I'm not going back to Constantinople.'

I looked up in surprise. 'Where will you go?'

'To England – with Saewulf.'

On my knee, Everard tugged at the sleeve of my tunic, peeved to find himself forgotten. I ignored him. The delicate peace in my soul, so patiently stitched together on the voyage, was torn apart again. 'To England?' I stared from one to the other. Neither looked happy with the decision. 'I thought you swore you would never return while

619

the Normans ruled.' Every atrocity, every insult, every obloquy that I had ever heard against the Normans raced through my mind, and I wanted to hurl each one back at him. 'You're a captain of the palace guard. Would you give all that up to live the life of a peasant in a captive land?'

Sigurd sighed. 'The emperor doesn't need me – any more than he needed Aelfric or Thomas or Nikephoros – or even you. If anyone asks, tell them I died at Jerusalem.'

Saewulf looked no happier than I did. 'It'll break your heart,' he warned. 'The country you remember vanished a long time ago. Better to stay here and cherish it as it was.'

Sigurd shook his head. 'If you believed that, you wouldn't have gone back yourself.'

'But Constantinople is your home,' I said.

'Constantinople is *your* home,' he corrected me. 'It was mine, too, for a time. Now I must go back. When you get to Constantinople, find my family and tell them to follow as soon as they can. They'll understand.'

I realised then that I could not dissuade him. I pulled myself to my feet and embraced him. As ever, it was like putting my arms around an oak tree.

'Try not to kill the first Norman you see.'

He grunted. 'Try to keep out of trouble yourself. Remember you won't have me to protect you any more.'

They sailed away next morning. I sat on the quay, watching the ship diminish until it slipped over the horizon. Then, surrounded by my family, I turned east and set out on the final stage.

*   *   *

Those last two weeks were the happiest of the entire journey. Though we were late in the year, the weather blessed us with a succession of clear days, each more brilliant than the last. The sun shone, and in the evenings a dewy haze descended to cloak the world in soft mystery. All around us we could see the world gathering itself in for the winter. Fields had been harvested and ploughed, flocks brought down from the summer pasture, firewood piled up ready for burning. If we did not speak much now, it was because we did not need words to describe how we felt. Each of us was seized with hope, and with sweet anticipation.

It was evening when we arrived at Constantinople. We came over a hill and there it was – the eastern suburbs of Chrysopolis falling away to the Bosphorus beneath us, and the domes and towers of the city rising in their splendour across the shining water. I could see Ayia Sophia, majestic on its promontory, and the many terraces of the palace cascading down the hill. The autumn sun was setting behind a cloud in the west, casting the sky, the water, the city, the whole world in molten gold. From across the strait, I thought I could hear the chant of the priests at vespers.

'I don't think I've ever seen it from this side before,' murmured Helena. 'It's beautiful.'

We went down to the water's edge, and waited for the boatman to ferry us across.

Τέλος

621

Historical Note

࿇࿇࿇࿇࿇

The capture of Jerusalem by the First Crusade in 1099 stands as one of the great cataclysms of history. Through a potent combination of zealotry, pent-up frustration and greed, the crusaders massacred more or less every man, woman and child in the city, depopulating it for generations to come and leaving a legacy of hatred whose effects are still being felt today.

As always, I have tried to be as faithful as possible to the facts and chronology of established events, while putting my own interpretation on the motives, meanings, and the gaps in the record. If the story seems to meander in places, it may be because the crusaders, who had been so brutally single-minded in rampaging across Asia Minor and grinding out victory at Antioch, dithered for months when the road to Jerusalem lay open. The princes seemed to lose interest completely, preferring to nurse their jealousies and quarrel over the spoils they had won that far. Even when they did manage to move on, first to Ma'arat and then to Arqa, they quickly stalled.

In those circumstances, the emergence of Peter Bartholomew as the angry voice of the frustrated poor is hardly surprising. My own sense, which I have tried to convey in the book, is that he was a charlatan who stumbled onto an unexpectedly successful ploy, who grew ever more extreme as he tested the limits of his newfound power, and who eventually came to believe his own hype, to suicidal effect.

But Peter had tapped into one of the most powerful forces at work in the crusade The historical debate over the crusaders' motives is as energetic as it is futile, but it seems clear that a strong thread of millenarianism inspired many of them. The key biblical text used to preach the crusade – 'If any man would come after me, let him deny himself and take up his cross and follow me' (Matthew 16:24) – is drawn from a passage where Jesus foretells the imminent second coming, and several chroniclers of the crusade show the link was clear in their minds when they begin their narratives with the omnious phrase, 'When that time [i.e., the last days] had already come . . .' The recapture of Jerusalem by God's elect has always been seen as a precondition for the end of the world (which is why Christian Zionists today encourage the Jewish diaspora's return to Israel), and in 1099 the time must have seemed particularly ripe. To the cosmopolitan armies of the crusade, fighting an exotic range of Turks, Arabs, Armenians, Berbers and Africans, it must truly have felt as though God had gathered up all the nations of the earth to wage war for Jerusalem. The fact that they were actually fighting to liberate the city from the forces of Babylon (as Cairo was inaccurately known) only added to the sense of destiny. In this context, Duke Godfrey's decision to leave the assault just as the city fell, strip off his armour and enter the city through the Golden Gate on the Mount of Olives looks less like humility and more like a conscious evocation – or consummation – of Ezekiel's prophecies: this was how Christ would return at the end of time.

The First Crusade effectively ended with the victory at Ascalon, three weeks after the capture of Jerusalem. But that was merely the opening chapter in the two-century story of the crusaders' attempts to master the Holy Land – and, some historians have argued, a far longer saga of western conquest and colonisation generally. Today's map of the Middle East contains plenty of borders as artificial and fragile as those of the crusader kingdoms, while from Tehran to Baghdad to Jerusalem, the region still draws zealots of many faiths trying to build their paradises on earth. At the time of writing, none has yet succeeded.

Acknowledgements

~~~~~~

This was not an easy book to write, but it would have been infinitely harder without the tremendous generosity of others. I owe an enormous debt to my editor, Oliver Johnson, who watched deadlines fly by with cheerful stoicism, and managed to keep my head when I was in danger of losing it. His insights on the first draft were key to shaping the final book, and gave me one of my most enjoyable days working on it (and a fine lunch to boot). Meanwhile, it would need more words than are in this book to justly describe how much my wife Marianna contributed to it: from tramping around Jerusalem to teasing out plot tangles, she endured every step of the journey with good humour and much-tested patience. I was and am lucky to have her with me.

I'm grateful as ever to the British Library, both in London and at their Boston Spa redoubt, and to the Minster Library in York. Susan Edgington generously supplied a pre-publication copy of her translation of Albert of Aachen's chronicle, which once again gave me access to a wealth of material that would have been otherwise unavailable. The prophecy in the book is adapted from a variety of contemporary sources, but chiefly from translations of the letter of Adso of Montier-en-Der and the *Revelations of Pseudo-Methodius* by Bernard McGinn. The biblical excerpts are generally adapted from the New Revised Standard Version, whose copyright is held by the Division of Christian Education of the National Council of the Churches of Christ in the USA.

Ariel and Sigal Knafo were wonderful hosts on my research trip to Israel, while Emma Pointon kindly showed me her holiday snaps. When inspiration ran dry at home, I found a happy substitute in the Danish Kitchen tearoom in York. Particular thanks go to my agent, Jane Conway-Gordon, and to all the people at Century who worked on giving form to the book: Charlotte Haycock, Richard Ogle, Rodney Paull, Alison Tulett and especially Steve Stone for his magnificent artwork.

The First Crusade ended in victory, but the crusaders' work had barely begun. The atrocity at Jerusalem left a hunger for revenge across the Muslim world, while in

Europe a new order had begun to assert itself. Demetrios'
journey may have ended, but the story goes on.

Tom Harper
July 2006

tom@tom-harper.co.uk